THE PIGEON DROP

By

Scott Faragher

Copyright 2015-2021 Scott Faragher
ISBN: 978-0-9863726-5-0
DeathCat Media
PO Box 50292
Nashville, TN. 37205
deathcatmedia@gmail.com

PREFACE

Nashville, Tennessee---Music City USA, Home of the Grand Ole Opry, recording studios, country music, famous entertainers, Andrew Jackson's Hermitage, Vanderbilt University, and Gibson Guitars. These are some of the images usually associated with the name 'Nashville.' To most people, the city of Nashville seldom, if ever, brings to mind the idea of murder. And yet, as a native Nashvillian, I do think of murder from time to time whenever Nashville is mentioned. Actually, I could give a fairly detailed tour of the city's most famous murder sites off the top of my head, just driving down the street. I can think of more than a dozen local murders right now, many involving members of so-called 'polite society.' While some of these murders have been random and senseless in accordance with current American fashion, a greater number have been spontaneous crimes of passion. In the South, especially, emotions of rage, love, lust, jealousy, or hatred, when fueled with alcohol, drugs, or hormones, make a particularly deadly combination, one which often requires an immediate release. Yet there are other killings here as well, like those which result from misunderstandings, domestic disturbances, robberies, differences of opinion, or just plain subjective dislikes.

Some of our murders even gain national recognition. For example, Senator Edward Carmack, owner of the Nashville 'Tennessean' newspaper was gunned down in broad daylight on a downtown street by two of the governor's thugs in 1908. Another sensational case in 1961 involved a woman who 'accidentally' ran her husband through with a sabre one night at the old Wilson Mansion in the 1960s. She claimed they were just 'playing.'

We've also had our share of high visibility unsolved murder cases. The most famous ongoing case involved the disappearance of Marcia Trimble, a young girl, who in 1974, left her quiet home in one of the city's best neighborhoods to sell Girl Scout cookies. After two weeks of the most extensive around the clock searching, her body was found in a garage, less than half a mile from her home, a place which had already been thoroughly checked. The crime took more than thirty years to solve despite its simplicity.

And then in the mid-1980s, only a couple of streets away from the Trimble murder site, in the most exclusive section of town, an elderly woman, Mrs. Lapidus was killed when her house was destroyed by a remotely detonated bomb, obviously, the police determined, a professionally executed murder for hire. Again, no arrests were ever made.

In 1996, another unsolved murder, this time in Nashville's exclusive and affluent Jewish community. The beautiful daughter of a prominent Nashville attorney suddenly disappeared without so much as a trace, leaving her stately Forest Hills mansion, two young children, and a husband ultimately named by the police as the prime suspect. In this case, the body has never been found despite an unlimited budget and the use of the most high-tech equipment available. And the murderer, finally convicted after a decade on the run will probably be out of stir again in short order, most likely stalking our city streets.

But, regardless of the underlying motives or methods employed, in a murder case, somebody always dies, whether or not a body is ever actually found. Perhaps this predisposition toward permanent solutions to personal disagreements in modern day Music City USA is an outgrowth of our frontier heritage, a holdover from the time of Andrew Jackson, Sam Houston, and Davy Crockett. In any case, murder is a popular pastime here in Nashville, and murders of revenge are possibly the most interesting of all. They are intriguing because they involve the greatest forethought, and probably even more raw emotion than the spontaneous crimes of passion which quickly find their resolution. A passion which is repressed, seethes and germinates beneath the surface, consuming its host to the extent that its expression and fulfillment ultimately become the driving force of life, as it was in the instance about to be related.

The circumstances attending the murder of Nashville socialite Mason Hamster are particularly unique in many ways. In the first place, the resentment toward the victim had been completely unknown to the decedent. He regarded the perpetrator of this crime as his oldest and most trusted 'friend.' He never even imagined the rage, hostility, jealousy and envy which the perpetrator had harbored silently for literally decades. That the murder was conducted so successfully in another country is indicative of the thorough planning and extreme attention to detail involved. There was nothing linking the murderer to the victim. It was in fact, the perfect crime, and would have remained so had not the murderer become overly greedy. But more of that later.

Nashville exists on several levels socially, but the most interesting Nashvillians of all are the bon ton. Though there are many rich people in this city, the so called upper crust, mockingly referred to by its envious detractors as the `Silk Stocking Gang' will be found in Belle Meade, a small area on the west side of town. Many of this group are very visible, and frequently involved in high profile charities and public organizations. They are people with social aspirations, people on the way up. They usually drive late model foreign cars and often live way beyond their means. Inhabiting Belle Meade along with this group are an elite, smaller set of the really wealthy. These people are not the nouveau riche. They are old money, and many of them are eccentric. They generally do not interact with their more outgoing peers, and for the most part, have no social aspirations at all. They don't seek or require the approbation of others, as they've already `arrived.' As a rule, they do not `work' per se, but live off proceeds from long established trusts or off of the income from investments established by their progenitors. They are inconspicuous for the most part, dress as they please, often drive older, and in some cases even `beat up' luxury cars. They are in a word, decadent. The late Mason Hamster fell into this category.

His son, Chip, the main character in this story, was the stereotypical spoiled brat. He wasn't spoiled by indulgence, as many imagined. He was spoiled by neglect. Neglect accompanied by an unlimited expense account. That he accomplished nothing noteworthy before the age of thirty is not surprising. That he became involved in an illegal loan scheme involving large scale fraud is no surprise either. That he was involved in a motoring accident, presumably drowned, and his body not recovered, provided his father's murderer the opportunity to carry his plans to the next level. He mistakenly assumed that young Hamster was dead, when in fact, he was not. The son's reappearance after a three month period of captivity by inmates at an asylum, was more than the murderer could accept. It upset all of his carefully laid plans. His (the murderer's) subsequent carelessness and foolish bravado eventually contributed, along with a series of meaningful coincidences, to his ultimate downfall.

The perpetrator, himself a man of wealth and prestige, was convicted of conspiracy to commit murder, served a brief sentence, and as is the custom for such offences in Tennessee, was released, and again moves freely among the members of upper Nashville social circles, seemingly more popular than ever. The assassin with whom he was involved was convicted 'in absentia' of first degree murder and remains at large.

Oswald Banks Lobrecue, IX

Located at the base of Lookout Mountain, the Double-Cola plant would soon become an unlikely, but crucial factor in those events which were about to occur.

CONTENTS

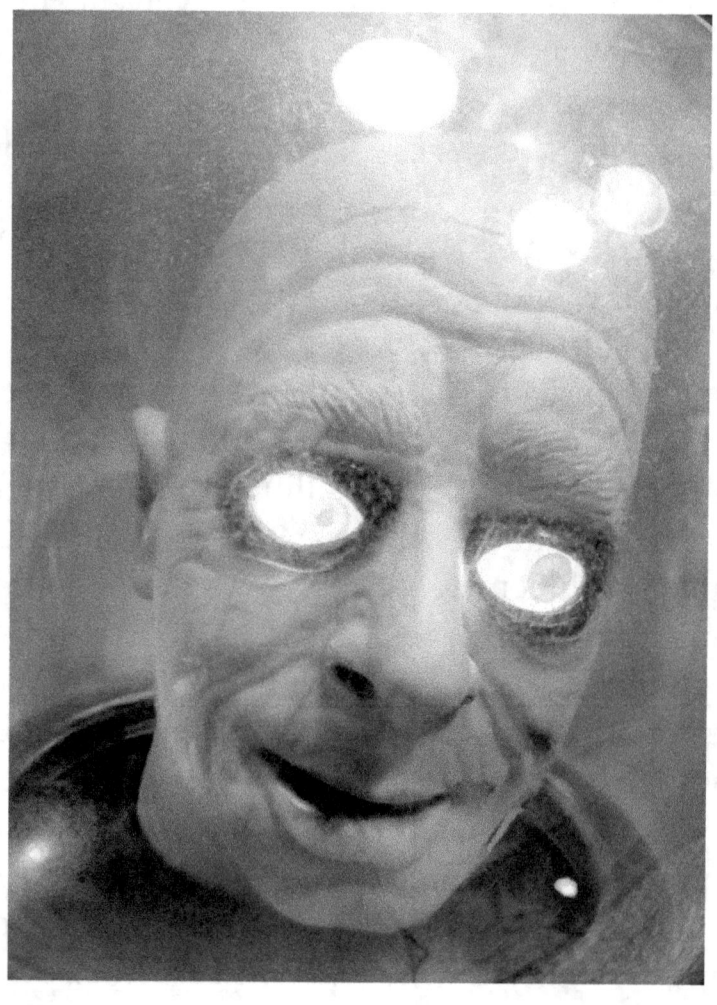

1.

COUNCIL OF THE TWELVE
WILDMAN SANITARIUM: NEAR CHATTANOOGA

Marduk shifted uneasily in his chair. As head of the Council of the Twelve, that august body of wizards who actually controlled the universe, he was deeply troubled. "I have received a directive from the Supreme Extra Universal Command. Our services are required elsewhere and we shall move our operations to another galaxy. It appears that our mission here has been deemed unsuccessful by higher authorities. I cannot disagree. We've held this place together as long as possible. Things seem to be going from bad to worse. There hasn't been a decent car made in America since the 1976 Cadillac Fleetwood, the music degenerates constantly, and the least intelligent are still the most prolific. The so-called religions we established to keep them in check have become counter-productive. The introduction of yet another disease, war, or religion," he continued, "are not enough to turn things around this time. Gentlemen." he said gravely, "the Earth needs to take a big crap. It needs to excrete these gnawing little human rodents."

"That is a heady statement, Your Excellence," replied Marcus, "What do you have in mind?"

"We've been instructed to handle this matter in a manner consistent with our modification of past so-called advanced civilizations in other locations. I think we should initiate a celestial disturbance of some sort on the outside edge of Earth's galaxy. We will target Earth specifically, and then prepare our departure, as whatever we decide to construct moves in this direction. We will leave this galaxy altogether a few days or weeks, as necessary, before it actually strikes the planet, and leave them to face the consequences of their own actions."

"Don't you think that's a bit extreme, Your Excellence?" Alexander asked. "Do you really feel we have given these creatures enough time?"

"Hell yes we've given them enough time," Marduk snapped. "How much time do they need? I can't...No, we've wasted enough time with these wretches. They were created as a slave colony to mine this planet, and that was all well and good, as long as we needed their services, which we obviously don't any longer, given the depletion of rotanium at this point. So technically, these animals should've been destroyed eons ago. Their arrogance is incredibly offensive, especially given their decided lack of both intelligence and morality. We, are of course amoral, as our circumstances dictate, but these foul creatures are detestable. Personally, I don't care whether they destroy this toilet which they inhabit, or whether we do it for them, and though I suppose they do have some merit, I can't seem to think of it now. Basically, they are redundant, which is reason enough to me for their elimination, but it's their arrogance which I find most offensive. These groveling little rodents should be destroyed entirely, but out of respect for the opinions of some of this group, I have decided that their so-called civilization shall not be totally eliminated, just partially, but personally, you know my feelings. I detest these vile disgusting creatures. Dogs are better pets."

"Your Excellency," ventured mighty Bustokus, "they are not all bad, and their antics have admittedly provided us much amusement. Take the Hebrews for instance, we sent them on a wild goose chase for forty years and then settled them in the only place in the Mideast without oil. That was some 'Promised Land.' And what about...."

Marduk interrupted, "Yes, yes, yes. I remember, and that was really funny, but back then humans still showed some promise, and I must admit that in the past century they accomplished much which was of interest to me personally. I liked Elvis. I enjoy their primitive machinery, and they do, or rather did have a sense of color. I loved the 1970s, when Negroes knew how to dress, and had some style. Now their music sucks and they look like bums. White people have become weak and lazy, and the Jews and the Arabs, hell, I can't tell one from the other. Enough is enough. You who are their advocates had better be content with the decision I have made, otherwise I might change my mind altogether and destroy this whole craphouse and all of them."

Some discussion followed, but surprisingly little debate. The Earthlings were judged to be hopelessly defective due to their

4

warlike nature, overpopulation, and the destruction of planetary resources. Ignorance, superstition, and wars still reign. There really wasn't that much to talk about. A vote was taken, the matter was passed, and Earth was targeted for significant but not total destruction in less than six months.

"One more thing," Marduk stated, addressing the Council. "What about Mazor?"

Mazor was a recently defected member who before, as a Council member, was known as Louie 'The Pencil' Guergleoni. He'd become the Council's accountant, in charge of world economics, and for the most part had served well, except for a few minor instances in which large sums of money, intended for other purposes, accidentally ended up in his own bank account. His departure from the Council was completely unexpected, and unannounced. He'd simply walked through the gate one day, without notice, stepped into a waiting car, and sped away. Sources outside the compound reported that he had taken the name Ron Di Lizardo and now operated a high end junkyard just beyond the Chattanooga city limits, less than five miles away from the Council's Central Command Center. It was both incredible and incomprehensible. Not only must he be replaced, but he possessed secrets of such immense import that, well....it was still too soon to determine the Council's course of action in the matter.

The mighty Corsican, who dutifully served as the Council's meteorological director, stood to address the remaining members. Before he could utter the first word, however, the meeting was interrupted by the intrusion of a psychiatric orderly, a rustic Caucasian-American with a low forehead and even lower intelligence quotient, someone called `Bim,' as if such could be deemed an appropriate name anywhere else in the world but Chattanooga.

"You boys need anything?" he asked, sarcastically.

"I've instructed you not to disturb us when you see the chamber doors closed," Marduk stated angrily. "The closed doors signify that a meeting is in progress. I've told you this repeatedly, yet you continue to disregard my commands. Any further interruptions will be at your own peril, I'll tell you that. However, since you have already disturbed us, yes, I suppose you might as well bring me a Double-Cola."

"I'm sorry Marty, I didn't mean to disturb you," the psychiatric

5

orderly mocked. "I just thought you might like some refreshments. Are you guys busy today?" he asked, "Controlling the universe and all? You better take care of that earthquake over there in Mexico, and, by the way, that shit is startin' up again over in Afgan. You better do somethin' about Haiti too, them boat people gonna' rurn Miamuh Beach...again."

As the orderly left the chamber, closing the door on the way out, Marduk observed, "Surely we can find better help than that idiot. Here we are, directing the affairs of this galaxy and subjected to intrusions by feral rustics. I suggest," he said coldly, directing a hard glance at noble Alexander, director of internal affairs, "that you review our staff appointments and make whatever replacements and adjustments as may be required. I do not wish to see that hayseed, or any more like him again. I trust I have made myself clear."

Alexander replied, "Yes, Your Excellence, I shall see that incidents of this nature are not repeated. I must state, in my own defense, however, that while Chattanooga may indeed be the geographical center of the universe, this significance doesn't seem to have been genetically impressed upon the population at large. In other words, as they say, 'it's hard to find good help.'"

This jocular remark elicited loud bursts of laughter from all of the Council members, with the singular exception of the Corsican, who had been standing quietly preparing to address the members on some matter of international moment, prior to the interruption. He dryly replied to Alexander's comment, "The little bastard should be eliminated," a phrase he'd picked up from some 1940s gangster film, and used in reference to nearly everything.

This response nearly brought the house down. Marduk wielded the gavel, repeatedly hammering it against his desk in an attempt to restore order, while wiping tears of laughter on the sleeve of his robe. After some few minutes the laughter died down, and the Corsican continued. "I feel that some action needs to be taken in the matter with regard to the defection from our ranks of our former member Mazor, who now employs the name Ron Di Lizardo. He is in possession of such knowledge as threatens not only our aggregation, but indeed the balance, and therefore the order of the universe. The fact that he has set up some business dealing in junk cars less than five miles from here is extremely dangerous, not only to our efforts, but to our entire order."

"He's right," interjected Alexander. "Since there has only been but one defection from our ranks since the dawn of time, I feel this to be an extremely serious and urgent matter. In consideration of the extent and type of information he holds, and its potential danger to all of us, I suggest that he be eliminated immediately."

"Precisely!" replied the Corsican. "If not, I fear it will truly be our Waterloo."

"Well, I think there seems to be a bit of an overreaction here." said Marcus. "While it's true that this is our second defection, I think the fact of the matter is that Louie, I mean Mazor, just got tired and couldn't deal with the pressures and responsibilities of the job anymore. He's always been very efficient and circumspect. If he were unbalanced...I just don't perceive any sort of threat. He has taken on a new identity, that's all. I don't believe he poses any danger at all. He just wants to be left alone."

"That may well be," continued the Corsican, "but the fact that he elected to settle down, almost within the shadow of our headquarters is unnerving. Not only that, it indicates to me a decided lack of judgment. If he was so cavalier in this instance what may we expect from him in the future? Even now, I am told, he makes snide little innuendos to some of his customers. I don't think it's a good sign. I expect trouble. It would be another matter entirely if he had packed his bags and moved to Switzerland, hell, even Montana, but just around the bend? I don't like it. Look what happened when Edison left our ranks. Oh yes, it was only one defection, but look at the consequences. The whole world was thrown ahead of schedule, the indirect result of which were the two world wars, and other social upheavals. I must say, 'Quod inferius est sicut quod superius.' If Earth is thrown off balance, then the solar system gets out of sync also. I wish to go on record now as saying that Mazor needs to be eliminated, or transferred to another dimension, if you think that sounds better."

"Let's not forget the connection between Edison and Carl Jung," Alexander stated loudly. "It was Edison who persuaded Carl Jung to venture here in the first place," he continued. "That was an extremely close call. It was fortunate that we were able to disguise ourselves as inmates of this medical research center and asylum. Jung came very close to our secret. And, as if that were not enough, he even mentioned being in Chattanooga in one of his books. He had a big mouth and thought that Chattanooga had become the geographical center of the universe as the result of an intergalactic shift. Fortunately he lacked the means to prove it."

"The same cannot be said of Louie the Pencil....I mean Mazor. He invented the lens of the Chile Palomar spectroscope telescope. He has the lens formula right in his head, right now. He invented it that time he ran away for two months and took a job at the Double-Cola Plant. That bizarre action should have alerted us to his instability."

"You're right again," replied the Corsican. "But there's more. We now know that the lens itself has been built into many 16 ounce Double-Cola Bottles; the bottom of the bottle is the lens itself, in miniature. While we've been able to retrieve and destroy many of those particular bottles, there are possibly hundreds, or even thousands of them still out there, floating around the country. What happens when some astrophysicist just happens to look through the top of an empty bottle? The peculiar light refractions of the spectroscope will manifest immediately. The consequences of such a discovery as I've just mentioned are too horrible to imagine, and yet, I venture to say that such an event could happen any day. This was the work of Mazor. He did it for a joke, just to see if it could be done. He's truly capable of anything."

So far Marduk had witnessed this exchange of opinions in silence. Now he spoke from the authority of his exalted position. "Gentlemen, I have weighed both sides of this issue, and have, to some degree agonized over the situation. This is what I have concluded. Mazor, or Ron Di Lizardo, as he calls himself now, is not a problem for us. As our work throughout the cosmos continues, hopefully the intergalactic populations will evolve as well. Was that not our purpose here? That one of our number, one of the enlightened, has entered the mainstream of Earth's society as a common tradesman, is perhaps our greatest achievement to date, possibly the greatest accomplishment in the history of this organization. In the distant past," he continued, "the enlightened have withdrawn from society, as we've done. I suggest that we send someone to ascertain Mazor's intentions. We should discuss those findings, and, if all is well, let him pursue his new life without interference from us for as long as he has left, if you catch my drift. As far as Edison is concerned, there was a true example of 'quid pro nimbus,' and as such was beyond our jurisdiction. I might further add that we, as a body, were not held accountable for his actions, notwithstanding that the results of his findings caused the unnecessary deaths of more than a hundred million persons. But again, they were merely humans after all, so really, what difference did it make?"

A vote was taken, and Marduk allowed it to stand. The decision was made to determine the intentions of their former colleague, and in the absence of any dangerous activities, he would be permitted to live out the remainder of his days unhindered. The second, and equally important order of the day, was the problem of replenishing their ranks. They were two down at the moment, and a constant membership of twelve was required by the Supreme Interplanetary Aggregation's bylaws. The methods of recruiting new members were limited by the externally imposed rule that they must not actively seek initiates, but instead must select from whatever candidates chance brought their way. This ancient rule had been established upon the premise that a perfect balance existed in the universe, and that whoever they ended up would be right for the job. Admittedly this might seem like a rather casual way to run the universe, but so far it had proved effective.

Marduk assured the membership that there was no cause for alarm and that their two new member candidates would be arriving unexpectedly any day, as ordained by the ancient charter. "In the meantime," he said, addressing the Corsican, "there is a trailer park in Sandusky, Ohio which requires some attention. See to it with a tornado, if you would be so kind. Symbion can give you the precise coordinates." With that, the meeting was concluded and the members returned to afternoon games of shuffleboard, bingo, and checkers.

The command post employed by the Council of the Twelve was established in 1943 as the Wildman Retreat, a front for covert government operators seeking to go beneath the third level of caves under the magnificent tourist attraction, Ruby Falls, a Lookout Mountain landmark. Their intentions in this exploration were to retrieve certain minerals, specifically rotanium, for use in the development of an explosive device far more devastating than the atom bomb. The atom bomb project was successfully concluded ahead of Operation Lookout, so the facility became unnecessary.

The Wildman Sanitarium. It was easier to get in than it was to get out.

After the war, the government sold the installation to a group of wealthy physicians, who continue to operate the facility as a sanitarium. As such, the Wildman Retreat continues to provide quality psychiatric care for approximately 200 mental patients. Beneath this serene exterior, however, the ancient Council of the Twelve controls the fate of nations, populations, weather, diseases, indeed the course of entire races and civilizations.

10

2.

COLLISION COURSE
THOMPSON OBSERVATORY: LOBSTER TAIL, ICELAND

"The entire international scientific community is well aware of the presence of SS396, and of its trajectory," observed world renowned astrophysicist, Dr. Debra Davis. "And yet," she continued, "nowhere has there been much public mention of the obvious danger its presence clearly implies. This is very unusual. It's as if SS396 doesn't exist, as if by not acknowledging it, it will simply disperse or change its course. I don't understand the international silence."

The problem seemed real enough to Dr. Davis. For some reason a large heavenly body approximately the size of the planet Jupiter, had suddenly appeared and then arbitrarily and erratically accelerated suddenly from a fixed position in another galaxy. While unexplained celestial movements were not unknown, or even unusual, that one of this nature had occurred was deeply troubling to her. It was, as far as could be determined, without precedent in the recorded history of astronomy or astrophysics. 'Powerball,' as Dr. Huji Kwami Entutu had named SS396, appeared to be headed straight for planet Earth at a velocity which was basically immeasurable with present scientific equipment.

"Your fears are without merit," Huji had told Davis. "It is one dimensional, that's why its apparent velocity can't be measured. Its movement is apparent, not actual."

"But, according to my calculations, Powerball will collide with our planet in less than 200 years," Davis said. "As far as I can tell, this is unavoidable. So why haven't the Russians, or the British, or anyone else for that matter, displayed any concern over the presence of Powerball? I don't understand it. This is potentially a problem of catastrophic proportions for all of us. I know that you discovered this 'thing,' and that you named it, but still…"

"They haven't expressed any concerns about it for the same reason we haven't. Nobody knows what the hell Powerball is. Is it a

11

planet? A star? A giant asteroid? What? I don't know yet, nobody does, but what we do know, what the world's scientific community knows and agrees upon, is that it appeared spontaneously, and that it exists beyond our galaxy, and is therefore one dimensional. Since it is one dimensional, its motions must of necessity be apparent, not actual. Consequently it poses no threat to us. In other words, to be more succinct, it doesn't actually exist. It's in another galaxy. I'm quite surprised by your concerns. Honestly Dr. Davis, it will likely disappear without notice, as quickly as it manifested. It's probably merely some sort of illusion existing solely as a convergence of cosmic light."

"I understand that it's one dimensional, but in a broader sense, in a cosmic sense, nothing can exist at all except in relation to something else," Davis argued. "It bears no resemblance to anything I've ever seen. It looks like a bright dot of light circumscribed by a larger ring of light or energy, or perhaps something else altogether. I really don't know what it is."

"Hell, it looks like the hubcap off of a `67 Eldorado to me," interjected a rustic sounding voice from the other side of the planetarium. "I've been noticing what appear to be the developing formation of broad spoke like structures emanating from the center area of intense light. It's still too early to say for sure, but given the rapidly changing nature of this thing, whatever it is, I'd say that's what's happening."

Satisfied with the brilliance of his own deductions, computer nerd Clarence Henry took a swig of Double-Cola and firmly smacked the bottle on the table for emphasis. Of course Powerball did not exist. It was outside the galaxy. It was one dimensional. Consequently, while it could be observed, it had no objective reality from Earthly points of reference. Its motions, while observable, were, in the final analysis, merely apparent, not actual. Entutu was right.

"Well," Entutu laughed, "that's the nature of quantum reality. I take back everything I've ever said about the Vanderbilt football team," referring to Dr. Henry's alma mater. "Still, I think one of us should call Hans Olv in Zurich, and see what he has to say about these new developments in its appearance."

"You know him best, Dr. Entutu."

"You're right, I'll call him immediately. That should put your mind at ease," he said, and left the room.

Drs. Davis and Henry continued to observe Powerball. It still appeared to be on a collision course with planet Earth. It was nice to know that it was merely an illusion. In a few minutes Dr. Entutu returned with the results of his conversation with Professor Olv. "Well," he smiled, "Olv said that SS396 is one dimensional, and that's why nobody has said anything about its changes. The members of the scientific community worldwide assume that the rest of us are aware of the phenomenon, and that we, like they, are watching it also. Since it does not exist objectively, there is nothing to be said. That explains the international silence on the matter, at least to my satisfaction. That and the exclusive, protective, and competitive nature of our colleagues in the field. It poses no threat to anything in this galaxy. Its motions and apparent physical changes simply don't matter. Dr. Olv sends his regards, and said that you, Dr. Davis, shouldn't worry about it at all."

"My unnecessary concerns make me look foolish," Dr. Davis stated dryly. "I think it's being in this God forsaken wasteland. It's really clouding my judgment."

"You two M.I.T.-wits should be embarrassed," Dr. Henry said laughingly as he stood to take a bow. "I, a lowly hillbilly from the Volunteer State, had to figure it all out for you two geniuses. Will my work never end? I accept your humble and heartfelt gratitude." With that, he bowed at the waist, and spread his arms, unintentionally striking the soft drink bottle and knocking it off the table. It rolled around for a few seconds and eventually came to rest at that spot on the observatory floor where the light from the spheres exited the telescope's eyepiece. Immediately there were a series of high pitched and almost deafening sounds accompanied by the rapid darting of laser like beams around the room. Everywhere a beam focused, something was immediately destroyed or disintegrated. Some objects incinerated instantly, while others melted. Some, simply ceased to exist, apparently vaporized by the darting energy beams. Some items, however, seemed to be unaffected at all by the fantastic display of flashing lights. The observatory's fire alarms sounded loudly as the room filled with smoke and particulate matter from the destructive actions of the energy beams.

All three scientists immediately hit the floor, and as they did, Dr. Henry's foot struck the Double-Cola bottle, pushing it out from under the telescope's eyepiece, ending the odd display as quickly as it had begun.

"What in the hell was that?" Davis shouted above the sounding alarms and buzzers.

"It must have been the bottle," Dr. Henry said, "Look, it's still glowing."

"Don't touch it!" shouted Entutu. "Leave it there. C'mon let's check for damages."

"Don't worry, I'm not about to touch that thing, at least not until it cools down."

"But look," observed Dr. Davis, "It's glowing with colors I've never seen before, colors existing outside the known spectrum."

"Stay back," cautioned Entutu. "There's no way to tell what has happened here."

Within an hour the bottle had cooled to the degree that the three scientists felt safe enough to approach it with a Geiger counter. Nothing. Other instruments indicated no activity of any kind either, nothing electro-magnetic or radioactive. The bottle looked like any other regular Double-Cola bottle. Having satisfied themselves that the bottle posed no further danger, Entutu retrieved it from the floor. Holding it carefully with gloved hands, he examined it visually in the presence of his associates. All it said was "Double-Cola, Chattanooga, Tennessee."

"It's a cold drink bottle," Entutu observed. "Nothing exceptional here. It's just a glass bottle."

"Let me see it," Dr. Henry said, taking it carefully. He held it to the overhead light and looked at its bottom. It was clear swirled glass, nothing more. He reversed it and looked through the small opening. Again, just a normal soft drink bottle. "It's just a drink bottle," he said, handing it to Dr. Davis.

The bottle on the right looked normal, but wasn't!

"I agree," she said, turning it over in her hands, "but we all know what happened. When the light from the telescope struck this bottle, or passed through it, or whatever it did, there were immediate and violent consequences."

"The bottle was fine until it fell under the light. I think that it was affected by the focused, concentrated light coming through the telescope eyepiece," Entutu observed. "Let's take it outside and try looking through it at the sky under normal light."

It was discovered when examined under normal outdoor night light that the Double-Cola bottle, when employed as a telescope directed skyward, revealed the presence of a negative refracting spectroscope lens built into the bottom of the bottle. The technical sophistication involved in the design and construction of this lens was so far beyond the realm of present scientific knowledge as to appear to have been constructed by beings of another order than human, a much higher order.

The scientists kept their findings to themselves but continued experimenting with the bottle. It was ultimately determined through the use of their discovery that SS396, though one dimensional at present, would become objective at the instant it entered Earth's galaxy. At this point it would accelerate even faster, disintegrating Earth, dislodging other planets from their orbits, and ultimately destroying the solar system. The time factor? Twenty years hence, plus or minus ten years.

That an instrument of such technical sophistication could even exist, let alone be incorporated in the bottom of a soft drink bottle postulated the active involvement of a superior intelligence. This was no accident. Several calls were made to the Double-Cola plant in Chattanooga, but to no avail. Nobody there had any idea what the scientists were talking about.

The fate of the planet, the solar system, and possibly even the entire galaxy was in the hands of these three scientists, stuck in some provincial outpost in the frozen wasteland. There was no time to lose. Whoever had invented this thing, for whatever reason or reasons, was the only entity on Earth who could possibly know how to avert the impending disaster, that is, if it could be averted at all. With this in mind, Drs. Davis and Henry made plans to travel incognito to Chattanooga, Tennessee with the purpose of locating the individual or group who designed this lens, and soliciting his, hers, or their help. There were no other options. Meanwhile, other astronomers and astrophysicists throughout the nations watched the approach of SS396 as casually as a child would watch the Aurora Borealis, oblivious to the impending doom its presence heralded.

The astrophysicists had reason to suspect that what appeared to be a normal Double-Cola bottle revealed the direct involvement of a superior race of beings.

3.

THE WILL

"Well, Mr. Hamster, that concludes our business," the lawyer stated dryly, handing the young man a small stack of papers.

"So I get everything?"

"Everything that is, except for your father's stock in Amalgamated Cheese, Inc. According to the original charter, that stock will be equally divided among the other stockholders, purchased by them actually, and that money is to be held in a trust account, administered by myself, until such time as you have a child."

"So I'm to be left financially bereft due to that `skip a generation' tax dodge. What if I don't produce any heirs? What happens then?"

"Well, that is more or less up to me. In the event, however, that no heir is forthcoming, the money returns to Amalgamated Cheese....eventually. It's all clearly spelled out in the papers that I have provided for you."

"Okay Mr. Filcher, when do I get my money?"

"You have but to sign these papers and everything is yours. It was your father's wish that I retain the title to your family estate to prevent you from selling it for any reason. When I die, it shall be passed along to you."

"Mr. Filcher, I'm entitled to the full use, occupation, and ownership of that property, and I resent the insinuation that I would be likely to sell the home of my youth."

"Chip, the place is yours. You may live in it, use it, etc. You simply can't sell it or borrow against it. There is no point in discussing this any further. If you want to have another attorney look over...."

"No, that won't be necessary."

"This is for your own protection Chip. With over eight hundred thousand dollars at your immediate disposal, and the house, its property taxes, upkeep and maintenance paid for, you should be comfortably set for quite some time."

"My father's estate should have been worth several million dollars, at least. I don't understand where the money went. There should be more than eight hundred thousand dollars left. I don't understand."

"Take my word for it," the lawyer smiled. "Your father was a big spender with an extravagant lifestyle. He had women everywhere, and had for years. Besides, he was 97 years old. Frankly I'm surprised there was anything left at all." The busy lawyer didn't want to waste any time answering stupid questions from some moron.

"I want the cheese then," Chip said off the top of his head.

"Unfortunately, that isn't possible. The company was set up in 1952 and it was clearly outlined at the beginning that the stock would be closely held by the original founders. As your father wished, your children shall be provided for."

"Mr. Filcher, that Hunter Ratcliff, or Ratlips, or whatever his name really is, he's working there. I suppose his father isn't going to give him stock now that my father has died? I should be running the whole operation worldwide. I know more about cheese than Ratlips. He doesn't know feta from fetid. Really, Mr. Filcher, I don't wish to sound ungrateful, but I probably know more about cheese than any man alive. Besides, I don't think anyone who has a name beginning with 'Rat' should in any way be associated with cheese, if you know what I mean. And since when did my old man become so concerned with children. I was an accident. He told me that himself. He hated children. I can't help but imagine that he would have had me sterilized if he'd had his way. He hated children. Hell, he hated me. He hated everybody, as far as I know."

"That well may be, Chip, but you can't make somebody do something after death that he was unwilling to do in life. If your father had wanted you to work at Amalgamated Cheese, he would have hired you himself. As president of the company, he could have done so anytime."

"I suppose you're right. Besides, the factory itself has a distinctly unpleasant odor. Still, considering that my father started the company, I don't think it unfair that I, as his only son and sole heir, should wish to derive some benefit from his life's work."

"There's nothing at all I can do about it," the lawyer stated

18

conclusively.

"Well, what about the Green Tortoise Club?" Chip asked.

"Six months ago," the lawyer replied, "your father made a large donation to the Tortoise for the purpose of resurfacing all twelve of the outdoor tennis courts. He also paid for the manager's daughter's honeymoon. You do remember Charlene, I trust?"

"Of course I remember her, half of Nashville does. I dare say that at the tender age of seventeen, she'd personally handled more penises than most middle-aged urologists."

"All's well that ends well, Chip," the lawyer stated dryly. "She married a doctor from another city, and her father is happy at last. You're suspension was cancelled, and you are again entitled to all of the privileges of membership. It has all been approved by the board of directors. You've taken over your father's membership. The Board was somewhat reluctant at first, but in consideration of your father's especially generous endowment...well, it has been worked out. Be that as it may, I would still suggest that you stay well clear of Charlene's father."

"Worked out? I would imagine so. My late grandfather founded the Tortoise after he followed the jeweled turtle into that cave. In fact he named it..."

"I'm familiar enough with the history of the country club," the lawyer replied curtly. "Just remember your father is no longer around to have you reinstated should you again fall from grace. Keep that in mind."

"All I did was...."

"Drying your golf ball on the Saudi ambassador's headdress was most inappropriate and was a great embarrassment to the governor. Now, if you will sign this other set of papers...."

"Just one more thing Mr. Filcher, what about my father's Rolls-Royce?"

"Your father left it to Therpis. Now if you don't mind, I would like to...."

"Therpis? He gave it to Therpis? That foolish hick doesn't even possess a driver's license. He and I are going to have a talk."

The lawyer looked over the top of his reading glasses at Chip Hamster. The loathing he felt for the spoiled, thirty-something little prick was beyond expression. It was all the lawyer could do to remain in the room with him long enough to conclude this unpleasant business. 'Look at the little son of a bitch, sitting there in bright purple shorts, raggedy tennis shoes, and a tee shirt covered with drawings of skeletons engaged in lewd acts. What an absolutely useless human being, a complete and total deadbeat,' the lawyer thought. Still, he didn't need the little bastard poking around or asking any questions, what lawyer ever does?

Meanwhile, Chip eyed the lawyer suspiciously. 'He's a slippery little son of a bitch,' Chip observed quietly to himself, and determined to keep an eye on him.

"That 'hick,' as you call him," the attorney continued, "is your father's cousin in some sort of roundabout way, and is, therefore, related to you. Chip, I'm going to give it to you straight," the lawyer swallowed hard, then proceeded. "I've been your father's friend, financial advisor, and attorney for over forty years. I've known you since you were born, and it is, quite frankly, my opinion that you're a playboy and nothing more. You've had every opportunity that wealth and prestige afford, and you've turned them to no purpose whatsoever. I stop short of saying you are a bum, solely out of respect to your late father. But you'd better make something out of yourself. You need to get a job, go back to work, do something. I don't mean to lecture you Chip, but I feel close enough to advise."

The words cut Chip Hamster to the quick. If only Filcher really knew how he felt, how much Chip really wanted to succeed, to make something of himself. Besides, Chip's old man wouldn't have been such hot shit if he hadn't inherited the family fortune, a pirate treasure discovered when Chip's grandfather had followed some creeping, jewel encrusted turtle into a cave. A God damned turtle!

Chip's grandfather. The family fortune rode in on the back of a turtle!

It was far easier in ancient times, Chip reflected. If a man wanted to prove himself, or wanted something, the gods gave him some specific task to accomplish, like bringing home the Golden Fleece, or something else equally difficult and pointless. While the task was almost always both stupid and impossible, it was at least tangible and definite. Today, it was a different matter. There were few great adventures left for the average young man. Everything is so vague now. You mostly got married, fat, in debt, and died early. But Chip believed in himself. There was some great purpose for which he'd been created. In the meantime, all he could do was wait. He addressed the attorney once more.

"Mr. Filcher, I appreciate your sincerity and concern, and yet surely you, of all people, must be aware that my life has not been as easy as it appears on the surface. As you know, my mother abandoned us when I was eight years old, running away to Arab, Alabama, with some bowling instructor in a stolen cheese truck. After that, I was sent to an endless series of private schools, all far enough away from home so that my father wouldn't have to fool with me except at Christmas and Easter. And now my father has been murdered. I suspect that I have suffered severe emotional and psychological depravation as a result. Since I'm still relatively young, it's perhaps too early to assay the full measure of my injuries, and eight hundred thousand dollars, more or less, offers slight recompense for being totally deprived of a nurturing family environment. If I am indeed maladjusted, is it any wonder?"

The lawyer honestly appeared touched for a moment. "Mason, your father, I mean, did the best he could. He was not a family man, it was just not his nature. He was aware of his shortcomings as a parent, and yet, I can say that he loved you as much as he was capable of understanding that emotion. In any case, I am available if you need legal counsel, and Mr. Crooke at the bank stands ready to help you dispose of your remain…I mean your inheritance. I suggest you visit him. Now, if you will sign these papers, I can make my lunch meeting at the Green Tortoise."

Mason Charles Hamster a.k.a. Chip Hamster, looked at the stack of papers and began signing them. It would have taken him weeks to read them in detail. He just wanted to finish this business, put the past behind him, and start his new life. When the papers had been signed he stood to take his leave.

Chip Hamster was a thirty-ish gentleman of the country club set. Tall and lean, with sandy brown hair, piercing blue eyes, and sharply chiseled features, he was handsome by anyone's standards, and stood in sharp contrast to attorney Leonard Filcher, whose gaunt look, pale and transparent skin gave him the appearance of a funeral director. Chip's manner and bearing, despite his baggy and brightly colored Bermuda shorts, spoke of old money. He was comfortable in the formal setting of the lawyer's office, but was equally at home at a dyke bar, a cock fight, or the men's lounge at the Trailways bus station.

So, matters were settled, at least for the moment. Chip would finally be able to fulfill his lifelong dream of purchasing a new Rolls-Royce convertible and returning to the Green Tortoise in the manner he deserved, now that his membership had been restored. They'd be kissing his ass now, all of them, all of those disgusting social climbing clones with their 2.3 kids, and their chubby wives, with their boxy looking Volvo station wagons. They'd laughed and called Chip a deadbeat because he aspired to be a writer. And the business with Charlene had been truly embarrassing, and being banned from Nashville's premier social gathering place was a horrible thing. But that was all over now. In fact, Chip had been very pleasantly surprised by the support of some of his former friends in the wake of his father's tragic death. Many of them, people he hadn't seen for years, had sent sympathy cards, or had dropped by in person. In fact, Chip would be attending an informal gathering this very evening in his honor at the charming Belle Meade address of his formerly close friends, Sidney and Stewey Von Snocker, of Nashville, Palm Beach, and Newport (Tennessee). It suddenly dawned on Chip that since he'd been living in Key West the last four years, there was really nobody in Nashville he could call for a date. While he certainly missed Ioveena , he wasn't married, and felt free to conduct himself however he wanted.

In Key West, Chip had been known by the nickname of 'Mr. Odom, the sausage magnate.' He'd told his friends that his father owned the Tennessee Pride Sausage Company in Nashville. It was a little white lie he'd fabricated, but at no damage to anyone personally, mainly because 'Tennessee Pride Sausage' sounded more impressive than 'Amalgamated Cheese.'

"Think about it," he'd said to Ioveena , the lovely Haitian refugee he'd found swimming toward the coast one morning, "Sausage, s.a.u.s.a.g.e. Sausage. There's something manly about the very word. In fact, when he hauled her out of the ocean, like a dark and sunburned mermaid, he'd comforted her with a quart of Blatz beer and one of those disgusting summer sausages, the kind wrapped in plastic that costs a quarter at the local Seven-Eleven store. That night, after Ioveena had recovered from overexposure to the sun and salt water, he massaged her exquisite body with John the Conqueror Oil and tucked her into his own bed on the upstairs porch, lulling her gently to sleep with the soothing words of the Tennessee Pride theme song:

'For real country sausage, the best you ever tried, look for me on the label of Tennessee Pride. It's real country sausage yessiree, but the secret of the goodness is the recipe, and before this song is done I'll say, Mr. Odom will tell you how it's made...'

As Chip softly sang those lovely and soothing words, he actually felt himself to be the real Mr. Odom. The next part of the song was his favorite:

'First you start with meat that's really grand, pure whole hog pork, the best in the land, then you add a dash of X and a pitch of Z, and for flavor and taste you add Y-9D...a touch of Odom's magic blends all three, and that's the secret of the secret....the recipe'

But what was Y-9D really? The question had no doubt troubled greater minds than his own. Worry over this matter had probably contributed to the deaths of Edison, Einstein, and Tesla. Something which sounded as esoteric as Y-9D couldn't simply be an off the cuff fabrication of some ad man. It was most likely a couched reference to something really deep, like the proverbial Philosopher's Stone. On the other hand, Y-9D could be some deadly synthetic toxin. Who could be certain? Someday Chip would know the true significance of Y-9D. It was at least as important as $E=MC2$. In the meantime, he would have to be content with the knowledge that millions of people had no idea that Y-9D had any meaning whatsoever. Like the ancients said, the world is literally a book of mysteries. The keys to the universe are in plain sight for those who take the time to look for meaning beneath the obvious.

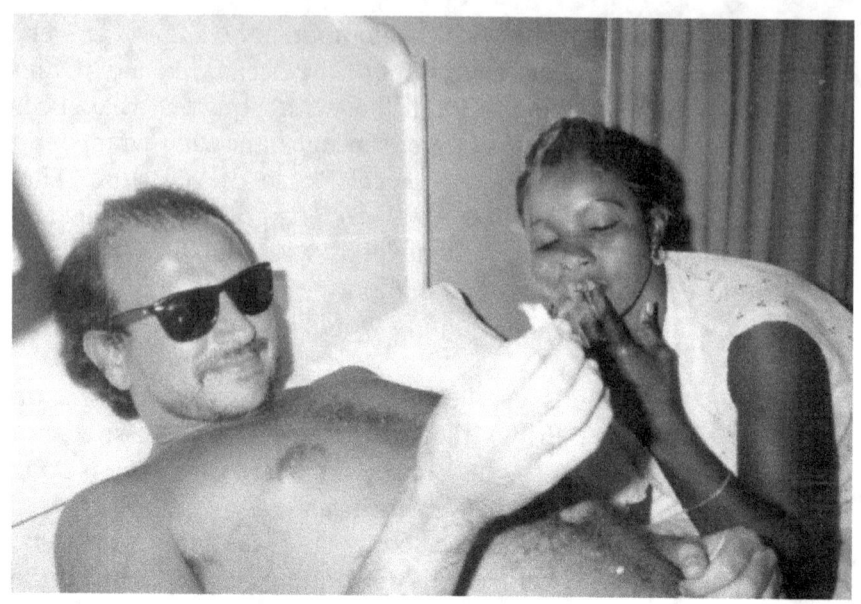

Chip Hamster with the lovely Ioveena in Key West

Later that night, after a Perry Mason rerun, Chip had slipped into bed beside Ioveena and found her sleeping like a baby. Bright and early the next morning Chip was awakened by the lovely Ioveena attending to his vibrant personal manhood. From that very instant she had become the love of his life, at least for the moment.

From what he was able to ascertain in spite of their problems with communication (she spoke little English), Ioveena had gone fishing with her brother off the coast of her hometown, Miragoane, Haiti early one morning. She took a nap and awakened at dusk to find herself alone in the middle of the Caribbean Sea, with no land in sight. She kept herself alive for several days by eating and drinking sparingly of the slight provisions she and her brother had brought along. Finally, on the morning of the fifth day, a great storm arose and capsized her small boat. She stayed afloat as long as possible, but finally gave up, resolved to find sanctuary in the dark embrace of Neptune. Just as she lost consciousness, she was rescued by a porpoise that gave her a lift on its back to a sandbar close to the shore of Key West, where Chip found her swimming pleasantly and leisurely toward the beach, at least that's what she said.

It must be admitted that this account seemed somewhat questionable, even to Chip, who was more inclined than disinclined to believe anything any woman told him. Still, had not Chip, himself, actually personally spoken to a group of porpoises through the underwater telephone before he got kicked out of the navy, he might have questioned certain aspects of her narrative. As it was, it mattered not, for she was exquisite in every way, and Chip considered her to be a gift from the god of the brinish depths, probably in appreciation of those two large bales of marijuana he was forced to dispose of rather hastily two years earlier.

At the news of his father's untimely death, about the same time as Ioveena 's arrival, Chip had been forced to return to Nashville to deal with the funeral and settling the estate. He'd reluctantly left the lovely Ioveena at his place in Key West under the care of some other Haitians. He missed her now, especially her many and ample 'charms,' as they are referred to in polite society.

It was lunchtime, so Chip sat down for some sushi. As he ate, he thought of her and made his plans. The first thing to go was that BMW of his. It was okay in Key West, since there weren't that many of them there. But in Nashville, there were three or four at every intersection. He would call the Rolls-Royce dealer in Miami, pick out a new convertible over the phone, and bank wire a deposit. He would then fly down, get the car, and pay his respects to Ioveena . After a little R & R, he would return to Nashville and begin his professional business career, whatever it might be.

It had all happened so fast, his father's untimely demise, fatally smacked in the head with a skillet by an unknown woman. A rather unsavory ending for a cheese magnate, but then the details were still somewhat sketchy. All Chip knew for certain was that 'the incident' had taken place at one of those remote and unpronounceable villages in the southernmost part of Mexico. Struck down in his golden years by a skillet. It took nearly two weeks to get the body home. According to the physician, Dr. Bumbleby, Chip's father was a dark brown, almost mummified in fact. It was a grisly business.

 **The murder weapon. An unsavory ending for a powerful cheese magnate. Struck down by a skillet.**

The vile murderess had escaped, according to the authorities, and most likely fled the country. In other words, the local police had no intention of seeking to solve the crime. A more or less reliable witness had reportedly seen a large, dark woman sneaking out the back door on the day of the murder, so the perpetrator, whoever she might be, was still at large, somewhere in the cosmos. Chip resolved that he would at some point avenge his father's murder. If necessary he would, like the great O.J. Simpson, devote his entire life to finding the real murderer or murderers, whoever they might be, even if he had to personally search every golf course in Florida.

And then there was the incident with the bee. It was not by mere chance that this event happened, and in retrospect, Chip concluded that its true significance had not been fully appreciated, or even understood at the time of the occurrence. Indeed, it was only the passage of time, aging and mellowing the memory like a fine grain-fed Kansas steak, or a 2014 bottle of Thunderbird Wine, which, along with a twenty dollar visit to the fortune teller, made known the bee's true import. The bee had served more or less as a harbinger of a series of seemingly unrelated events, which, through an acausal connection, would be deemed in the final analysis to be synchronistic, at least in the Jungian sense. While Chip's conclusions were subject to some argument, the facts were a matter of record, that is, they were reported to several reasonably sober patrons of Captain Tony's bar, who believed the narrative to have been accurate at the time.

Here's what happened:

Chip had been sleeping late and awakened just in time to notice a rather large bee buzz through the open window. It was nearly 10:30 in the morning, and he should have been at work. Alas, he had no job. He'd told his father that he intended to be a writer, and that's why he was in Key West, following in the footsteps of Hemmingway, Tennessee Williams, and Mike Hunt. He did intend to be a writer; that is, he wanted to be rich and famous. He would begin writing his masterpiece any day now. The fact of the matter was that the only things Chip had written during four years in Key West were checks on an account reluctantly funded by his father.

On that fateful day, Chip had continued to lie there watching the bee casually buzzing around the room. It was very pleasant, with the breeze blowing through the open window, the rustling palms, and the heat. He watched as the large bee flew around the room, moving ever closer to the spinning ceiling fan, but managing to avoid its blades. The sight of the bee gave rise to many significant but splendid and fond speculations. Was the bee there by chance, or was there some guiding purpose that directed its activities? Do bees think? Surely they must have some self-consciousness, since he'd read that they communicate by dancing. And what about those so-called African killer bees, are they better dancers than domestic bees? These lofty and uplifting daydreams were suddenly and disastrously interrupted when the bee, seemingly without reason or provocation, dove straight for Chip, stinging him several times in rapid succession. He'd barely escaped with his life, and was literally unconscious for an indeterminable period, which may have lasted hours, days, or even weeks, given his reaction to the insect's venom. Its effects caused him to experience visions of a possible previous life as a pirate, during which he was rescued by a beautiful mermaid named Debbie, whose kind attentions saved his life after his galleon had been torpedoed in the Caribbean by a German submarine. Metempsychosis was no mere myth.

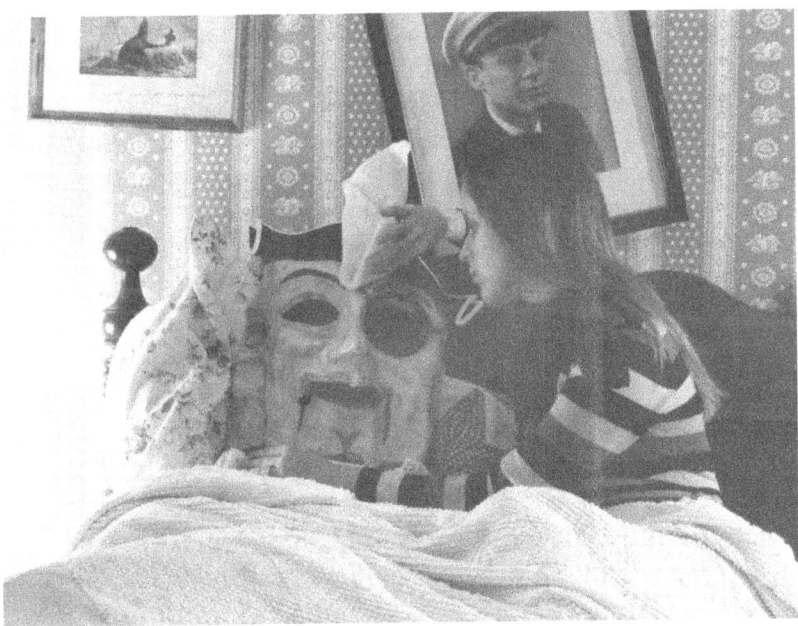

In his delirium Chip imagined himself a pirate rescued by a mermaid.

For most people this event would have held no particular significance over and above the mere fact that it happened at all. There was no reason, therefore no explanation was required. A bee simply flew through an open window and stung someone. It is an occurrence that is no doubt repeated hundreds, if not thousands of times daily throughout the world.

It was less than half an hour later that Chip received the news of his progenitor's untimely murder. He subsequently ascertained that his father had died at exactly, or within a couple of days, one way or the other, of the time that he had been so savagely attacked by the bee. While there was admittedly no direct correlation between the two events, there was no question, at least in his own mind, that there was a connection beyond mere coincidence, and that the bee had come to inform him of his father's demise. But something was missing. What was the link between the two seemingly unrelated events?

For several days Chip discussed the matter with anyone who would listen, even the Iguana man on the bench at the entrance to Pirate's Alley, who surmised that it wasn't a bee at all as they are, generally speaking, capable of stinging once, an act which rips the stinger out of the bee's own abdomen, causing it to die in the process. Ok, so it could have been a wasp. Does it really matter? What mattered was the event itself. Who gives a shit whether it was a bee or some other equally useless and pernicious insect? It was finally the sage observation of an elderly Cuban gentleman that clarified the matter once and for all, and brought everything into proper focus: "If yo aizz hadn't uh been in de bed at lebben o'clock, duh bee wouldn't uh gotcha." This simple statement struck Chip with the force of a revelation. It was a Zen experience, like Satori, Karezza, or like the sound of one hand clapping, or one cheek flapping. Why it had happened at all had no relevance. Chip had missed the point completely. If he hadn't been in bed at eleven o'clock, it wouldn't have happened at all. From that moment forward, Chip resolved to follow the wisdom of the bee, or whatever the hell it was, to do something with his life, to make something of himself. He would return to Nashville, attend his father's service, and seek his fortune.

After the funeral, Chip returned to his late father's mansion, for indeed that's what it was, a big place on Belle Meade Boulevard, situated on four acres, with a perfectly manicured lawn. Chip

28

reasoned that he should have no problem getting all the women he wanted now that he had the house and some money. Just as he prepared to turn into the driveway, some numb nuts in a red Porsche blew past him at a high rate of speed. "Slow down you son of a bitch!" Chip yelled uselessly at the blur as it whipped around the bend and out of sight. "Another disgusting yuppie!" he muttered. "This place is oozing with them, but if I'm going to be living here I might as well join them. I have always wanted a Porsche. It is exactly 1:45 pm. I shall have one today."

Chip's house itself was stately and elegant, three full stories and about 14,000 square feet, much more than he actually needed. It was appropriately furnished in an admixture of styles, blending harmoniously together. Eighteenth century English was predominant, with a number of standard pieces such as breakfronts, highboys, and so on. Actually this was all a bit too pretentious for Chip personally, but at least there were no hunting prints, thank God for that. Since Chip intended to resume his role as a socialite, he would leave the house as it was. In the meantime, he wanted to get a Porsche, today. Hopefully the dealership had a turbo cabriolet in stock. Actually Chip had always hated Porsches. Even he knew that having the engine hanging behind the rear axle was poor engineering, if not downright stupid and dangerous. And the cars look like bugs, especially the earlier 911s. The only decent looking one of the bunch was the former 928, and the back of it resembled a bathtub. In Hamster's opinion, a 911 Porsche is nothing more than a glorified Volkswagen, and everybody knows it, even the people who own them. A new Porsche roadster, however, would appeal to the feeble herd-like minds of his peers in this town of sons in law.

Chip called the Porsche dealer. They had one turbo cabriolet on hand, and he could get it today. That was the good news. The bad news was that it was a putrescent vomit green.

"When can I get it?"

"When would you like it?" the salesman asked with an audible smirk.

"I would like it in exactly one hour. I will pay you cash when I get there and I want all of the papers ready when I arrive. I'm not prepared to wait around for some stooge to have to fetch it off the showroom floor or start looking for the keys or anything like that. Is that clear? Are you with me?"

"With whom am I speaking?" asked the salesman, sensing he had some adolescent prankster on the line.

"Sir, I am Mason Hamster, III, of Amalgamated Cheese. You have no doubt heard of my company," Chip said, stretching the truth a bit. "In any event, you just have my car ready when I get there. Can you do that?"

"Yes Mr. Hamster, it will be ready when you get here, sir." Even the salesman had heard of the Hamsters, and of the strange and recent death of Mason Hamster in particular.

Chip next called the Rolls-Royce dealer in Miami Beach and purchased a new Phantom convertible, in much the same manner as he had bought the Porsche. The cost of the Rolls-Royce was $600,000, more or less. He agreed to bank wire a deposit of fifty per cent that afternoon, and arranged to fly down and pick it up late morning on the forthcoming Friday. It was good to be back in Music City, USA, home of the Grand Ole Uproar, the Gerst House, and the Silk Stocking Gang, even though this tragedy had brought him home.

Next, Chip drove his BMW to the end of Belle Meade Boulevard, through the large stone gates of Percy Warner Park, around to the right, up the hill, and stopped at the top of the driveway. As he looked down from the highest point and beyond the steps below, Belle Meade Boulevard stretched out before him like two serpents on a putting green. This was where he always came whenever he felt on the verge of some major change in life. For more than a few moments Chip was nearly overwhelmed by an inexplicable and almost overpowering urge to put his car in gear and watch it tumble down the long series of descending steps, but quickly realized that if he did, he would have to walk back home in the heat. His shoes were rather uncomfortable, therefore he reluctantly let the feeling pass. He stretched his arms out to his sides, parallel to the street, and stated joyously but firmly to the universe, "I am Charles Mason Hamster, III. I know more about cheese than any man alive, and it's not for nothing that I am possessed of such knowledge. Though I have returned to the Music City to follow my destiny, the world is truly my stage. I have no idea where fate may lead, but wherever it may be, I'm prepared to follow. It is so, and cannot be otherwise."

4.

CHARMED, I'M SURE

"Well, well, well Chip," prated the host, Sidney Von Snocker, "I see that you have a new Porsche. Your father's will must have provided well for you," he said with an obvious trace of envy.

"Yeah" he said, overlooking Von Snocker's rudeness, "I picked it up this afternoon so that I would have something to scoot around town in until I can get my new Rolls-Royce."

The comment sliced Von Snocker like a razor. He laughed, but knew he would never have a Rolls-Royce, no matter how much money he might make, his father would see to that. Sidney Von Snocker's grandfather was also one of the original founders of The Green Tortoise, Nashville's premier country club. It was also a yacht club since many of the members also lived in seaport towns like Ft. Lauderdale, Newport, and Kentucky Lake, during different parts of the year. Anyway, Von Snocker's old man was still alive, although he must be at least 150 years old, or so it seemed to Sidney. Would that old bastard never die?

"That was too bad about your father's untimely demise," Von Snocker mused enviously.

"Yes, it was a real tragedy. It seems that my father slipped on an anchovy and unfortunately fell and struck his head on some kitchen implement," Chip replied.

"Oh hello Stewey," Chip continued as Von Snocker's wife approached them. The once lovely woman had obviously been spending some time at the trough since Chip had seen her last, four years ago. It was really a shame, Chip reflected, that she'd become so porcine. Von Snocker himself, once the pride of the Vanderbilt Commode-doors offensive line, had broadened his horizons similarly, not to say that he was not still almost as offensive as he had once been as a football player back in the early nineties.

"Permit me to re-introduce my valet, and cousin," Chip bowed, "Therpis Monroe, PHD, Pearl High Diploma, or Professor of Hoo

Doo, either one," Chip said, waving his arm graciously toward the aging and rustic distant relative, once removed, thrice re-instated, and frequently arrested, who'd been standing behind him and to his right.

"Therpis, as you may perhaps recollect, procured us our first marijuana some little while ago."

"Oh yeah," the host replied, "Therpis. I remember you now. Both of you, do come in." Von Snocker remembered him well enough. He was some sort of country cousin of Chip's late father. The exact nature of the relationship had never been clearly explained to anyone's understanding, not that it mattered. Whenever Chip was asked, he merely passed along what information he had been told by his father. "Therpis is from Tomachichi, Mississippi. Some of our relatives were from that part of the country before the war, that is, your grandfather's father's cousins on your great aunt's side. I think that probably Therpis's aunts and uncles all slept in the same bed." While the genealogy was difficult to follow, that explanation always seemed to be understood immediately by anyone who'd asked. Whoever he really was, Therpis had always lived in the Hamster's guest house with his wife, Matti Pearl, a large corn-fed, country woman, who still insisted on hanging her laundry on a line in the back yard. Therpis had served as their driver, and taken Chip and Sidney to the movies as children, and later, on dates into the seedier parts of town. He would buy them beer, whiskey, and marijuana too, as long as he got some for his trouble.

There were about thirty or so people at the party, mainly ambassadors of the bon ton, former friends, and friends of friends. Chip found their company pleasurable enough and renewed many long standing acquaintances that had lapsed to some extent due to the passage of time. He was especially attentive to all of the men, not wishing them to be concerned by the attentions of their wives and girlfriends whose behavior on his behalf was somewhat reminiscent, generally speaking, of female elephants in heat.

Chip was indeed a charismatic and charming man, and regarded himself as such, not in any conceited fashion, but rather in much the same manner as the fat lady at the circus is fat. It was merely a matter of fact, nothing more or less. Chip's skin color was darkened by continual exposure to the tropical sun of Key West, but not yet to the degree that it resembled finest Corinthian leather. He stood in marked contrast visually to the other men there, whom, for the most part were attractive enough, though possessed the appearance of spiritual hardness frequently conferred by wealth and a life of leisure. A certain pudginess throughout the face, no doubt the result of a long standing friendship with alcohol, characterized many of those present. All in all, a charming slice of Nashville's upper crust.

The conversation was spirited and interesting, with Chip asking many questions of his hosts and their guests, seeking to ascertain their interests. After all, he'd been out of circulation for awhile, and it was his desire to again join their ranks as a respected member of society. He also intended to enter the world of business in some as yet, undetermined capacity. With this in mind, he sought the opinions and advice of many of Nashville's most respected sons in law on a variety of timely matters. None of their particular endeavors, however, proved very interesting, and it became clear at length, that unless he married someone's daughter, himself, he would most likely be forced to start his own business. Whatever he decided to do, he hoped that he would make some money, but, more importantly, that his chosen profession would be amusing.

At length a toast was proposed by Jody and Nipper, very unmarried ladies whose dowry was only exceeded by the volume of incessant chit-chat, which always overflowed from their plump, chipmunk-like little mouths. The toast was made and several gentlemen called for a speech, at which time the subject of the evening's festivities distinguished himself as an orator of considerable merit, pausing here and there to express his joy and gratitude at having returned to that "Athens of the South, Music City USA, home of Vanderbilt University, Tennessee Pride Sausage, the Grand Ole' Uproar, the Gerst House, and Cantrell's Bar-B-Que on Cleveland Street, in the darker part of the city."

Fifteen minutes later Chip and his valet departed, leaving both his hosts and their guests with the warm glow of a most pleasurable evening still lingering, like the stench of a cheap cigar. At home Chip and his valet smoked a marijuana cigarette and reflected upon the day's activities, and talked about cars.

Therpis had been the family chauffeur ever since Chip was a boy. Ole' Therpis, or Uncle Therpis, as he called himself, had involuntarily relinquished his driver's license about ten years ago, as the result of numerous DUI convictions. Chip referred to him as his valet, a term which Therpis had suggested, and seemed to enjoy.

The conversation reminded Chip that he must get his Porsche insured right away. He had thirty days under Tennessee law, as he recollected, to add it to his existing policy. The matter could be easily handled tomorrow with a simple phone call.

5.

AN OLD FLAME

"Damn!" Chip reflected, "I'm out of money. That's the bottom line, that's what this really means. How could I have gone through more than $800,000 in just a few months? Well, it's easy enough to figure out. $600,000 for a Rolls-Royce convertible, $225,000 for a Porsche Turbo S, $20,000 for three weeks island hopping in the Pacific. A new state of the art recording studio. I've got $1,500 to my name, I mean forever. Shit!"

Chip walked over to the window and looked at his Porsche out in the driveway, sitting there crushed and broken like a stomped Katydid. The tree was still on top of it. The car was completely destroyed. Less than ninety miles on a $225,000 car, struck down by a windblown tree in a freak storm. It was strangely ironic. He hadn't even wanted the car but had purchased it merely to impress some old friends he didn't particularly even like. Well, that's the way things go. If only he had taken the time to call his insurance agent, none of this would have happened. Now he was out all that money with nothing to show for it. What a pain in the ass!

"I'm out of money," Chip stated flatly, turning to his cousin Therpis.

"Go get a loan Chip, 'til you get some money. The bank is overflowing with money. Tell the bank man that you's Chip Hamster. They'll give you as much money as you want."

"Look," Chip said, "you don't understand. I can't borrow against the house. I have no collateral."

"Well, what about your car?"

"It's wrecked, you fool. Crushed like a bug!"

"Naw, naw, naw, I mean your otha car."

"No Therpis, I don't want the bank to own my Rolls."

Their conversation was interrupted by the long ring of the front doorbell. "Therpis, go see who that is." Chip continued to ponder the situation. There must be some way to get some money from the

35

bank, but how? And even if he could, there was no way to pay it back. He might actually have to get a job, but doing what? Yes, sure he was a genius and could probably run any company in the US better than it is being run now, but he couldn't just walk into the door of Sealtest Ice Cream, for example, or Frosty Morn Sausage and announce that he was here to replace everyone at the company. He should really be in cheese. Amalgamated Cheese was where he belonged. But the truth of the matter is that he did not particularly even like cheese, and the entire plant was permeated with an offensive `cheese-like' odor.

Therpis returned to the library and stated ceremoniously, "Miss Cissy Flambeaux to see you."

"Send her in" Chip replied. Cissy Flambeaux. Now there was a blast from the past. In high school, many a lad had lost his innocence between her plump thighs. She'd been possessed of a highly developed sporting nature in those days. It had been almost ten years since he'd seen her. She'd married some rich oil man from Louisiana, but Chip had heard that he'd died of a heart attack some months back. What could she want now, after all this time? He rose to greet her. "Cissy," he smiled, "You look charming. Time has been kind to you." And indeed it had. In fact, at a bit over thirty, she probably looked the best she'd ever looked in her life. She still had a head full of blonde shoulder length hair, and her figure was more angular now, having lost some of the plumper quality it possessed in adolescence. He was genuinely surprised and pleased to see her.

"And how is Nashville's most eligible bachelor?" she asked, as she gave him a quick peck on the cheek. "I was sorry to hear about Mason, your father, I mean. It was such a shock."

"Yes it was," Chip stated gravely. "It sent ripples throughout the cheese industry....worldwide. I guess though, that he probably died happy. He'd lived a rich, full life, and done everything he'd ever wanted to do, still...."

"It was rather sudden," Cissy stated solemnly.

"He really didn't know what hit him, figuratively speaking of course," Chip answered with a trace of sadness.

"I heard it was a skillet," Cissy said, without thinking.

"Yes, well...a terrible tragedy, to be sure. But what about you? I know it's been years, but I'd hear of you from time to time or see your picture in the paper. I heard about your husband."

"Well Chip, my late husband is gone too, but I can assure you that he died happy as well..."

"No doubt," Chip mused quietly. "Well Cissy, How are you holding out? I mean are you okay personally?"

"I'm still wearing black," she said with a smile as she raised her shirt and displayed her two splendid breasts barely contained within the grasp of a black lace bra. "Mosquito bites, still," she laughed.

Cissy Flambeaux

"Indeed! Well, to what do I owe the honor of this visit? It's literally been years." He remembered the time he pawned his over coat to old Mrs. Friedman just to get a bottle of wine and a cheap hotel room so he could wrestle with her. It was worth it too. She rode him like a horse. But he almost froze to death getting there, as God is his secret judge. That is, if there's a God listening.

"Well, I am your neighbor now, and I thought that I might come over and borrow a cup of sugar," she said flippantly.

"I didn't know you lived around here."

"Well actually, I live three houses down. I'd heard that you were back in town. I missed you at the Von Snocker's party. I must have arrived right after you left. I've come by a couple of times but they said you were out of town."

"Yeah, I had some business to wrap up in Key West, and I also spent some time in 'Honaruru,' as they say. I've moved back here for good, I think."

"Well, what are you doing tonight? Come on, I'll take you to dinner."

So off they went into the night in Cissy's bright blue Miata with the top down. Chip held onto his nuts all the way. The last thing he wanted was to die in some Jap car that resembled a tadpole. She drove like a bat out of hell, and he imagined himself lying in the street bleeding to death with a bunch of morons staring at him. They finally settled on some Italian joint where they reminisced on their lives and what had happened to each of them during the last ten or more years.

Later that night, Chip lay in the darkness smoking a Hoyo De Monterey Sultan, a fine cigar. To his left lay the sleeping Cissy. In the background he listened to the immortal sounds of Jackie Wilson singing 'Baby Workout.' The tip of his cigar glowed as he took a big puff. When one is 'en flagrante delecto', he reflected, everything happens so fast, but here in the afterglow, this is reality, the ultimate time for thinking things over.

He turned on the bedside light, and thumbed through the pages of the latest issue of ' *Wheels and Deals,*' a local used car magazine. He always looked at the antique cars first, then the old Cadillacs, and finally the old Lincolns. Chip had been wanting one of those giant `77 or `78 Lincoln Town Cars for some time now. The prices had been steadily declining. Not even the hicks or pimps wanted big old Lincolns anymore. Now they wanted low rider Toyota and

Nissan trucks, with crappy 'boom' noise blasting out of the speakers and annoying the public. There were several examples of old Lincolns advertised, at less than two thousand dollars. It irritated Chip to think that he could easily have had fifty of them instead of that stupid bug-looking Porsche. Now he couldn't afford to buy even one. Chip had squandered his inheritance. What a pity. He turned a few more pages and stopped at a full page ad that featured individual photographs of wrecked and burned cars. There were Volvos, BMWs, Porsches, and Corvettes. Under each picture were descriptive words and phrases, such as, "light rollover", "theft recovery," or "minor water damage." Some of the cars looked like they'd been hit by a train or dropped off a cliff. There was one new Jaguar that was as flat as a pancake. Underneath the picture the caption read, 'easy fixer, good title, 1400 miles.' It was priced at $15,000. "Good God!" Chip exclaimed loudly. "What moron would pay $15,000 for that piece of junk?" It might serve as a ship's anchor or as an addition to a fishing reef, but beyond that it was absolutely useless. There wasn't one single piece on the whole car that wasn't crushed, flattened, or dented.

He again looked at each picture, this time more carefully. All of the cars were very expensive, way, way overpriced. The guy running this place must be either very stupid or very rich, most likely the latter. Nobody would be advertising crap that couldn't be sold at all, unless he were stupid or the operation was some kind of front for something else. Chip determined then and there that this was the type of business for him. He looked at the top of the page and saw that the ad had been placed by Mid-South Auto Brokers, Intergalactic, Inc. in Chattanooga. Chip felt at once that he'd finally found his calling. He and Cissy would drive down there in the morning and check out this guy's operation. Chip didn't exactly know how all of this would come together yet, but he knew that it would. That much was certain.

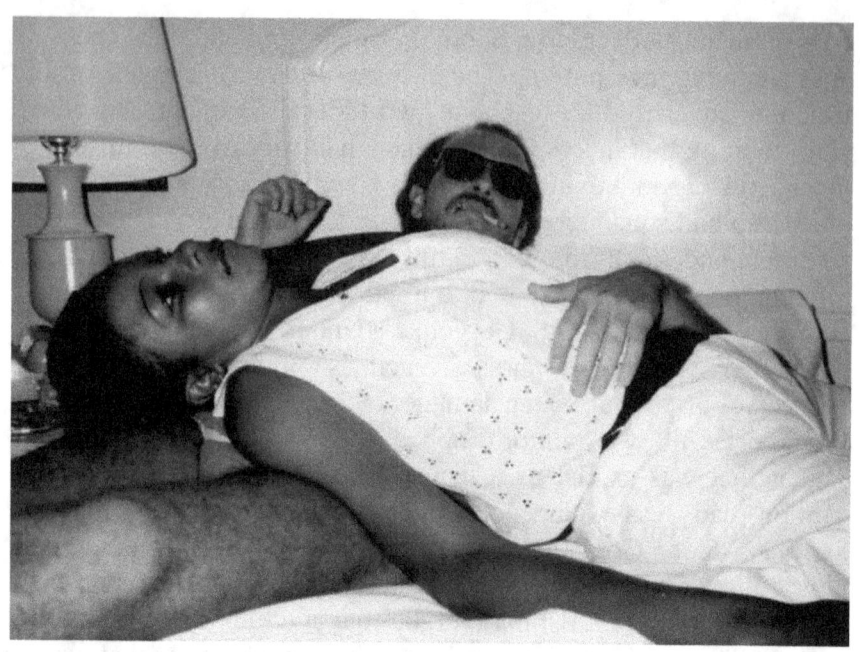

As he dozed he dreamed of the lovely Ioveena .

The magazine slipped from his fingers as he dozed off, dreaming of the lovely Ioveena . He'd been unable to find her in Key West when he'd returned to south Florida to pick up his Rolls-Royce, and nobody knew where she'd gone. It looked like she was lost forever. Damn! If only he'd brought her with him to the funeral, but it was too late now. She'd probably gone to Miami, where by now, some other man was floating and bobbing pleasantly between her exquisite thighs, like a raft adrift on a rolling sea.

6.

MARVIN HOCKER
OHIO STATE PRISON: COLUMBUS, OHIO

A petulant Marvin Hocker looked through the bars of his small cell at the Ohio State Prison in Columbus. He was here serving time for arson and four counts of attempted murder. Facing a combined sentence of 150 years, he had successfully plea bargained to a mere 40 years. With five months served and time off for good behavior, he'd be eligible for parole in another two months. He shouldn't be in the slammer at all, since what had happened was certainly not his fault. It was the media. Take the news for instance. While the press and television networks appeared to be liberal, the fact of the matter was that they constantly and intentionally did everything they could to fuel the fires of racism and anti-Semitism, all in the name of impartial presentation of the facts. By reporting events and incidents in such a way that these tensions were magnified, they intentionally and willfully incited the masses for their own commercial purposes. The emotions of the public were constantly manipulated without notice by the so-called liberal news media. But most people were too stupid to figure that out. Marvin Hocker had figured it out though, and didn't watch the news anymore, or read the paper. If something didn't either bring him pleasure or make him money, there was no point in fooling with it. He wasn't as stupid as he looked, that's for sure. In his case, there was no doubt whatsoever that television caused crime. His life was a perfect example. He lifted one cheek slightly off the thin mattress and released a short burst of gas. SBD,

41

silent but deadly. Hocker attributed his present misfortunes to Paul Newman. While it was true enough that Newman had made good popcorn and salad dressing, before he croaked, that is, if he actually, really made them, it was his role in the movie, 'The Long Hot Summer' that had started Marvin Hocker down the path which would eventually become a highway of crime. He envied the barn burner's life of freedom. But Paul Newman had probably sold the use of his name to some Yankees, and let them put his picture on the jars and packages to promote sales of the various products. He probably couldn't even boil water.

While some of Hocker's problems could be traced directly to English singer Arthur Brown, and American guitarist Jimi Hendrix, it was Newman who started it all. `Barn burner!' `Pyro!' It was the fascination with fire that had become his obsession. A fire swept away all pretense. It was the great social equalizer. The prisoner again detected portentous intestinal rumbling which fortunately dissipated prior to its expression.

Marvin Hocker looked like a moron, with his blank expression and flat, saucer-like head, the latter amplified by a flat top hairstyle. He was indeed an idiot; at least that's what his own lawyer had said in court to get him off the hook. A psychologist had been summoned for the defense as an expert witness. He had, in the defendant's best interests, explained in great detail, to the bewilderment of all present, the difference between a moron, an imbecile, and an idiot. These terms are decidedly unpopular in this age of mediocrity, where bird-brains and dimwitted stooges are called "slow learners," and the obviously feeble-minded are given comfortable government jobs. The prosecuting attorney had countered, saying that while Hocker certainly looked stupid, and was probably retarded, he wasn't, clinically speaking, an idiot.

When all was said and done, the jury proved sympathetic to Marvin Hocker, feeling that his own attorney had sold him out, and that it was uncharitable to have called him unpleasant names in public. They could tell, after all, by looking at the defendant, that he was a product of rural inbreeding, extending perhaps over many generations. The individual members of the jury were, of course, too socially conscious to express their obvious conclusions in this matter, even within the privacy of the jury room. Hocker was consequently acquitted of all charges stemming from the unexplained fire at the Rent-Em-Up Center, which one juror was overheard to have remarked, seemed like an example of 'Jewish lightning,' whatever that is. It was subsequently determined by the insurance company with able assistance from the fire marshal, (who received a new Toyota), that the mysterious fire had indeed been set by the owner, a corpulent Italian American of Sicilian descent. So Hocker was innocent after all...not that he wouldn't have torched the store immediately, had they not credited his $3.15 overpayment on the vibrating chair rental to the following week's accounts receivable. Had he not burned down his attorney's residence in angry retaliation for having been called an idiot at one point during the trial, (when he was actually, at least in his own opinion, a moron), he would have avoided or at the very least, postponed his trip to the big house.

But Hocker was malicious and obnoxious like an insect that gets in one's face on a hot day. The malice was worse because it was not directed by any great intelligence. The blatant and public affront to his dignity, at the hands of his own attorney, demanded immediate retribution. That the Molotov cocktails which Hocker had thrown chanced to have been made from Double-Cola bottles was a matter whose significance couldn't have been suspected by the vengeful Hocker at the time of the firebombing of his lawyer's house. Or perhaps, as they say, some criminals leave clues to their identity as part of a subconscious desire to be apprehended by the authorities. Chances are, that in this case, Hocker's actions on the day of the crime were the result of carelessness and stupidity rather than any hidden or unconscious motives. In any case, his fingerprints were found to have been liberally applied to the bottle fragments at the scene of the crime.

With less than a month remaining before the scheduled parole hearing, one would think that Hocker would be on best behavior as that eagerly awaited date approached. Such indeed was the case, more or less, but the more he thought about it, the less the whole business appealed to him. There was in his estimation, no way that he would be released. He must take matters into his own hands. Being far more intelligent, or so he reasoned, than anyone in his immediate environment, he was certain that a perfect escape plan would be forthcoming. Since he worked in the prison laundry, and the machines were operated by natural gas, an explosion was not out of the question. In the resulting confusion he could somehow escape. He would figure that part out after lunch. The first thing he needed was an explosion. He ripped down the warnings posted by the gas company and stuck them into his pocket with the intention of studying them in great detail in his cell after `lights out.'

IF YOU SMELL GAS, HERE'S WHAT TO DO:

You can't smell gas in its natural state, so we add a distinctive odor to make leaks easier to detect. Natural gas is clean, safe and efficient, but if you smell gas in your home, there are certain things you should do. If the odor is light, the source of the leak is probably one of your gas appliances. Occasionally, pilot lights will blow out, so first check each of these. While you're doing that, make sure each of the burners of your range and oven are turned completely off. In most cases, these two checks will solve the problem. If the odor grows stronger and you can't locate the source, here's what to do:

1. VENTILATE your home by opening all windows and doors. Doing this will prevent a concentrated build-up of gas in your home.

2. EXTINGUISH all open flames. DON'T use matches. Don't turn on light switches or use electrical or battery powered equipment that might create a spark.

3. GET OUT of your house and call the gas company from an outside phone. Wait there until our service representative arrives.

4. If you know where your meter is located, TURN OFF the gas to your home by using the shut off valve at the meter.

Some wise ass had taken a heavy black marker and crossed out the instructions with a single large black "X" At the bottom of the page he had written **"RUN LIKE HELL!"**

"No shit!" laughed Hocker. "Pull my finger and I'll give you some global warming to go with it," he mumbled.

Blowing up the prison laundry would be no problem. He would put a container of flammable liquid in one of the machines. It would blow up, and he would escape in the confusion. It was that simple.

The flammable liquid he had in mind consisted of one gallon plastic jugs of 'Little Rhonda's' floor cleaner, one for each of the huge gas-fired dryers. The label on the jug showed a smiling four-year old girl with a bucket in one hand and a mop in the other. Her parents should have been horse whipped for letting their daughter pose for her picture on the label of this toxic shit. Little Rhonda was probably already dead, or had three arms or something from being around the floor cleaning solution. The label itself had caught Hocker's eye not for Little Rhonda's picture, but for the much larger 'HIGHLY FLAMMABLE! Script and the skull and crossbones emblem denoting that the contents of the bottle were not only flammable, but poisonous as well. He'd read the 1/16th inch tall warning label with a magnifying glass and found out that among other things, exposure to its vapors could be fatal, and that as little as two drops applied to the skin caused a necrosis of the exposed tissue. Blindness was likely were not the eye irrigated with a constant stream of salt water for an uninterrupted period of at least twenty-four hours. If, God forbid, even a minimal amount were ingested, an exclusive four week diet of plain yogurt was mandatory. Who could eat that crap for four weeks but a bunch of needle-nosed hippies? He'd rather die a death.

The prison laundry. Key to Hocker's escape.

And thank God. At least he didn't live in California, where it was known to cause unsavory genetic mutations to the reproductive

45

organs and an 'abnormal' and certainly inconvenient lengthening of the toes. To make matters worse, the contents were 'orange scented for freshness.' Hell, it smelled like an Orange Crush. It was like the manufacturers were intentionally seeking to poison children. "The government shouldn't let companies make crap like that," he mumbled to himself, but the substance was readily available throughout the prison laundry, like his own private cache of explosives hidden in plain sight. "I'll blow this son of a bitch off the face of the earth."

That was Plan A, well actually Part 1 of Plan A. Plan B would require a body. Or would that be Part 2 of Plan A? No matter, he could figure all of that out after dinner. There had to be a body, however, and the prison officials must know it was his. Since badly burned bodies were almost always identified through dental records, it would be necessary to get his dental records from the prison hospital, copy them, return the copies to the files, so as not to cause suspicion, and be sure there was a copy on the body, probably in the pocket. He wanted to be sure they knew it was his body in the fire. If his dental records were on the body, there would be no question that it was his body that was discovered in the burned out remains of the laundry. He would be home free.

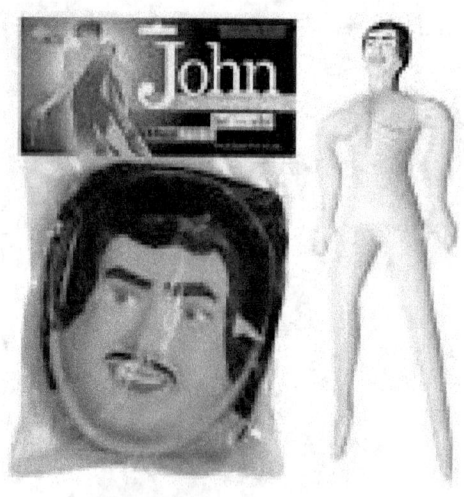

But he needed a body? Now where could he find a body? It should doubtless be easy enough. He just ordered a life size male love doll from some nice advertisement on the back page of '*Bend Over,*' a popular prison magazine. When it arrived, in a plain brown box, so as not to create suspicion, he would hide it in the laundry. On the day of the big explosion, he would simply inflate the doll, dress it in his own clothes, and stick the copies of his dental records in the pocket. What could be easier?

The love doll even looked like Hocker (or Wayne Newton), and was about the same physical size. The only problem upon its arrival, was the doll's 'weiner' was missing. After some deliberation, Hocker determined that in a fire, a man's hot dog would probably be burned off anyway. Besides, anybody looking at, or for, a dead man's pee-pee is a pervert. The important thing is that that Hocker's dental records would be found, and indeed they would.

These things would require time, and by his calculations he had just about two or three weeks to prepare everything. He would act normally and pretend to be excited about his upcoming parole hearing. When that day arrived, he would attend the hearing, then blow up the laundry room the next day, before he got the bad news that his parole request had been denied. Nobody would suspect him. It was a perfect plan, foolproof. He was a genius. All in a day's work. Nothing could be easier to accomplish. How dare that bastard lawyer call him an idiot, when it had been clearly established that he was a moron.

After his escape he would retire to Florida and start an oyster ranch. On the way down, perhaps he could stop at Marineland for a nice lunch at the Dolphin Restaurant.

But first he would stop in Nashville to see the world famous Grand Ole Opry.

A portent of things to come?

7.

UNDERWAY

The next morning they departed at a reasonable hour, Chip, Cissy, and Therpis, who that very morning had received a promotion from valet to 'Chancellor of the Vine,' a promotion solemnly attended by the presentation of a crisp five dollar bill and a six pack of Blatz beer. The two hour drive to Chattanooga was accomplished in a leisurely fashion with Chip at the wheel and Therpis asleep in the back seat. En route, the pert and vivacious Cissy toyed with Chip's manly affections, but not during that part of their journey when they descended the treacherous bit of highway known as Monteagle Mountain.

On the outskirts of town, with the wheel of the Rolls-Royce still in the casual but expert control of Chip Hamster, they located Mid-South Auto Brokers Intergalactic, Inc., and Chip made the acquaintance of Ron Di Lizardo, a rather large, pop-eyed, fortyish gentleman, who professed to be the proprietor of this rather unusual used car lot. Ron was understandably impressed with Chip's new Rolls-Royce convertible and they became fast friends at once. As a matter of consequence, Chip was indeed able to glean much knowledge that would have most certainly been withheld otherwise.

Chip looked around him, and then into the distance. Almost as far as the eye could see, there were wrecked, burned, crushed, smashed, flattened, twisted, mangled, mutilated, dented, and destroyed cars. Chip had no idea that there could possibly be that many wrecked Porsches, Mercedes, Jaguars, and BMWs in the entire South, let alone in one place, especially Chattanooga. Strange indeed. Over to his right a burned and rusted Rolls-Royce Silver Spur with melted aluminum doors, had fallen victim to large leafy vines.

The majority of these wrecked automobiles, Chip later discovered, were purchased from insurance companies that were only too pleased to get whatever money they could for them. Di Lizardo made his money by keeping a large inventory of wrecked luxury cars, and parting them out at rather high prices. Some he sold as 'builders,' cars that someone could buy cheaply and fix up. The condition of the vehicles varied. Some were in fairly good shape. Others were almost unrecognizable. All were damaged in some way.

"What are you getting on that Ferrari?" Chip asked casually, looking at a car that was burned to a crisp except for the first foot and a half of the front end.

In response, Ron Di Lizardo ceremoniously grabbed his belt with both hands, pulled his pants up, hocked a quid into the dust, looked studiously at the wreckage for a moment, and then replied gravely, "That one, by God, had a light interior fire, but hell, with some imagination it could be good as new. Son of a bitch has a clear title. I would, by God, ask around $27,500 for it, but if you want it today, since you like cars so much, it's yours for $26,995. Hell, it's a good car. That's a Goddamn deal. Take it or leave it!"

Chip was about to respond to Di Lizardo's outrageous price, but was cut off before he could speak.

"Don't move Goddamn it. Freeze! It's a snake, by God!" their host shouted. Everyone stood still and looked down to their horror, shocked by the sight of a large coiled snake in striking position. The snake looked particularly menacing, and appeared to be poisonous.

"It's uh Coba! It's uh Coba" shouted Therpis in spite of their host's warning to be quiet. The sound of Therpis' voice so startled the snake that it instinctively lunged toward Cissy's leg, which was its closest target. The serpent was instantly snatched from the ground in mid-strike by Ron Di Lizardo, who grabbed the snake's body halfway between its head and tail with his right hand. With lightning speed he took hold of the snake's tail with his left hand and gave it a powerful tug, bringing the serpent's head into his closed right hand. He immediately brought his closed fist to his open mouth, closing his mouth over the protruding head of the snake. He blew one powerful burst of air right into the nose and mouth of the bewildered serpent and then triumphantly cast it to the ground, apparently lifeless. The entire incident was over in a matter of seconds.

Chip, Therpis, and Cissy stood quietly for a moment scarcely able to believe what their eyes had just witnessed. Finally, Cissy broke the silence. "You killed him," she exclaimed, her horror now turning to sympathy.

"Wadn't no Cobra, by God, it was a spreadin' adder, a faintin' spreadin' adder. He'll be all right in a few minutes, you just wait."

"You killed him," she repeated, almost as if in a trance.

"I told ja, he ain't dead, by God, just fainted. You can do the same thing, by God, to a crawdad, just blow down his mouth and see what happens. He'll faint every time. Just grab him, by God, and see for yourself. Son of a bitch ain't dead. Just fainted."

The snake looked dead enough to Chip alright. Di Lizardo continued talking as if nothing had happened, and sure enough, in about ten minutes the snake began moving, slowly righted itself, and slithered off quietly into the bushes beside a flattened Aston Martin Lagonda.

Chip did not quite know what to make of this Ron Di Lizardo. It seemed, if language and accent were any indication, that their host was extremely uncultured and rustic, and most likely a native of rural Wisconsin. The frequent conversational interjection of quaint expressions such as "by God" and "Goddamn," indicated clearly, however, that Di Lizardo had spent some considerable time in Alabama, and most likely had some religious exposure in his youth. And yet the eyes protruded unnaturally, as with many northern Floridians. Di Lizardo was a mysterious individual, there was no doubt of that, one who would bear close watching. Chip determined to observe him carefully.

"What about that Maserati Indy?" Chip asked, pointing to a rusted out shell of a car with no engine, windows, or interior.

"That one is a Goddamn Indy, by God. Do you hear me? Ah said it's a Indy, by God, a very rare car and I'm a gonna' fix her up good as new, one of these days."

Chip's reference to that particular car obviously sparked some deep seated emotional response on the part of their host, one, which should, Chip decided, perhaps remain unexamined. Di Lizardo's face had assumed an unusual, and somewhat sinister expression as Chip's casual inquiry was answered. Judging from the size of the tree growing out of the engine compartment, Chip surmised that the restoration must yet be awaiting the arrival of a few more important parts.

Ron Di Lizardo had quite an extensive and unusual inventory, to be sure. Nonetheless, one could not help but wonder if this entire business was not perhaps a front for some type of illegal operation. Not that such a possibility particularly bothered Chip personally. His suspicions in that regard, however, were soon put to rest as their host browsed them through a large warehouse filled with engines, wheels, doors, bumpers, and other car parts, all neatly stacked, numbered, and catalogued. Di Lizardo had an actual salvage mill in full operation. Despite his lack of conversational skills, he must really be a genius. He must be netting hundreds of thousands of dollars a year, perhaps even millions. The place was a gold mine.

Chip's first thought was how wonderful it would be to own a business like this, more specifically, this particular business. He knew, however, that he couldn't afford to buy this operation from Ron Di Lizardo. It was making way too much money. In addition it was the type of business that would require full time, daily attention, and as such, would be too restrictive to Chip personally. Last, but not least, this was a big, high profile operation, one where a great deal of money changed hands. These days, Uncle Sammy wants his share, and yours too. Chip didn't feel like being audited or investigated. He wanted to be as low profile as possible so that the 'Gub-ment' wouldn't be on his ass. Besides, touring this place had given him an idea. He now knew exactly what he wanted to do. He wanted to get titles to late model luxury cars so that he could use them to get loans from various banks. He imagined that he had come to the right place.

"What happens to the titles of these cars once they are dismantled?" Chip asked casually.

"I used to just throw them away, by God, but now the state makes us turn them in. I have to stamp each one with a special stamp that says 'SALVAGE.' The government has everything pretty well under control. It's just a lotta Goddamn paperwork for me. What are they gonna do with those useless titles, by God? Just throw them away their own selves...or wipe their ass with them. Huh."

"No doubt. Do you send in every title?" Chip asked.

"No, some of them come in after the cars have already been stripped, junked, and crushed. I got a stack of 'em, by God, in the 'Tiki Hut,' I mean my office.

"Hmmm. I see," said Chip, as he thoughtfully ran his fingers across his chin. Throughout the tour of the junkyard, Therpis had remained unusually quiet, and followed along with a large feather brush with which he frequently dusted Chip and Cissy. It was truly an interesting and informative excursion, and their host proved most cordial, displaying sufficient familiarity with his guests that he did not forbear to expectorate or pass gas whenever necessary. It was one of those rare and beautiful days, clear blue skies, charming companions, pleasant chit chat, an unexpected gift from life. The rapport between Di Lizardo and Chip was so great that Chip and his fellow travelers were afforded their host's ultimate gesture of hospitality. They were invited for drinks and small talk to that part of the property known as the 'Tiki Hut.'

The Tiki Hut was a casually constructed A-frame, made of two by fours, and roofed with inexpensive green fiberglass panels. In size it was not more than eight feet square. Three sides were open, with the rear wall actually affixed to the back of a storage shed. The interior appointments were equally tasteful; four woven nylon and aluminum lawn chairs, resting comfortably upon a rich green carpet of Astroturf. There were primitive cement statues reflecting Polynesian influence, as well as some ashtrays gathered from various motels and restaurants. In all, a most refreshing oasis in this wasteland of rusted, wrecked, and burned luxury cars.

"This son of a bitch, by God, is the Tiki Hut." Di Lizardo exclaimed proudly, as he directed his guests to their seats, with a wave of his arm. "Welcome, by God, to the Tiki Hut. As you can see, there are two phones, count 'em, two, a stereo, ashtrays, by God...everything you need right here in the Tiki Hut. If the phone rings, by God...I can get it right here...Where? Hell yes, right here in the Tiki Hut. Make yourself to home."

Di Lizardo pushed a buzzer, and as if by magic a big fat woman attired in a grass skirt and halter top arrived a few moments later, bringing refreshments for all. "Orange Crush, Double-Cola, by God, Moon Pies....whatever you want, I got it ... where?"

"That's right," Chip answered, taking the cue, "at the Tiki Hut."

"That's right," interjected their host, "at the Tiki Hut...well, Goddamn."

As the three visitors whiled away the afternoon with pleasant conversation and delicious rustic snacks, Chip began to formulate his plan more specifically. At one point during the conversation, their host laughed and said "Well....hmmm..., you was askin' about titles and here's one right here from a Mercedes S 550. I was using it for a coaster. Hell, I ain't even stamped this one yet, by God."

Di Lizardo handed him the wet, limp, Georgia title to the almost new Mercedes. This was just what Chip had in mind. The title to the Mercedes was regrettably too stained for his purposes, and yet, there were, no doubt, more. Chip must have them all, but he must be circumspect in his demeanor so as not to arouse his host's suspicions. He would have to come up with a credible reason for wanting titles to nonexistent automobiles, one that would not unduly arouse anyone's curiosity. This would require some time, but not too much.

While Di Lizardo was obviously ignorant, he was definitely not stupid, or at least not as stupid as he acted. Chip resolved to call upon him later, next week perhaps, either by phone or in person, and begin getting titles on a regular basis. First though, he had to have a plan.

The obvious and honest thing to do would be for him to simply tell Di Lizardo why he wanted the titles. If he did that, however, Di Lizardo would, if he possessed any decency whatsoever, refuse outright. Even worse, he might notify the police and tell other people in the junk car business to be on the lookout for Chip. No, it would be best to fabricate some elaborate and high sounding scheme. Chip would have to think about it. There was also the physical problem of the cars themselves. Chip didn't particularly want the wrecked and burned out hulks of these cars. He just wanted the titles. To get the titles however, he would most likely have to take the wrecked cars as well, in order to avoid arousing suspicion. If he actually had to take possession of the cars, there was the problem of transportation and storage. Where could he store, or otherwise dispose of several dozen or perhaps even hundred, junk cars? There were also certain legal aspects to consider. What if someday things went awry and his dealings actually caught up with him? Wouldn't it be better to have those junk cars in his possession? He would be much more likely to explain his actions satisfactorily if he had the cars. He could say that he was borrowing money from the banks to fix them up with the intention of selling them later for a profit. Yes, that would work. It isn't against the law to make mistakes in business or to exercise bad judgment. Keeping the cars would create the perfect alibi. Not that he would ever need one, but just in case...

As the party from Nashville prepared to leave, they ceremoniously presented their host with a full six pack of Blatz Beer in convenient 12 oz. easy open aluminum cans, a kindly gesture of extreme generosity that was most appreciated, especially considering that it was so unexpected. "One final question, Mr. Di Lizardo, if you please," asked Chip. "Why is your company called 'Intergalactic'?"

"When the famous psychologist C.G. Jung visited Chattanooga, he told the doorman at the Read House Hotel that he'd discovered that Chattanooga, Tennessee is indeed the geographical center of the Universe. Did you hear me? I said the center of the Universe, by God. Carl knew that all those thinking people up east, people like the Kennedys, and the Pope, and all, would've shit a brick if he had made this knowledge, available, by God, to the masses, not to mention the fact that the UT football fans in Knoxville wouldn't go for that shit at all. So, even though he was right in not telling the public at large what he'd found out, I was aware of it myself, since the ancient doorman told me, and I chose to honor his discovery by calling my company 'Intergalactic' instead of 'International,' I mean with my company being in Chattanooga and all."

"I had no idea that Carl Jung had ever been to Chattanooga," Chip replied with amazement, not that he was overly familiar with the work of Mr. Jung. "What could he possibly have been doing here?"

"Well, they say he was snooping around the Wildman Sanitarium, by God, on the outskirts of town, looking for some inmates, by God, called the Secret Chiefs, who he thought ruled the world, or some horseshit like that. All he found was some nuts dressed up in foolish looking costumes playing shuffleboard. He stayed in town about two weeks but didn't find a thing. I've heard rumors myself, by God, but maybe I've said too much already."

"Well," Chip observed, "There must have been something to it. He's a famous chef. He wouldn't have come all the way from France if he didn't have some idea that he was going to make an important discovery of some kind. But why Chattanooga? What do you think?"

"I think, by God, you orta read his autobiography, 'Memories, Dreams, and Reflections,' that is, if you're so interested, but maybe I've said enough. I don't know nothin' about that place. It was just some rumors, by God, but if I were you I'd stay away from the Wildman Sanitarium. I'm sure that it's easier to get in there, by God than to get out. A word to the wise should be deficient, if you get my drift. Have a nice day, and y'all come back now. And thanks for the Blatz. We don't see much of that around these parts."

With that, they bid a fond farewell to their host and motored the short remaining distance to the Sky Harbor Motel on Lookout Mountain.

"Why are you interested in those junk cars?" Cissy asked, completely ignoring the fact that she had just found out that Chattanooga, Tennessee is perhaps the geographical center of the universe.

"I fully intend to make my fortune, and to mark my place in the financial world with a similar undertaking. That Di Lizardo is a true genius," answered Chip.

"Why don't you just stay in cheese?" she asked, not understanding that Chip had been forced out of the business.

"There is no place for me at Amalgamated Cheese, Cissy. Ratlips and his ancient father have seen to that, notwithstanding the fact, the incontestable fact, that I personally know more about cheese than any man alive today."

Later that night in room # 1 of the Sky Harbor Motel, the room with the double bed, Chip Hamster sought, with the help of a large cigar and a chilled bottle of Blatz, to plot the course of his glorious career of high finance. His head still reeled to some degree from the pistol whipping which the pert and saucy Cissy Flambeaux had so recently administered with her large and shapely, though not to say pendulous tetas. At the height of their passion he had, like the great Dante, swooned, perhaps as a result of one too many bottles of improperly chilled Blatz. He awakened from a most terrifying dream of being chased by a roaring tiger, only to behold the loudly snoring form of the tart and delectable Cissy, sleeping blissfully, yet perilously close to 'his side of the bed.'

He pondered the events of the last several days, but more especially of this day in particular. He'd had no idea that Chattanooga was possibly the geographical center of the universe. It was not as absurd as it seemed upon first consideration. Why else would such a man as the great Carl Jung have spent time here? It was also no mere coincidence that Chattanooga was the birthplace of the internationally revered 'Moon Pie.' Why every schoolboy learns early that the Moon Pie was created in 1917, but to what degree has the knowledge been lost that the Moon Pie, when used in conjunction with an Orange Crush, or a Royal Crown Cola, is reputed to be the most effective form of birth control known in the South? * (This claim has not been recommended by the FDA.)

And what about the dark and sinister presence of the Double-Cola Plant situated quietly at the bas e of Lookout Mountain? And why were Double-Cola aluminum cans not available in Minnesota? And who had taken it upon himself to shrink the Moon Pie from its original diameter of 7 & 1/2 inches? These and other uninvited questions now pressed heavily upon his sense of well-being, leaving him at a loss to explain their origin or purpose. The old adage that the universe is an infinite circle whose center is everywhere was no longer acceptable to great minds like his own. Other men, no doubt accepted such vestigial concepts without question, but then they'd never, at least most of them, known the mind altering and most transcendental experience of being held prisoner within the powerful loins of the lovely Ioveena . He missed her now, her large, sensual mouth, her heady fragrance. It was almost too much to bear. They should be together tonight, frolicking like two sea cows in the tropical waters of Key West, but alas, there was work to be done. Chip would soon be to junk cars what Gates was to computers. Then he and Ioveena , wherever she might be, would stroll with impunity through the front door of The Green Tortoise. When that glorious day arrived, and it certainly would, he would finally feel justified in telling the world to kiss the better majority of his ass. Until then, the two lovers must be apart, for now, but not forever. He would find her, no matter where she was, but first he must prove himself to the world.

At length Chip went and stood out upon the balcony overlooking the mighty Tennessee River, which glowing under the moonlight, wound like a quiet serpent through the fertile area known thereabouts as Moccasin Bend. He looked out across the river and beheld the Wildman Sanitarium beneath the starry sky. How tranquil it seemed, how trivial, and yet it was rumored in certain circles, as he now knew, that the inmates of that institution were none other than the Secret Chiefs, the great adepts who secretly directed the affairs of Earth, controlling at their discretion meteorological conditions and astronomical upheavals, wars, diseases and plagues, droughts, famines, indeed the very destiny of nations. It was not difficult to imagine now, as he stood there in the silence, in fact it was almost a certainty. Strange to think that thousands of tourists passed within sight of that installation daily as they trekked their way up Lookout Mountain to Rock City, and Ruby Falls, completely unaware that they passed Earth's likely command center, the Wildman Sanitarium, to which, in comparison, the Kremlin and the Pentagon were nothing more than two insignificant ant farms.

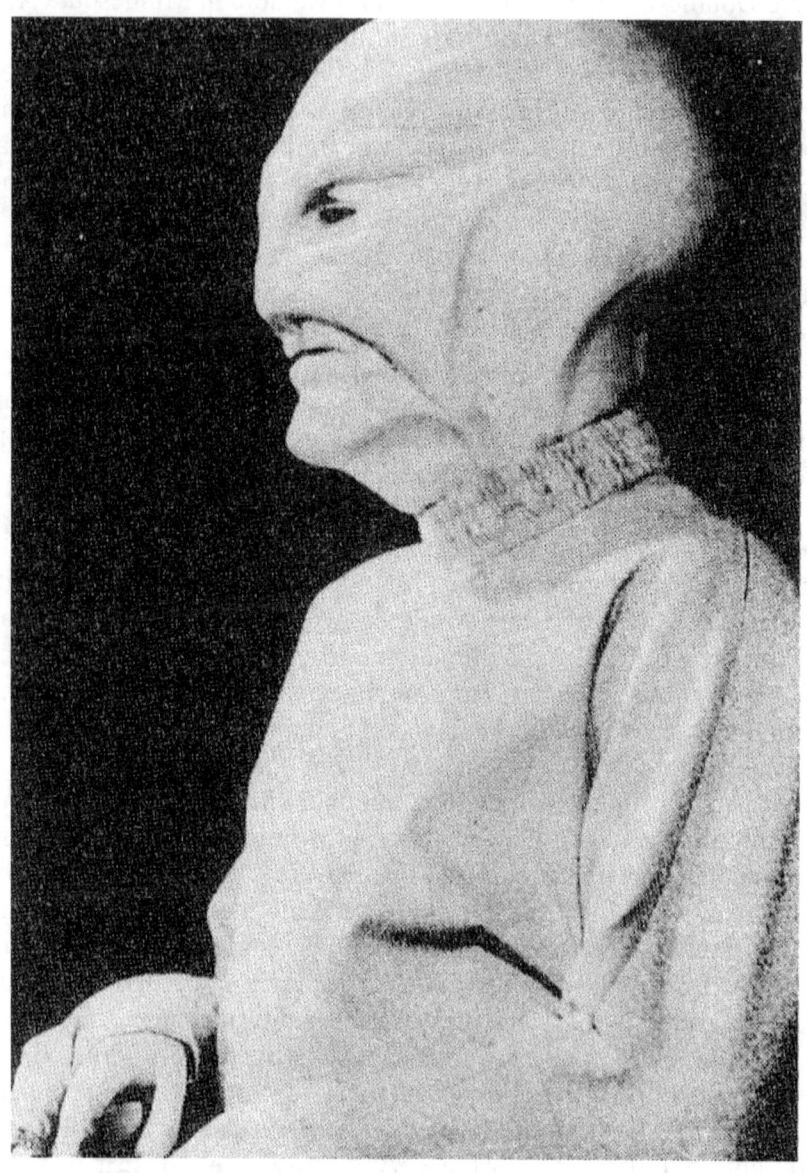

One of the Secret Chiefs?

8.

THE SHORT DRIVE HOME

"The Bank! Mr. Crooke! That's it!" Therpis was right. He would get a loan from the bank. It came to Chip in a flash of divine inspiration as he passed a Sovran Bank sign on the way back to Nashville the next morning. The vague and ill-defined plan he was formulating as the result of his visit to Di Lizardo now took on specific direction. He could start with his own Porsche. He owned the title to it free and clear. He would get a loan on that title. If that worked, then he could start getting titles from Di Lizardo, and from other sources, establish some fake car lot, and live like a king. His credit was excellent, and so was his family name. The name Hamster was known and recognized worldwide. In fact, people all across this great land were likely to reflect fondly upon hearing the name Hamster, if for no other reason than the hamster is such a cute, cuddly animal. Poor Hunter Ratcliff. Imagine a name starting with the word 'rat'. The very name creates suspicion. Nobody would even imagine the possibility of questionable financial dealings initiated by someone named Hamster. It was settled then, the Porsche would be an experiment. He could work out the details for his future business on a grander scale later. At least this would give him some quick seed money.

There was no doubt whatsoever, Chip reflected, passing a Sovran Bank sign, that the Sovran Bank founders had intentionally misspelled the bank's name. 'Sovran' indeed! Why? One reason is because the average citizen is incapable of correctly spelling 'sovereign.' As a confirmation, Chip asked Cousin Therpis to spell the word himself.

"Souveroun!" Therpis stated with authority.

"Quite so." Chip exclaimed, feeling correct in his hypothesis. Nonetheless, he mused privately, there could be no honorable justification for intentionally altering the spelling of such a weighty, even if difficult word. This is especially true when those undertaking the alteration are capable of doing so on such a grand scale. They had no doubt reasoned that the public at large wouldn't know the difference. They were right, and the bank appeared to be successful, but for how long, and at what cost to a society whose literacy diminished daily? No wonder 'Johnny can't read.' He can't read because he can't spell. He can't spell because of incidents like this one. Such atrocious spelling was on the rise nationally, and the implications were far more sinister than one might at first imagine. The communists had stated that they intended to destroy America from within. The destruction was indeed well underway. This was but one example. It was bad enough when some hick named a restaurant, for example, 'Kountry Kousin's Katfish Kabin.' While there was deliberate intent to mislead, the damage to the public was questionable, since the error was so blatant. In the instance just mentioned, it could possibly be argued that some good was accomplished, since patrons of the establishment, as well as passing motorists would note the error, and correct it in their own minds, possibly even subconsciously. The word 'sovereign' however, was another matter entirely, and could not be dismissed so casually. It denotes royalty, and its intentional alteration was no doubt intended to place the word in further disrespect by the masses. There was nothing Chip could do about the situation. The damage had already been done. He could but hope that some larger banking conglomerate would in time devour Sovran and change the name to something more appropriate.

"What does that have to do with anything?" Cissy asked petulantly.

The question vexed Chip considerably. The tender-loined Cissy was already seeking to control and direct the affairs of soon to be financial wizard Chip Hamster. For someone as intelligent as she seemed to be, she sometimes came out with some stupid crap.

"Look Goddamn it!" he shouted, "This country is going to hell in a hand basket. Self-service gas stations, self-service restaurants. Hell, you're supposed to feel guilty if you don't pick up after yourself at some crappy fast food joint. 'Sovereign' is a word denoting royalty. By chopping it up, altering it and dishonoring it, the wealthy are held in further contempt by the masses. It was crap just like this that started the stupid French Revolution."

"Chip, you're acting crazy. I don't like it when you're like this. I had forgotten you had this evil other side to your personality. I remember now when you set that man's pants on fire at Varallo's back in high school."

"Look," he continued angrily. "It's just like Dracula, and Frankenstein, or the Mummy."

"What in the hell are you talking about?"

"In those old movies, some loud-mouthed bastard always stirs up the peasants. And what happens next? There they go with their rakes, clubs, axes, and torches, destroying the only interesting person and decent architecture in town."

She continued to harass him about junk cars. All the way back from Chattanooga she sought to interrogate him, asking him deeply personal questions like, "How are you going to make a living fooling around with wrecked cars?" and "What are you going to do with them?" Chip politely suggested, more than once, that she drop the matter, indicating that he as yet had no specific plans. Strangely, this only served to incite her further. Her questions might not have been so offensive if he intended to ask her for a loan to tide him over until 'his ship came in.' Even then, however... Well, no matter, his course was clear now, at least the first step. Beyond that he did not know, but he was a man of destiny in an age of mediocrity. His success was assured. His way would become clear, if but one step at a time.

"Why are you thinking about starting any kind of business right now?" she asked with irritation. "You know Mercury is going retrograde. You should wait until the signs are more auspicious."

There was an audible and disdainful snort from the back seat. Therpis had been raised around all of that kind of thing back home. His mother was considered to have been a successful root doctor back in Tomachichi, Mississippi, an equal of famed New Orleanian Marie Laveau. Therpis had never been able to live it down. 'There goes Hattie's son,' they'd say, 'he's got the gift too.' Therpis' mother was still greatly feared among certain elements of the population even now, despite the fact that she was in her nineties. Therpis had been raised in that tradition.

When they returned to Nashville, Chip was glad to have some time away from her. She was already acting as if they were married. The fact of the matter was that his plan was so ingenious that it must be developed in absolute silence, away from inquisitive eyes, growing quietly but steadily in the darkness, like a marijuana plant under a light bulb in the basement of one's grandmother's house. Cissy's incessant questions disturbed his concentration. He must have time alone. Nobody must have the slightest clue as to his intentions, otherwise he would be 'rurn't' as they say in east

Nashville.

"Why that ho axe you so many questions? Ho!" Cousin Therpis asked as they sipped two chilled 16 ounce cans of Blatz in the kitchen of his splendid Belle Meade residence. "Mercury going renegade. Humph! The forces that control shit ain't constrained by any table of planetary days and hours. She's talkin' shit. I know that fo' a fact. She needs to quit telling you what to do. She reminds me of Mattie Pearl. Always sayin' 'don't do this and don't do that.' If you don't keep the upper hand now you'll end up like me. I'm telling' you that she wants to get a clamp on you. Why they like that?"

"I can't answer that," Chip responded dreamily.

"Dey'll make a fool outcha every time, every trip of the whip, Mistuh. How many times that done happened to me? But I'm wise to them cows now! My thing jes as important as they thing. If it wadn't for the bull and his great big rod, they wouldn't be no meat or butta by God."

Chip considered the wisdom of those weighty words so graciously proffered by his rustic cousin Therpis, who daily reaffirmed the correctness of his appointment as Chancellor of the Vine, by his sage and salient observations.

"Hey Chip, what about that Coba?"

"Yeah, Therpis, that was funny as hell alright," Chip replied, "but like I said, I don't believe that the Cobra is indigenous to the southeastern region of the United States. Nonetheless, that display by Ron Di Lizardo was one of the strangest things I've ever witnessed. Why would anybody put the head of a live snake in his mouth? And then blow on it? It was an interesting diversion but pointless as well as dangerous. It didn't make any sense to me."

"Do them snake handlas in Knoxville make sense that they gonna kiss uh Rattlesnake?" Therpis asked. "You gonna paint cho lips orange and we gonna kiss? Goddamn, I can't handle no snake in God's name, Jesus either. Can you?"

"Only snake..."

"No, I can't do it!" Therpis shouted.

"This is the only snake I can handle son," Chip stated proudly, grabbing his crotch.

"Yeah, he gonna charm a Coba. Shit! If a Coba ran up on me, you ain't got no...I'm gonna have uh heart attack. You ain't..."

"I'm gone," Chip laughed, "All you're gonna see is assholes and elbows."

"You...I'm gonna be somethin," Therpis continued. "I ain't gonna go try tuh kiss him. Kiss my ass man. Snake...Who gonna go face a damn lion on Jesus's name? You believe three little Heeb-yu chillun was in the fiery furnace and didn't get burnt up? Or Jonah...a whale swallowed some somitch and thowed him up? Do you believe that shit?"

"Well," Chip replied, "It is held on good authority that...no, not particularly."

"I don't. Hell, it might be true. I'm not sayin' it ain't true. But I don't believe no three somitches was in a fiery furnace and come outa theah. I don't believe three iron somitches could come out. Now I might go along with Daniel being in a lion's den, messin' with them little lions. I might could eat that up. But I ain't gonna eat up no Goddamn whale swallowed uh somitch, but I might eat that up better than I would thuh fiery furnace."

"Wait a minute, Therpis. Are you saying that the Bible isn't true?"

"I don't know what choo talkin bout! I'm sayin' what I feelin...Is that thuh Bible or something some somitch wrote?"

"I think that it's something some son of a bitch wrote," Chip replied with certainty, prodding Therpis toward further, and hopefully, even more absurd and amusing conclusions.

"Well, talk to me. What Choo talkin bout when you talkin bout the Bible? I don't know what thu Bible is. It might be thuh King James version."

"King Jimmy," Chip laughed.

"Jimmy my ass. Hell with King James! Is he livin' or dead? Has he done got up and come back? That ain't nuthin' but a bunch of man-made bullshit."

"Are you saying you don't believe in the Bible?"

"What is thuh Bible?"

"Well, I've got one in there. Do you want me to get it? "

"Do it say King James Version?"

"Yeah."

"Well then, keep thuh somitch in theah!"

"So you don't believe in the Bible?"

"I...what is thuh Bible? King James ain't God. I might have uh version. That's right. They tell me thuh most important stories of thuh Bible haven't ever been found."

"Why's that?" Chip asked, obviously provoking Therpis to even more salient observations.

"I don't know! Goddamn it. Go get on thuh ship and find out. Who do you think....? Damn King James!"

"Well," Chip replied matter of factly, "I hope you get outside before lightning hits you."

"Shit. Damn King James. King James Version....Shit. It might be my mammy's version."

As the effects of the properly chilled Blatz coursed through the well-worn neurological circuits of Therpis' mind, he frequently expounded loudly upon subjects of personal significance, the discourse usually triggered by something conversationally in his present environment. In this case the sequence logically followed the discussion of the snake which they had seen in Chattanooga. From there it progressed to snake handlers in general, and then to the religious aspects of snake handling, and from there to the Bible, a subject particularly distasteful to Therpis. Had an investigation into his past been conducted, it would have revealed that as a child Therpis had been spanked with the Bible as a disciplinary measure, and then told "Go ahead and cry. The more you cry, the less you piss. If you cry, maybe you won't piss in de bed."

9.

MONEY

Monday morning:

Chip arrived unannounced at the main Nashville office of the downtown executive branch of the First Mercantile Agrarian Trust Bank of Commerce and Industry. There was no place to park so he drove the Rolls-Royce up onto the sidewalk and parked it there, much to the chagrin of some no doubt envious members of the bovine masses, stockbrokers, lawyers, etc. He had anticipated an immediate audience with Mr. Crooke, and was more than slightly annoyed to find that Crooke was not there. He did not wish to have to deal with some lackey vice president, and there were no doubt several dozen of them in residence. On the other hand, he was there for a loan, and Mr. Crooke would most likely want to know how Chip had managed to squander $800,000 so quickly. As it chanced, fortune was kind enough to place Chip Hamster in the hands of an old school chum, Mark O'Lepty.

Chip parked his car on the sidewalk, as usual.

Mark had dozed off in night school at the military academy one evening and Chip had inserted a lit match in the side of his shoe. When the heat reached its zenith, the fire ignited the glossy leather shoe, which suddenly burst into flames due to an abundance of highly flammable polish. Mark awoke and dashed down the hallway, almost as if instinctively guided by the divine intercession of the formerly highly esteemed god, Mercury. Chip remembered the orange flames and thick black smoke trailing behind Mark as he raced for the bathroom. Even now, Chip remembered the loud hiss as Mark's flaming foot sought comfort in the tranquil waters of the toilet.

Mark had threatened to whip Chip's ass, but inasmuch as they were both minors in exile, a case of Falls City Beer, in returnable amber bottles, succeeded in placating the angry cadet.

A formal inquiry was instituted nonetheless, at the behest of the student fire marshal, an obnoxious and obsequious little turd, with a jealous and unprovoked vendetta against anyone who enjoyed life. The proper placement of several crisp five dollar bills provided detailed testimony from a few more or less reliable witnesses, who, in the absence of any specific causal evidence, jointly concluded that this unfortunate incident was indeed an authentic textbook case of spontaneous combustion, in all probability occasioned by Cadet O'Lepty's fermenting socks.

As Chip made his way down the long corridor of the 35th floor of the Mercantile Agrarian Trust Bank of Commerce and Industry, he considered it unlikely that Mark would remember such a trivial occurrence after all of this time. If the banker did remember the incident, he proved to be too much of a gentleman to refer to it. After the exchange of some casual pleasantries, Chip got quickly to the point.

"I'm here for a loan" he stated precisely, finding his old school buddy to be fairly congenial. Chip was nonetheless justifiably intimidated by the presence of a computer screen on the desk, which the banker activated at once.

"Business or personal?" The banker asked as he checked the computer records on Chip's behalf, a gesture which made the visitor somewhat nervous.

"Why business of course," Chip responded authoritatively, chancing accidentally to notice Mark's white patent leather shoes protruding ever so slightly beneath the desk. The banker instinctively withdrew them from Chip's gaze.

"Shit!" he thought, "The son of a bitch is going to deny me a loan based on some trivial thing that happened a quarter of a century ago. I must take the offensive and disorient this needle-nosed yuppie with my considerable skills as an after dinner speaker."

"Mind if I smoke?" Chip asked most courteously...after ceremoniously lighting a Royal Jamaica Goliath, one of the largest production cigars in the world. In an effort to distract the banker, he rose and began pacing back and forth through the office, a thick trail of blue smoke following in his wake.

"It seems that you've written some rather large checks lately, Chip," said the banker, as he continued to view the computer screen, undaunted by Chip's diversionary tactics. The banker retained his keen powers of concentration right up until the moment that Chip surreptitiously tripped the computer's power cord with his foot, thus shutting down the terminal.

"Well, it looks like something is wrong with this darn computer again," the banker stated flatly, still looking at the screen as if by staring at it long enough, he could somehow reactivate it. "Mr. Crooke is going to be out for two weeks. Is this something that can wait?"

"Not at all Mark. I have an important investment opportunity that must be acted upon immediately or risk being lost altogether," Chip exclaimed, hoping the banker wouldn't ask him what he had in mind before he had time to fabricate something that sounded worthwhile.

"How much do you need?"

"I need $50,000 at your preferred rate for 90 days initially, with an option to extend and renew for a total of six months, at which time I would be prepared to pay the note in full or perhaps convert to an installment loan."

"The bank examiners aren't looking favorably at installment loans right now. I can give you $50,000 easily enough on a 90 day note. I know your father was a founder of this bank, and believe me, I don't want to insult you, but in Mr. Crooke's absence,....but, do you have any collateral?"

Chip had anticipated this question to some extent, and consequently was able to quickly produce the title and current registration to a brand new Porsche Turbo Cabriolet. "You will note," he said with a flourish of his splendidly manicured hand, "that there are no liens or encumbrances of any kind on this vehicle."

"This will cover me," the banker replied immediately. "I had no idea you had a Porsche Turbo. What a magnificent car," he continued, thrilled to be able to hold the very title to such a car in his own hands.

"That's great, it's nice to know someone who appreciates the finer things in life. It is obvious that you are very well informed about such matters," Chip oozed.

"Don't you have to worry constantly about somebody stealing it? I mean a car like that..."

"Oh, don't worry about that. I really don't think it will be going anywhere."

"Did you drive it today? I mean, I'd really like to see it," the banker said excitedly.

"Actually," Chip replied with a smile, "It's at home in the driveway at this very moment, parked under a large shade tree."

"Gee, that's too bad," said the banker.

"It is indeed," Chip agreed.

"I think that particular body style is one of the best looking automotive designs of all time."

"The Porsche Turbo doesn't resemble an absurd looking crab with protruding eyes without purpose," Chip replied. "Despite its insect-like appearance it was not designed to mock the owner's lack of proportion and style, as it might seem to do at first glance. Nor was the engine placed improperly and dangerously behind the rear axle solely to make the car back-heavy, off balance, and with minimal front traction. Quite the contrary. The 911's, the 930s, and even the ancient 912s are indeed a testament to the superior engineering of German craftsmen. The car speaks for itself."

"What do you think of the 928?" the banker asked.

"Interesting that you should ask. The Porsche 928 was, in my estimation, the finest closed sports coupe in the world, bar none, that is, for its era. Do you think that the stern was arbitrarily designed to resemble a bathtub?"

"Uh, well, I ..."

Chip cut him off. "Not at all. The stern of the 928 was designed to afford superior collision protection in the event that the car strikes a solid object in reverse gear at a high rate of speed."

"But I thought that..."

"Yes, you knew that already, being the enthusiast that you are. I should have known," Chip continued.

"But what about...?"

"About the lightweight, soft alloy doors, fenders and hood? They were not intended to protect the vehicle's occupants from a rampaging Buick. That's true enough. It is, however, much more important to the average driver to sacrifice the safety afforded by heavy steel doors for reduced weight and wind drag at speeds in excess of 140 mph. After all, how many of us have actually been broadsided by a late `70s Buick anyway? I believe I've made my point."

"But I..."

"Yes," Chip interrupted, "I know that you need to attend to more important and pressing matters of commerce than these minor investments in which I dabble."

The conversation ended as suddenly as it began, and Chip Hamster departed Mark O'Lepty's office with a cashier's check payable to himself in the amount of $50,000, a check which he promptly exchanged for cash on the first floor of the Mercantile Agrarian Trust Bank of Commerce and Industry, lest the banker's computer suddenly regain power and tell a tale of over $ 800,000 squandered in a very short period of time. Chip was taking no chances. He got the cash and was glad to have received it. If Mr. Crooke hadn't run off with his beehive-coiffed secretary (as Chip subsequently ascertained), chances are he wouldn't have gotten the money at all. The gods of commerce and industry were protecting him, for the moment at least. Still, a triangular Blatz neon beer sign from his personal, museum quality collection of advertising art would be delivered to Mark O'Lepty's 35th floor office first thing tomorrow, as a genuine token of Chip's heartfelt appreciation. A truly noble gesture from a man of steel. Mark would be speechless. A Blatz neon was nothing to be taken lightly, and Chip was certain that it would be a welcome addition to Mark's den or office.

Chip and Therpis left the bank and proceeded to the old Howard School building to fetch the new custom license plates that he'd ordered for the Rolls-Royce several weeks ago. "NOTABMW." These plates, affixed to his convertible, along with his custom designed sterling silver alligator mascot atop the radiator shell would certainly incite the wrath and envy of the upwardly mobile heard in this city of sons in law.

They then motored to the Satsuma Tea Room on Union Avenue, parking directly in front of the restaurant in his reserved parking space, designated by the "NO PARKING 24 HOUR LOADING ZONE" sign. Once inside the restaurant, they were escorted to a semi-private table at the rear of the place, where Chip discussed financial matters of grave import with his cousin Therpis, who visually ogled a fashionably attired female sales clerk with quaint and rustic verbal expressions accompanied by a rapid up and down movement of his eyebrows, much to the amusement of the restaurant's other patrons, but to the chagrin of the object of his attentions.

"I'm a pipester," Therpis observed for the benefit of his employer and relative, "My daddy was a plumma and he sho taught me how to lay some pipe! Now I'm thru with that."

Throughout the meal, Therpis talked constantly as Chip held his fork in one hand and his plate with the other, moving the latter quickly as circumstances demanded in order to avoid occasional bits of food that fell indiscriminately from the rapidly flapping lips of Therpis.

"How did you put the touch on that banker?" Therpis asked.

"It was easy enough. I just double talked him. I told him that....I established control of the meeting early. And as you know, the early bird gets the worm, figuratively speaking."

"Yeah, and the late bird gets the snake," Therpis laughed.

"It was just a high class version of the old 'pigeon drop.'" Chip observed.

"Only he was the pigeon," Therpis laughed. "I can dig that, baby."

"Ha," Chip laughed. "I set his foot on fire back in high school. I'm surprised he gave me the money." The memory caused Chip to immediately start laughing loudly, much to the obvious disgust of the restaurant's other guests. As usual, Therpis kept right on talking,

70

oblivious to Chip's loss of control.

"You're one low down....how could you do that Chip? Set a boy's feets on fire? He didn't do nothing to you. That's just low down. Why do you act like that? I just don't understand you sometimes."

Chip was silent now except for hysterical gasps as he sought to regain his composure. He was now laughing like a hyena, becoming weaker with every passing moment. His laughter was probably just the involuntary release of nervous tension, a relief that the matter at

the bank had been so easily and successfully concluded.

"Talking about pigeons, now, we used to eat pigeons when I was a little boy down in Mississippi," Therpis recalled. "Oooo-weee. Now that's some good eatin.' We'd thow rocks at the dumb bastards and they'd just sit there 'til you hit one. Then we'd fetch 'em off the ground and take 'em on home to Aunt Inez. She'd fry 'em up real good. Now let's see. She was your daddy's first cousin's mother, after the divorce of his uncle's sister's brother's third cousin. That would have, let's see. That would have made her your daddy's first, no, probably third. Oh damn all that, but she could cook pigeons like I never ate since. That woman could cook mister, oooo-wee. Fried pigeons, pickled pork pig's feets, what a meal. She's gone now. I think she got mowed down by a Trailways bus back in 1979. Hell, that was....let's see, no, it might have been a Greyhound. It's hard to get fried pigeons anywhere these days. Ain't none on the menu here, you see that don't cha? These Nashville restaurants are missing the boat. That's just all there is to it."

Chip jumped up from the table and ran for the restroom, on the verge of screaming, completely overcome by his companion's humorous remarks, observations, which from a literary standpoint, would be considered as belonging to that genre universally known as 'stream of horseshit.' Loud animal-like sounds emanated from the rear of the restaurant as Chip continued to laugh uncontrollably. In about five minutes Chip emerged calmly as if nothing had happened, but his face was red as a beet and there were still tears in his eyes. He avoided looking directly at Therpis, grabbed the check off the side of the table and proceeded silently to the front door.

On their way out of the restaurant, Therpis removed his dentures, and, holding them aloft, inquired loudly of their host, "Hey David, you got somewhere I can wrench off my teeth?"

Chip imagined that he noticed several of the more timid patrons gagging, while others witnessed the scene in stunned disbelief. A good time was had by all. Outside, a corpulent thug of a policeman prepared to ticket Chip's car.

"Is this your car Buddy?"

"Yes sir," Chip replied pleasantly, but feeling otherwise. He was always nice to policemen, especially since they had the authority to detain anyone for up to 48 hours without explanation. A frightening thought indeed.

"Well then, read this." he exclaimed as he handed Chip a $50.00 ticket for parking in a loading zone.

As they pulled gracefully away from the curb, Therpis observed, although not too loudly, "Why they make them cops so fat? That somitch is so fat he ain't seen his nuts in forty years! Why they wanna be like that Mistuh? Givin parking tickets to cheese magnets when these sto clerks gettin all shot up and they can't catch 'em? I don't go for that shit now! Why? Why? Yaaaa!"

"Well," said Chip, having resolved himself to the situation, "at least the fat son of a bitch didn't have my car towed. Nonetheless, it is in decidedly poor taste to give a Rolls-Royce a parking ticket under any circumstances, but then, as they say, "Pearls before swine."

"Yeah, and age 'fo beauty ho!" interjected the ever jocular Therpis.

It had indeed been a magnificent morning, a visit with an old school chum, lunch with a friend at a fashionable restaurant, and $50,000. Chip would surely turn that $50,000 into millions.

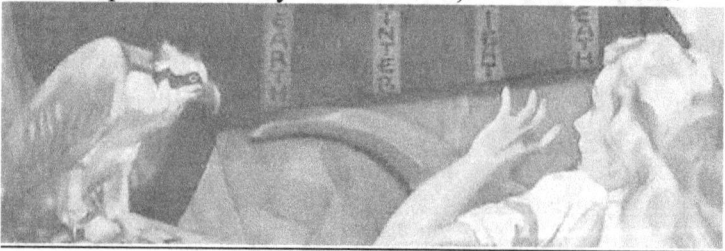

10.

SUMMER AFTERNOON

Chip peered down the long hood of his Rolls-Royce as they entered his driveway, catching sight of his new Porsche Turbo, "Turbot" as he called it, having added the letter 'T' to the end of 'turbo' for the express purpose of disorienting the upwardly mobile masses. There it was, crushed under the tree, like a stomped June bug. Fortunately, it couldn't be seen from the street. It would be necessary to dispose of the body, figuratively speaking of course, and soon, but not right now. The summer heat had temporarily drained him of his energy. He needed a few moments to collect his thoughts. It had all happened so fast, really; the rescue of Ioveena from the briny depths, his father's untimely demise at the business end of a skillet, his new Porsche turbot destroyed by an act of God, the discovery that Chattanooga, Tennessee might be the geographical center of the universe, the blatant and too rapid attempt of Cissy Flambeaux to control his masculinity through the influence of her powerful womanhood. It was almost too much.

"Chancellor!" he called, summoning Therpis. "I think that it's time for a couple of Blatz 'Negaritas'."

"Yes suh Mistuh Chip, two Negaritas comin right up!"

The Blatz Negarita is a sort of black Margarita made with Blatz Bock, carefully prepared under the very closest supervision of a master mixologist. The recipe is enclosed for the benefit of the reader for informational purposes, but for obvious reasons, should not be attempted by amateurs. Fortunately Therpis had initiated the lengthy and laborious process earlier that morning.

1. Take a 12 oz. can of Blatz Bock. Open the pop top and let it stand (in the can) at room temperature for exactly two hours and twenty-three minutes. (It is best to employ a digital alarm clock at this step for the sake of precision, this being a crucial aspect of the all-important decarbonization process).

2. Carefully take a can opener and remove the entire top of the can, in much the same manner as would be used in opening a can of dog food.

3. Stand the container upright in the freezer for several hours until frozen solid.

4. Empty the frozen contents into a blender, mix thoroughly at low speed, adding a measured four ounces of lukewarm tequila as it is mixing. Insert three Doritos (Preferably Nacho Cheese flavor), a dash of Bruce's Tango Sauce, top with a Jalapeno and serve with a straw in a Margarita glass or a snow cone cup. There you have it, a Blatz Negarita.

In less than five minutes the finance minister appeared, drinks in hand. "I made you a double" he said, meaning of course that there were two Jalapenos instead of one. Chip expressed his sincere appreciation and accompanied his words with yet another five dollar bill. "It's not as crisp as I would prefer, but then this humidity is oppressive, and in conjunction with this heat. Well...you understand."

"Yooze the boss and I'ze the hoss. My names Jimmy and I'll take what you gimmee! Now I'm thru with that."

But he wasn't through. As the alcohol began to travel through the well-worn and seriously frazzled neurological circuits in the Chancellor's rustic brain, Chip sensed an impending philosophical discourse. He was not mistaken.

"If all of the wimmenz in the world was to zipper theyselves, the world would come to an end. That's right. If all of the wimmenz in the whole world zippered theyselves, then the world as we know it would come to an end."

"Therpis, that well may be, but I don't see that it is germane to our activities or conversations of today."

"Germans, French, your Negroes, Chinese, everybody! The world would come to an end. I tell you mistuh that the world as we know it would cease to exist!"

"Well Therpis," mused Chip, "considering human nature, that is rather an unlikely possibility."

"Yeah Chip......but if all the rapists was to stop rapein' and all of the snakists was to stop snaking,' well that would be it." Therpis kept rambling but Chip had shut him out. He was thinking about his own life up to that point, up to that very moment in fact. He was more or less unfit to work at any real job, and he knew it. In the first place he did not possess any particular skills. He didn't have a law degree, or a barber's license, or any other marketable professional credentials. But then, with the exception of a few doctors he knew, neither did the majority of his friends. They had for the most part taken over the family business or married well. Chip was certain that he possessed executive ability, as much as anyone else in America, he just had to find his niche. The world had changed. Chip had been led to believe as a youth that anyone with a college degree was set for life. That may have been true thirty or forty years ago, but those days were long gone. A college degree now meant less now than a high school diploma had after World War II. Furthermore, the days of company loyalty were gone. It used to be that a person could work for a company for twenty-five or thirty years, and get a good retirement and medical benefits. Now, companies were bought and sold, and employees were dismissed with little notice, only to find that their pension fund had been gutted and their medical benefits withdrawn. So much for corporations and large companies. Smaller companies were even worse. They were under so many government restrictions that they could hardly move. Since there really was no real job security, Chip determined that he might as well be insecure working for himself. Besides, what other employer would pay him an exorbitant amount of money for doing whatever he wanted to do, whenever he wanted to do it? Chip would be much better off on his own, engaging in his car business, and operating as much as possible in cash, and off of the books.

He'd led an easy life up to this point and readily accepted that this was the case. That he had not turned his life to any purpose so far was both understandable and acceptable. Henry Leland, the genius who started both Cadillac, and Lincoln motorcars, had been over seventy years old when he began each of those admirable undertakings. And what about Col. Sanders, or Oswald Lobrecue? The list of late bloomers was indeed extensive. By failing to enter into the accepted mainstream of the social work ethic, he had set himself as an outcast to some degree. That everybody in Nashville assumed he was a millionaire gave him a certain air of legitimacy. And yet it bothered him that he wasn't in any kind of established vocation.

He saw people his age at lunch in nice restaurants. They were well dressed, with crisp white starched shirts and ties, and wedding rings on their fingers. They no doubt spoke about important deals they were working on. They probably had attractive wives at home, and rosy faced children at one of the many exclusive private schools in the Nashville area. They most likely went to church, and had life pretty much figured out. Most of them were probably stock brokers, after dinner speakers, or lawyers.

Chip had originally wanted to be an after dinner speaker himself, or a lawyer, like Perry Mason. That had always been his dream, but by the time he got kicked out of the Navy, it was too late, there were already far too many lawyers. There was no point in getting a law degree by then, and the problem had only gotten worse with the passage of time. Every few months several hundred more lawyers passed the state bar exam and were excreted into an already over saturated marketplace. This had been going on regularly for over thirty years, with the result that lawyers were now as common as flies, and equally as pernicious. It was Perry Mason's fault, not Raymond Burr's personally, but Perry Mason's. No, it was Raymond's fault too. He was, is, and shall always be Perry Mason. He single handedly ruined law as a profession nationwide. The popular television show began in the late 1950s and persuaded an entire generation to become lawyers. Raymond Burr had even been the featured speaker at Tennessee Bar Association's Gatlinburg conference in 1959. Prior to that time, law had been a respectable profession, and most lawyers seemed to be rich, successful, and respected, not the ambulance chasers and hucksters that they are now. They didn't have to advertise or keep a police scanner in their vicinity at all times so they could rush down to the scene of an accident and beat the competition. They knew by instinct when there had been an accident or a crime. It was an inner knowledge, a Zen thing.

Perry Mason could sense a murder from miles away, and has personally discovered more bodies than any man alive. He had it all, wealth, prestige, power, self-respect. He drove a Lincoln convertible, a real American iron, not some rice rocket like a Honda or a Lexus. Not only that, he could ride down a busy L.A. thoroughfare at sixty mph. with the top down and speak to his secretary at a normal conversational level without the wind blowing his hair sideways. He was a man of steel, a man of honor, known

76

and respected by all. He never knowingly defended a guilty client. If somebody couldn't afford to pay him, Perry defended him anyway, as long as the client was really innocent. Nor did he burden the taxpayer with lengthy court trials. He almost always forced a confession from the true criminal at a preliminary hearing, and not in violation of the criminal's Constitutional rights either. When Perry got a confession, it was in a courtroom full of witnesses, and it always stuck. He never suffered through any moral dilemmas. He never had to get a criminal off the hook or defend a guilty party in order to pay his bankcard bill. But it was too late for Chip to have that kind of life. It had all been ruined by a television show.

Chip opened his ever present black book and found Perry Mason's phone number. Madison 5-1191. He got the number off of one of the episodes when some guy had told his secretary to call Perry Mason at that number. Chip had jumped up, grabbed a pen, and written down the number in his phone book immediately, and had carried it around for years. Since he had never been charged with murder, he felt no real need to call. Now, he picked up the phone, entered the area code for L.A., 213, and then dialed the number. He might as well see who in the hell's number it really was. It rang a few times and someone answered. "Is Perry there?" Chip asked casually.

The party at the other end hesitated, then answered, "Who?"

Chip asked again, "Is Perry Mason in?"

The person at the other end of the line again asked, "Who?"

"Excuse me, Gertie?" Chip asked, thinking that perhaps he'd gotten Perry's receptionist. "I was looking for Perry."

"Who?" came the reply once more.

"I'm looking for Perry Mason but it seems I've made a mistake. He probably lives in Denver now, and I must've dialed the Owl's residence by mistake."

The confused recipient of the call for the fourth time asked, "Who?"

"If I'd wanted Owls, I'd have gone to the Children's Zoo," Chip replied, laughing, and slammed down the phone.

"Who?" asked Therpis, "Who you callin'?"

"Et tu Therpae?"

"No thanks, Chip. I done had me a little sandwich fo lainch. I probably won't eat again today."

The heat was oppressive, but nonetheless enjoyable. At length, however, after four cocktails, Chip dozed off, and was besieged by many odd dreams, the type that only come during an afternoon nap on a summer day. The sandman brought him many strange images, some of which were not particularly soothing. In one segment Chip was underwater and unable to breathe. In another, he was seated at a small table in the darkness, surrounded by angry men dressed in robes. Later, it seemed, Chip had been caught by the authorities and was standing trial for interstate bank fraud. At last, he was led in chains and shackles down a long dark corridor and strapped into the electric chair. He would die for having poisoned his aged valet Therpis, with a tainted glass of 'Milwaukee's Finest' The phone rang in the execution chamber, the guard answered, nodded in affirmation, and then announced that the stay of execution had been lifted by the governor.

"Chip. Hey, Mistuh Chip," Therpis shouted from the back porch, "Phone call."

Chip rubbed his eyes. Thank God, it had only been a dream. He lifted the cordless phone, flipped the switch and brought it to his ear, feeling his surroundings swirl. "I am so drunk," he laughed. "Hello."

"Is this Charles Hamster?" The voice asked from the other end of the line.

"Yeah, who's this?"

There was a moment of silence and then a loud blast of horrible music "Da da da dada!" followed by a pre-recorded message of extremely poor sound quality, "Hey, have you been injured on the job? Slipped and fallen down three flights of stairs? Been run over by a truck? Bitten by a neighbor's dog? If so, help is on the way. Stay on the line now for a personal consultation with one of America's top legal experts."

Chip knew precisely how to handle the situation. When the operator came on the line, Chip was asked the nature of his injury, to which he replied gravely, that he had slipped on a big green quid in the parking lot of the K-Mart.

"What were the nature of your injuries?"

"Well, it's very personal and I don't know if I can speak about it over the phone, especially to someone I don't know," Chip replied.

"It sounds as if you have been severely traumatized," the salesman said sympathetically, thinking he had a sucker on the line. "Would you like to schedule a free consultation with one of America's top legal professionals?"

"Yes," Chip answered, "perhaps that would be the best thing. Let me put my assistant on the phone and he will take the necessary information." He covered the mouthpiece and motioned for Therpis to pick up the phone. Therpis picked up the phone in the kitchen, and the conversation continued.

"OK, my assistant, Therpis, is on the phone with us and he will take down the information. Therpis, write down their name and number and then, if you would be so kind, please flap your jaws for our friend."

"Wait. Just one more question Mr. Hamster. I have to write down the nature of your injury so that we can begin to assess your situation in order to determine an appropriate damage figure for your claim."

"It's really too personal to discuss over the phone," Chip stated quietly.

"I promise not to tell anyone," the caller stated. Chip thought he detected heavier than normal breathing on the other end of the line. Either it was a fat son of a bitch, a pervert, or both.

"Well," Chip answered demurely, "When I slipped, I fell and..."

"Yes, yes, and what happened?"

"Well...I fell, and when I got up, there was...there was...a crack in my ass."

"You mean that you cracked your pelvis?" the caller asked.

"No, I told you that as a result of my fall, I now have a big crack in my ass."

"Well, how big is it?"

"Well," Chip replied, "I haven't actually measured it."

"I mean, is it large?" the caller inquired. "What I mean precisely is, is that it must be fairly large, or it wouldn't be able to accommodate that bulbous, hydro encephalitic water balloon head of yours."

"Avast, you vile rodent! Mind your manners. Here's my assistant," he said, handing the phone to the outstretched hand of Therpis.

"Aboogala…" Therpis shouted as he flapped his jaws rapidly from side to side, "Don't make me put my lawyer on you. He'll put a clothespin on your ass and hang you out with the laundry."

"That guy's good," Chip slurred, "I think he's getting the best of you. Tell him you're going to jump through that telephone wire and kick his ass."

"He's laughing," Therpis said to Chip. "Hey Mr. Phone Man, come on over to 1267 Belle Meade Boulevard and have a drink. We just clowning on a hot day. Naw man, come on over. Nashville. Where you? Vanilla? Where's that? Hold the phone.

"Chip, he said he's in Vanilla, in the Philistines."

80

Hey Chip, he said he was in Vanilla, in the Philistines and he can't get here. Chip said that didn't make no difference," Therpis spoke into the phone, "and just to come on over. All right, we'll see you when you get here. Yeah, it might take a while but we ain't goin' nowhere. Yeah."

"Therpis, here's five dollars, get me another drink."

"You is the boss and I'ze the hoss."

11.

LET'S MAKE A DEAL

"Who did you say you are?" the voice on the other end of the phone asked suspiciously.

"I told you," he repeated, "I'm Chip Hamster, from Nashville, Tennessee. You know, as in cheese, as in AMALGAMATED Cheese."

What an imbecile, Chip thought.

"Look, is this the Mandrake Detective Agency or not? A simple yes or no will be sufficient. Jeeeee-sus," he said, covering the phone. "What an absolute bird-brain."

There was no response initially, other than the sound of what seemed to be rapidly turning pages. Eventually the voice replied dryly, with a simple "No."

"No what?" Chip asked. This is unbelievable. What an idiot.

"No."

"No what?" Chip shouted. "No dice? No shit? No way? No news is good news? No time like the present? No what?"

"No," the dull voice replied. "This is not the Mandrake Detective Agency, it is the Manroot Detective Agency. Furthermore," the voice continued, "There is nobody named Hamster in the Miami phone book, therefore it is...."

"I'm not in Miami. I told you I'm in Nashville. What does the phone book have to do with anything? I don't need a phone number."

"It only stands to reason," the voice replied curtly, "that if the name Hamster is not in the Miami phone book, that it wouldn't likely be in the Nashville book either, what with Nashville being a considerably smaller metropolis."

"Well, just what is it you're trying to say?" Chip asked.

"I'm saying precisely that there is nobody with a name like 'Hamster' anywhere other than a pet shop or a zoo. In other words, it is obviously an alias. I don't speak with pseudonyms. If you wish to engage my services, then I suggest you provide me with your correct name."

This was almost more than Chip could bear. He quietly gathered his thoughts before replying to this insane allegation. He would have immediately told this dim-stooge to kiss the better majority of his ass, except that the Manroot Agency had come highly recommended, and he must find Ioveena .

"I'm sorry that my name doesn't meet with your approval," he said coldly, gritting His teeth, "but Hamster is my real name. Now here's what we can do. I can fax you a page out of the Nashville phone book, and a copy of my driver's license, if that will satisfy you."

"I would accept that as sufficient documentation for further conversation." the detective said dryly.

"Alright then, give me your fax number, and call me when you get it. I'm going to do this right now, so stand by."

Chip faxed the information immediately and waited patiently by the phone for an hour before becoming disgusted with the wait, and again calling the Miami phone number of the Manroot Detective Agency. The phone was answered and he was immediately put on hold. He was starting to get pissed. Five minutes later, a robot secretary answered and said, "Mr. Manroot will be with you in just a moment. Your call is important to us, so please continue to hold. The Manroot Detective Agency is South Florida's premier investigative service. Catering to the carriage trade for nearly fifty years, Manroot has specialized in locating missing persons, recovering lost family pets, confirming allegations of marital infidelity, investigating accident and injury claims, and engages in a variety of other specialized investigations and surveillance services. Listen carefully as our menu options have changed..."

Chip put his hand over the phone as the recording continued and said to Therpis. "Listen closely because our menu options have changed. Who gives a shit? That's something some dumb son of a bitch somewhere, came up with, foolishly thinking it sounds intelligent, now you get that crap every time you call anybody anywhere in the US. Our menu options have changed. Like we knew what they were originally? Who cares? What a bunch of stooges!"

"You's right," Therpis mumbled.

"If you require missing persons, the recording continued, press seventeen now. If you feel your significant other may be unfaithful, press eighteen now. If you are in need....." Suddenly the robot cut off.

"Chip Hamster," the voice said, "born at St. Expedite Hospital to cheese magnate Mason Charles Hamster, and the former Deloitte Haskins in 1980. Raised in Nashville on Belle Meade Boulevard, attended several military schools before entering U.S. Navy in 1998. Kicked out in 1990. Various mediocre colleges, then a move to Key West for four years, posing as a writer, but living off the reluctant support of recently deceased father. Chief interests; expensive cars, women, and cigars, not necessarily in that order." That was all the voice said.

"Pretty good for an hour's work," Hamster said, his anger quickly diminishing, "but listen to me. If I tell you something, you can count on it being true. It may or may not be pleasant, but I will not lie. I said my name was Hamster, and indeed it is."

"Very well, Mr. Hamster, my apologies," the voice said. "I am very much into details, and I always check out every potential client. Now, what can I do for you?"

"I want you to locate an attractive Haitian woman of mixed ancestry, who had been residing with me at my place on Duval Street in Key West since last spring. I think she got pissed that I didn't bring her to Nashville with me for my father's funeral, but there were too many things going on in my life at just that moment."

"You returned to Key West and she was gone?" It was more of a statement than a question.

"Yes. I think she moved to Miami, but I'm not certain," Chip said.

"And now you want her back," the voice spoke plainly.

"You got it," Chip answered.

"What's it worth to you" the voice asked.

"Whatever it takes." Chip replied without hesitation.

"$5,000 in advance, $1,000 a day, plus expenses, and another $5,000 when I find her."

"That's kind of steep," Chip replied. The phone immediately went dead. "Son of a bitch!" Chip shouted, not knowing whether the phone had cut off or if the detective had hung up on him. He called back, was put on hold again for ten minutes.

"I don't tolerate indecision. I don't have time for indecision. I am the best at what I do." the voice said coldly. "I told you my price. Take it or leave it."

"I'll take it," Chip said quickly.

"Very well, email me what information you have; her full name, a complete physical description, photographs, if available, last known address, names of friends, and anything else that might be of assistance. I'll look it over and call you when I need you. You will be billed monthly, and payment is required within five working days. Failure to pay, or late payment will result in the voiding of this agreement. Is that understood?" the voice asked.

Chip agreed to the rude son of a bitch's terrorist demands because he had to have Ioveena in his life. She was the first real woman he'd ever met, and probably the only woman he had ever really loved. He now seriously regretted not bringing her to the funeral. He must find her. Perhaps she was wandering the streets of Miami, alone and desperate, feeling that he no longer loved her. That she might think that, was the worst thing he could imagine. She was his everything. Sex with her just went on and on and on. Anywhere, anytime. More than that, she was a magical person, not to mention a real exotic showpiece. Von Snocker would dump his tubby wife Stewey instantly for one roll in the hay with the lovely Ioveena . Hunter Ratcliff would beg like a dog for any favor she might bestow, no matter how trivial. What man wouldn't? Someday, he hoped, they would get married at St. George's Episcopal Church, at the entrance to fashionable Belle Meade Boulevard. He must have her back at any price.

Chip did not like the attitude of that boring jerk Manroot, but if he could find Chip's lost love then it didn't matter if the guy was a prick, or what it ended up costing him financially. Whatever he spent, it would be worth it to have her back in his arms, back in his life.

Now to the business at hand. Chip had $50,000 with which to launch his career as a 21st century giant of finance. From now on it was dinner at Vestibula, Ruth's Chris, Antonio's, and lunch at Satsuma, the Indian joint Sitar, and snacks at the Krystal, yet another Chattanooga-based company. There would be big parties at his charming and fashionable Belle Meade address, a second, new concert grand piano, and weekend trips with his consort, Cissy, and cousin Therpis. In short, it was nice to have a little spending money again.

Chip finally decided to risk everything by laying out all of his business plans for Ron Di Lizardo, and told him how he intended to use the titles to wrecked cars to secure loans with which to fund ultimately legitimate business endeavors. This was always, Chip explained, the way most great Americans had started what later evolved into lasting and well-known businesses.

He really hadn't known exactly what to expect in terms of a reply. Di Lizardo could have easily called the police. He could have notified the state banking commissioner, or he could have politely instructed Chip to get off his property. What he did, however, was to take a big swig of Orange Crush, lean back in his aluminum lawn chair and peer off into the distance quietly, looking far beyond the bamboo walls of the Tiki Hut. At length he turned to Chip and asked casually, "What's in it for me?"

"What do you want?" Chip asked.

"I am an honorable man," Di Lizardo replied, choosing his words carefully. "I would never intentionally defraud, cheat, or in any other way, even unintentionally beat another human being out of any money, not that I'm especially fond of 'humans,'" he exclaimed with an air of unmistakable derision, which Chip let pass, in view or the reason for his visit. Chip was disheartened by this reply.

"But," Di Lizardo continued, "on the other hand, banks, insurance companies, and other similar large corporations which become rich off the backs of honest and sincere businessmen like ourselves, by God, are another matter altogether. I'd be happy, by God, to provide you with certain titles for an amount of say, 20% of whatever you are able to receive as the result of your activities."

"20% might be a bit excessive," Chip replied, pinching his chin thoughtfully between his thumb and forefinger. "With the interest I will have to pay to these fly by night title loan companies, and to the banks, 20% doesn't leave me much of a cushion."

"How much 'cooshun' do you need?" Di Lizardo asked.

"I was thinking in terms of, perhaps, 10%," he answered.

"What do you intend to do with the money?"

"I haven't decided yet, exactly. I've been thinking about investing it in some musical projects. You know," he continued, "I live in Nashville."

"Of course," Di Lizardo said thoughtfully, "there could be no connection to me personally, or to Mid-South Auto Brokers, Intergalactic, at all. Any transactions between us would have to be on a purely cash basis."

"That's most acceptable, Ron," Chip answered, daring to address this possible future business partner by his first name."

"I don't know," Di Lizardo replied, appearing to hesitate. "I have a good business here. There isn't much reason for me to jeopardize things unless there is a low risk opportunity to make a substantial amount of money, over an extended period of time. I'm sure you understand my situation."

"OK, then" Chip answered, "20% it is," he said, extending his hand to the car dealer. They shook on it, and the deal was consummated. Chip just wanted to get started.

"Before I give you any titles," Di Lizardo said, "I want you to give me a complete rundown of your specific business plan. I need to feel reasonably secure that what you are contemplating has some chance of succeeding."

And so Chip laid it out for his host in as specific detail as possible. He told him how he had successfully borrowed $50,000 from the bank on the title to his Porsche. He intended to borrow money from other banks in much the same way, depending, of course, on the loan value of the cars to which Di Lizardo supplied legitimate titles. There were, he continued, also less reputable car loan companies, known as title pawn shops, or auto pawn shops. These places loaned up to a third of the 'Gray Book,' or wholesale value on car titles, keeping the car's actual title, but permitting the borrower to retain physical possession and use of the actual vehicle. Chip planned to drive up ceremoniously to these places in his new Phantom convertible, present his Tennessee operator's license, showing his prestigious Belle Meade address, and state that he had lost some money gambling, and that he needed to make it up before his wife found out. He would say that he couldn't bring the car in because it was his wife's, and he didn't want her to get suspicious. He would offer to sign whatever papers were necessary, would have the title to the car in his hand, and would hopefully leave the premises with a check in a matter of moments. It was that simple. Based upon who he was, that is, a well-known Nashville socialite, his plan seemed credible enough. After all, he reasoned, he wasn't some hick off the street. The auto pawn places only loaned money for thirty days. At the conclusion of that period, the borrower had to renew the note and pay the total interest due for the past month. It came to 20%.

"Your plan seems well thought out," Di Lizardo announced pleasantly. "This will be on the honor system," he stated. "I'll give you five titles to start with. Let's see what you can do with them. I have a stack in my file, and you can choose whatever make and model of vehicle you please. After you've received your initial loan, I'll expect a cash payment of 20% of that amount, as well as 10% received from subsequent loans off of any of my titles. I don't want any checks, money orders, cashier's checks, or bank wires. Cash only. I want nothing connecting us in any way. No paper trail. Is that understood and agreed?"

"That's fine with me," Chip replied happily. "I think, as much as I like Ferraris and Rolls-Royces, that I had better stay away from the really exotic stuff. Some two year old BMW 700 series, and a few S or G series Mercedes are probably the best thing for the Nashville market. They'll bring some good money, but won't arouse any suspicions. What do you think?"

"That's the right decision. If you start pawning Ferrari titles all over town, somebody might get to asking questions."

"Yeah," Chip deliberated, "I can also conduct business out of state, with banks and other major financial institutions. I can say that

I've come out of state so that my wife won't find out about it. Since my credit record is excellent, nobody will suspect anything."

"This sounds a little bit like a pyramid scheme to me, by God" Di Lizardo observed, "not that I particularly care, personally, but you're going to have to do a lot of floating and juggling. The banks will be easy enough to handle, given the current artificially low interest rates, and you can most likely do renewable 90 day notes. That will buy you some time initially. Those monthly places however, represent a much greater threat and are therefore more dangerous. Maybe you should start with legitimate banks. They never ask to see anything other than a title and your credit rating, at least as far as I know. I've never gotten a loan from any bank by God, so I can't say for sure. All in all, however, it sounds like a good plan. I would imagine that your first loan will be the most crucial."

Di Lizardo turned, reached into his file, and pulled out a stack of about 150 car titles. Chip thumbed through them carefully, settled on a new top of the line Toyota Lexus, a year old Mercedes sedan, two big BMWs and a five year old Mercedes SL 550. He bid Ron Di Lizardo a fond farewell and returned to Nashville before Therpis or Cissy had even missed him. Not bad for a day's work. He strolled through his back door like a strutting Bantam rooster, leaving a trail of rich smoke from a Hoyo De Monterey Sultan in his wake. He paused to look admiringly at a gigantic oil portrait of his grandfather as he passed the door of the drawing room. He then walked into the large dining room and paraded proudly before one of the giant gold leaf pier mirrors at each end of the room. "Am I not magnificent?" he asked, looking proudly at his image. "Am I not a genius?"

And indeed he was, at least by his own reckoning. He had thought about the situation on the way home and decided that he would be free of Di Lizardo soon enough. He would get loans on these titles, pay Di Lizardo, get a few more titles from him, and then recirculate the titles he already had among different lending institutions. It was simple enough. He truly was a brilliant man.

Later:

"You seem to be in a good mood tonight," Cissy said cheerfully, happy to see the man of her dreams. Chip was so cool. He was much different from most of the other young men she knew. He was smart, always thinking about becoming a successful businessman, always seeking to further his career, and to make the most of himself. It wasn't love yet, at least not on her end, but it could be any day. She'd allowed herself time to recover from the unfortunate and still fairly recent demise of her first husband, who'd been gone less than a year. Chip was much better sexually than the old man she'd been married to. He'd made her carry a spoon in her purse for whenever he wanted to 'do it.' It was disgusting, really, but worth it. She figured it was a little like robbing a bank, or selling drugs. You make a bunch of money, stash it away, get caught, do your time, and then come out rich. That's basically the way she viewed her marriage....time served. Oh, she had liked the old bastard well enough. He'd been much younger when they'd met. She'd been only 20 then and he'd been nearly 70. It was his idea to get married. They'd lived together for fifteen years, and he'd taught her a great deal, and shown her parts of the world she would have never seen otherwise. He'd died 'in the saddle' so to speak, and had left her with vast financial holdings, including a beautiful house in Nashville, and another in London.

"I am in a good mood," he replied looking at her and winking. "If you play your cards right," he joked, "you might just get lucky tonight."

"Well," I like that," she said with a smile.

"Where to?" he asked, trying to decide where to have dinner.

"It doesn't matter to me," she said, "you decide."

"Ruth's it is," he replied looking at her to see if the selection met with her approval. It did, so they were off into the night with the top down and music blasting.

Ruth's Chris is a steak house, part of a small chain of restaurants, with locations in New Orleans, Memphis, and elsewhere. The one in Nashville opened in the early 1980s and had been one of Chip's favorite joints, one he'd seriously missed while in Key West. It was frequented primarily by music people on week nights, and locals on Fridays and Saturdays. The place was vaguely reminiscent of the old Cock and Bull that used to be on Sunset, out in L.A., but had since become a parking lot. The vibe was great.

Cissy sought to engage Chip in casual conversation. He was only too willing to oblige, and told her of his trip to Chattanooga that morning. She was quite angry that he hadn't invited her. Ever since 'that night' at the Sky Harbor Motel, in room # 1, the room with the double bed, she had felt that Chattanooga was 'their town.' It was something they'd shared together, an 'us' thing, a 'couple' thing.

That he had driven to 'their town' on a magnificent summer day and hadn't been considerate enough to ask her was unpardonable. It was unforgivable, a serious breach of trust. This oversight set the tone for the entire evening, a decidedly unpleasant one.

"Why didn't you invite me to go with you?" she asked finally, trying to conceal her anger, and the hurt feelings underneath.

"Well," he replied, "It was a business trip. I went straight down there and came straight back. I didn't take Therpis. I didn't even stop for lunch. It was down, meeting at the junkyard, and then back."

He hoped his explanation would be sufficient. He didn't feel it necessary at that point in their relationship, or for that matter, at any point in any relationship with anybody, to explain his actions in any business matter. He needed to 'take a meeting' as they say in LA, and he didn't want to have to explain what he was doing, or why he was doing it. He used the time available on the drive down to make his plans, and the return trip time to reflect on the meeting and formulate his future plans. He didn't have time to entertain her or make pleasant chit-chat. It was nothing personal. He hoped she had sense enough to understand.

"I can't believe you didn't even call me. I would have enjoyed the ride down. It was a beautiful day. I just ended up wasting time at the pool, reading and doing my nails."

Women think they have some kind of clamp on you. Therpis was right. They're all the same. They want to own you. He looked at her for a moment and started to answer her, but was suddenly frightened speechless by what he saw. For him, and probably for most men, women are initially sex objects. It's a biological imperative. It doesn't mean that men are no good, or that they don't respect women, or any of that other crap they've been accused of. It simply means that men want to get laid. It is this desire, or need for sex, that brings a man around a second, third, and fourth time. If it's good, he keeps coming back. This is what Chip had done. Of course he was in love with Ioveena , and actively trying to find her, but she wasn't here, and Cissy was. What frightened Chip was that, just now, for the first time, as he looked at Cissy, he glimpsed her humanity, her unique nature as an individual manifestation of the cosmic or archetypal woman, and not just another sex object. He saw the incredible depth and beauty beneath the surface. It was just a flash, a brief glimpse of Cissy Flambeaux, as she really was, someone who was really just a pretty little girl, someone to be loved and protected.

It would be criminal to mislead or take advantage of her. In this instant he felt sorry for her, and realized that what he was contemplating was wrong. He intended, even at this very moment, to drop her like a hot brick as soon as Ioveena was located. She knew nothing about Ioveena . There had been no reason to even mention Ioveena .

Chip had a couple of immediate options. He could be honest with Cissy and tell her all about Ioveena , or he could continue his relationship with Cissy just as it was, not mention Ioveena at all, and see what developed. He could also just not see her anymore, tell her that he had to concentrate on business, that this was all happening too fast for him, that he wasn't ready to be tied down. She was tough, she could handle that. After all, this wasn't love, it was more of an amorous friendship. Like some banks have "Check Plus" for their checking customers, this was "Sex Plus," sex plus friendship. He didn't know what to do, but determined that he wasn't going to mislead her, or to make promises he couldn't keep. He was a whore dog, always had been, always would be. It would probably be best if he didn't see her. Otherwise, he was likely to really be swept into her undertow, and never come out. She might absorb him into the cosmic womb. It was an extremely frightening prospect, Mother Nature's greatest and most successful trick.

One day you're at a restaurant explaining your private business, and justifying your actions to some woman who has no right to know. The next thing, you're sitting at her mother's house along with a fat wife and 2.75 howling, yapping brats, when you'd rather be watching football. But she'd asked for nothing. She just wanted to know why he hadn't taken her with him to Chattanooga. It was a reasonable request. Perhaps this was all in his head. He looked at her again, and thought her eyes were somehow deeper than usual, and her mouth was very inviting. He suppressed a sudden urge to kiss her and instead answered her question in as conciliatory a manner as possible, assuring her that he would take her next time, and apologizing very profusely for his thoughtless and unkind oversight.

Later, he found himself in her bed three houses down the street from his own, but not before he had unintentionally divulged every word and detail of his meeting with Di Lizardo, and his specific plans for making his fortune.

12.

HOG WILD AND PIG CRAZY

Chip Hamster was feeling his oats. Armed with five car titles with which to start his financial empire, he was pumped and ready for action. Perhaps it had been the inspirational music, "Hunka burnin love," which he'd found so edifying on this most splendid summer morning. Or possibly it was the memory of his late father's loving advice on the subject of career management. "When are you going to get a job you little bastard? You need to get busy and make something of yourself. If you think I'm going to support you the rest of your life, you've got your head lodged. Get a job at the Goddamn Pizza Hut, Wal-Mart, or somewhere. Get off your ass and do something!"

Chip's late father, a cheese magnate.

Those kind words had been both encouraging as well as uplifting, but Chip had much bigger plans than Pizza Hut. His father would be proud of him now. He could just imagine the old man standing there in the entrance hall with a drink in one hand, a hot looking woman on his arm, and a cigar hanging out of his mouth. "Get a job you little son of a bitch!" he would shout, spit dripping down his chin. "You want to end up like me don't you? All right then, get moving.

95

Cut some God damn yards or something." It had been difficult for a nine year old to cut a four acre yard with a push mower, though Chip had certainly tried. Well, no matter. His father would be proud of him now.

"The first thing I'm gonna' do," he said to himself, "is to pay off that existing loan with the Agrarian and Mercantile Bank, in order to lull O'Lepty into a false sense of security, before I sucker him out of even more money."

There were plans for other banks too, both within Tennessee, and out of state, but he would use O'Lepty's bank, the bank which his grandfather had help found, as his principal base of operations.

"I am brilliant," he reflected proudly. "First, I'll get loans from some of those trashy fly by night auto title pawn shops. Next I will put that money in my bank account along with the money still remaining from the first loan on the Porsche. Those title pawn places don't give a damn about anybody's credit rating, cash on hand, financial statement, current indebtedness, or anything else. All they want is to loan as little as possible, make their twenty-whatever per cent and hook another fish."

He didn't know how much he'd be able to get from any of those places, but whatever he got, he'd add to the growing pile in his checking account. After he'd snookered several auto title joints, he would approach another major bank, and get a larger loan, with which to repay the original loan on his Porsche. With thirty or forty thousand cash already on hand, and an excellent credit rating, his financial statement would look good to any bank.

The best way to put it is simply to say that Chip had gone crazy, 'hog wild and pig crazy.' It seemed as though he wanted to make up for something he had missed in childhood, and thought that by obtaining as much money as possible, this unknown void might somehow be filled. But his plan was not quite as brilliant as he imagined. If he were preparing to invest this money wisely, things might have turned out differently, but he had no specific investment strategy at all. He was simply borrowing money indiscriminately and spending it relentlessly. For example, he started "dino-sizing" all of his bulldog's meals at Crappy D's. He bought Cissy an expensive and unsolicited fishing reel at K Mart. He had also started giving Therpis ten dollar bills instead of fives, and with much greater frequency. He'd switched from medium octane to the highest possible fuel grade. But more than any of the above mentioned blatant and obvious extravagances, Chip seemed possessed of a strange look about him. He had started whispering and laughing to himself, often at inappropriate moments, like after sex, for example, or especially at the bank.

"I don't like you when you're like this," Cissy had told him, after he'd started laughing once while they were making love. He didn't care though, her criticism meant nothing. He was on a mission. "I gotta thoo what I gotta thoo," he said, quoting actor Jack Nicholson in his role as Jimmy Hoffa.

"Today is the day that I'm going to reel in my first sucker," Chip stated proudly. He dressed in the typical Southern summer style, casual but elegant, with a freshly pressed, heavily starched white shirt, khakis, and a loose fitting sport coat. His brown alligator loafers had just been expertly polished by the talented Therpis, and possessed an enviable and reflective shine, one which, were it not for the presence of the alligator grain, would have no doubt permitted him to look up any woman's dress in town.

"Well done, noble Therpis," he smiled, and handed his elderly valet/cousin a crisp ten dollar bill which would, before the end of the day most likely be exchanged for a dime bag somewhere on 12th Avenue South, near the former sight of Bradley's Pressing Club. Chip had always been intrigued by the name 'Bradley's Pressing Club.' There didn't appear to be a swimming pool or tennis courts anywhere near the structure, but there were always plenty of new Cadillacs, most of which had been in some way customized by their owners, for that unique 'personal touch.' You didn't see cars dressed up like that much anymore, at least not with propeller driven bug deflectors, fox tails, chrome plated fender skirts, and long chrome whip aerials. That kind of died in the mid-1970s, at least in the rest of the world. And what a pity too. It was hard for the serious minded customizer to dress up a Ford Probe or a Toyota Lexus. All of the cars now were blunt, chromeless, and lacked individual identities. You couldn't even put long chrome lake pipes on a car anymore. The EPA had seen to that with catalytic converters. Well, no matter. It was still possible to make money in the car business, and that's what he intended to do.

Chip stood admiringly before his image in the mirror, and practiced his best Clark Gable look, raising one eyebrow slightly, and sort of twitching the left side of his face from side to side.

"Charming," he remarked, "charming indeed." With that, he bid a fond farewell to Therpis, grabbed a clean dishcloth off the handle of the Sub Zero, and left his house through the kitchen door. His black Rolls-Royce glistened in the sun, like a mirage in the desert. Waves of heat radiated from its liquid black surface. It was only 10:00 a.m., but the car was already much too hot to even touch. With the insulation afforded by the dishcloth, he carefully opened the door and slid across the hot seat, his olfactory senses immediately assailed by the musty combination of leather, wood, and mildew which is characteristic of every Rolls-Royce, regardless of its age. He closed the door behind him with a firm thump, raised his butt off the seat and fumbled around looking for the keys. When he finally found them he transferred them to his left hand and sought to insert the proper key into the ignition switch. As always, the cluster of keys fell to the floor, and as usual he cursed the English under his breath for doing everything backwards.

"Gin swilling bastards," he exclaimed.

The English, for all their uppitiness, don't know shit about cars. Take the car he was driving for instance, a Rolls-Royce convertible, or 'drophead,' as they called it. If this car belonged to an Englishman, it would be driven only in the best possible weather, which in England means about ten days a year. The oil, water, and brake fluid would be checked religiously every day. It would hardly ever be driven over fifty miles an hour, would always be parked in the garage, and never left in the sun with the top down. In short it would be worshiped rather than enjoyed. Sooner or later somebody who knew how to drive the son of a bitch would end up with it, not change the oil for ten thousand miles, get sex stains all over the back seat, burn a hole in the carpet with the ash from a reefer, and leave the top down in the rain. To hell with the leather. And has anybody, anywhere, in the history of the world, ever made a fast getaway by starting a car with his left hand? Hell no! Never had, never would.

The car came to life, and as it did so, Chip remembered what happened to some Country singer's husband. He had bought a new 1988 Rolls-Royce convertible, back in the day, probably with her hard earned money, and had hardly driven it for over 20 years, saving it for who knows what. One day he had started the car, and left it running in the garage. A short time later it came to his attention that the car was on fire. Not only did it burn itself up, but set his house on fire as well. The cheap son of a bitch.

And so off Chip went, pulling gracefully out onto Belle Meade

98

Boulevard, hanging a right toward Harding Road, and taking a left on White Bridge. His first destination was some title pawn joint over near the interstate, in a less than splendid part of the Music City. He wheeled up slowly, making certain that his car was seen by whoever might be inside the former drug store. He looked in his rearview mirror, checked his hair, and then reached over to the passenger seat and retrieved the large envelope which contained the crisp Tennessee title to a 2014 Toyota Lexus.

The large room was empty except for a counter and two inexpensive desks, side by side, in the middle of the room. An attractive and intelligent, but wrong side of the tracks kind of woman, addressed him without getting up from her desk.

"May I help you she asked?" emotionless, a cigarette hanging between the fingers of her left hand.

"Yes," Chip replied meekly, "I'm here about a loan."

"I believe I can help you," she said, unconsciously sizing him up. "First of all," she replied flatly, "I'll tell you how it works. Have you ever had a title loan?" she asked. He was very handsome, she thought, and found herself immediately attracted to him.

"No," Chip replied, "This is my first, and most likely my last time."

"Well," she said, looking at his left hand, "Here's how it works. We can loan you up to one third of the wholesale value of your car, according to the prices posted in the Gray Book. You can continue to use the car, but we hold the title. There is no interest for the first thirty days. In other words, if you pay the money back within that period, there is no interest. The note is due and payable in full at the end of the second thirty days, plus twenty-two percent interest. Checks or money orders are not acceptable as payment for the loan. Cash only. These notes are not renewable. The note and the interest must be paid in full. Only then can a new loan be made. Any questions?"

"No," he said.

"What type of car do you have? Not that thing you drove up in I hope. What kind of car is that anyway?" she asked, becoming more friendly.

"That is a Rolls-Royce Phantom," Chip said proudly.

"I've never seen one before," she replied, obviously impressed. "I've seen them in movies, of course," she said. His eyes met hers, catching her off guard, piercing her tough redneck persona, and leaving her feeling strangely exposed.

"Who are you?" she asked, thinking she had seen him somewhere before.

"I am Charles Mason Hamster, III," he said warmly." Just call me Chip."

"Hey Rene," the man at the other desk interrupted, "come here a minute." The man whispered something to her, and she whispered something in reply. Chip thought that he overheard the words 'cheese,' and 'skillet,' but he couldn't be sure.

She returned to the counter, and looked at him admiringly. "What kind of car do you have Mr. Hamster?" she asked, lowering her voice.

"It's a 2014 Lexus LS 400," he answered, handing her the envelope containing the title. She removed the title and looked over it carefully, making certain that it wasn't a forgery. Everything appeared to be in order.

"How small of a loan would you like?" she asked him.

"Well, I'd like to get as much as possible," he said, leaning closer to her. "Listen," he said, almost whispering. "I went to Tunica, Mississippi, last week, and wasted seven thousand dollars gambling with some friends. It was the first time I've ever done anything like that, and the last. I feel like such a fool," he said, playing her along, as he reached into his inside jacket pocket and withdrew his checkbook. "As you can see," he said, showing her his balance of thirty-eight thousand dollars, "I can easily pay whatever loan you might be prepared to make."

"I 'm sure that we can loan you the maximum amount," she said. "That is, if the car is in good shape, but first let me get back to my desk and see how much that would be." She fumbled with her calculator for a moment, tore the printout slip from the bottom, and said," The best we can do is $8,366, which is one third of the wholesale value.''

"That would be perfect. I need some money, and I don't want my wife to find out."

"Well, we won't say anything about it if you don't," she winked. "Of course, we'll need to see the car," she said, almost as an afterthought.

Here came the dangerous part, the part he had to get beyond if his scheme was going to work at all. He must convince her to let him walk with the money without actually seeing the car that went with the title he had. There was no telling where the real car might be. It might lie flattened in Di Lizardo's weed covered junk yard, or it may have been crushed and sent to the smelter months ago. This was going to be a delicate line to walk. If he appeared too desperate, the woman might be suspicious. On the other hand, if he wasn't sufficiently convincing, he was also likely to be turned down.

"Listen," he said, resting his elbows on the service counter, "here's the problem. I can't bring the car in because my wife is driving it."

The young woman suddenly straightened and said, "I'm sorry, but we have to see the car, or we can't make a loan on it."

"You don't understand my problem. The car is paid for, as you can see from the title. There are no liens of any kind on it at all."

"I can see that," the girl replied, "but I don't think I can help you."

"Now listen," Chip continued. "I came for a loan. Why don't you call the credit bureau and check me out?"

"It's not about the credit bureau," she said. "The only things we are concerned with are that you have appropriate collateral, and that you are able to repay the loan."

"I've got enough money in my checking account at this very moment to cover the amount in question more than four times over, but my wife would notice."

She stood there with her arms folded, looking at this handsome stranger and sincerely wanting to give him anything he wanted, anything. She smiled flirtatiously, but shook her head from side to side. Chip laughed and looked over at the man, who had been watching the transaction silently from his desk. He had a wedding ring on his finger. "Help me will you? You're married, aren't you?"

Billy Bob rose from his desk and sauntered up to the service counter. He didn't like the uppity woman who served as his co-worker. She was, he surmised, most likely grinding away on his boss, that goofy turdmaster, Trey Turner, at the downtown office. How else would she have ever gotten this job? No way was she anywhere near as smart as Billy Bob, at least not in Billy Bob's estimation. Here was a fellow married man in distress. Billy Bob had seen the article in the paper about the death of Mason Hamster. He knew that Chip Hamster was rich. Hell, they had shown a picture of that big house of his on Belle Meade Boulevard. That thing alone had to be worth several million dollars. This offered the perfect opportunity for Billy Bob to step in and establish himself clearly as the heavyweight at this office. "What seems to be the problem?" he asked.

Chip explained everything again for his benefit, stating it carefully so the goofy bastard wouldn't miss anything. Billy Bob rubbed his thin beard between his fingers and struck a thoughtful pose as he considered the facts. He looked like a fat Steve Reeves, the guy that used to be in the Hercules movies back in the late 1950s, with his thin moustache and beard. While he was still thinking about it, Chip took the lead.

"Why don't we do this?" he suggested. "Why don't you call my bank, any branch you want, and tell whoever answers the phone that you have someone at your place of business by the name of Chip Hamster? Tell them that you have a check from him for, say twenty-five thousand, and that you are calling to find out if there is enough money in the account to cover the check."

It was a brilliant idea. Chip hesitated and then said, "I can cover any check I write. I paid cash for the Toyota, I mean Lexus. I just can't let my wife find out that I blew any money playing craps, drinking and hanging out with other women."

Chip and Billy Bob exchanged a knowing look. Rene, a single mom, caught the exchange of glances between the two men. She might have been irritated under other circumstances, but in this particular situation, she was starting to wonder just how married Chip Hamster might actually be. Was he married a lot, or just a little bit?

Billy Bob thought Chip's suggestion about the check was an excellent one. The banker confirmed that there was enough money in the account to cover a twenty-five thousand dollar check, and that was all the information Billy Bob needed. He agreed to assume full responsibility for making the loan. He wanted to assert his authority over his female co-worker. He also wished to ingratiate himself with Chip Hamster. Who knows, some day he might need a job at the cheese factory. Being on the good side of a man like Chip Hamster was certainly a good thing. Chip signed some papers, presented his driver's license, and walked away with a check for $8,366, as well as a crumpled piece of paper which read "955-4949 Call me, Rene."

The faces were different, but the game was the same. By the end of the day Chip had also obtained loans on the two Mercedes sedans and the two late model BMWs, securing a total of thirty-eight thousand and change. Not bad for a day's work. It had been like shooting fish in a barrel. He celebrated with a big lobster supper in one of those quaint and peculiar avant garde bistros in Nashville's famous 'pink' section of town. Later that night, at home over cigars and Blatz with Therpis, he thought how easy it had been to dupe those suckers. "If people think you're rich, they will do anything to gain your approval. It's like they just want to kiss your ass."

At drill in military school, some idiot had always shouted "Preeeeesent aarms!" and everybody had to snap to attention immediately. Chip felt like standing out on the corner of 5th and Union, in the financial district, at noon, and having some lackey order "Preeeesent aaasss!" on Chip's behalf. Chip would then present his ass for obeisance by the more important citizens of Music City. He imagined Hunter Ratlips, Sidney and Stewey Von Hocker, the mayor, all Nashville lawyers, the police chief, and the entire police department, all passing in review. "Eyes Right!" the mayor would shout, as the marchers approached the review stand. He would finally receive the respect he truly deserved. Oh well, it was, after all, just a summer night's dream, perhaps the result of a too fond recollection of the day's many accomplishments, and too much to drink. He made a mental note to call that Rene. She was saucy, just the way Chip liked 'em. She wasn't, as Therpis would say, the type to "freeze up on yuh."

There was only one dark cloud on the horizon, and hopefully it was a passing one. He wished he hadn't succumbed to Cissy's considerable powers of sexual persuasion. She now knew everything about his plans, solely because of his own big mouth. She had teased him, toyed with his manly affections, and then sexed him down and forced him to tell her everything before she would give it up. He'd sung like a bird too. Now, he regretfully wished he'd kept his lure in the tackle box. It was too late for that now. She already knew everything he had planned. But he had no intention of telling her anything further, that was for sure. He would just let the matter drop. If she mentioned it again, and she certainly would, he'd just say that it had been a foolish idea, something he can't believe he ever even thought of in the first place.

"Them cows done made a fool of me too many times," Therpis shouted angrily, as if reading Chip's thoughts. "How many times they done done that to me? But I'm wise to 'em now. They just evil. They'll be lying up in the bed laughing and kissing on each other, talkin' bout how they done made a fool outa so and so. Why mistuh?

Why they wanta do a man like that?"

"It's just their nature," Chip speculated idly.

"That's right. It's just their nature. They do it cause they can. But I'm wise to them cows now. They can't do me like they used to. If Matti Pearl was to stand naked in that door right now, it wouldn't mean no more to me than uh elephant. I mean that."

Chip laughed.

"I mean it," Therpis repeated with deep conviction. "If Matti Pearl was tuh come and stand naked in that doorway right now, it wouldn't mean no more to me than uh elephant. I mean it!"

"I know you do," Chip laughed.

"I my ass. Get out the way bitch. I'm comin thu." And the drunken Therpis marched proudly but clumsily out of the house, through the kitchen door, apparently anxious once again to thrill to the sound of a chrome vacuum cleaner pipe smacking him upside his head, expertly wielded by Matti Pearl.

Chip's cousin Therpis. "Get out thu way bitch. I'm comin thru!'

104

13.

HELL HATH NO FURY

Cissy was pissed. That was the only way to put it. She had given her all to Chip Hamster, had sacrificed her virtue repeatedly, under a variety of different circumstances, and in some unusual locations, and unnatural positions, solely to satisfy his depraved carnal appetites. At the movies, in the K-Mart parking lot, under the tablecloth at Cafe Apa Dapa, and in other places and in ways too indelicate to mention here. That she had enjoyed herself immensely was completely beside the point. This wasn't about her, it was about him, particularly the way he'd been acting recently. It was really a combination of things. To start with, Chip frequently and loudly called that big convertible of his a "ho magnet." Now, how was that supposed to make her feel, when she was sitting right there in it?

And he and that no good Therpis, that long lost cousin, or valet, or whoever, or whatever he is. The two of them together were up to no good at all. Chip was constantly handing over money to that man who, in return, regaled him non-stop with exaggerated details of female treachery and infidelity, talking about how he had found his third wife in bed with another man, and his second wife in bed with another woman. He also constantly warned Chip not to get married and incessantly talked about a woman 'gettin a clamp on yuh.' Talk about beating a dead horse. To make matters worse, he constantly both praised and condemned one particular part of a woman's anatomy, and spoke of its incredible power over a man. If this kind of talk didn't frighten Chip, what would? Worst of all, he used the 'P' word all of the time, and continually said such things as "If women didn't have a P- - - -, there'd be a bounty on 'em." Then they would both just laugh themselves silly, with Therpis actually falling out of his chair and rolling on the floor. How was it possible for their love to flower under such adverse and hostile circumstances?

She needed to get rid of that fool Therpis. He was a bad influence on Chip. Perhaps she should send him and that stick-wielding cow of a wife of his, Matti Pearl, on some sort of exotic sea cruise. Cissy was rich, she could afford it. Maybe two weeks at sea with her beating the shit out of him all day and all night might give him the attitude adjustment he needed.

And then there was that shady financial stuff Chip was involved in. He had snuck away from town like a slinking dog one day, gone to Chattanooga without her, and made some dirty under the table deal with that slimy snake Ron Di Lizardo. That Ron had said he was from Florida. What a joke. Cissy had never seen anyone like him in Palm Beach, or anywhere else in Florida, except maybe the St. Augustine Alligator Farm. And that 'Tiki Hut,' as he called it looked like something from somebody's back yard in Madison. It was a hideous affront to even her questionable tastes. Di Lizardo was a crook if there ever was one. Nothing good could come from him. What they were doing was wrong. Chip had been borrowing money from a variety of financial lending institutions, using titles to cars as collateral, cars that didn't even exist. If that wasn't illegal, nothing was. Where was it going to end?

She'd told Chip that she would set him up in business if that's what he wanted. But no, that wasn't enough. She had offered to buy him his own Hickory Farms cheese store at the mall, if he wanted to be in cheese. But no, that wasn't good enough either. Chip Hamster wanted to be a big wheel, driving around town in a half a million dollar car, so that everybody would look at him and think, "Well, there goes 'Mr. Big Shot.'" She had enough money for both of them. All he had to do was behave like a gentleman, and do what she wanted him to do, and he could be set for life. How difficult could that be?

He'd also been acting strange recently, and had come home with another woman's perfume on him, at least she thought so. It was hard to tell though. He said that it was 'garden scented bug spray,' and it might have been. Nobody from their part of town would be wearing that type of fragrance, at least not intentionally. So she let the matter pass, but determined to keep an enhanced eye on him anyway. And then there was the SEX. Chip had been trying some new moves lately which he hadn't used on her before. He had to have picked them up somewhere, and he certainly hadn't learned them from Cissy. And then they weren't making love as much as they used to either. When a man suddenly loses interest in SEX, it's always a bad sign. She mentioned this to him, but he apologized and explained it away, saying that he was preoccupied with business concerns as of late, but then mumbled something vague about a 'delivery truck' and 'two routes.' She had intended to question him about that, but was side tracked by the light and gentle attentions of his tongue at just that particular moment.

Nonetheless, these thoughts, forebodings, and suspicions were making her both angry and afraid, afraid that she could be.....losing him. She broke down sobbing, releasing the emotional firestorm which had been building like a toothache over the past several weeks. After a few minutes, her tears turned to anger. She remembered how her late husband, even at ninety had been caught trying to do it with his secretary.

"If I ever catch Chip with another woman," she vowed, "any woman, it will be the worst day of his stupid, self-involved life. This is my solemn oath." Well, she felt better now. It was probably nothing, an overreaction on her part due to the unwelcome and uninvited presence of a sudden increased level of hormones.

It was probably all in her mind, anyway. She did talk to Chip every day, and saw him several times a week. After all, he was trying to make his way in the world, so the least she could do was to attempt to be supportive, even if what he was doing was illegal. They'd be married soon enough, she reasoned, and then he would have to tow the mark or bear the consequences. Besides, Chip had told her that he had a 'special present' for her, and not what he usually meant when he talked like that. This was something special, he had said, something he had picked out just for her. He was going to give it to her this weekend. Since he had several important business meetings downtown and wouldn't be seeing her today, she decided to drive out to the Rivergate Antique Mall on Dickerson Road.

ELSEWHERE

"Then you aren't really, actually married?" Rene asked, somewhat disappointed at being denied the opportunity of one-upping some woman she'd never met.

"Oh, I'm married all right," Chip replied. The last thing he wanted was this woman to start thinking of him as more than a temporary stop on his delivery route. "But what made you ask me that?''

"Well," Rene replied, "you never wear a wedding ring".

"I didn't want to insult you," he replied, reaching into the console and removing the three dollar band he'd purchased as insurance for just such circumstances, from some carney at the State Fair. The whole business of marriage was something he'd rather not think about. In the first place, he didn't know anyone who was actually happily married. Hell, his own mother had run off with a bowling instructor. That should tell him something. Von Snocker's wife ordered him around like a dog. Plus, Therpis had constantly advised him to avoid marriage, advice which had definitely had an impact, even if subconsciously.

"Them cows want to get a baby by yuh. 'Oh I'm gonna get me uh baby by him.' I done heard em say it," Chip remembered Therpis warning him.

And that Cissy had been driving him crazy, calling him at all hours, wanting to monopolize him, and then getting mad when he had work to do. This little diversion with Rene was proving quite amusing, and it was also placing some much needed distance between Chip and Cissy. Rene was hot, with a cute little body, which she certainly knew how to use. More importantly, she made no demands of any kind and was not inquisitive or even interested in Chip's financial affairs. She had a taste for the exotic and always dressed hot, with lacy silk stockings and a garter belt, so that Chip never knew quite what to expect. Regrettably, there wasn't much for them to talk about either before or after sex, but then neither of them were there for conversation. It wasn't that she wasn't as intelligent as Chip, it's just that their life experiences were basically different, except for sex. But sex proved an excellent point of reference for both of them.

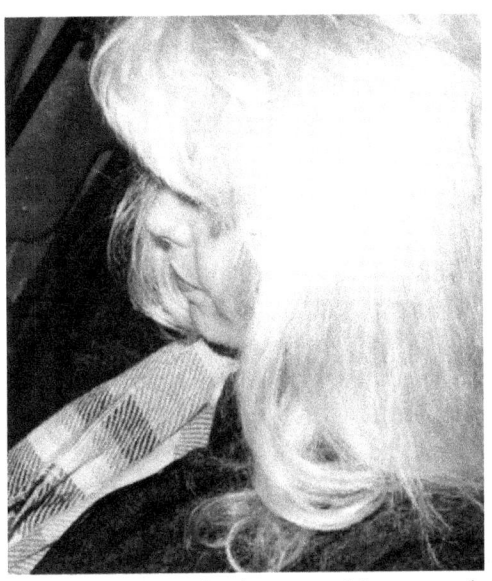

Rene liked Chip sexually too, and he always made it good for her. He wasn't afraid of her passion, like some other men, and was uncontrollably excited by everything about her. They usually snuck off for a quickie during her lunch hour, but today, she had the day off while Billy Bob was minding the store. Chip was to pick her up at the Crown Chalet Apartments off Gallatin Road, and they were going to Rivergate to look at an old car, and then to lunch at El Chico, her very favorite Mexican restaurant. They probably wouldn't get a chance to 'grind' today, as Chip called it, since her daughter was with the baby sitter at her apartment, but who knows? Where there's a will, there's always a way.

Chip arrived punctually, dressed in loose Madras shorts with a bright red cotton golf shirt, his basic summer uniform of the day. This never varied much, the only difference being that at night he usually wore a buttoned long sleeve shirt, which Rene liked to slowly peel off of him, a few kisses, and a few buttons at a time. He looked really manly in his black Rolls-Royce convertible, with that silver watch against his dark skin. The top was down, as usual, and Rene was excited about riding in a convertible, and about being with him. He always said something encouraging and uplifting that made her feel good about herself. It was hard being a single parent, and he told her how much he respected her for getting a good job and being able to handle the heavy responsibilities of motherhood by herself. Most men had no idea what was involved in that undertaking. Anyway, she reflected, today was going to be a really great day. She was waiting by the window, and hurried out the door when she saw him drive up.

"Hey," he said, raising one eyebrow, "You really look great. It's good to see you." And she did look great, with short shorts, and a sleeveless halter top that exposed her trim midriff and shapely arms. How nice it is, Chip reflected as she walked toward the car, to see someone who is genuinely happy to see you for no particular reason.

They decided to eat lunch first in order to beat the crowd, and went directly to the Mexican joint. Chip selected the appropriately entitled luncheon special # 2, which consisted of a cheese covered soft taco, and a cheese enchilada swimming in a brown chili gravy, an excellent choice. Rene ordered some breaded, deep fried nasty looking cylinder, called a chimichanga. He doubted that there actually was such a dish in Mexico as a chimichanga, but couldn't be certain. He imagined instead, that it was something invented by some American at some factory in Mexico, in an attempt to appeal to that fairly large segment of the public which actively sought death by way of heart attack. No matter, he reflected, whatever it really was, Rene enjoyed eating it immensely, licking it around the edges, and looking at him seductively.

After lunch, it was onto the interstate headed back toward town. It was an incredible day, with intense dry heat, just the way Chip liked it. The wind noise in the car with the top down made conversation all but impossible at eighty miles an hour, so there wasn't much opportunity for after lunch chit chat with his lovely passenger. The next thing Chip knew, he detected a certain rustling of material in the area of his personal manhood. He looked down to see two slender hands undoing his shorts, and Rene's pretty face giving him a suggestive smile. Within a matter of seconds, she had gone down on him like a pair of flea market socks. In light of this new distraction, Chip thought it prudent to slow the car to 55, and enjoy the scenery.

Meanwhile, a blue Mazda Miata, a tadpole looking wisp of a car, was also driving toward town on I-65, approaching what appeared to be a mid-60s Studebaker convertible. Cissy hadn't seen one of those in a long time. The Cones, on Lynwood Boulevard had owned a white Studebaker when she was a mere child. The car was ahead on her right in the slow lane. Since it wasn't moving too fast, she could probably catch up to it for a closer look. As Cissy Flambeaux drove ever closer to the object of her pursuit, she also moved more closely into that strange realm known as the synchronistic, in which random, meaningless, and unrelated events suddenly take on very definite significance for the individuals involved. As she approached what first appeared to be a Studebaker, it became obvious to Cissy that she had been mistaken. It wasn't a Studebaker at all, but something else, another kind of car. Now all she knew for sure was that it was black, but as she continued her approach, she recognized the stern of a Rolls-Royce convertible. She would have to tell Chip she had seen one just like his. "Wait a minute," she thought, "that looks like Chip." She hit the accelerator as hard as she could, and the powerful lawn mower-like engine surged to full power as the car hit sixty miles an hour. She had to be sure. That is Chip, she smiled. She'd pull up next to him and wave. Imagine running into him out here on the interstate. What a pleasant surprise.

It proved to be a surprise indeed, for all concerned. Chip was driving along pleasantly, oblivious to the occasional loud horn of a passing truck, and enjoying the delicate and exquisite sensations building steadily in his powerful, rock solid manhood, or his 'meat item' as they say at Turdley's, a famous local Cafeteria.

"What's that jumping up and down on his lap?" Cissy asked herself, as she pulled up beside his car. It looks like a little dog, and a very frisky one at that. What's he doing with a dog on his lap? It certainly isn't Steve, his bulldog. It's got kind of silver and blonde hair. It looks like a Yorkie. "Oh yes, yes," she thrilled. "It is a Yorkie. Chip bought me a Yorkie. He's so considerate. This must be the surprise he's been telling me about. He made up those excuses about meetings just so he could drive out to east Nashville and pick it up for me. This really is a wonderful surprise."

He still didn't see her, preoccupied as he was under the circumstances. "What's he doing?" Cissy wondered, honking her mosquito sounding horn. He's shaking all over and throwing his head back and forth. I don't hear any music though. And the Yorkie is jumping higher and faster in his lap.

Suddenly Chip saw her driving along next to him. "Son of a bitch! It's Cissy!" Instinctively he pushed Rene's head down hard, as far as it would go. Rene hated it when men did that. Damn, she was doing the best she could. Now Chip was trying to choke her to death. She sat up quickly gasping for air, and locking herself in the full, upright position. "Why the hell did you do that?" she shouted angrily.

He pointed to the car to their left and said, "My wife."

LATER THAT AFTERNOON: A phone booth, somewhere in the Music City.

"Is this the Internal Revenue Service snitch line?" she asked, speaking from a pay phone.

"Yes, this is the Internal Revenue Service," the voice replied calmly.

"I suggest that you investigate the financial affairs of Mason Charles Hamster, III, social security number 444-93-67825." the emotionless female voice said, and then hung up the phone with a pronounced click.

"Tennessee Banking Commission," a pleasant female voice answered at the organizational headquarters in Nashville, "May I help you?"

"Who I am is unimportant," the caller said, "Just take this information down for your boss."

"Who is this?" the receptionist asked.

"Look," the caller continued, "there is a well-known public figure who has been getting loans fraudulently at various major banks in Nashville and elsewhere, using valid Tennessee titles to wrecked cars as collateral. I felt that the commissioner might want to know. There are large sums of money involved."

"I see," said the receptionist in a tone which betrayed an equal amount of sarcasm and curiosity. "And who might this person be?"

"His name is Mason Charles Hamster, III, and his Social Security number is 444-93-67825."

"He's dead," the receptionist answered automatically. "I read about it in the paper. He was in New Orleans, or somewhere, and got hit in the head with a brick, for messing with somebody's wife at Mardi Gras."

"No, that was his father who died. Chip Hamster is alive and well, and defrauding banks out of large sums of money on a daily basis."

"If you don't mind me asking," the receptionist wondered," Why are you telling me this?"

"Have you ever been in love?" the caller asked quietly.

"Well, of course. I'm in love now," the receptionist replied happily.

"Has anybody ever done you wrong? Taken your heart, used you for years, and then left you for someone younger?"

"I was married for seven years and caught my husband with some cocktail waitress. I believe I'm familiar enough with that sort of thing. Is that what happened to you? Did this no good man do this to you?"

There was a moment of silence, followed by a whimpering and tearful "Yes," on the part of the caller.

It was truly tragic. Some no good son of a bitch had mistreated this poor woman, and had brought her to this sad state of affairs, all because she'd sought to love him. Well, this Chip Hamster, whoever he was, had done it for the last time. He had broken his last heart. It was time women stuck together. Burn baby burn! "Whoever you are," the receptionist said, trying to console the caller, "the buck stops here. I will personally see that the commissioner gives this matter top priority." Sisterhood is indeed a powerful thing.

... love affair with a female demon!

I don't think lipstick will be enough this time.

14.

TROUBLE

Banker Mark O'Lepty sat down to a comfortable Sunday morning breakfast on the balcony of his fashionable, near Belle Meade condo. He had started his financial and social ascent twenty years ago, entering the banking world with a degree in home economics. Fresh from Vanderbilt University, he'd established himself quickly at Mercantile Agrarian Trust Bank of Commerce and Industry as a successful branch manager in some of the music city's less desirable and more provincial outposts, such as Madison, Antioch, and Donelson. Now, many promotions, (and asses kissed), two point-five children, and two wives later, the world was his oyster, in a manner of speaking. He was now literally within the shadow of Belle Meade. As soon as his current wife's ancient father kicked the bucket and left them set for life, they would make the short move to one of the nearby streets which adjoined one of the avenues actually connected to Belle Meade Boulevard itself. The old man, however, was taking his own sweet time about croaking. Well, Mark reflected, unwittingly paraphrasing soul singer Chuck Jackson, "Any Day Now." The days, however, had turned into weeks, months, and now, years.

Everything had been 'upwardly mobile' for Mark, and still was, except for the severe trauma he'd suffered initially when he chanced to visit that fool Chip Hamster's house one day, unannounced. To his astonishment, Mark had discovered the Porsche that he had loaned $50,000 on, crushed beneath a tree in the back yard. It had obviously been there several months. If there was one unspoken rule in banking, it was that you don't, under any circumstances, lend money to anybody who has ever set one or both of your feet on fire. It's just not done. Mark had bent the rules on this one occasion, but fortunately things had turned out alright.

He'd been extremely upset at first, understandably so, but Hamster had assured him that everything would be all right, even though, as he mentioned quietly, the car "wasn't actually insured," due to some technical oversight. What the hell kind of oversight it could've been was never fully explained to the banker's satisfaction. Instead, Hamster invited him in for a cool Blatz on tap. Once in the house, Mark O'Lepty had been overwhelmed by his host's graciousness as well as by the splendor of Hamster's residence itself, which was truly magnificent. The furniture, art, and antiques, practically shouted 'old money.' Any fears which Mark O'Lepty had evidenced at first were put to rest. There was no doubt that Chip Hamster would be able to repay the loan, probably from pocket change. He was obviously a millionaire many times over.

Hamster's valet, Therpis, had been equally attentive, making certain that Mark's glass was never empty. It had truly been a splendid afternoon visit, and marked the beginning of a financial relationship between Hamster and the banker which would hopefully prove profitable for both. When the first 90 day note was due, Chip came in, paid the interest and renewed the note for an additional ninety days. When Mr. Crooke returned and found out what had happened, he instructed O'Lepty to inform Chip that the note would be due and payable in full at the end of the second ninety day period, and would not be renewed. Chip paid the $50,000 note in full, on schedule, as Mark knew he would.

In the meantime, Mr. Crooke had left the bank rather abruptly and unexpectedly, after nearly thirty years, with no other explanation than that he needed to "find himself." Mr. Crooke's secretary, the buxom 29 year old, Shawniqua left quietly at the same time on the same day in fact, presumably for the same reason. They both found themselves, several months later, face to face with Crooke's angry wife in divorce court. The proceedings were rather nasty and ended with Mr. Crooke being divested of everything but his toothbrush and pajamas. How Mrs. Crooke exacted her womanly revenge on her wandering husband is certainly worthy of mention as an example of a woman's superior cunning.

If Crooke had merely come home one night with 'Lipstick on his Collar,' as 1950s crooner Connie Francis phrased it, chances are the incident might have been satisfactorily explained and ultimately forgotten. Lipstick on one's underpants, as was the case in this instance, is another matter entirely, one which defies a credible explanation altogether. After hiring a detective, gathering evidence and preparing her case, Mrs. Crooke confronted her errant husband late one night when he was too tired to mount an adequate defense. Within the space of less than twenty minutes, he had confessed to everything, accused his secretary Shawniqua of being an evil Jezebel, and begged his wife's forgiveness. Mrs. Crooke, however, was not that easily satisfied in the matter, despite her generous proposal. If, she suggested, Mr. Crooke were truly as penitent as he claimed, then she would feel less ashamed and embarrassed if Mr. Crooke confessed his adultery before the congregation at Sunday service, as was the custom within the Church of the Exalted Christ. Nothing, she assured him, could ever make up for the cruel betrayal of her sacred trust, which his careless actions had caused. She would, however, feel better about the matter and would agree to take him back in if he would confess his sin publicly in the manner she suggested.

Shawniqua

This was certainly a sad state of affairs for the banker because his wife definitely had him by the short hairs. If he refused her generous but embarrassing offer, she would definitely drag him through court and take him for everything the law allowed. If he agreed, however, he would likely be shunned socially as a result of his great sin, but at least he would be back in his wife's good graces to the degree that he could live in his own house. He really had no choice and accepted her generous offer, never even slightly suspecting the full extent of her anger, or the genius which guided her revenge. When Crooke stood up before the full congregation on that fateful Sunday and confessed his shameful adultery, his wife's attorney was conveniently present to tape the public confession. At last report, the former Mrs. Crooke had sold the family residence, bought a house in Palm Beach, and was having her garden attended regularly by a suave and handsome Cuban yardman.

Mark O'Lepty had taken advantage of his predecessor's misfortune and moved quickly and easily into the spot vacated by Mr. Crooke. He had not expected, however, to move up the financial ladder as rapidly as he had. He was, in fact, rather an unlikely candidate for bank president, due both to his youth, and to his quiet and extremely conservative nature. Perhaps it was his personal reservation in demeanor that caused him to be placed at the tender age of 39, as the head of Nashville's oldest and most traditional bank. The Mercantile Agrarian Bank was the bank of choice for Nashville's so-called polite society. Mark, from an old and respected Tennessee family, seemed the logical successor, at least to the bank's board of directors. His appointment however, was still a shock to Mark himself, even several months later.

Everything had gone very well, very quickly. But there was just that one outstanding loan to Chip Hamster of $90,000. Mark had thought that he would be replaced with an outsider as soon as the dust settled after Crooke's departure, so in looking after his own future, he had loaned Hamster this large sum without collateral, based upon some vague business proposal Chip had fabricated. He knew Hamster was full of horseshit at the time, but figuring he was about to be moved to the mail room and replaced by some big-time banker from up north, O'Lepty had decided to loan Chip the money while he still could. Chip had promised Mark ten percent personally, of anything the undertaking made. While this was both unethical and illegal, Mark did it anyway. When Mark O'Lepty had been called into the directors' meeting, he expected to be introduced to the new bank president, probably some other old bastard like Crooke. Instead, he was appointed president, and had his salary immediately increased from $57,000 annually to over $200,000. Now he had to walk the straight and narrow. Every move he made was under constant scrutiny not only from the workers in his immediate environment, but also from the bank's owners, the board of directors, and those fiendish federal bank examiners. While Mark knew that Hamster was rich, the loan Mark had made that fool was beginning to haunt him and to cause him sleepless nights, especially since that wormy little sissy, Clarence Snoidwell, down in auditing, had started sniffing around.

As Mark sat there he suddenly felt an all-encompassing sense of dread, as if something terrible were about to descend upon his household, something of biblical proportions. He resolved at that moment to contact Chip on Monday morning, get the loan paid back immediately, and put the whole business behind him forever. He should never have loaned that foolish bastard such a large sum of money. Well, fortunately, nobody had mentioned the matter, perhaps because Chip's father had been extremely well liked by everyone at the bank. The matter would not go unmentioned forever. It had to be dealt with now.

Mark's lovely third wife Debbie handed him the Sunday morning *Tennessean* as she sat down. "You know that rich socialite Chip Hamster, don't you, dear?"

"Yes, we went to school together. Why do you ask?"

"I was just watching the morning news and they said he was missing. They found his car in the Tennessee River just outside of Chattanooga, but they haven't found him. I wonder where he could be."

Mark jumped to his feet. "What?"

"Yes, dear, I'm afraid it's true, I saw it myself. They were dragging his car out of the river. I know you admired him. Well, it said in the paper that he had received a swimming merit badge at Camp in 1990. I'm sure they will find him, sooner or later."

Mark quietly sat down and stared off into the distance for several hours, unresponsive to any external stimuli. There was no doubt that his career as a banker was over. It was true enough, alright, there it was, in black and white, right on the front page of the Sunday paper, in bold headlines: "Nashville Socialite Charles Hamster Missing and Feared Dead." There were two photographs, a head shot of Chip, and another of his battered Rolls-Royce being hauled from the murky depths of the Tennessee River.

A sad sight to be sure. Chip's car being pulled from the murky depths of the Tennessee River. He was missing, presumably devoured by giant mutant catfish.

There was a lengthy history of his family, detailing the origin of the Green Tortoise, the discovery of the treasure, and the founding of Amalgamated Cheese. The recent and unfortunate demise of Chip's father was delicately represented in the most socially and politically correct manner with the phrase "skillet wielding Negress" replaced by "Renowned African-American Chef."

The accident had occurred just before nightfall on Saturday evening, about five miles outside the Chattanooga city limits. Witnesses at the scene, including several extremely alert truck drivers, indicated that the black Rolls-Royce, left the road without warning, crossed the median, plummeted down an embankment and plunged into the swirling waters of the Tennessee River. By the time the witnesses reached the scene, the car had already been swallowed by the water. It was not immediately known how many occupants were in the car or if there were any survivors. One of the truck drivers thought that he had seen three people in the car, but so far, no bodies had been recovered. Fortunately, divers at the scene had been able to retrieve a nearly full case of "Milwaukee's Finest" in the convenient imperial quart bottles.

Therpis was found at dawn by a search party of Boy Scouts about a mile downriver, bruised and battered, but basically none the worse for the experience. He indicated to the reporter from the *Chattanooga Tattler* that he had been rescued from the swirling waters and carried to shore by a large Sturgeon. Based on this account, a field sobriety test was administered at the scene by a Tennessee State Trooper, and it was determined that Therpis had been intoxicated at the time of the accident. In light of this development, certain aspects of his narrative were subsequently open to question, particularly his account of being rescued by a Sturgeon. The officer determined that the rescue had been most likely performed, if at all, either by a large Carp, a Catfish, or even a Snapping Turtle, although the latter was unlikely inasmuch as Therpis was still possessed of his genitalia. Since the Sturgeon is a cold water creature, these were the only possibilities.

Based upon the account provided by Therpis, it was further ascertained that there had indeed been three people in the vehicle at the time of the mishap; Therpis, Chip Hamster, and some hitchhiker they had picked up at a truck stop at the edge of Monteagle. Therpis only remembered that their passenger was named "Booger", "Hocker," or something similar, and that he had acted very strangely.

Therpis refused the ambulance and asked a bystander for a ride to the Kingfish Lounge, downtown, on what was formerly known as 9th Street. Chip's badly damaged car was towed to the impound lot operated by Mid-South Auto Brokers, the crowd disbursed, and the search for bodies continued for several days before being called off. Since nothing was found, it was speculated that the bodies had been carried downstream by the current or devoured by certain large unknown aquatic animals, mutated as a result of the toxic, and most likely, radioactive slime formerly oozed into the Tennessee River by several foundries in the Chattanooga vicinity. A truly sad and terrible ending for young Hamster, one who had so much to offer the world.

A truly tragic ending for someone who had so much to offer the world.

15.

THE WILDMAN SANITARIUM

"Where am I?" Chip asked, his eyes slowly beginning to focus. "I've had this terrible dream. I must have dozed off," he laughed. "Hey Therpis, bring me a cocktail." There was no answer. "Therpis! Bring me a Blatz." There was no reply. Chip propped himself up and looked around. The sight that greeted his eyes was not what he expected. He was definitely not at home. What he saw were several unfamiliar faces whose features were unpleasantly distorted by the strange light. He tried to jump off of the table but was prevented from doing so by a sharp and sudden pain which cut through his left leg like a knife. He didn't like the look of the situation at all.

As his eyes gradually became accustomed to the light, he determined that he was most likely in the embalming room of a funeral home....not a pleasant thought. He was resting upon a large stainless steel table, probably a morgue table, and surrounded by six whispering stooges. His predicament required immediate action. It wasn't for nothing that he had spent perhaps hundreds of hours studying reruns of the 1960s show "The Avengers," memorizing every technical aspect of the martial arts skills of Emma Peel. She was an admirable fighter, especially during the show's introduction, when the viewer was presented with her splendid profile as she gave a petite kick toward some imaginary assailant, followed by a knife hand strike, which could only be described as 'crisp.' She'd truly been subject of many adolescent masturbatory fantasies, worldwide in her day.

"If I kick the fat one in the nuts," Chip reasoned, "I can grab these two bastards by their throats and pull them over the table, and then jump to my feet, grab that steel trocar, and dispense with the other three. Then I can get the hell out of here. I believe I was on the way to Chattanooga. I was with Therpis, and some hitchhiker. That means that they are also most likely being held here against their will."

His hand instinctively reached for the derringer in his pocket. Chip was shocked to find that he was in some type of hospital gown and that his pistol as well as his pants were missing. The movement made him instantly and nauseatingly dizzy.

"Don't even try it," said a darkly robed figure in the corner.

The pain again sliced through Chip as he settled back on the shiny table. He was outnumbered, injured, and uncertain of his whereabouts. It was clearly their move. "Where am I?" he asked. "How did I get here, and who are you?"

Marduk, Supreme Leader of the Council, answered his questions. "Where you are is of no consequence to you at the moment. Let it suffice to say that you are our guest, in a manner of speaking, and are under our protection from hostile outside forces, from those who would destroy you. You were in an automobile accident yesterday evening en route to Chattanooga and were rescued by certain members of this elect group, whom you now see gathered about you in this room."

Chip began to protest, but was instructed to be silent as Marduk continued.

"The authorities have already sought you here. We informed them that nobody from the outside had been seen. They seem, for the moment, to be satisfied with our answers to their queries, but, I suspect they shall return again soon enough, and most likely with a search warrant."

"What authorities?" Chip asked in disbelief. "I've done nothing. I demand to be released immediately! I'm being held here against my will."

"No one is ever held here against his will," The Corsican quickly interjected.

"You are free to leave whenever you please," Marduk continued. "I feel, however, that you should become aware of the exact nature of your external circumstances before leaving the safety of our company."

"What are you talking about?"

"Four agents from the Federal Bureau of Investigation have been monitoring your activities for several weeks now, seeking, I am told, to gather enough evidence to charge and convict you with interstate bank fraud. Were you aware of their presence?"

"No. Are you serious?"

"I thought not. They are very elusive. It seems that you're a prime suspect in some form of loan fraud involving the misrepresentation of certain vehicles for illegal purposes. It is, I've been informed, a Federal offense punishable by a lengthy prison sentence."

"Why didn't you turn me over to the FBI then?" Chip asked flippantly, displaying a false bravado which his circumstances at present didn't warrant.

"We have other plans for you," Marduk replied, "and in a few days, after you have fully recovered, we shall offer you a rare and unique opportunity. It will alter the course of your destiny in a way which at this time, would be incomprehensible to you. We invite you to remain with us as our guest for a few days, during which time you will find out who we are, why we are here, and what we do."

"First of all," Chip replied authoritatively, "all of you get out of the shadows, turn on the lights so I can see you, and tell me who you are, and where in the hell I am. This is not a request, it's a demand, and it's not negotiable. I am Chip Hamster, cheese magnate, businessman, and financier. I demand immediate and intelligible answers to my questions. You...you there in the corner..... come out here where I can see you. What are you doing in that foolish costume? Who are you? You people all look crazy. Just wait until I get my lawyer on the phone. He's gonna chew some ass. I mean it. I will not be held here in this dark funeral home. I'm gonna whip some ass myself, Goddamn it! Turn on the lights! And where is my car? Get me out of here! Wait. I can't swim....I told you that I know more about cheese than any man alive, and I meant what I said."

Ahmedis, a wrestling fan, and veteran of many Saturday afternoon matches at Chattanooga's Memorial Auditorium, reached over and put the sleeper hold on Chip, rendering him immediately unconscious.

"I think," he said, addressing the others, "that our guest is somewhat disoriented. Perhaps we should let him sleep here for a while. When he is rested, I think he should probably be assigned to one of us until he learns the ropes. All of this at one time would be enough to overpower anybody. He'll be alright in a few days. The molecular scanners indicated no specific or significant physical injuries."

"Ahmedis is right," interjected Marduk. "We'll keep someone with him. Prescott, you stay with him, but notify me as soon as he wakes. Now where is the other one? Is he still in the laundry room? Good. Nobody is to know that we have these two, at least not yet anyway. I mean nobody. I'll arrange their admission papers immediately through the usual channels, and nobody will suspect anything. Gentlemen," he continued, "I told all of you that we would soon be at full strength again. We have our two new council members as was ordained. This is truly a great day in the history of our organization, and the beginning of a new era."

"It has been so ordered, Your Excellence, and shall be done."

In the Laundry Room of the Wildman Sanitarium, Marvin Hocker plotted his getaway. His escape from the Ohio State Prison had been easy enough. He reflected proudly that he had destroyed the entire prison power plant, as well as the laundry, had blown them to kingdom come. When the firemen arrived, Hocker, in the confusion of smoke and flames, smacked one of them on the head with a pipe, hauled him around back of the dumpster, traded clothes with him, and took his place at the pumper. With firemen from all over town at the scene, it was easy enough. After a while, when several of the firemen were overcome by smoke and hauled down to St. Expedite Hospital in one of those giant ambulances, Hocker was among their number. By the time he arrived at the hospital he was understandably feeling better. After a brief examination by an intern, he walked out of the emergency room a free man. It had been that simple.

He'd kept the fireman's driver's license as well as his credit cards, phone card, and other identification. In fact, Hocker enjoyed a big lobster supper that night at The Gulas, courtesy of MasterCard and fireman Hugh Grundy, before he boarded the bus to Nashville, also courtesy of the aforementioned.

Hocker put on the feed bag at Gulas Restaurant.

He had several hundred dollars in cash, but might as well use the credit cards and keep the money. There was some possibility that he would leave a paper trail if he used the credit cards, but he'd thought of that already. Anyone who could single-handedly blow up the Ohio State Prison and just walk out of the place wasn't likely to overlook any details. Besides, he reasoned, inmate Marvin Hocker had been burned to a crisp in the explosion. Nobody would be looking for him. When the fire marshal and his boys sifted through the burned out rubble of the laundry and power plant several days later, after things cooled down, the officials would find the badly charred remains of the life-like rubber love doll he had left, dressed in prison clothes, with Hacker's dental records neatly stuffed in the pocket. He would immediately be pronounced dead. The police don't look for dead people, that is, not if they already have the body and the dental records. It was an open and shut case. Hocker was a free man.

He had stopped by the Grand Ole Opry in Nashville and seen some hillbilly singers, and then started thumbing his way down I-24 toward Florida, that Sunshine State, where he expected to get a job at the Riviera Hotel in Daytona. He'd work as a doorman until he could steal enough from guests' rooms and suitcases to get his oyster ranch going. He hadn't expected to be in a car wreck when he'd hitched a ride to Chattanooga with those two fools.

At this particular moment he was surrounded by some stupid looking men in magician costumes. While it was readily acknowledged by anyone who'd ever spent any time whatsoever with Hocker, that the lamp of intelligence burned low, he was spared the complicated and lengthy process of ratiocination. He didn't spend too much time with such questions as 'how' or, as in this case, 'why.' He dealt only with facts and objectives. In the day to day business of life, he possessed a decided advantage over those whose superior intellects required them to look at all sides of a situation rationally before taking action. Hocker bypassed all of these mental gymnastics and operated solely on the basis of instinct and intuition. He went straight to the point. Facts, objectives, and methods. Fact: He was being held prisoner, most likely in the nut house, since he had seen a sign for the Wildman Sanitarium just before the accident. Presumably he had been either rescued or captured by some of the inmates. Objective: Escape and continue journey to Florida. Method: As Malcolm X said, "By any means necessary."

"By any means necessary!"

The wreck had shaken him up a bit, especially when the car overturned and the water started coming in. He'd easily covered the short distance to the opposite bank and sought refuge in a very large drainage pipe, safe from the police. The next thing Hocker knew, he was in a mental institution surrounded by persons who were obviously insane. Were he not an escaped felon, he would walk right out the front gate and be on his way. He was willing, for the moment at least, to rest for a day or so and then sneak out of this joint. If there was the slightest delay of any kind, he'd simply blow the sanitarium off the face of the earth. He did not intend to waste any time at all with anybody. He'd blow this son of a bitch to smithereens if need be, but first, he'd play along with them for a day or so and see what happened.

While Marvin had most likely made the perfect escape from the Ohio big house, he hadn't actually waited around to be sure he had been declared dead as a result of the explosion. The cops could be looking for him right now. Anything was possible, so for the moment he would humor these people. After all, they were insane. How much trouble could it be? He'd play along with them, as if they weren't out of their rabbit ass minds, then, if he had to, he'd blow the place up.

The tallest and most foolishly dressed inmate approached, flanked by two burly attendants in white coats. They were probably along to see that the inmate didn't try to cut anybody up or anything like that. The nut cake started the conversation.

"Good afternoon. My name is Marduk. I apologize for the accommodations. We will see to something more appropriate at the first opportunity. Inasmuch as you were not carrying any identification, we did not know who to contact. We don't know who you are. What is your name?"

Snocker had thrown the fireman's wallet and credit cards off of Nashville's Shelby Street Bridge into the Cumberland River as a precautionary measure, taking care, however, to memorize the

129

number on the AT&T phone card, in case of emergency. Now, he cocked his head to one side as he considered the question he'd just been asked. At just that moment, Marvin Hocker bore more than a passing resemblance to an opossum, though he would most likely have been offended by the observation. After a moment, he replied. "Tom Smith, yeah, that's it, I'm Tom Smith," Hocker said.

Marduk looked at the two attendants and raised his eyebrow. "Well, no matter," he said. "You'll be assigned another more suitable name soon enough."

"I don't think I'll be here that long, but thanks anyway." As Hocker looked at Marduk, he could already see flames in his mind's eye licking the walls of the very room in which they were standing.

Later that afternoon, 'Tom Smith' was officially escorted out of the laundry room, through the admissions office, and after an interview with Dr. Lowenstein, was situated in a semi-private room with Astaroth, Minister of Interplanetary Transportation, as his temporary roommate.

Throughout the day's activities Hocker kept his cool admirably, checking things out, noting the number and size of the guards, determining the physical layout of the facility, and quietly planning his escape. He pleasantly submitted to the admission procedures in an effort to appear docile and passive. During his interview with the doctor, he felt like saying, "Look Doc, I'm an escaped felon, just camping here until things quiet down outside. I'll be outa here in a few days, and on my way to Florida to start an oyster ranch." Hocker could have something cool with a western cowboy theme with a sailor instead of a cowboy, riding a bucking oyster instead of a bronco, and oysters instead of cattle. He could re-activate the famous 'Oyster Loaf,' once Miami's oldest oyster joint. He'd be rich like that Amazon guy, what's his name, Jeff Blazos...Blutos? Whatever. Who gives a shit? He could think about that later.

For the moment, he made up what he thought were appropriate answers to the questions asked by the doctor, questions such as, "Do you hate your father?" and, "Would you rather be hit on the foot with a hammer or have your toes cut off by a lawnmower?" No shit! What the hell kind of questions are those to be asking a newcomer? He might be stupid, but he wasn't crazy. It was like in the story by Edgar Alan Poe about Doctor Tarr and Professor Fether, where the inmates had taken control of the asylum and posed as doctors. Hell, everybody here was crazy, if not in fact, then at least by association. Oh yeah, instead of Smith, they had given him a new name, "Meeztor." Since it sounded like 'Mister,' it didn't bother him too much. In fact, he sort of liked being called Mister; it was a sign of respect.

In his travels throughout the compound, Hocker discovered that the place was indeed the Wildman Sanitarium, that it was, for the most part, a minimum security operation situated on approximately thirty-five acres and surrounded by water. It was indeed only a few miles from Chattanooga and Interstate 75, en route first to Georgia and then to Florida. There was one segment of the compound which appeared to be a maximum security installation, since all of the windows and doors were covered with thick steel bars. His questions about that area were casually dismissed with a number of conflicting and evasive replies, depending upon who was doing the talking. He was curious, that was all, nothing more. He didn't care what they did or who they had locked up there. It didn't mean shit to him. He just wanted to be sure that the eighteen-foot fence wasn't electric, in the event he had to hop over it.

From what he'd been able to ascertain, most of the inmates were from rich families and had been dumped here because their relatives either didn't want to fool with them, or wanted to steal their money. As a matter of consequence, some of the inmates were not as foolish as their getups might suggest. Perhaps not all of them were completely insane. That, of course would remain to be seen. Some of them did have strange names though. Ahmedis, Marduk, Astaroth. All phony sounding names, probably stolen from some comic books, but what did it matter to him? They called themselves "The Council." He had known some counselors at Camp Sea Gull, when he was a kid, but they had names like Wilson, Jones, and Chapman.... normal names.

Hocker found out some other things as well. That fool Hamster, or whatever he was called, was also being detained at the sanitarium. He'd been injured in the wreck and had been raging incoherently about "cheese magnets," whatever that was. They'd been forced to drug him to keep him quiet. No matter. Hamster had bragged so much about what a genius he was, for so many miles, that Hocker probably would have set his car on fire anyway sooner or later. If Hamster was so damn smart, he wouldn't have driven an expensive car right off the road and into the water. He would have been paying attention to the highway instead of rooting around on the floor looking for the Elvis CD "In the Ghetto." But no, he just had to hear Elvis Presley, that fat, Dracula looking oaf. As a result, Hocker's career as a doorman at the Riviera, and subsequent position as oyster baron had been unnecessarily and needlessly postponed. Well, no matter, Hocker was going to break out of this bug house soon enough. The Council members had some strange job titles, one of which was called the "Interplanetary Meteorologist." He had said to Hocker, with absolute authority that the afternoon was going to be warm and sunny, "...without a cloud in the sky." By 2:30 p.m. it was raining cats and dogs. He couldn't predict a fart after a Mexican dinner. Hell, if you want to know if it's going to rain, all you have to do is look at the bus stop and see how many people are wearing shower caps. How is it that they always know, even days in advance whether or not it's going to rain? They just do. You don't have to go to some expensive school to figure that out. Just look out the window.

And his roommate "Astaroth," was supposed to be in charge of transportation throughout the universe. He was nice enough, but didn't even know the delivery schedules to the sanitarium. They were a strange bunch, crazy as hell, and always talking some big bunch of high sounding bullshit. They were probably rich though. Maybe Hocker could beat them out of some dough before he hit the road.

Hocker's most important discovery was a telephone. He had asked to use the phone but was told by some portly nurse with a beehive, that "use of the phone by patients was not permitted." He would've stuffed her big fat ass in a laundry chute and burned the entire hospital down at that very moment had it not been lunchtime. He decided to sneak out and make his call later, at night, after everyone had gone to sleep. Lights out came at 9:00 p.m. sharp, as some scratched up record of a bugle played "Taps" through the intercom. Hocker had to call the prison and find out whether or not he was dead. He had to know. If he'd been declared dead, then he would be able to move throughout America without fear. On the other hand, well...he didn't care to think about that possibility.

He just needed to use the phone. He'd asked, but had been rudely refused, like he was some prisoner in this bug house of freaks. Now he'd really use the phone, one way or the other, the hard way, if necessary. The hard way consisted of taking a big hammer, a pointed spike, and a wire coat hanger. You knock a small hole in the side of the coin box, and call whoever you need to call, anywhere in the world. The coat hanger is inserted into the hole in just such a way that it triggers something to make the operator think you've put in a bunch of quarters. It's easy enough. Well, he reflected, he didn't have the appropriate tools just as yet. It would be necessary to either use the phone at the watch station on his floor or sneak down to the visitor's lounge on the first floor. He chose the latter course of action and easily eluded the on duty nurse and watchman.

He dialed the number of the Ohio State Prison, preparing to enter fireman Hugh Grundy's AT&T card number. Instead of the familiar AT&T tone, he was greeted by a robot's voice, "Thank you for choosing Opticob." He entered the card number anyway, but to no avail.

"Your call cannot be completed as dialed. Thank you for choosing Opticob, please try your call again."

133

This bullshit drove him crazy. More unnecessary government interference in the lives of everyday citizens. When would it stop? Now there were petty tyrants and pirates setting up independent phone companies at every two-bit town, across America, each exacting some tribute. Goddamn thieves. Probably senators or congressmen, who took advantage of the so-called antitrust laws to break up a big company in order to invest in small regional companies themselves, and further gouge the public. Fueled by these thoughts, the urge to totally destroy the phone swept over Marvin Hocker and possessed him body and soul. He pressed his face hard against the front of the phone and clasped the sides with each of his hands. He trembled with rage, and would have torn the phone from the wall with his bare hands and dashed it to the floor, but after a lengthy and emotional battle, reason prevailed. He had to make the call. Now he had to try to remember the access code as well as the card number, and the number at the prison, a total of thirty numbers. God have mercy if he misdialed and had to try and remember all the numbers in the proper sequence a second time.

"Ohio State Prison, Walters speaking, may I help you?" It was that foolish turd Walters. What the hell was he doing there on the night beat, the goofy son of a bitch? Hocker pinched his nose and attempted to disguise his voice.

"Sgt. Waltuhs, Hoy, this is Rabbi Bowevilitz I'm sorry to distub yuh evenin', but I wonda could yuh be so kind as to summon Tyrone Moshe Jones to the phone. Theaz been an unfortunate death in his immediate family."

Tyrone Moshe Jones, a former Black Panther activist and political radical, had shunned the so-called religion of Islam (unlike many of the other black prisoners), and embraced the Hebrew faith. Rather than re-name himself some fake pseudo-African name, like "Kwame," he preferred to identify with the most successful element of the population at large. He felt himself to be a member of one of the lost Hebrew tribes that had wondered into Ethiopia, and therefore, one of the real Jews. The others, most American Jews, for instance, he considered to be Arabs and not Jewish at all. He had studied the Bible, both Testaments, as well as the spurious 6th and 7th Books of Moses, not to mention the Book of Splendor, and other works, such as the Talmud, and concluded that the Negroes were the only true Jews, and that they had wandered into Africa during the Exodus. The rest of the Semites, the Arabs as well as the Jews, he classified simply as Arabs. Not only that, but the Jews spread a fine table after services. That certain members of the Jewish faith took umbrage with the prisoner's claims was more or less to be expected. Nonetheless, Tyrone Moshe Jones was tolerated, and actually encouraged in his studies by Rabbi Bowevilitz, especially since Jones was technically, the only Jew in prison.

Rabbi Bowevilitz (not a happy camper)

Sgt. Walters wasted no time bringing the prisoner to the phone. He had felt the wrath of the stinging tongue of Rabbi Bowevilitz once and did not wish to endure the same again. In less than five minutes, the prisoner was on the phone. Sgt. Walters walked back down the corridor to the watch station to afford him privacy.

Tyrone Moshe Jones placed the receiver to his ear and answered, "Hello?" as courteously as he could, wondering why Rabbi Bowevilitz was on the other end of the line at this hour.

"Moshe, listen quietly, it's me, Hocker."

"Who? Hocker! What? Where are you?"

"Shhh! I'm, well, never mind where I am. The phone might be tapped. Do they think I'm dead? That's all I need to know."

"That was one hell of a getaway, Hocker. Very theatrical also, I might add. How'd you do it?"

"I'll write you a letter. I can't talk now. Just tell me, Moshe, are they looking for me?"

"You'd better believe it, brother. They're mad as hornets. You almost burned the whole place down. The fire spread all the way over to C block. It almost caused a riot."

"But what about my body? Didn't they find it?"

"That was really great, man, a love doll in prison clothes. The brothers really dug that, man. Too cool. Ice baby. Too cool."

"Yeah, but..."

"Ice baby. Don't shit brother Moshe. You're my favorite turd."

Hocker had reason to be concerned now. This meant that there

135

was probably an APB out for him at this very moment. He might have to spend his life on the run like that fugitive, what was his name? Yeah, like Dr. David Jansen, pursued and hounded forever, from one place to the next by some vengeful cop with one arm and unlimited public funds and nothing better to do.

"But what about my dental records? I put them on the body."

"I said, don't shit me, you're my fav-O-rite turd. I don't be knowing nothing about that, bro. I do know that they found a fireman behind dumpster number three in his skivvies and a lump on his head, but they didn't find you. They found a dead love doll, all browned up and toasted and melted, and all that kinda stuff. They didn't find no Marvin Hocker. You're a hero round here man. The sands dig yuh too. Oh yeah, one other thing....your parole request was granted, although I don't think that applies now, if you know what I mean. Dig it bro. Salami."

"No. Man you're shitting me."

"Fo' I shit cha, I wouldn't fool wit cha."

"You mean they were going to release me? My parole request was granted?"

"Was, my brother Hocker, was, but as Carole King said, 'It's too late baby'."

A greatly dejected Marvin Hocker bid his prison buddy a sad farewell. Now he wasn't feeling so well, and walked up the stairs and down the hall back to his bed, not even bothering to sneak around.

"I toldja I had to use the phone," he said blankly as he passed the nurses station. He had planned everything so carefully. What went wrong? Well, he reflected, at least he was out of the big house. But, now, he was in the nut house, a prisoner of freaks in choir robes. He hesitated to imagine the future. It had all seemed like a bad dream. They at least had television in the slammer, and you could smoke. This was awful, just awful.

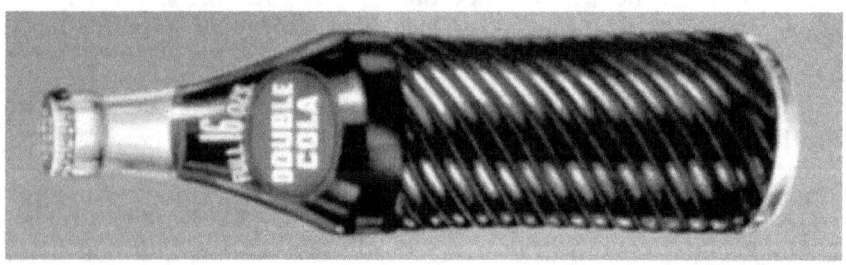

16.

WITHIN THE INNER SANCTUM

"It's difficult to keep this place on the road so to speak," Dr. Langley stated flatly to his chief orderly, a burly cross-dressing ex-marine.

"I understand your predicament sir," the orderly replied, "but keeping this many stone ass freaks from going ape shit, tearing things up, hurting themselves, or each other is equally as great a task. I've..."

"Please don't use those derogatory terms anywhere in or out of this facility. In the first place, they are not freaks, they are psychologically challenged. Better yet, I like the phrase 'psychologically challenged Americans.' Adding the 'Americans' will keep them from feeling disenfranchised and possibly damaging this facility."

"Okay boss."

"Thank you. That was easy enough," the doctor replied dryly. "Now, to the matter at hand. The reason I've called you here is that I keep hearing reports that one of your team has been interfering with the 'Council.' I believe you know who I'm referring to."

"Doctor, I know I agreed not to use the term 'freaks' anymore, but I'm severely tempted. Those guys are crazy, I mean really crazy. Look at the way they dress, those stupid looking robes and all. I mean it. I don't know whether they look more like idiots on graduation day, the psycho Supreme Court, or halfwit choirboys. They really are freaks."

"Bob," the doctor replied," this is a psychiatric facility, a sanitarium. It isn't a school or a camp, it's a nut house. Pardon the expression. Be that as it may, however, it is a business. It is a revenue producing operation tailored primarily for the privileged. More importantly, for both of us, it is our main source of income. This place provides our jobs."

"I know, but these weirdos in the Council have adopted stupid sounding space names. That fool Tyrone Davidson calls himself 'Bustokus' or some stupid bullshit like that. What's worse, he insists that the staff address him by that name. If we don't, he won't do anything he's told. It's the same with all of them. They all have some bullshit space name. Ahmedis, Marduk, Astaroth. Horseshit! My orderlies don't want to have to humor these people to that degree."

"Again, Bob," the doctor continued, "these people are like children. Play with them. If they want to pretend that they are part of Star Trek or the command fleet, it really doesn't matter. Besides, most of them are from very wealthy families. They were probably spoiled as children, especially from the point at which their parents determined that they were disturbed. So humor them. Remember, they are like children. They're just playing dress up. So please just ask Bim and the rest of your staff to try a little harder to humor them. If they are in some meeting planning to take over some distant planet, just let them be. They're innocent enough."

"Innocent? They were overheard planning to kill that former inmate Louis Guergleoni. They called him 'Louie the Pencil,' or Mazor, or some off the wall shit like that. They were planning to kill him just because he was released from here. As if it's some kind of crime to own a junkyard. Bim discovered the reason they were going to off him was because he left without their permission. And what about all of that electrical equipment they have? What is that shit? It emits weird groans and hums, and lightning bolts and electricity are always flying around down there in that so-called lab. Whatever it is that they are doing interferes with television reception in the employee's lounge. What is all that stuff?"

"Bob," the doctor laughed," I think you are over reacting just a bit. Those guys couldn't kill a fly. You know how psychotics fixate on someone. Guergleoni spent some time here, recovered as a result, and was again ready to enter the productive mainstream of American society. The Council members probably resent the fact that he was released and that they're still here. That's all. It's human nature. As far as their so-called laboratory is concerned, think of it as their playroom. There was some outdated radio equipment left by the government after the war when this place became a private facility. We decided to let them play with it. I think one of them was a ham radio operator or built a Heathkit radio in the boy scouts. It's not like there is any nuclear facility down there. It's all in fun. If they play like they are talking to people from outer space. What does it matter?"

"Well," the orderly answered, "I guess you're right. It's just that their high-handed and superior attitude is offensive to the people who work here, the normal people. But I'll try to keep Bim and the rest of my staff out of their way as much as possible."

"I really appreciate it Bob," Dr. Langley said warmly. "When the inmates can be kept calm without the administration of drugs, I feel that genuine progress is being made. There are many patients who, in the past have come to this facility for treatment, have become refocused, and have again returned to society as productive and well-adjusted members. That's our goal here, to serve our patients and their families. Admittedly, not all of the patients will return to the general population of society at large. I think those inmates who call themselves members of the Council most likely fall into this latter category. Let's just try to make their lives as comfortable as possible during their stay here, whatever its duration may be. Thanks again, and feel free to contact me about anything that might be a problem. I count on you guys. We all do."

The orderly rose to leave, but turned to the administrator again, "Oh yes," he said, "there was one thing I forgot to mention. Our staff has heard rumors that there are two new patients being housed in this facility whom we haven't met. I can't do my job if I don't know what's going on."

Dr. Langley swallowed hard. He had suspected that the members of the Council had somehow abducted those two persons missing from that motoring accident a short while ago, but he'd been unable to ascertain for sure. The orderly's inquiry caught him off guard. This was not a good sign. These two innocent travelers were probably being held here at the sanitarium, and certainly against their wishes. This was not good at all. If Langley denied their presence it would create suspicion among the workers. Once again, he had to cover for someone else's bullshit. He attempted to sound relaxed in his reply.

"Yes, there are two new inmates on the premises, but they are being housed in some vacant space adjacent to the Council's make believe laboratory. Both of these inmates are severely psychotic and are under heavy sedation and constant observation by another psychiatrist who is new to our hospital. I will bring him around to meet your group in the next few days. As far as these new inmates are concerned, I feel that it will be weeks, or possibly even months before they are ready to become part of the overall patient population. They are at present very disoriented and delusional, and I felt that their introduction into this institution through the normal procedures would be potentially upsetting to some of the other patients. It's best that their presence at this facility be kept secret for the moment, at the wishes of their families, of course. In other words, nobody other than ourselves should know of their presence here."

"Well, it's your call Doc," the orderly replied, seemingly satisfied with the explanation he'd been given.

"Their respective families have fabricated credible tales for their friends and associates at home to account for their absence. The less said about the matter the better, at least for the moment."

With that, the orderly took his leave, and walking down the corridor, came face to face with the robed and regal presence of the inmate who called himself Marduk, another razor walking psycho freak just one stitch shy of a strait jacket. The two eyed each other uneasily and without speaking, like two lizards passing on a tree. As the distance between them continued to diminish, the one who called himself Marduk fixed the orderly with an unrelenting basilisk eye, known throughout the civilized world as the "madman stare." The orderly averted his eyes as they passed each other, but thought he heard Marduk growl.

"Weirdo space freaks!" the orderly muttered inaudibly to himself, but only after he was safely and well past the dark robed figure.

Dr. Langley was furious. He could not permit a bunch of inmate freaks......that is, psychologically challenged American patients, to dictate the operations of his institution. He was the hospital's chief resident physician, its administrator, and one of its owners. He had a responsibility to the patients housed here, to the public at large, and to the other owners. He could not, nay, would not further permit the members of the Council to tell him how to run his own hospital. They were the inmates, not him. And now they were holding two private citizens as prisoners. PRISONERS! It was unbelievable. This is what happens when you're too nice. Permissiveness and appeasement never work. It's just like in grammar school. You have to fight the bully, win, lose, or draw or he will never give you a moment's peace. It was time to make a stand once and for all. And there was no time like the present.

140

As if reading the physician's thoughts, Marduk stepped silently through the office door, unnoticed in fact, until the doctor looked up, startled by Marduk's unexpected and unannounced entrance. Dr. Langley was a typical southern doctor in every respect. Tall, imperially slim, perfectly groomed and manicured, and elegantly dressed in a thousand dollar suit. His thin blonde hair and wire rim glasses gave him the look of someone from an affluent background. His appearance was in stark contrast to that of Marduk, who was also tall and thin, but whose face and hands were the only visible parts of his body. The rest of him was covered by a long purple robe of ancient design, produced at a cost of perhaps ten thousand dollars. He wore no flashy gold watch or other jewelry. The two men regarded each other coldly before the visitor spoke.

"I believe you wished to see me, Dr. Langley."

The doctor's rage had been building like nausea until he could no longer control it. "Look," he said to the robed figure, "there are going to be some changes around here, beginning immediately. Your reign of terror and intimidation is over. If you think that what you've got on me is that strong, go ahead and lay your cards on the table. Do what you gotta do, and may the best man win. I'm through being given ultimatums. I'm not taking any more orders from you or any of your friends. You are the inmates at this institution, not me. Do what you gotta do."

Marduk listened quietly to the ravings of the hospital administrator and then got to the business at hand. "I told you last week, Dr. Langley, the new sub-atomic particle accelerator must be in our possession by the 15th of next month. Have you attended to this?"

Dr. Langley stood up, walked to the window of his office and looked out at the thick summertime foliage and at the exquisitely manicured grounds. "This son of a bitch is ignoring me," he said angrily to himself. He then turned and faced Marduk, glaring at him intensely, his eyes filled with hatred. "Did you not hear anything I just said?" he asked.

"I want my particle accelerator by the 15th of next month. I will accept no excuses."

"Accept no excuses?" the doctor asked indignantly. "Accept no excuses?" he asked again. "I'm not your goddamned delivery boy. If you want some more equipment get it yourself. You can stick that accelerator in your ass. I don't work for you. This is not your hospital. You are a patient here, you and all of your ridiculous cronies. If you mess with me I'll have all your heads shaved and see how you like being clothed in the raiment of the criminally insane. Don't fuck with me, I'm warning you!" The doctor was shocked by his own profanity but pleased with his forcefulness. Desperate circumstances require desperate measures.

Marduk's first inclination was to smite this insurgent and force him to his knees with a touch of his electric cattle prod. The fact of the matter, however, was that despite this sudden show of courage and its subsequent insolence, the Council had, for the most part been well pleased with the administrator's performance. Furthermore, if it became necessary to replace this director, much valuable work time would be irretrievably wasted in breaking in his successor. For these reasons the supreme leader of the Council elected not to be offended by the insulting and arrogant remarks which had just been delivered so unkindly.

"I regret the necessity of reminding you that the Council is in possession of certain compromising photographs involving you and a former patient of this institution."

"I told you," the doctor said. "Do what you have to do. I have done everything you have asked, but the demands just keep coming. I never know what to expect. If you want to wreck my life go ahead. It will probably be worth whatever happens just to be free of you bastards. I got some tail, so what? It happens everyday. She was certainly willing enough."

"Perhaps you should consider your words more carefully, Dr. Langley. I'm on the very verge of taking offense at your decidedly hostile manner. Let me remind you that the object of your affections was a minor at the time of the incident you are referring to. More unfortunate is the fact that she was a patient of this hospital, a seriously troubled and maladjusted youth entrusted to your care. By taking advantage of her dependency you transgressed the first rule of psychiatry. You seduced her, robbed her of her innocence, and violated her sacred trust, the trust of a child. This hospital cannot afford any publicity of that nature, and neither can you personally. I don't believe that your wife would be as forgiving as the Council has been."

Dr. Langley's ardor for battle cooled appreciably at Marduk's words. The Council had him by the nads. "What in the hell do you want?" he asked in desperation.

"I want that new accelerator," Marduk answered, "I need it for the research we are doing. Have you placed that order as we directed?"

"Yes, I placed the order, but how in the hell am I going to justify to the board of directors a purchase order for a $ 2.5 million piece of equipment whose purpose I am unable to explain?"

"As usual, it's a mere formality," Marduk replied." These equipment purchases have never cost this institution as much as one penny. No justification is necessary."

"But my board of directors?" the doctor asked again. "They have to approve every expenditure in excess of $10 thousand."

"In case you haven't noticed, Dr. Langley, there has never been any objection to any purchase we've ever made, regardless of the amount involved. A bank transfer has always been made in advance to cover any costs. Don't you think it odd that nobody on your board of directors has ever objected or contested anything we've ever wanted to do?"

"That is odd, I must admit, but so what?" the doctor replied, relaxing a bit now.

"The reason is that your owners and board of directors are the most highly paid in the world for their services. That money comes directly from the Council members' families, both in America and elsewhere. There is no reason for you to rock the boat. All of you are on a gravy train. The best thing for you to do is just to sit back and enjoy the ride."

"But," Dr. Langley interjected, you people are inmates in a sanitarium."

"All the more reason to comply with our minimal requests. Of course we are crazy. Why else would we be here?"

"But you are crazy, I mean really."

"Yes," Marduk replied. "I know that. You are not mistaken. You are the one with the medical degree. We are the ones with the silly names and peculiar clothes. We are the ones who play act. But we do have a good time for the most part, considering our limited mental capacities. So please, just humor us."

"But what is all of that stuff? I got a bill for over $100 thousand for a Fazioli? What in the hell is that? And what is a sub-atomic particle accelerator anyway? I know damn well it isn't part of any ham radio rig. And anyway, I thought you already had one."

"The Titan is a musician and he wanted a piano. We thought he ought to have a nice one. The newer sub-atomic particle accelerator is something we need for our new recording studio. We require a hundred tracks digital and a hundred tracks analog. It is our desire to record the same piece of music.... Look, never mind all that, it's too complicated to explain."

Once again, Marduk had prevailed over Dr. Langley. He always did. The problem with the administrator was that he had become too accustomed to comfort. "You like the prestige of running this famous facility and the perks that come with the job," Marduk stated. "You are addicted to your flat Jaguar convertible, your big house, and that young wife. People who require such things become slaves to their desires, and are easily manipulated. There is nothing wrong with luxury per se," Marduk reflected. "I surround myself with it, but it makes most people weak. I can live comfortably anywhere, under any circumstances, you, Dr. Langley could not."

"Who are you people?" Dr. Langley asked. "No, really. Who are you?"

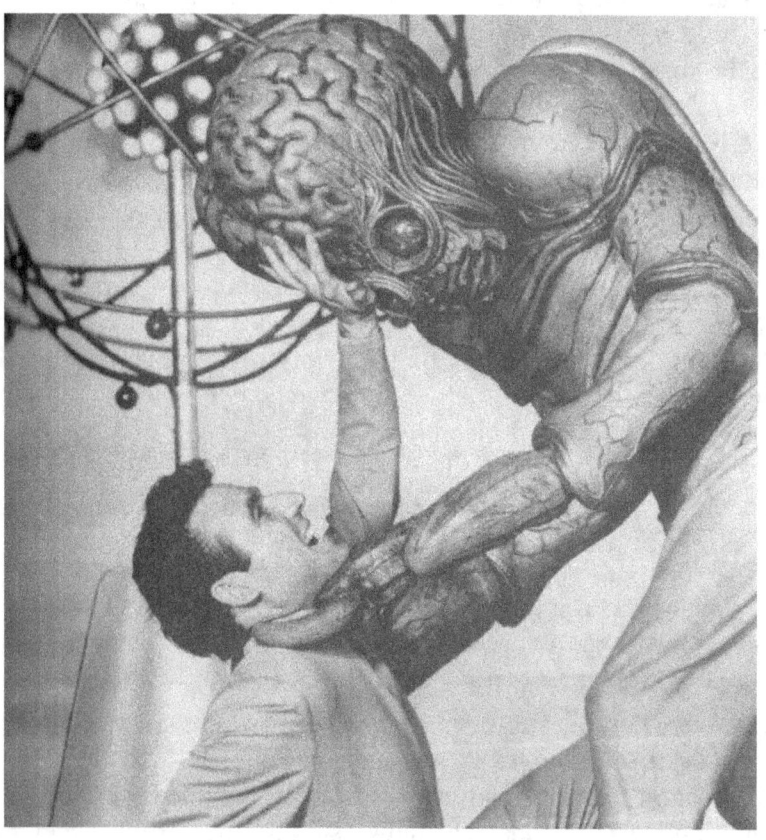

17.

DOUBLE-COLA

Meanwhile, in Iceland, Drs. Henry and Davis continued their experiments on the Double-Cola bottle for another week, but their conclusions remained the same. Somebody, somewhere possessed of a supernatural intelligence had, for whatever reason or reasons, designed this futuristic lens and incorporated it into the bottom of the 'soda' bottle, as they say in Indiana. Considering that the planet was about to be destroyed and life as it exists at the moment obliterated, their mission was one of top priority and absolute security. The problem, however was much more involved than merely stepping into the Double-Cola plant and asking to meet with the designer of the company's bottles. Or was it?

"I think what we need to do is to walk right into the place and ask to meet with their chief design engineer and say that we are interested in submitting a new bottle design proposal," Dr. Davis stated.

"Anyone intelligent enough to design that lens will be sharp enough to see through us immediately."

"Not at all," she replied. "Double-Cola is not exactly an internationally known household name. That company needs some help, and that's why we are here. Design proposals are submitted daily to businesses throughout the world."

"I don't know Debbie. What if the place is some kind of CIA research or training center or something like that? I don't think that we can just walk in and start asking technical questions."

"Look," she argued, "this is not the Pentagon. It's a soda factory, they make pop, not nuclear warheads. We're probably the only people in the world who know about this. The rest of the scientific world has no idea of the impending cataclysm. We have to get the information we need. It's not an option."

"You may be right about the rest of the recognized scientific community, but whoever made this lens knows exactly what's going to happen when that formation, or space gas, or whatever it is hits our galaxy. It will become objective, at which time it will have mass, velocity, acceleration, and although I hesitate to say it, most likely volition as well."

"Volition?" Dr. Davis asked with disbelief. "You mean you think this thing has a consciousness? That it is deliberately aiming itself at us? That is preposterous. It's not possible. There is no way."

"Alright then, how do you explain its activity and motion?" Clarence asked.

"Its movement, its very existence in any dimension is both spontaneous and random. The whole thing is unquestionably random, everything about it," she said. "It may have been artificially created, but its actions appear random to me. It could just as well be moving in some other direction. This is where we disagree."

"No, I think not. I don't know what to think. It's possible that it either is directing itself, or being manipulated. I'm not sure. Both of those suggestions are so absurd I hesitate to mention either of them, even to you. But I swear Debbie, I think the thing, whatever it may be, is intentionally aimed at Earth. Don't ask me how or why. I hope I'm seriously mistaken, but it's a gut feeling, something I can't shake."

"But what about its initial erratic movements? There was nothing specific or directed there. That's why Entutu called it Powerball, due to its total unpredictability."

"That may have been a smokescreen for our amusement, a light show to throw us off guard. Or," he speculated, "those movements may have been some aspect of its creation. Nobody, anywhere can define the movements of SS 396 as erratic now. It's headed straight for us. Hell, I venture to say that it's aimed at us."

"Clarence, do you realize what you are saying?"

"Yes, I do." There were a few minutes of silence as the two scientists weighed the implications of Dr. Henry's speculations.

Dr. Henry broke the silence. "Powerball has intentionally been programmed to destroy our planet. Something tells me that it won't take twenty years either. It will be much sooner than that. Like maybe six months to a year, yeah, less than a year."

"Good God," Davis exclaimed, "All this is making me dizzy. Are you really talking about the destruction of Earth?" I mean, nobody knows this except us."

"Us, and whoever invented this lens," Dr. Henry said. "This all sounds a little too 'Star Trek' for me."

CHATTANOOGA

Drs. Davis and Henry proceeded from Iceland to New York, to Atlanta, and finally to Chattanooga, changing planes at every stop, finally arriving in the Lookout City, worn to a frazzle. They rented a car at the airport, checked into the Read House on Broad Street, had a strategy dinner at the Green Room, and then returned to their respective suites.

Bright and early the next morning the two scientists met for breakfast in the coffee shop of the hotel, then drove the short distance to the Double-Cola plant at the base of Lookout Mountain, next to a Bojangles restaurant.

The plant itself was dark and foreboding, notwithstanding the brightness of the day. It was a large brick building with a circular driveway situated on a flat piece of land. If this was an active cola manufacturer you would never have known. There was nothing happening outside the building. There were no cars in the parking lot, no trucks loading or unloading. The place was as quiet as a tomb. To the local residents of Chattanooga, however, there was nothing unusual about the fact that this cola plant seemed to be closed down.

147

There had never been any visible activity there as long as anyone could remember, at least not according to the aged bell captain at the hotel.

The two scientists approached the structure with trepidation. As soon as they turned into the driveway it was as if the world had gone from color to black and white. Looking across the street, to the left or to the right of the building, everything seemed normal, but on the Double-Cola property itself, all seemed colorless.

Clarence parked the rented white Lincoln Town Car in the empty parking lot in front of the tall red brick building, but hesitated before opening the door. Dr. Davis suppressed an involuntary shudder as she saw the building up close for the first time. It was definitely sinister. Decidedly bad vibes. For a moment she thought they should forget all about their self-appointed mission and return to Iceland. This was obviously a mistake. She would probably wake up any moment in her own cozy bed at the observatory compound, with a fire in the fireplace and her cat resting quietly at her feet. Too bad, she wasn't going to get off that easily. She really was in Chattanooga, and really on a mission to save the world.

"So what approach are we going to take with these people?" Dr. Henry asked.

"Well, I've got the bottle designs I sketched last night, if we go that route," Dr. Davis said. "I think the best thing to do however, is to see who we end up with and play it by ear."

"That sounds good in theory," he replied, "but as soon as we enter the building we're going to have to have some sort of story already planned, some logical and valid reason for being here."

"I guess you're right, so what's it going to be?"

"Ok, I got it. We're post graduate students from the University and we want to do a report on this well-known Chattanooga landmark for an urban planning class, and wondered if we could tour the plant. That will work."

"But is there a university here?" Dr. Davis asked.

"Yeah, there's a University of Tennessee extension here."

"Well then, that's it," she said, as they approached the building and opened the front door.

The interior was as strangely silent as the grounds had been, with no activity of any kind. There was however, a perky receptionist, who provided a strange contrast to the drab lobby.

"May I help you please?" she chirped brightly between smacks of her chewing gum.

Dr. Henry answered. "Yes, I'm Clarence Henry," he said, careful to avoid any reference to the designation 'doctor.' "And this is my friend Debbie Davis. We're doing an advanced thesis on architecture and its utilization in the field of urban planning. I know that the Double-Cola building has long been a Chattanooga landmark. We were just wondering if we might tour the plant and get some ideas for our paper."

"That certainly sounds interesting," the receptionist cooed without the least trace of sarcasm. Apparently Clarence Henry passed 'mustard' as they say in that part of the Lookout City known as Moccasin Bend. "I'm Darlene," she smiled. "Let me see if I can find someone to help you."

With that, she pressed a buzzer under the left side of her desk. It wasn't the normal buzzer she generally used to signal that a group of school children or cub scouts had come by for a visit to the world headquarters of Double-Cola. It was the other buzzer, the one indicating that the visitors might be somebody coming to snoop around. This was not as unlikely a scenario as one might initially imagine. In the first place, especially with the opening of the eastern European block to free trade, the actual formula to Double-Cola had become a highly desirable property on the international market. Secondly, several persons from a so-called consumer safety group had acted very strangely regarding a particular 16 ounce bottle that had been released inadvertently into the marketplace a short while ago. For these and other security reasons, anyone other than school children or cub scouts were regarded suspiciously, at least until their true intentions became known.

The receptionist was very attractive in a local sort of way. She was flashy and vivacious, actually, somewhat saucy. Gaudy gold necklaces, rings, pendants and a rich dark tan, failed to detract from the prominent projections at the front of her dress, projections which engaged the attentions of Dr. Henry, though no doubt, for purely scientific reasons. Her pouffy sprayed and ratted blonde hair, as well as her pink bubble gum-colored lipstick, highlighted with dark purple liner, only served to further distract Dr. Henry, who hadn't seen much action of this sort in Iceland. She seemed completely relaxed and chatted amiably with her guests on a broad array of interesting topics as she chewed her gum and filed her nails.

"Have you been to the new aquarium?" she asked Dr. Henry.

"They tell me it's wonderful. I haven't been myself," she said looking up flirtatiously. "They say it's the number one fresh water aquarium in the United States. Wait. Is it salt water or fresh water? I don't remember. I think it's mainly fresh water, but I'm not really sure. It could be salt water, or it could even be both. I wonder if they have a Coelacanth. That would be a salt water fish, wouldn't it?" she asked.

"Uh, yes, yes it would," he answered distractedly.

Dr. Davis had been watching the way the receptionist ogled her associate. She chatted aimlessly like some big busted rodent, a squirrel or chipmunk perhaps. It irritated Dr. Davis the way this woman flirted so brazenly with her companion right in front of her very eyes. Dr. Henry had introduced her as his 'friend.' When a man introduces an attractive woman as his 'friend' it generally indicates at least to the genteel, the existence of a relationship. That this was not the case in this particular instance was, in Dr. Davis' opinion, entirely beside the point. It was as if the receptionist was deliberately trying to intimidate her. Fortunately, Dr. Davis' wrathful musings were interrupted by the arrival of someone who had presumably been sent to answer their questions.

Darlene looked up and announced that Mr. Lear, the company's general production supervisor, would be pleased to show them around.

"Thank you very much, Darlene," Dr. Henry beamed. "You've been very helpful."

The receptionist smiled to herself as she watched the trio walk down the long hallway. "Hot stuff," she remarked to herself, regarding Dr. Henry. "What I could do with that. Mmmm girl!"

"Bobby Joe Lear," the supervisor said, holding out his hand as they walked down the hall toward a large conference room. "This way," he said cheerfully, directing the two visitors through an open door. If Lear entertained any suspicions, he concealed them very well. "Have a seat," he said, "and tell me what I can help you with."

Dr. Davis spoke first. "First of all, Mr. Lear," she said, "thanks for taking the time to see us. We are both pursuing post graduate degrees in the field of urban planning. As part of a joint thesis, we are examining the utilization of large manufacturing buildings within the dual contexts of initial manufacturing function, and secondary use in cases where the initial manufacturing purpose is no longer feasible. We thought we could begin with properties such as yours, which are well known local landmarks, still in use in their original configuration. With that in mind, what can you tell us about your company? For example, when was this building constructed? Who was the architect, the construction contractor, and so on?"

Bobby Joe Lear felt like asking the pair to produce current student ID cards. If these two were students he would kiss a bumble bee's ass mid-flight over the Grand Canyon. He was inclined to throw both of them out immediately. However, he wasn't paid to play the role of strongman. He lived to make Double-Cola. That was his only concern. Regretfully, security was also within his job description, to some degree. He needed to find out what these two were up to, and what they really wanted. Industrial espionage in this world of high technology was nothing to be taken lightly.

"We here at Double-Cola are glad that the public is interested both in our company and in our fine line of products. I'm going to give you some printed material which will probably provide answers to all of your questions." With that, the supervisor reached into a large drawer, withdrew two press packs and handed them to his guests.

Dr. Henry looked sideways at his associate. This was not what they wanted at all.

"Excuse me, Mr. Lear," Dr. Henry interrupted, going straight to the point. "Could you tell me who designed the bottle? It is certainly an attractive container."

"It's all right there," he said, "right in that envelope, including pictures of our first bottles, and labels, as well as the ones we use now."

This was going from bad to worse. Fearing that the interview was about to be concluded, Dr. Davis asked their host if it would be possible to tour the plant.

"Well, of course," said the supervisor with a smile. "This is one of my favorite things, to take our many visitors around the facility." He rose and escorted them through a padded red leather door.

"This is our 'tap room,'" he said. "It's sort of a party room. People can rent it for weddings, gatherings, you know, that kind of thing. How about a taste?"

"Sure, that would be great," answered Dr. Henry, as he stepped forward to receive a freshly tapped frosty schooner of Chattanooga's finest. He held the glass aloft, watching the light filter through the amber liquid, and brought it down again to eye level, swirling it leisurely and gently like one would a fine glass of `94 Boars Head or a `93 Golden Harvest.

"The color is excellent, the bouquet exquisite, and the carbonation exactly as it should be," he said, as he brought the glass to his lips for a taste. Their host eagerly awaited Dr. Henry's comments, apparently forgetting for the moment, that his guests were possibly agents of industrial espionage.

"Divine," Dr. Henry stated genuinely. "Truly divine."

Dr. Davis was also treated to a fresh draught of Double-Cola, and was equally transported by the magnificence of the experience. "This is," she said, "I'm....this is heady stuff." She suddenly became aware of certain physiological stimuli that were, quite frankly, sexual in nature. She asked for another glass, a larger one this time, if possible.

"I thought you would like it. Even though our patrons enjoy our products in the convenient family size 16 ounce bottles, and the 12 ounce Kwik Kool alloy cans, there is nothing quite like Double-Cola on tap. Now for a thorough tour of the plant."

If the plant or its supervisor were intending to hide something, it was anything but obvious to the two visiting scientists who were being afforded every courtesy. They were puzzled indeed. There was nothing out of the ordinary here.

"If you will follow me," Mr. Lear stated pleasantly, "we'll see how Double-Cola is actually made. Now I regret to say this, but I will be unable to answer any specific questions for you regarding this process. In this era of industrial spies and espionage, we can't be too careful. I hope you understand."

"Oh yes. It pays to be careful," stated Dr. Davis. "We understand completely."

"One other thing," their host added, "You'll need to wear these safety glasses. Insurance regulations and all." He handed them some cheap, flimsy looking, red and white cardboard glasses like they pass out at 3-D movies.

The two scientists donned the foolish-looking glasses, and were taken on a most excellent tour of the plant. At its conclusion, they were each ceremoniously presented with a six pack of Double-Cola in the convenient 12 ounce Kwik Kool alloy containers for their drinking pleasure at a later time. They were escorted back the way they came, and out through the reception area.

After they left the building the supervisor was called into the conference room and asked about the two visitors. "I was suspicious at first," he said, but they didn't ask any unusual questions. Standard stuff. I think they were as they represented themselves to be," he concluded.

"I hope so, for your sake," the voice stated coldly. "In any case, I've ordered them followed for the next 24 hours, just to be sure."

I Hope so, for your sake.

18.

I THINK NOT

LATER: The Read House Hotel Bar
Clarence Henry took a sip of Guinness and remarked casually, "It was too slick."

"What was?" Dr. Davis asked, snatched from her summer daydreams by his unsolicited observation.

"Hell, everything. That whole place was suspicious. The parking lot was empty, the lobby was empty. I don't think there was anybody in any of those offices. I didn't see one delivery truck anywhere. And what about those guys in the white lab coats? Employees don't dress in lab coats in a cola factory."

"It's hard to say," Dr. Davis answered with some skepticism. "He didn't look like he was hiding anything, or trying to hide anything."

"Yeah," he laughed, "Sure. You can't buy Double-Cola in most of Chattanooga or Nashville, but you can get all you want in Moscow or Saudi Arabia. Please, give me a break."

"That is a bit peculiar, I must admit. But why were you poking me in the ribs?"

"I was trying to show you that a couple of bottles on the conveyer were broken."

"What do you mean broken?" she asked.

"I mean that those bottles on the conveyer were the same ones just re-circulating. That machine wasn't bottling anything. It was just the same several hundred or so bottles going round and round. I tried to show you."

"No," she said," that was impossible. I saw the soda going into those bottles and overflowing. Those bottles were overflowing."

"They were overflowing because they were already full."

"Are you sure about that?" she asked in disbelief.

"Yeah, didn't you notice how quickly he moved us out of there? And what about those guys in the vat room?" Henry asked.

"What do you mean?"

"What I mean is that I think they were robots," he said precisely, delivering the statement as effectively as a nine year old dropping a water balloon from a third floor balcony.

"You've got to be kidding," she said, scarcely able to grasp what her associate was saying. "You mean the workers we saw weren't real?"

"They were real enough alright," he laughed, and took another swig of stout. "But they weren't human. I think they were on some kind of mechanical track or something."

"Now wait a minute Clarence. One of them smiled and waved at me."

"Yeah, he turned around and waved alright, but did you see how mechanical it was? He was still waving after we left the room. Come on, you had to have noticed what was going on. That whole place is a hoax. There's nothing right about it."

"You mean they're not really making sodas there?" Dr. Davis asked, still unable to believe that they'd been so thoroughly duped, if indeed they had been duped. The Double-Cola plant was perhaps a bit strange, but so what? They'd been treated cordially enough during their visit. She was satisfied that the Double-Cola plant made Double-Cola. As far as Dr. Davis was concerned, that part of their investigation was closed.

"Please, give me a break," he continued, refusing to let the matter drop. "And, what about those hokey cardboard glasses? What a bunch of crap, I mean *really*." It was possible that Dr. Henry had perhaps had a wee bit too much to drink on this hot summer afternoon. Both sat there in silence for a few minutes, each deeply absorbed in their own thoughts.

Dr. Davis noticed two lovers sitting at a nearby table. They were about to do it right there in the cafe, groping each other under the table, laughing and kissing passionately. They were about her age, both of them. She'd been in love herself once, really in love with someone wild and free, and had acted the same way. "This is the way people in love act," he'd told her. He'd really loved her too. She remembered it now and felt a stabbing pain in her heart, a pain all the worse because she'd thrown him away to pursue her all-important scientific career. Back then, everything had been more important than him. He'd just wanted to be with her. Finally he tired of waiting and found someone else. Guys like him always do. She'd had other boyfriends since him, but nobody even came close. Since losing him, her life had never been the same, never would be the same. She'd traded the love of her life to be stuck in some stupid observatory in one of the most barren wastelands on the planet. Jesus, what a fool she'd been. But it was too late now. She looked over at Dr. Henry and wished that he was more...something. She liked him but he just wasn't her type.

Finally, he broke the silence, "I'm going back there. We accomplished absolutely nothing today. We got the same tour the girl scouts would have gotten. The answers we're looking for are in there, I just know it. We came all the way down here to get some answers, and by God, I'm not leaving here until I've got what we came for. The fate of the world is literally in our hands. Failure is not an option. I'm going back."

Dr. Davis was puzzled by her associate's logic. If the people at the Double-Cola plant hadn't told them anything the first time, why would they tell them anything their second trip? That is, if there was anything to tell.

"It's 7:30 Clarence," she said. "The place is probably closed. Besides, what makes you think they will answer our questions this time?"

"What makes you think I'm asking any questions this time?"

"What?" she asked.

"I'm breaking into the place, right now in fact, that is, as soon as I can get up to the room and get my tools," he said.

"You're kidding, of course?" she said.

"Not at all."

It was pointless to try to talk him out of it, although she did make the effort. At length, Dr. Davis decided to go with him, not because she wanted to, but because she didn't want to be left alone or to have to come looking for him later. Despite her maturity as a scientist, she was still a woman in a strange, unfamiliar, and possibly hostile environment.

"When do you propose to involve us in this illegal act of breaking and entering?" she said loudly, causing other patrons of the bar to look in their direction.

"Be quiet," Dr. Henry whispered. "Let's get out of here. Do you have any dark clothing?"

"Well, sure, I lived in Manhattan for a couple of years, so about two thirds of my wardrobe is black. But it's summer. Yeah, like I wear black in the intense heat of this oppressive southern climate. But wait," she paused. "I do have a dark flannel bathrobe. You know how cold hotel air conditioning is," she added, as if some explanation were required. Men could be so ignorant about the necessities of even the most basic women's attire.

They paid the check and caught the elevator back to the sixth floor. "I'll see you in ten minutes," he said seriously.

When Dr. Henry arrived at her room, she was not quite ready. "Debbie, c'mon, let's get out of here. I thought you'd be ready."

"Ready?" she asked indignantly, "You said you would be here in ten minutes. It hasn't been ten minutes yet."

"You're right. It certainly hasn't been ten minutes. It's been almost a half hour." Although Dr. Henry was understandably irritated, he'd logged enough past experience with women to know that any further exhortations in the interest of expediting their departure would be unfruitful, and possibly even counter-productive, so he sat silently while Dr. Davis attended to some insignificant last detail of her coiffure.

"Now tell me once again. Why are we breaking into a building?" she asked as she adjusted her robe.

"I told you," he said. "We have to find out what's going on there, and we have to do it now. We don't have time for the formality of playing questions and answers with some jerk at a cola factory. Somebody there knows something. We must locate them and find out what they know."

"But whoever it is won't be there. I still don't understand why..."

"Let's roll it, Debbie. You look great. This isn't a fashion show. We're busting into the Double-Cola factory. Now let's go."

They parked at the rear of the Bojangles parking lot and decided to leave the car there. Dr. Henry produced a black gym bag, withdrew some grease paint and darkened his face."

"You look like Al Jolson," she laughed.

"Here, put some of this on," he instructed her curtly, handing her the tube.

"No way," she said. "Not even a remote possibility. I already look ridiculous in this silly bath robe. There's not going to be anybody here anyway. This is not some defense installation for God's sake, it's a soda factory, you know, S-O-D-A, as in soda-pop."

"You must be from Indiana," Dr. Henry said, as they got out of the car and stepped quickly to a very large group of bushes.

"Well, of course, you knew that already. So what?"

"Nobody south of the Mason-Dixon has ever used the term 'pop' or 'soda.' Down here, everything is a Coke. This applies equally to every carbonated dark soft drink, including Pepsi. Under formal circumstances, the designation is 'Cocola.' Anything else, that is, any other soft drink, is generically known as a '7 Up.' Down here, the term 'soda,' in polite society, broadly refers to any carbonated fountain drink containing ice cream."

"I don't see what that has to do with anything," she said curtly.

"Lay back and follow me," he said, ignoring her. "And if I tell you to stay somewhere, stay there." He'd seen enough adventure movies to know that every time the hero tells the woman to stay put, she waits until he leaves and then immediately disobeys orders, usually to the detriment of the mission. "Ok, let's hit it." With that, Dr. Henry crouched close to the ground, and ran down the side and then to the back of the plant, zig-zagging back and forth wildly all the way. Dr. Davis followed behind, only not feeling it necessary to zig-zag. "Shhh!" he said, "Follow me." As they continued walking he said to her, "The first thing is to secure the perimeter. Then we'll determine a point of entry."

"Guys are so stupid," she thought to herself as she followed him down the rear of the building. Dr. Henry wanted to build this whole thing up and make it into some kind of covert military commando operation.

"Good God, Clarence," she said none too quietly, "we aren't sneaking into the Pentagon."

"SHHH!" he whispered loudly.

The building was longer and much larger than it had looked during the day, and if it had seemed sinister then, it appeared much more so now, looming like a dark presence, as they slowly walked behind it beneath the loading dock. Suddenly they came upon someone standing under a spotlight on a landing about halfway up the loading ramp. It appeared to be a guard, but whoever it was didn't seem overly concerned with security. The back door was propped open, and it looked like his rifle was leaning against the rail. He appeared to be smoking a cigarette.

"There are trucks everywhere," she whispered, "large route trucks, the kind that deliver soft drinks," she said angrily, smacking Dr. Henry in the back of the head.

"Shhh! Cut that shit out. Be quiet," he whispered loudly. "Now wait here."

"Where are you going?"

"Just wait here," he said again, and then quickly jumped up on the loading dock. It was a very dark night but she could see his outline clearly enough as he moved slowly in the direction of the guard, crouching low to the ground like a large dark rat. The tension was almost more than she could handle. What if the guard saw her associate? What if he shot him?

Suddenly Dr. Henry was beside the shadowy form. He raised his arm and struck him in the head with something. Down the guard went with a heavy thud. It was just like in the movies. Dr. Henry looked from side to side, checking for any other guards. When he was satisfied that no one else was patrolling the rear of the building, he motioned for her to join him. Dr. Davis jumped up on the loading dock, careful not to entangle herself in the folds of her bathrobe. She should have worn what she wanted to begin with, she reflected, and vowed then and there to never let any man select her clothing, not for any reason. Nonetheless, in an instant she was at her associate's side. The victim was stretched peacefully, if not blissfully at their feet, his cigarette still smoldering on the asphalt beneath the loading dock.

"See," Dr. Henry said proudly, "smoking is bad for your health."

"Why did you have to do that?" she asked, feeling sorry for the man unconscious at her feet. "You got the janitor."

"He had to be neutralized," Dr. Henry replied, still using the macho military talk. "He wasn't going to give us a guided tour."

"Well, he looks 'neutralized' to me all right. You 'neutralized' the janitor, poor bastard. By the way, that isn't a rifle," she said pointing to the rail. "It's his broom. I can't believe you hit him in the head. This whole business is absurd. Really, Clarence, let's get out of here. I can still take a hot bath and catch the late show." She looked at the poor fellow stretched out on the cement loading dock. She didn't want to just leave him there, but she didn't want to wake him either. He wasn't bleeding or anything. She bent down and checked his pulse. Normal. What did you use to 'neutralize' him?" she asked, again placing particular emphasis on 'neutralize.'

Dr. Henry produced the heavy swirled glass returnable 16 ounce Double-Cola bottle, the same one that contained the lens.

"Now let's go," he said, moving silently and quickly through the open door. "We don't have much time."

160

And in they crept, slinking down the dimly lit hallway, pressed against the wall. The ground floor, at least in the rear of the building consisted primarily of stacked cases and boxes, all of which bore markings indicating that their contents were nothing other than bottles of Double-Cola in various sized containers, packed, labeled, and awaiting delivery. At first Dr. Henry was concerned that there might be other guards or night watchmen, but apparently not. They made their way to the front of the building without hindrance.

The front entrance to the building, as best as they could tell, considering the low light, consisted of a large walnut paneled reception room circa 1953, judging from the sparse, streamlined appointments, the same they'd seen earlier in the day. A long, office-flanked hallway originated from this central area, running along the entire front right of the building. Another hall of approximately the same length ran down the other side of the building. There might be some information in one of these offices, or possibly in the large conference room, but there wasn't time to look through all of them. Furthermore, the only light on this level was that afforded by the lights in the front parking lot. It would be too risky to turn on any of the ground floor's interior lights. What the two scientists were looking for was much more likely to be found in the engineering spaces, in that specific part of the plant where the cola production took place. That is, if there actually was any production.

They moved silently through a heavy steel doorway, up a flight of stairs, and exited into a large light colored tile room in the building's tower. The room was well lighted and spacious, with a highly polished floor. There were tile covered cement columns, also highly polished, throughout the room supporting another, upper level. Inside this room was a smaller enclosure made of highly glossed white brick and glass. Within this structure the answers they were looking for would most likely be found. Their tennis shoes squeaked as they attempted to quietly approach the large enclosure. The place was absolutely spotless, if not sterile; an excellent environment for the production of a soft drink, or something even more significant. Dr. Henry tried to open the door but it was locked. He peered through the glass wall, holding his hand up over his eyes, hoping to obtain a more clearly defined view. What he saw were a number of chrome and copper pipes of varying diameters snaking into, out of, and around several large bright stainless steel containers.

"We have to get in there," he said to his associate.

"What is it?" she asked. "What do you see?"

"I'm not sure," he said, reaching into his black bag and retrieving a flat piece of metal that resembled a finger nail file. He inserted it into the space between the door and the frame, on the striking plate, right next to the lock. The heavy door opened quietly and Dr. Henry stepped through cautiously, motioning his associate to follow him. Once inside the room, he closed the door so they could speak more openly without fear of detection.

"This looks like where they make the syrup, or whatever it is they put in colas," Dr. Davis observed dryly.

"I hate to say it, but I think you might be right," he said, removing a large brushed aluminum disc off the topside of one of the kettles. He aimed his flashlight into the darkness of the vat and discovered a dark, thick-looking liquid, not unlike maple syrup or molasses. He started to stick his finger into the slowly swirling liquid.

"I don't think I would do that," interrupted Dr. Davis.

"Hell, it's just some Double-Cola concentrate," he laughed, ignoring her and tasting it anyway.

"Well?" she asked, pleased to see that he hadn't keeled over.

"It's concentrated Double-Cola, just as I suspected."

"Well, what do you think?" she asked.

"Son of a bitch!" he exclaimed angrily. "I don't know what to think. This place looks like what it purports to be, the Double-Cola factory. So far I haven't seen any evidence that would indicate anything to the contrary. Maybe those guys weren't robots. It was probably my imagination. But who knows? This building is so big it would take probably weeks of searching, and that's with unlimited access. Hell," he admitted, "I don't think there's anything at all here out of the ordinary."

"I don't either," Dr. Davis replied. "You probably shouldn't have hit that man on the head like you did. I hope he's okay."

"Yeah, me too, but he's going to be waking up any minute, and when he does he's going to wake up mad, and he's also going to call the cops. We better get out of here. This place may be a dead end, but the bottle came from here, or if not actually from here, it certainly is a Double-Cola bottle."

"Yeah," she agreed, "It was definitely bottled at this plant, so it came from here at some point. I mean, the bottle says Chattanooga. What's next?"

Their speculations were brought to an abrupt halt as large steel grates slid silently and rapidly down the outside surfaces of the enclosure on all sides, locking into place with a loud click, sealing the two scientists within the glass and brick structure, like lizards in a terrarium. Dr. Henry tried to open the door but it would not budge.

"It's too late now," he said. "I must have somehow triggered some security system or silent alarm."

"Or maybe you didn't 'neutralize' the janitor well enough," she said sarcastically.

"I guess we are stuck here until morning, or at least until somebody shows up."

"Yeah, this is really great. Let's see," Dr. Davis said angrily, counting on her fingers, "trespassing, assault, possibly aggravated assault, breaking and entering, damaging property, and espionage. This will really look great on my resume. Damn you Clarence! I'm pissed."

"What is that smell?" Dr. Henry interrupted, sniffing the air. "I smell something."

"I don't know, I smell it too. It smells like sulfur or...something. I don't know what it is, but it stinks. The perfect end to a truly wonderful evening."

"We might as well sit down here," Henry said, sliding down the thick glass wall and taking a seat on the floor, suddenly feeling very relaxed. "I guess I was more tired than I thought."

"Yeah, me too," she shrugged. "I feel very sleepy. I might as well take a little nap too. I mean we sure aren't going anywhere. You've seen to that. This is all your fault. And to think, I could have had a quiet, pleasant evening by myself. Damn you!"

The Steep Grade of the Incline
Lookout Mountain,
Chattanooga
Tenn.

19.

WAY ON DOWN

"I must be at sea," Dr. Henry reflected silently as his body rocked gently from side to side. "What a pleasant thought. I've always liked the sea."

"Look directly above you into the far reaches of what we call Crevice Gallery. A fault, or shifting in the rock caused this crevice ages ago."

"Shhh, listen. The captain's addressing the crew over the intercom," he reflected drowsily.

"Look directly above you into the far reaches of what we call Crevice Gallery. A fault, or shifting in the rock caused this crevice ages ago." The announcement repeated.

Possibly it was the cool air in the tunnel, a constant 58 degrees year round, or maybe it was the sound of the recorded message he'd heard as they passed directly beneath the famous Lookout Mountain attraction, Ruby Falls. Or perhaps it was the sense of motion which revived the scientist. In any case, he awakened to find himself strapped into some kind of small trolley or cart which was moving slowly, along two narrow tracks through a long, dark, and narrow tunnel, transporting him and, presumably his associate, to some unknown destination. As he regained consciousness he became fully aware of his circumstances, and consequently somewhat alarmed. His physical movement was severely inhibited by the presence of two bright steel restraining bars. He was also unable to move his head more than a few degrees in either direction, or to speak, due to a large mask which had been affixed to his face. The thought crossed his mind that the mask might be his source of oxygen so he made no attempt to remove it, not that he could have if he'd wanted to. A moan from behind him told him that Dr. Davis must also be on board.

The cart seemed first to ascend gradually. It then lurched, turned right and followed the track down a steep but gradual decline, before leveling off for a distance of probably half a mile, and then ascending slightly once again. Throughout this trip the dark tunnel was dimly illuminated with enclosed lights placed on either side of the roughly hewn walls at intervals every thirty feet or so. As the cart passed each series of lights, the passengers noticed strange signs and symbols etched into the walls.

In fifteen minutes, more or less, the car slowed and suddenly once again began a steep ascent, this time approaching two swinging doors that opened and then closed again as the car passed through and leveled off. When the vehicle had come to a complete stop, two large, expressionless attendants in crisp white cotton coats approached the scientists, one from each side of the cart. These two removed the passengers' masks and inserted a key of some sort into the side of the cart, unlocking the bars holding them in place. The steel restraints opened silently, releasing the car's occupants and permitting them to exit the vehicle.

"Step this way if you please," said a tall robed figure who, with a wave of his arm, directed the two new arrivals down a brightly illuminated passageway.

"Where are we?" Dr. Davis asked, still feeling groggy.

"It ain't Disney World," her associate replied, "but I'm glad to see that you are alright."

"Of course, you realize this is all your fault," she said curtly, addressing her associate.

"Welcome, my friends," the robed figure interrupted gently. "You are in no danger here. Just follow the two attendants to the end of the hall and turn right."

Obeying the robed one's instructions, the two scientists soon found themselves in a large conference room, standing at the foot of a solid rosewood table of immense proportions. There were four persons seated at either side of the table, another standing at its head, with another at his side.

"Be seated," the man at the head of the table ordered pleasantly.

The two reluctant guests took their seats, looked at each other, and awaited further instructions.

"You are here as our guests," Marduk stated graciously. "As you can see," he said with a flourish of his elegantly clad arm, "we have prepared a little welcoming reception of sorts, for your pleasure. Kosher corned beef, fresh nova and lox, bagels, peppered beef, pumpernickel, half cured kosher pickles, kippered Tennessee

River catfish and, of course," he paused, "Double-Cola, a particular favorite of our small group, and I suspect, of yours as well."

"First of all, who are you, and where are we?" Dr. Henry asked indignantly.

"Let it suffice for the moment to say that you are our guests," the one known as The Corsican replied graciously. "The duration and nature of your stay with us will depend upon a number of factors, not the least of which will be your attitude. With that in mind, why don't you meet the members of our distinguished aggregation, and partake of some light refreshments. After that, we will be happy to answer most of your questions. And then perhaps you will be kind enough to answer some of ours."

Dr. Davis and her associate eyed each other briefly, then glanced at their surroundings. The walls appeared to be tastefully covered in a pale lavender silk wallpaper, bordered at the top by a white crown molding. Down one wall there were seven large paintings of strangely attired older men, perhaps judges or college professors. There was no way to be certain. The paintings themselves certainly didn't resemble the portraits businessmen usually commissioned, although they were elegantly bordered in ornate gold leaf frames. Their hosts, or rather captors, were also a strange looking bunch, dressed as they were, each in some different kind of brightly colored robe. They looked theatrical, more than anything else.

There was no way to know how much time had passed, whether hours, minutes, or possibly even days. Neither had any memory of anything that had transpired after they'd been captured at the Double-Cola factory. It was also impossible to determine whether it was day or night. Presumably they were being held in some sort of underground compound, judging from the manner in which they'd arrived. Not knowing where they were would make it more difficult to escape, should that become necessary. As far as Dr. Henry could tell, looking around the room, there was only one way out, and that was through the large double doors through which they'd entered. There were most likely guards on the other side too, probably the same two hulks in the white coats who had released them from the contraption that brought them here.

"Look," Dr. Henry said, standing to address their captors, "This is not some sort of cocktail party. We've been gassed and kidnapped." He continued, "And under the circumstances, we can't just pretend that we're all real chummy, and buddy buddy. Now where are we? Why have you kidnapped us? And, more importantly, which way is out?"

The Titan suppressed the urge to remind Dr. Henry that he and his associate had been apprehended upon illegally entered property after striking and injuring an innocent citizen.

"Very well," The Titan replied, with irritation, glancing briefly at his associates, "We had hoped we would be able to establish a cordial relationship with you, our guests. But as you wish. Let's suspend the usual courtesies and get down to business. You were found to be in possession of a certain soft drink bottle. Where did you get it and what are you doing with it?"

Ahmedis interrupted before either of the two scientists had an opportunity to respond. "Before you answer The Titan's question, let me interject, for your edification, that we already know who you are, where you are from, and the nature of your professional occupations. Therefore permit me to suggest that you weigh your replies carefully. We have neither the time nor the patience for any inaccurate answers."

Dr. Davis looked around the room at the various strangely dressed figures and unusual faces seated at the large conference table, and prepared to answer their questions. She was ready to get out of there, and subsequently out of town. She hesitated and then glanced at her associate, as if seeking his approval. But Dr. Henry appeared to be very agitated at being held against his will.

"Don't tell these people anything." he cautioned her strongly. "They can't keep us. I'm getting the hell out of here right now. C'mon Debbie," he said, rising, "let's go."

He started toward the large double doors at the rear of the room, but stopped just short of them and turned to face his captors.

"If anybody tries to stop me, I mean anybody," he said looking at all of them intensely, "I'm gonna whip me some ass. Now if you want some shit, just come on."

As he reached to open the door, a bright burst of light flashed near his hand and Dr. Henry immediately fell to the floor unconscious. Before Dr. Davis could move to help her fallen comrade, the double doors swung open quietly and two giants in white coats lifted his limp body and carried him away to an undisclosed location.

"Now, Dr. Davis," Astaroth interjected, "perhaps we can return to the matter at hand."

Slowly she turned from the door to again face her captors, now certain that she had at the very least, entered the company of those who had created the lens and placed it in the bottom of the Double-Cola bottle. They might appear foolish in their brightly colored robes and with their phony sounding names, but there was no doubt, at least in her mind, that if she was going to get the information she wanted, she would have to play ball with them. In the meantime, the food placed on the table at the side of the room looked very appealing.

"Look," she said standing to address her hosts. "I don't know who you people are or what you want, but it appears that I'm at your mercy, at least for the moment. Let me say on behalf of myself and my partner, that, despite his rude behavior, we mean you no harm."

"That's refreshing," Marduk reflected, impressed by the young woman's attitude. "Be certain that we mean you no harm either, despite the circumstances attending your arrival at our installation. Now, I saw you looking at the refreshments we have prepared for you, so let's have a little something to eat," he said pleasantly. "I know you must be hungry."

For the next forty-five minutes Dr. Davis conducted herself as charmingly as possible, subtly flirting with the men, complimenting them when appropriate, on their splendid garments, tasteful selection of fabrics and colors, and other fashion matters in which they shared mutual interests. They expressed their approval of her attire, the bathrobe in particular, especially its elegant gold collar trim. After the delicious meal, they again seated themselves at the conference table. The atmosphere was this time, much more relaxed. They questioned her about the Double-Cola bottle and she explained how she and her associates had chanced accidentally to discover its incredible power and technological sophistication. Her purpose in coming to Chattanooga, she explained, was to seek the person or persons who had created this masterpiece in the hopes of increasing mankind's overall store of scientific knowledge. Whoever had created this marvel, she observed, obviously possessed knowledge of an order far beyond anything known in scientific circles at present. She failed however to mention that the lens had revealed the immediate and impending threat to Earth posed by Powerball, or SS396, as it was known in the scientific world.

She was, despite her openness, unable to ascertain who her hosts were, where she was being held, or what they were really up to.

While the members of the Council were understandably unprepared to release any vital information to this newcomer, they were certainly pleased to have a true scientist and fellow astronomer in their midst, especially such a pleasant and attractive one. Satisfied with her explanation, they decided, after a brief consultation, to invite her into their observatory.

They left the conference room, the Council members and their lovely guest, and strolled pleasantly through a large tropical garden, entered a short hallway, and then stepped onto a waiting elevator. The elevator was large, like a freight elevator, and heavily padded with thick green blankets, the kind furniture movers use. It was difficult to tell with certainty whether the elevator was going up or down after it began to move. In any event, when the door opened, she found herself inside some kind of highly sophisticated command center. There were lights flashing, banks of equipment all along the walls, and video monitors like those at NASA's Mission Control Center. The screens were, for the most part focused on various celestial locations.

As they walked past one bank of monitors, she noticed SS396 on one screen. She was familiar enough with its configuration to recognize it at once. The Corsican noted her attention to that particular screen and whispered something to Marduk.

"Are you familiar with that particular formation?" Marduk asked her.

"I've seen it once or twice before," she replied, attempting to sound unconcerned.

"Tell me then," the Council leader stated firmly, "What exactly do you know about it?"

"What's to know?" she replied casually, trying hard to seem disinterested. "It appeared totally spontaneously a short while ago, displayed erratic movement initially, and then began transforming its shape. It appears to have stabilized recently, but is considered to be one-dimensional, at least by the majority of my fellow astronomers and physicists. I would class it as inconsequential. Any movement, or even its existence, as far as that's concerned, is obviously apparent, not actual."

She may have wanted to seem casual, but her rapid divulgence of specialized knowledge about this obscure formation indicated to the trained ears of her hosts that Dr. Davis' interest in SS396 was much deeper than mere general knowledge or curiosity.

Marduk pinched his chin whiskers gently between his thumb and forefinger and then asked by way of comparison, "How would you compare SS396 to say, ZTNDX6, in the Zebulon Chantelle Nebula, Dr. Davis?"

"ZTNDX6 is stationary of course, despite its apparent motion. But then, it is three dimensional, although I'm certain you already know that." The question was an obvious set up, an attempt on the part of her hosts to catch her off guard for some reason, but her specialized knowledge of ZTNDX6, off the top of her head, indicated that her knowledge was extensive, so suspicions were put to rest.

"Who are you people?" she asked sincerely.

"How would you like to have a look through our telescope Dr. Davis?" Astaroth asked proudly, ignoring her question.

"Do you really think that wise, Astaroth?" Marduk interrupted.

"I believe it to be acceptable under the circumstances," Astaroth answered.

"In that case, I defer to your judgment," Marduk stated, bowing gracefully with a wide sweeping gesture of his robed right arm.

Astaroth and several other Council members directed their guest down a narrow passageway, this one also well beneath the earth's surface, judging from the absence of natural light. After walking several hundred feet, the party came upon a large cylinder about the size of the fuselage on a 12-passenger Lear Jet. As they approached, an eight foot section on one side of the tube opened, with the lower half dropping toward the floor and the top half opening upward toward the roof.

"After you," Astaroth said, extending his arm and bowing graciously. When everyone had been seated, an automatic prerecorded voice cautioned the passengers to fasten their seatbelts, and to withdraw their hands, arms, and legs into the craft in preparation for departure. The tube's sensors, indicating everything properly secured, issued a sequence of inaudible electronic signals with the result that the two halves of the tube closed, sealing them inside with a loud hiss. The tube then seemed to lift magically from its mooring and to hover in place briefly before moving forward. Dr. Davis cast a puzzled glance at The Titan who, assuming a fatherly tone, reassured her, saying "Compressed air, my dear, just like they use at the drive through window of the bank."

After traveling for about a minute and a half, the tube suddenly switched to an entirely vertical position and continued its ascent, straight up for another one or two minutes before again righting itself and docking at its destination, somewhere just beneath the earth's surface, at the highest point of Lookout Mountain.

"Amazing," Dr. Davis stated, genuinely thrilled to be there. Another brief walk interrupted by several electronic security checkpoints, and there they were, in what appeared to be the lounge of a modern recording studio. Passing through a large, heavy, wooden door, they found themselves within the studio's control room. There were a number of different machines, presumably recording machines of some sort, as well as a large knob-covered console, probably the mixing board. In front of the board was a large wall of glass, on the other side of which she could dimly see a piano, some drums, an organ, and a few microphones.

Her observations were interrupted by the sudden disappearance of the studio's rear wall. In its place appeared several rows of standard sized television monitors. To their right was a large screen television, of the type usually found at sports bars. Marduk, remote in hand, activated all of the screens at once. After surfing past MTV, CMT, ESPN, and the Gomer Pyle show, where he hesitated for a moment, Marduk stood and pressed his hand flat upon the screen of the third monitor from left on the second row down. Immediately the lights in the control room dimmed and the night sky came into focus with a clarity Dr. Davis had never seen in any observatory. "What do you think?" Astaroth asked.

"This must be a movie," Dr. Davis laughed, thrilled by what she saw on the largest monitor.

"This," said Marduk proudly, "is unquestionably the most sophisticated telescope on this planet. It is without equal. We are able to see any constellation from any direction, that is, from any vantage point. We can literally view anything out there, from any position."

"Good God," Dr. Davis exclaimed, "This is unbelievable. But where is your actual telescope? All I see are TV screens."

Marduk pushed a button on the hand held remote, and another wall opened, revealing the presence of a large telescope, over two stories tall.

"But that's a General Semantics Celestia-Sphere," she said with bewilderment. "It's probably a Mark I, which would mean that it was made sometime before the Second World War, I'd say prior to

1940, at the latest. Where did you get that dinosaur?" she asked without thinking.

"She knows her stuff," the Corsican laughed, looking at his associates.

"You're right," Marduk agreed, "but off just a bit. Actually it's a '41 Celestia-Sphere, and it's a Mark II, not a Mark I."

"But that's a Mark I eyepiece," Dr. Davis stated firmly. "At least that's what it looks like from here, and as far as I know, they weren't interchangeable."

"You amaze us," The Titan stated, beaming with approval. "That is indeed a Mark I eyepiece, and they are not interchangeable. We modified the refractor housing in our machine shop. Louie the Pencil....I mean Mazor.....that is, one of our former associates, altered the fittings to our specifications."

"Still," she observed, "No modification or upgrade, no matter how sophisticated, could ever render that antiquated relic functional on the level portrayed on these screens."

"You are both right and wrong," Astaroth observed, "but first things first. We acquired the Celestia-Sphere as government surplus after the war. It was rightly considered to be obsolete, and useless by the geniuses who operate what is now known as NASA. We bought it as scrap for $150. It was classified obsolete because they had no idea how to properly operate it. True enough, without audio, its uses are certainly limited. Siegfried Vonnumnutz designed this incredible instrument under contract for the US government in 1938, knowing that the government astronomers and scientists wouldn't be able to use it at full potential. It was truly designed for someone who would come later, someone who would know what to do and how to upgrade it. We have fulfilled that function."

"I see," Dr. Davis said reflectively. "But what do you mean by 'audio?'"

"My dear," The Titan replied, "I mean the, proverbial 'music of the spheres,' of course." With that, he activated the remote, and suddenly the room was filled with a music of such quiet and soothing depth that it could only be described as 'celestial.'

"Oh God," she swooned, moved to the depths of her soul, "What is this?"

The music was sort of a strange but very melodic humming, unlike anything she'd ever heard, or even imagined. It consisted of unfamiliar notes beyond the normal scale, balanced and blended harmoniously with the familiar sharps, flats, and minors she was used to. The overlapping melodies were beautiful and otherworldly, but absolutely indescribable. She was instantly transported emotionally to a dimension of pure joy, and also of absolute knowledge, and felt at once like laughing and crying.

Suddenly, Marduk retrieved the remote from The Titan and shut down the audio. "You aren't ready for this yet," he observed. "Perhaps in time," he said.

"Look," she interrupted, still reeling from the impact of the music. "I've seen enough. I want to work with all of you. I've devoted my whole life to science, and yet, what I thought I knew seems so primitive in light of what I have seen and heard today. I have to work with you. You must take me in and teach me what you know."

"But what about your partner?" Astaroth asked. "What would we do with him? And how would you explain your own absence? Our work here is top secret. You would not be able to leave this facility during your stay, nor would anyone be permitted to know your whereabouts."

"And no visitors of any kind would be allowed," Marduk added.

"Could you live with that?" the Titan asked.

"Gladly," Dr. Davis answered without hesitation. "I want to stay here."

"This is a surprise. Let us discuss the matter among ourselves and we will give you our decision tomorrow morning. In the meantime, please excuse the restrictions we've placed upon your movements. Also, if it is your sincere wish to join us for a while as an understudy, you must mention none of what you have seen or heard today to your associate. He will be joining you for dinner shortly. Hopefully his attitude will have improved."

"But what about the Double-Cola bottle?" she asked.

"It is in our possession. If you are permitted to work under our direction, its origin and purpose will become known to you at the proper time," Marduk replied. "In the meantime, I would suggest that you dissuade your associate from making any further escape attempts. This entire compound is protected by a highly sophisticated, and very dangerous security system. We are unable to assume responsibility for any injuries incurred by anyone seeking to override or disarm it. Good night Dr. Davis. We shall see you in the morning."

"Thank you for a most incredible day," she said warmly pressing the hands of each of the scientists firmly within her own. "You must let me stay."

"We shall see, my dear. Goodnight," Ahmedis said, as Dr. Davis was escorted to her quarters by the two orderlies.

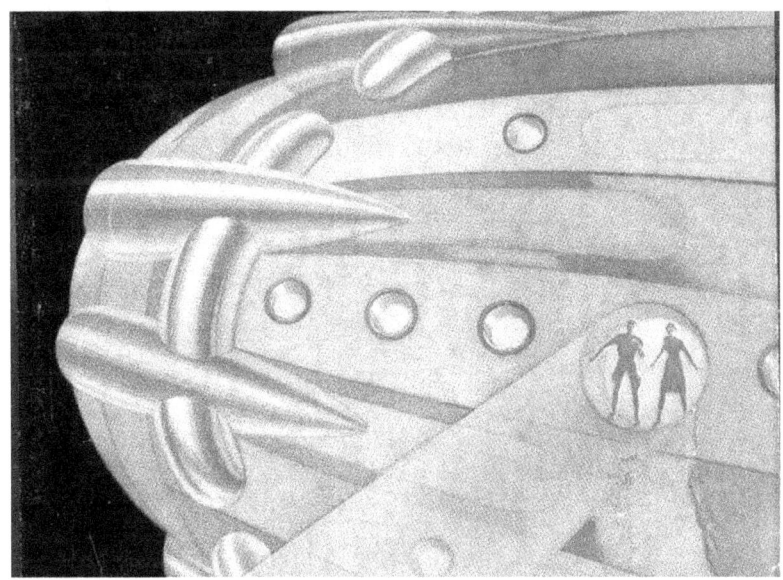

The Aural Particle Accelerator

20.

SAY WHAT?

The Secret Chiefs did not summon Dr. Davis the next morning as promised, but instead sent word that she would be contacted soon, and brought before the Council. Her request, she was told, was still under consideration. The term 'soon' was a bit more nebulous than she would have liked, and the delay was disappointing. On the other hand, remaining here was something she really wanted to do, and she was anxious to make as good an impression as possible. With this resolved, at least to her satisfaction, she decided to settle into her quarters and make the most of it. They would notify her soon enough.

Her quarters were not so bad. Actually, the accommodations were quite excellent. She was being housed in something similar to a hotel suite, one which adjoined her colleague's. There was a large ornate French bed with brass trim, and the sitting room furniture was also gilded French, covered in blue Scalamandre. There was an absolute state of the art entertainment center equipped with cable TV, international radio, a CD player, and a large selection of various types of music. The food was especially excellent, at least so far. Whenever she became hungry she had but to activate the menu channel on her TV monitor and the selections for the day appeared instantly on the screen. A push on her remote enabled her to scroll to whatever type of food she wanted. Under Italian, for example, she could select from Northern or Southern. Under Mexican, she could select from traditional, or Tex-Mex. There were also pastry, dessert, and bread menus. There was even a help feature within each selection, in the event that she was unfamiliar with a particular menu item. She'd never seen anything like this and had the feeling that she could really get used to this type of living. Everything was served on the finest English bone china with heavy sterling accessories. It was truly incredible.

There were a few downsides to her situation, however, which she imagined would be rectified as soon as the Council decided to let her join them. In the first place, she had only seen artificial light except once during her brief stay. She needed real light, sunlight. The other problem was that she didn't know what time it was. There were clocks placed throughout the facilities, and she imagined that they were accurate, but her body didn't have any sense of the passage of time. It was not really a problem, it just threw her off balance. All in all, she was thrilled with this unique opportunity fate had placed in her path. All because Dr. Henry had knocked a soda bottle off his desk. But beneath the exuberance of scientific advancement was the very sobering reality that the safety and preservation of civilization worldwide depended on what she learned. There was no time for delay of any kind. She had to discover the secret behind the Double-Cola bottle and it must be now. The dilemma was very real. How could she ask the necessary but pointed questions required without at the same time arousing their suspicions?

Dr. Henry, on the other hand, was not so easily satisfied, at least not at first, and Dr. Davis was involuntarily subjected to his wild ramblings.

"I'm going to kick those bastards' asses, all of them," he said. "What a bunch of disgusting sissies. Oh yeah, they're real tough. It takes a lot of guts to shock some poor bastard."

"I don't think that's the answer to our predicament," Dr. Davis volunteered calmly. It was obvious to her that the fragile male ego of her associate had been injured. "In the first place, we don't know where we are. Secondly," she continued, "we don't know how to get out, or even which way 'out' actually is."

"Well," Dr. Henry observed angrily, "We got in, ergo, we can get out."

"We're being held, at least for the moment and, considering the powers possessed by our captors, I think the best thing is to just wait and see what they have to say. Let's find out what they want. Obviously they want to know more about our reasons for being at the Double-Cola plant."

"You didn't tell them anything, did you?" he asked quickly, appearing suspicious of her conciliatory manner.

"Yes I did" she said, "but no more than necessary. They asked me about the bottle, and I told them how we found it, and that we wanted to find whoever made it so we could learn from that person or persons. No big deal."

"I can't believe you told them that." Dr. Henry said angrily. "Why would you tell them anything at all?"

"Look, Clarence," she said. "They're not stupid. They know who we are. We had the bottle with the lens in our possession when they got us. Last but not least, we had broken into the Double-Cola plant, and we were apprehended snooping around. I didn't feel like I had any choice."

"What?" he asked sarcastically. "Did they torture you into spilling your guts?"

"I really don't know what's gotten into you Clarence, I mean it. They were all very nice, as you would have found out, had you chosen to stick around instead of trying to pull all that G.I. Joe crap."

He sat sullenly, now beginning to suspect that perhaps he had indeed acted too hastily.

"And did it ever occur to you that these people might just possibly have the answers we're looking for, or that they might be willing to work with us, or help us out?"

Dr. Henry sat silently for a moment immersed in his own thoughts. "Well," he said finally, "did you learn anything about them, or where we are? And when they are going to let us out of here?"

"I didn't find out anything about them at all, other than that they are scientists of some sort, supposedly working on a number of top secret government projects. But they didn't state specifically what any of their work dealt with."

"Well then, where are we?" he asked.

"I don't know any more about that than you do," she said casually.

"You don't seem too overly concerned for someone who is being held as a prisoner."

"The way I see it is this," Dr. Davis speculated. "We accidentally stumbled into the middle of some top secret government project. That lens had probably been intentionally placed inside the Double-Cola bottle so that its presence would be inconspicuous. A maid or janitor, or somebody accidentally put the bottle in the recycling bin, understandably thinking it was an empty. Eventually it found its way back to the Double-Cola plant, was refilled along with other returnable empties, sent to a store somewhere, and purchased unknowingly by some average customer."

"Well how do you account for their strange dress, and those stupid names?" Dr. Henry asked. "That definitely ain't regulation G.I gear. I was in R.O.T.C. at Vanderbilt, and I know those costumes definitely ain't Government Issue."

"Don't interrupt," Dr. Davis said. "I'm not finished yet. Now," she continued, "that bottle was probably one of a kind, and whoever lost it was most likely in serious trouble as a result of their carelessness. It's probably worth millions of dollars. I imagine that a covert search was launched nationally. The government, that is, the president and military cabinet, probably don't even know the lens exists, let alone that it was missing. Whether they do or not has no bearing on my theory, however."

"What do you mean, Debbie?"

"I mean that whoever these people are, they couldn't put a billboard on the side of the interstate saying 'ten million dollar reward for unusual Double-Cola bottle.' Instead, the only thing they could do under the circumstances, was to enlist the help of the Double-Cola personnel in finding the bottle. Even this would have to be done very discreetly."

"Wait a minute," Dr. Henry interrupted. "You mean you think the Double-Cola plant isn't some kind of front for something else?"

"That's precisely what I mean. The president of the company was probably apprised of the situation in a much diluted manner and told to be on the lookout for the bottle we found. It's just lucky somebody didn't throw it off a bridge or dump it in the trash. It might never have been found."

"Well," he said," I imagine that whoever made it could make another one easily enough."

"Obviously not," she ventured. "It might be like replacing the sphinx or the Empire State Building, possible....but not necessarily practical.

"Well," Dr. Henry concluded, "I don't know what to think. Maybe they can help us after all."

"Promise me," Debbie said, "that you won't say or do anything further to irritate these people. One of them told me to make certain that you fully understood the dangers as well as the futility of attempting to escape. Any moves in that direction could cost you your life. I think we should resign ourselves to the likely prospect of being here for a few days, and see what we can find out."

Dr. Henry reluctantly agreed that the best thing to do was just wait and see what happened. He returned to his quarters and spent the remainder of the day happily watching ESPN, MTV, playing chess with the TV, drinking Double-Cola chocolate floats, and snacking on fresh strawberries dipped in hot fudge sauce.

ELSEWHERE

The ten Secret Chiefs sat down to an informal working lunch at the psychochemical lab. "Let's get down to business and wrap this up. I've got work to do," Marduk stated assertively. "Our visitor, Dr. Davis," he continued, "has asked to join us for a while and assist with our work. As usual, we shall vote on the matter, but first is there any discussion?"

The room was silent for a moment, except for the sounds of the various Council members cracking the lobster shells on their plates. "I think we ought to take her in," the Titan stated flatly.

"Yeah, I say she stays," mighty Astaroth ventured.

"Count me in," agreed Ahmedis.

"Same for me, only make it double," Alexander interjected brazenly, following his observation with a lewd, tongue-flicking gesture. "Ahdahdahdahd."

Everybody laughed except Marduk. "While it would certainly spruce the place up to have an attractive female scientist hanging around, I can't help but worry that her presence might interfere with our work. We have too much to do. 'Our project' will be striking Earth very soon. I'm not certain that we have time to fool with her at all under the circumstances. And again, what would be the point? It's doubtful she will survive `IT.' Cybrion," he ordered, turning toward one of the intergalactic transportation coordinators, "report to us as to the status of our departure arrangements."

"Just a moment," celestial Cybrion said, wiping the melted butter from his face with the bright orange sleeve of his exquisite tunic, much to the amusement of his colleagues. "Alright," he continued, "everything is in order. Our craft is being fitted even as we speak by the Skipjack Yard in Jennings, Louisiana. As you know, I was down there last week, and am happy to report that all is in order, on schedule and, at least for the moment, well under our initial budget estimates."

"That's really of top priority," Marduk said sarcastically, referring to the fact that the craft was not going to cost as much as initially expected. It didn't matter to any of them what the thing cost.

Where they were going, money, at least in the Earthly sense, was totally meaningless.

Cybrion ignored the caustic remark from their leader and continued his report. The craft will be delivered via the Tennessee River at the end of the month, as scheduled, and will then be assembled with our modifications at the Nimbus Foundry here in Chattanooga. This final fitting is expected to take an additional three weeks."

"And launching preparations?" Marduk asked.

"We are using the tracks of the Incline up the side of Lookout Mountain as a launching site," Cybrion reported. "The bottom of our vessel has been equipped at the Skipjack Yard with rotanium locks and fittings that will enable us to launch easily from that location."

"Wait a minute," Marduk interrupted. "Why the Incline?"

"The Lookout Mountain Incline, one of Chattanooga's most famous attractions, has 5,100 feet of track at a 72.7 degree angle. It's the prefect launch site. Actually, it's the only acceptable launch site in the area for a craft the size of ours."

"Engineering?" asked Marduk dryly.

"The solid fuel rockets will be installed at Nimbus by our own technicians, Your Excellence, right here in Chattanooga," replied the handsome Galactoso, the Council's chief engineer, and Marduk's Mexican-American cousin from another life.

"I've arranged with the president of Nimbus, for all of its regular employees to receive a three week paid vacation, beginning on December 10. This will allow us the time we need to add the sub-nuclear exponential injectors."

"It sounds like everybody's on the ball around here. We appreciate your work, but I still need to know how you intend to move an object the size of our ship, from the river to the Lookout Mountain Incline and prepare it for launch without arousing the suspicions of the police, the public, and the press, not that we are unable to deal with any interference. I simply like things to function smoothly, like a well-oiled machine."

"Easily enough," replied mighty Atlas. "I have arranged for the annual Christmas parade to take place a week later than usual, on December 21st. Our festively decorated craft has been entitled 'Santa's Helpers,' and will serve as a float for the Chamber's booster club. Nobody will suspect anything at all. When the parade turns off of Broad in front of McDonald's and heads toward St. Elmo, for that

182

loop of the procession, it will experience mechanical difficulties directly at the base of the Incline. Since ours will be the last float in the parade, nobody will think much of it one way or the other. St. Elmo is the last leg of the parade anyway. The kids dressed as Santa's helpers, will be transferred to another conveyance, chains will be attached as planned to the rotanium locks, and the vessel will be winched into launch position.

"Of course, we'll already be on board. At 1630 hours, on December 21, our group will be transported through the underground tunnel to the Double-Cola plant. There we will board a tour bus and proceed directly to the parade site and take our positions within the Craft, which will already be in the parade lineup."

Cybrion interrupted, "Off duty metro police officers will secure the area at a considerable distance from the launch site in order to assure the safety of the general populace. Not that it particularly matters."

"Very well, it seems like everything is in order. Thanks for your reports. Let's return to the business at hand, with Dr. Davis. Is there any additional discussion?"

"I am not opposed to the temporary admission of Dr. Davis into our order as an associate probationer," observed Alexander the Quiet, "just as long as nobody gets too attached to her. Our bylaws prohibit us from accepting anyone into the Council as a full member who hasn't come to us solely as a result of pure chance."

"I don't think any of us are thinking of our association with Dr. Davis as anything other than temporary, especially in light of our impending departure." Marduk replied. "Besides," he said, "we have Chip Hamster and his hitch-hiker friend, Marvin Hocker. But we can talk about them later. I merely remind this august body that our two new candidates are already on board, so to speak."

"Well, I don't see any point in taking her into our confidence if she is going to be left behind when we depart this planet for our future base of operations," Ahmedis stated frankly.

"That," replied Astaroth, "is precisely the very reason we should give her as much instruction as possible before we leave. When Earth is forced outside its orbit through the intrusion of 'our little surprise,' those remaining on this planet will need someone possessed of the knowledge to address the planet's new circumstances. Those so-called scientists, astronomers, and world leaders running things now will not be able to provide guidance for those surviving the initial impact. As usual, they will be useless."

"This well may be, my friends," interjected The Corsican, "but I believe, as they say, that 'cream rises to the top'. I imagine that an appropriate world leader will emerge at the proper time."

"No. Look at the scientific community now. We monitor their activities daily. Those imbeciles are too self-important, and ego-centered to even speak with each other about the blatant and obvious movements of 'you know what.' Each is afraid that another scientist knows more than he does, so his pride forbids him to speak. Their very doom is upon them," Astaroth continued, "yet they refuse to even address the matter. Though they don't know what 'our very special present' is, they pretend among each other that they know exactly what it is, but that it doesn't exist. If it doesn't exist, they reason, it is of no consequence. They are idiots, all of them."

"You might be right, noble Astaroth," suggested The Corsican, "but what does it matter to us? Our Council has held this planet together as much as possible for as long as possible. While it was a laudable undertaking initially, and a gracious gesture on the part of our ancient predecessors, these Earthlings are of a decidedly lower order than the original Council had imagined. They are not likely to change. I think it best that we move on and leave them to stew in their own juices, if you catch my drift."

"But what about their art? Their music?" asked Ahmedis. "And their beer?" he asked as an afterthought.

"That has all been sampled and transmitted already," replied The Corsican casually. "We've got everything from the King," he said, crossing himself reverently, "to Bach, to Hendrix, to those 'fabulous Louie boys,' the Kingsmen. Let's face it, their musical decline began with the Bee Gees, and has gone downhill from there, with Nirvana, Counting Crows, the so-called Dave Matthews Band, and, above all, Rap, representing the absolute worst crap ever to assault the human, or any other ear."

"But what about the Harley Davidson? The Hammond B-3 organ? The 1959 Eldorado?" Ahmedis asked, appearing to be extremely concerned at the possible loss for all time of these world icons.

"Nothing worthwhile has been left behind," Marduk replied reassuringly. "Everything from the original Falstaff Beer to Tennessee Williams has been stored on rotanium ledgers. If you want a 1959 Cadillac, Ahmedis, or a Quarter Pounder with Cheese, or a Goo Cluster, it's all available instantly."

"Hey, cut that shit out!" Alexander the Quiet shouted uncharacteristically at The Corsican, who had dropped to one knee and again crossed himself reverently at the sacred mention of the very holy name of the true patron saint of all literature, Tennessee Williams.

"Tennessee Williams rules!" replied The Corsican defiantly.

"Boys, boys, boys, simmer down," continued Marduk. "Listen, we all voted to create a celestial disturbance that would send Earth into another dimension. Isn't that the very purpose of 'the project?' Well then, let's quit the whining and moaning and get on about our business. It will be here soon enough."

"But millions of people are going to be killed outright," Ahmedis observed.

"You knew that when we voted on the matter initially. We've discussed this for years. It's not like something we just came up with on a lark. Yes, some people will be killed, but that's not the concern of the Council. They're all wicked," The Corsican continued, "there isn't one great man among them, not one."

"If there were even one," interjected Marduk, "there might yet be some hope. I would personally be willing to spare the Earth if there were truly one great human somewhere. This however is very unlikely, and in light of the pressing concerns of the moment, extremely doubtful. Besides, who cares?"

"You're right Your Excellence," the Corsican continued. "The great ones are all dead now. Look what refuse remains? The various gene pools have become so diluted that in most of the world, the general populace is scarcely more advanced than animals. Let them all fry. They are animals, evil, low-life animals."

"As is my right as a member of the Council," replied Ahmedis, standing, "I call upon the very words of Marduk, the Supreme Leader. I accept his judgment in the matter, as do we all. I also call upon his statement that..."

"Oh no you don't, you leftist goody goody..." the Corsican interrupted, sensing the direction of Ahmedis' pronouncement, and pounding his fist on the table.

But Ahmedis was not to be deterred from his intentions by any interruption. The Supreme Council Leader had stated, from his own mouth, in the presence of the full Council membership, that he would be willing to spare Earth for the presence of 'truly one great human.' "I call upon the very words of Marduk," Ahmedis continued. "If one truly great man can be found, the Earth shall be spared."

"I was merely stating," Marduk replied, "that..."

"I call upon your words, Marduk," continued Ahmedis.

"We shall not spare this planet. It has been decided and ordered by an authority higher than ours. If one truly great human can be found, that is if one exists, he, or she, will come forward in the aftermath of his own accord. But it will have nothing to do with us either way, and be advised, none of you are obliged to engage in any search for any such person. In fact, your duties in preparation for our departure must continue, and shall take absolute precedence over any other considerations. If you wish to waste your slight remaining time here searching for a unicorn, or a leprechaun, or a truly great man, Ahmedis, that is your right. Now, we've wasted enough time. Let us vote on the admission of Dr. Davis without any further delay."

A vote was held, and there were eight in favor, with Marduk abstaining, and Bustokus voting against. The measure was passed and the new candidate was summoned.

21.

WELCOME ABOARD

Ahemedis, The Corsican, Alexander the Quiet, Atlas, Cybrion, Galactoso, the Titan, Bustokus, and Marduk, sat around the large conference table, comprising what was to be the official welcoming committee for Dr. Davis.

"Before we bring her in," Marduk began, "I think it wise to once again review the extent of her access to our inner workings. First and foremost, she is not at this time permitted to know anything further than she might have already gleaned with regard to 'SS396,' as the Earthlings call it. Under no circumstances is she to know anything about its impending arrival, or of our departure plans. If we decide to tell her of our intentions, it can be done later, but only after a full vote. Are we agreed on this matter?" Marduk looked around the room as all heads nodded in assent.

"Very well," he continued, "let's bring her in."

"Welcome," Ahmedis said, addressing the young woman. "All rise. We are prepared to render our decision. After much consultation and deliberation, Dr. Davis, we've reached the decision to accept you into our ranks, with certain stipulations. Welcome aboard," he said with a smile, shedding his serious demeanor.

Dr. Davis relaxed visibly at this pronouncement. She had expected to be allowed to study with these members of the elect, but there was always the possibility that they could have decided otherwise.

"Now, here are the conditions under which you will be permitted to remain with us," Marduk stated gravely. "You will listen to each rule as it is read. If there are any questions, or if there is something you don't understand, you should clarify that particular point before we proceed to the next one. Is that agreed and understood?"

"Yes," she replied nervously, looking around the room at the strangely attired men who surrounded her.

"At the conclusion of the rules, you will be required to take an oath. When you have completed this oath you will be given a guided tour of our entire facility and introduced to some additional support personnel. "Proceed mighty Atlas," Marduk instructed.

"What you see and what you hear, when you leave, leave it here. In other words, everything you may learn about this installation, this group, our operations and activities, is absolutely confidential. It is to be discussed with no one outside this room, with the exception of the missing members who are, at present, on other assignments. Everything we do and everything we are is strictly confidential. You may not discuss our work, our findings, or even your own findings with anyone other than the members of this Council. This means any support personnel, or anyone else who is not a Council member or member candidate. Any violation will result in your immediate expulsion from this facility.

Atlas resumed. "You are to be here for an indefinite and unspecified time. You may depart whenever you wish, but should you decide to do so, you will not permitted re-entry. Additionally, when you do leave us, for whatever reason, the above still remains in full force. You must agree to never mention anything you have witnessed here.

"You are here at our pleasure, as an understudy. You may be asked to leave with or without cause, notice, or explanation, at any time. Should circumstances arise where this is required, you are to leave quietly, without protest, questions, or delay.

"You are not to fraternize with any of the hospital patients, staff members, or attendants. That's basically it. There will be some questions that will undoubtedly arise which we will be unprepared to answer. In such cases you will be informed that the subject in question, or some particular aspect of it is off limits, and that reply must be sufficient. That means the subject is closed."

"Now," Marduk said, "having established our rules of conduct, we shall tell you a bit about our installation, who we are, and what we do. Again, this is strictly classified information, and shall never here, or hereafter be discussed with anyone outside this facility. Perhaps the best way to approach this would be for you to ask whatever questions you might have. If something you ask is too sensitive we'll tell you so. Begin."

"Well," Dr. Davis, said, looking around the room. "There are many things I don't understand, but before asking anything, I first want to thank all of you for taking me into your confidence. I pledge to you here and now that your trust has been well placed. I appreciate the opportunity to learn from you, and will never divulge anything I may see or hear while under your guidance, without your permission. Thank you again."

The Secret Chiefs of the Council looked at her and then at each other. They were pleased with her attitude, and even in light of their impending departure, suspected that the time Dr. Davis might require, would most likely be time well spent. They nodded their approval as Marduk took a slow sweeping bow, and urged her to ask whatever questions she might.

"First of all," she asked with a quizzical expression on her face, "where am I?"

"This is a reasonable enough question," handsome Galactoso replied. "At present you are in our compound, which is located at the Wildman Sanitarium, situated at a bend of the Tennessee River, on the very outskirts of Chattanooga."

"Are you?" and she hesitated, looking for the right word. "I mean," she resumed falteringly, "Are you...?"

"Inmates?" Marduk asked, providing the missing word. All of the men either smiled, or chuckled outright at this question, a response which did little to put her mind at ease, especially in light of their strange, brightly colored costumes and peculiar names.

"Yes," mighty Atlas replied. "We are 'inmates' of this institution," he smiled, "but not in the traditional sense. "We're free to come and go as we please, in or out of this facility, and do so at will, worldwide."

Marduk added by way of clarification, "The Wildman Sanitarium provides an excellent cover for our activities. While it is at the moment unpopular to use the term 'insane,' everyone in the general public realizes that there are people who are insane, crazy, not all there, stupid, or whatever terms they may use in private. So this is technically a psychiatric hospital. We, on the other hand do not mind being called crazy, weird, peculiar, or anything else. Crazy people are usually left alone. People who are left alone, are generally free to pursue their endeavors and to accomplish their objectives without interference."

"In other words," the Titan interrupted, "don't be put off by our unusual and individual fashion statements. We dress this way because we can."

"More importantly," Marduk interjected, "our robes distinguish us from the general inmate population. Since there is a high turnover of staff at the hospital, our robes serve as a visual 'hands off.' We have absolute freedom to move anywhere, on or off the premises, without the need for explanation or permission."

"You are obviously possessed of incredible, if not actually superhuman knowledge," Dr. Davis continued, "so why Chattanooga? Why not Zurich or London, Vienna, or somewhere notable, like that? Or even Atlanta? It's more centrally located than Chattanooga."

"In the first place," Marduk replied, "that would be too obvious. Our work would have been discovered immediately. There are far too many spies, both military and industrial, snooping around such cities. In addition, there are unusually large population bases and attendant security problems. The weather also leaves much to be desired in all of the places you've mentioned. Over and above these important practical considerations, however, we are here primarily because Chattanooga is the geographical center of this galaxy. That might seem a difficult point to accept, but it is a cold statement of fact. Others have suspected as much, not the least of whom was the late C.G. Jung, but they have lacked the means to confirm their suspicions. Jung mistakenly thought that Chattanooga was the geographical center of the universe. Actually it is the center of the galaxy, not the universe. He was here snooping around after the war, but went home disappointed. He was not permitted to locate us, and was not granted an audience.

"And Atlanta? Hardly. What morons decided to locate the Center for Disease Control in such a highly populated and centrally located area? The accidental release of even one of the deadly bacterial and viral agents being created and synthesized there is a certainty, not a question of if, but when. The CDC should be located underground in some remote part of the northwest. The arrogance and stupidity of humans is one reason…never mind."

This information was truly astounding to Dr. Davis. What was even more amazing was that while they would permit her to join them, they would refuse to allow someone as important as Carl Jung to even speak with them. Perhaps he was too high profile as a result of his international renown. As far as Chattanooga being the center of the galaxy, that was hard to swallow, and of no consequence, even if it were true. And Carl Jung being in Chattanooga? Since he had died in 1961, there was no chance of asking him. These people were decidedly eccentric. But first and foremost, Dr. Davis was a scientist, and she had definitely stumbled onto something remarkable here. She was only too willing to overlook their quirks. There was still the business of saving the planet to attend to. She would hold off asking any questions about that just yet, but surely they must know more than they had indicated about SS396.

"Well, in any case," she said again, "I'm honored that you would grant me this opportunity. Now," she continued, "tell me, if you would, a bit more about your facility. How did you manage to transport and install something the size of the Celestia-Sphere?"

"The Celestia-Sphere, as I mentioned, was purchased by us as government salvage," Marduk, replied. "What is now the Wildman Sanitarium, was originally the site of a top secret government project, code named Operation Lookout. This was prior to the development of the atomic bomb. When the atomic bomb project was completed, ahead of Operation Lookout, the latter became redundant. It was kept in operation until shortly after the war, at which time it was sold to a group of physicians and converted to its present use. The caves and tunnels, as well as the telescope were purchased by our group under a silent arrangement with the defense department. Technically, at least as far as the United States government is concerned, this place doesn't exist. It never did. The only thing which actually existed was the development site for Operation Lookout, which was switched over to a private psychiatric facility, at the close of the war."

"Well, where did all of your highly sophisticated equipment come from?" she asked, amazed by what she'd already learned.

"Again," Marduk continued, "courtesy of the government. Since this was a top secret project, none of our equipment ever existed, at least not officially. What does not exist need not be accounted for. It was also considered to be so much scrap metal. Those in charge of the project were far closer to a major discovery than they ever imagined, something so far beyond mere atomic energy as to make any comparison impossible. The equipment and instruments which they abandoned served as the basis for what we have since developed. They were already working on an aural theory of particle acceleration. They just didn't know what to call it. We have since expanded upon their initial efforts and mastered the technique which they could then only dimly envision. A universe controlled by sound."

"That would explain the strange noises emitted from the Double-Cola bottle at our lab when it accidentally fell under the light from the telescope," Dr. Davis surmised.

"Precisely," observed Ahmedis. "The sounds you heard were, no doubt, very discordant, and actually quite dangerous. You are lucky your observatory was not destroyed completely, and all of you killed. The lens must align with the light particles at a precise angle and from a specific distance. The bottle must be in place before the light is introduced. When this procedure is properly executed the discord disappears and you hear instead, the 'music of the spheres,' which you briefly enjoyed the day before yesterday."

"That is precisely why you were brought here," Marduk stated calmly. "That bottle, in the hands of the wrong person, could destroy Earth in a number of different ways. I am not even necessarily referring to evil intentions, I mean accidentally."

"Well, how did such a thing as that ever end up floating around the country?" Dr. Davis asked in amazement. It was a valid question, even though the answer was a source of great embarrassment to all of the Council members.

"This was indeed a black mark on an otherwise spotless record, the result of carelessness and an intentionally misdirected sense of humor on the part of one of our former associates. Louie the Pencil, that is, the Council member formerly known as Mazor, basically went crazy and left this compound without permission. He took a job, unknown to us, at the Double-Cola bottling works on Broad Street. I believe you are familiar with that facility," he smiled. "Anyway, he'd been in charge of the development of that particular device, and had taken the knowledge of its construction with him. The only explanation as to why he placed the lens in the bottom of a Double-Cola bottle is that he was able to do so. He did it because he could. We think it must have been some kind of challenge to him. There were several dozen of them floating around the United States, and possibly in Europe and the Middle East as well. He refused to tell us how many he actually produced, so another may turn up at any moment. Fortunately, the technology involved in the construction of the lens, and the high degree of sophistication required to actually use it, make it extremely unlikely that its secret will ever be discovered, at least not in the next two hundred years. Indeed, even your discovery was an accident, was it not? And yet, the possibility for catastrophe exists as long as even one of those bottles is floating about anywhere in the world."

She nodded her head in assent.

"What is to become of my colleague, Dr. Henry?" she asked, suddenly changing the subject.

The Council members looked at each other sheepishly, and appeared to hesitate before Marduk undertook to answer her question. "Dr. Henry is, at this very moment," he said, pausing to look at his watch, "sleeping soundly in his room at the Read House Hotel. He will awaken in approximately two hours, most likely with a rather pounding headache, several empty champagne bottles scattered on the floor, a reasonably attractive naked woman beside him, and many unanswered questions. You'll need to call him later today, tell him that you are alright, and that you have decided to take a leave of absence to visit relatives in Florida, or elsewhere."

"If there are no further questions..."

"Wait," Dr. Davis interrupted, "What exactly is it that you do here, and what will my duties be?"

The Council members looked at each other, as if trying to decide which of them should respond. The one known as the Corsican rose to address the matter.

"Our basic work," he said "consists primarily of research directed study in a number of scientific disciplines, with astronomy, physics, metaphysics, and music being of primary concern. Under these various headings there are specific projects we're involved with on an ongoing basis. You will most likely work for a while in each of these fields in order to gain a general overall knowledge and perspective, which will subsequently enable you to specialize in one particular area."

"Excuse me, learned Corsican," Marduk interrupted, "but I think it necessary to mention our operational procedures. We are able to come and go as we please here, and do what we want. You personally, may go anywhere within this facility you like as well. Nothing is off limits to you anywhere within the hospital or on the grounds. The same does not apply, however, to the hospital staff, other than to specially designated service personnel. Nobody from over there is allowed over here. Ever."

It had been an interesting and full day for Dr. Davis. At its end, however, there still remained many unanswered questions, some of an urgent nature. For example, who was that handsome, well-tanned young man she'd briefly glanced through the window in the

Council's music room?

Davis had been renamed 'Deb-O-Ra' by her hosts, who felt that the Ra, being of Egyptian origin, possessed some especial significance. Who was she to argue? Nor did she protest when she was handed her new attire, a brightly checked robe which was more than vaguely reminiscent of a table cloth at an Italian restaurant. She had also been taken around the rest of the installation, observed some of the patients, and been introduced to the staff, including Dr. Langley, whose words were somewhat unsettling.

"These people," he had told her privately, after being certain that she was not being held against her will, "are insane in the clinical sense. I believe them to be harmless enough, just extremely delusional. They are rich, so, quite frankly, we permit them to do as they please. They like to pretend that they control the universe, so we allow them to have their little meetings, play spacemen, and, for the most part, do whatever else they want to do. They also have some obsolete and non-functional radios, transmitters, and generators left over from the war. They turn them on, the instruments light up, and they pretend they are doing scientific research. It's all harmless enough, and we, in deference to their financial status leave them alone. You have been presented to me as an understudy, but rest assured, unless you are writing a book on freaks or doing research at college for some paper on the highly delusional, you won't be learning much here."

She hadn't known how to respond, or even what to think about Dr. Langley's observations. There were obviously two different realities existing here. The Council members were rich, and they were registered inmates, that much was agreed upon by both sides. Here, however, is where opinions split. Dr. Langley maintained that the Council members were merely eccentric, but well-to-do patients whose antics and charades were tolerated due to their financial status. The Council members, on the other hand regarded Dr. Langley as an imbecile, whose sole purpose was to operate the hospital as an acceptable cover for their scientific work, whatever that might really be. Both sides of the issue were most likely valid to some degree. What Dr. Davis knew for certain was that the inmates, whoever they might actually be, were extremely advanced Technologically. In the meantime, the planet was in very obvious and immediate peril. Surely the scientists had to be aware of the danger. For the moment, she needed to be calm and learn the ropes.

22.

LET MY PEOPLE GO

Dr. Davis had only been at the compound for four days, but had already adapted extremely well. Perhaps the fact that she was attractive and brilliant, and also female, had something to do with her rapid and open acceptance. Already, she had become aware of very sophisticated research in a number of scientific fields. First and foremost, their research dealt with what they called the 'Aural Theory of Particle Acceleration.' The central hypothesis of their theory being that, by accelerating sound waves through the use of various instruments, it becomes possible to reach an altogether different musical spectrum, or dimension. Within that dimension, it is possible to alter the structure of mass, and even to create energy and matter. The basic scientific paradigm, since the seventeenth century has always been that 'matter or energy can neither be created nor destroyed,' merely transformed. The inmates of the so-called psychiatric hospital had advanced physics to the degree that the theory of energy transformation, the very backbone of all physical sciences, was as obsolete as the flat earth theory.

"It's true enough Deb-O-Ra," Bustokus told her. "As you know, under what we call 'normal circumstances,' matter and energy can neither be created nor destroyed. In the case of matter, for example, H_2O becomes ice, steam, or water, depending on external conditions. If, on the other hand, the basic elements of hydrogen and oxygen are accelerated through the use of sound, then they cease to be hydrogen and oxygen, per se, and may be manipulated 'genetically,' for lack of a better word.

"It's not that complex," he continued. "If you hear a song on the radio, for example, you are hearing it in stereo, that is, through two speakers. The sound level of the instruments is fixed. If you want the guitar to be louder, you turn up the volume. When you do that though, you are also turning up the volume on the singer, as well as on the guitar and every other instrument.

195

"The average radio listener knows this, and accepts that 'that's the way it works.' The recording engineer, however, knows otherwise. He can return to the studio, and play around with the levels of any or all of the instruments, setting their individual levels wherever he desires, without affecting the others. He can turn the guitar up as loud as he wants, without increasing the volume of the other instruments, or even the overall volume of the recorded composition. We are basically doing the same thing. We go into our 'studio,' and increase or reduce the level of energy or matter. To get into our studio, we have to accelerate sound waves to a degree that they change radically, and almost become something else entirely, something of a different order. This different order, or dimension, if you will, is our studio. When we are operating within that dimension, or in our 'studio,' we are free to manipulate both matter and energy, actually to create or destroy. Admittedly, my dear," he concluded, "this is a very, very, gross oversimplification."

And indeed it was. They were involved in medical research, for example, and based upon the application of their knowledge, had succeeded in isolating and changing cells completely, from one type to another. In other words, muscle cells, could become fatty tissue, bone cells could become nerve cells, brain cells, or anything else. While any transformation at the level of cellular medicine was possible, and even demonstrable, it was only so at the level of advanced aural acceleration. In other words, when removed from its artificially induced condition, a cell would then return to its previous condition. The twelve had not yet reached the level, at least in medicine, in which cellular transformation could be sustained outside of the accelerated particle state.

"Like the light bulb," Bustokus said. "As long as the light is turned on, it isn't dark. But turn off the light, and it gets dark immediately."

Such was not the case in certain other fields of research. In astronomy they had been able, through applied aural particle acceleration, to create the illusion of celestial bodies, which was how Dr. Davis officially found out about SS396. She was shown the formation as an example of how something could be created from nothing based upon the theory of aural particle acceleration.

"Well," she said, "that's incredible, but it looks like it's heading toward Earth."

"Yes," Bustokus answered. "It certainly looks that way. However,

196

if we were to shut down the aural accelerator, that celestial formation would drop from the screen like a brick. After all," he continued, "it doesn't really exist. Well, I take that back. It does exist, but its existence is artificially sustained."

"But it looks like it's moving to me," Dr. Davis observed, "and it certainly appears to have mass."

"It does appear to have both mass and velocity and, in fact, it actually does, but since it exists artificially and beyond this galaxy, its motion is meaningless. We can bring it forward or move it backward, as we please."

"But what happens when it penetrates our galaxy?" she asked.

"Why nothing, of course," Bustokus replied. "Since it doesn't exist, it can't penetrate our galaxy."

"But if it did," she insisted, "wouldn't it gain mass as well as increased velocity? In other words, wouldn't it suddenly become as tangible as, say, Jupiter?"

"That's an interesting thought. In fact, that was one of our initial concerns when we created it. I could see how you might think that. It's a logical supposition, Deb-O-Ra, and shows your excellent grasp of astronomy and physics. Be that as it may, however," Bustokus concluded, "it doesn't exist, and can't ever become objective. It's like going to a movie. It looks real enough, but turn off the projector and you are no longer in Egypt, or Florida, or anywhere else. You find yourself sitting in a chair at some junky mall cinema with your shoes stuck to the floor."

Bullshit. It was much more than a logical supposition, it was a fact. And now, Bustokus had deliberately lied to her about it. Even back in Iceland Dr. Davis had learned through the use of the Double-Cola lens that SS396 was headed toward Earth, and that it would have both mass, and increased velocity when it hit our galaxy. From that point it would accelerate. Dr. Henry had been right, more so than he'd ever suspected. These scientists were deliberately targeting Earth with SS396, and she knew it. With their aural accelerator, they would be able to make SS396 so fast, that it might even be undetectable at its point of entry. You wouldn't be able to see it, hear it, or even track it. It would just hit the planet one day, and that would be that. But why? They lived here too. Why would they want to destroy themselves? It was illogical. She felt she needed to talk to somebody about this, to report the matter to someone, somewhere, but who? Nobody would understand or even believe what she was talking about. And if they did, so what? If the President of the United States knew about the deadly approach of SS396, he couldn't do anything to stop it. She needed to talk to Dr. Henry, but the chances of that were very slight. While she believed that the Council members trusted her, she knew she was still on probation. The phones were certainly monitored. She couldn't call anybody.

And now, the words of Dr. Langley haunted her, that 'these people were crazy.' But the Secret Chiefs had been right about him also. Dr. Langley had no idea what was going on anywhere. All he cared about was his social profile. The end of the world was truly approaching and there was nothing she could do about it, and no one she could talk to. Perhaps she could somehow disable SS396. Before she could do that, assuming that such a thing were even possible, she would have to know more about it. It might already exist apart from the machinery that created it. In other words, even if she destroyed the entire research center, SS396 might already have enough energy to complete its mission. This was going to be much more difficult than merely destroying some lab equipment. The situation appeared hopeless.

ELSEWHERE

The private phone rang in Marduk's office, indicating that the hospital switchboard had been bypassed. No telling who could be calling. There weren't that many people who had the Council leader's private number, so whoever happened to be calling would consequently be a very important person. Marduk answered the phone on the third ring. "Hello."

"Please hold for Mr. Di Lizardo," a country sounding voice announced. Normally Marduk didn't hold for anyone. On the other hand, this was former Council member Louie the Pencil, formerly known within the Council as Mazor, now generally regarded as 'Mazor the Defector.' Still, he and Marduk had once been very close, before Mazor had become ill, and suffered some sort of nervous breakdown that had impaired his judgment to the degree that he would voluntarily depart their sanctuary. They hadn't spoken since before Mazor's defection, well over a year ago. Louie, that is, Mazor, had not returned any of the Council leader's calls in spite of the fact that without Marduk's direct intervention, the Council would have certainly voted to have him killed or transferred to another dimension. Finally Marduk had ceased calling his former friend. Even now, Marduk was upset by the sudden and unexplained departure of the Council's most brilliant scientist, and yet he also understood and sympathized. Being a Council member was a very high stress job. Decisions were made daily, indeed almost hourly, which had far reaching implications for millions of people, and basically living forever, was no picnic.

"Choice gospel greetings," Di Lizardo spoke jocularly into the phone.

The casual greeting offended Marduk, who was seldom amused by levity. "To what do I owe the honor of this call?" he asked coldly. There was a distance between them now, which both sensed at once, the distance between two worlds.

Di Lizardo couldn't care less. He respected the remaining Council members well enough, but the bottom line was that for all their research, manipulation, pretense, and self-imposed exile, nothing worthwhile had ever been accomplished by the Secret Chiefs. The world was still, for the most part, a terrible place. Little did he know that the remaining Council members had reached the same conclusions, and were acting on them even at that moment.

Di Lizardo was much happier on the outside. True enough, he dealt with a much lower rung on the evolutionary level in his day to day transactions, but this was the human condition. Real people, real problems, real clothes, by God. Baseball caps, overalls, and T-shirts, not expensive and foolish looking robes.

"You've got my business associate Chip Hamster, by God," Mazor accused. "And I want the son of a bitch back, God damn it."

"I'm frankly appalled by the extent to which your language has degenerated. You sound like a hillbilly," Marduk replied, genuinely disgusted.

"Well then, go Vols, God damn it!" Di Lizardo shouted, intentionally provoking the Council leader. "Go UT! Hey Big Orange, by God! Kick some ass Vols! How's that for hick?"

There was a moment of silence before Marduk deigned to reply. "What makes you think we are holding anyone captive?"

"C'mon Marduk. I wasn't born yesterday. It said in the paper that the sumbitch had a swimming merit badge in the damn Boy Scouts, so I know the bastard can swim. Plus, they towed his car to my junkyard. The paper said they thought he might uh been et by some radioactive fish, by God, but we both know that's a bunch of horseshit. You've got him, and I want him. He owes me money. It's that simple."

"Assuming that we did have him, what's it to you?"

"I told you, by God," Di Lizardo answered. "I want my money. You know that the by-laws prevent you from holding anyone against his will."

"That well may be," Marduk answered defensively, "but those same by-laws require that we maintain a constant strength of twelve members. Those same laws also require that our new members must come unsolicited, and by chance. Our two new candidates fall well within the scope of both provisions."

"You mean to tell me that Hamster isn't being held against his will?" Di Lizardo asked angrily.

"This is an internal matter. It's none of your concern," Marduk replied coldly. "You are no longer a member of the Council, and have no voice or influence in any of our actions or decisions." The resentment and hostility in Marduk's voice were unmistakable. Mazor's departure had resulted in an increased level of responsibility for the other members, but especially for Marduk, the Supreme Commander of the Secret Chiefs.

"You got one of my boys, someone I do bidness with. You've violated his constitutional rights by God," Di Lizardo flashed angrily.

"Since when do the arbitrary laws of some ant hill matter to you?"

"I'm talking about the Constitution by God, plus the son of a bitch owes me money, Marduk. I want my money."

"Look, Louie........Mazor, this bickering is getting both of us nowhere," Marduk said. "Why don't you let me send you a check for whatever he owes you? Hell, we'll triple it, since you are so concerned with money. As if you didn't have enough already." This seemed to Marduk like a perfectly reasonable solution to the matter. The Council could send the fool $10 million, for all Marduk cared. When that thing they had generated struck Earth, they wouldn't be 'doggone,' as Marvin Gaye said, they'd be 'long-gone.'

"How much does he owe you anyway?"

"Let me tell it like it T-I-IZ," Di Lizardo replied sarcastically, reverting to his hillbilly argot. "It ain't about money. It's about business.....something you wouldn't understand at all. That pissy little amount of money I make messing with Hamster wouldn't pay the light bill at the God damn Tiki Hut. But Hamster's my boy. I like that son of a bitch, by God. He's got style. His girlfriend ain't too bad either. And that country cousin of his, Therpis, is OK too. They's my kind of people, so I'm a telling you, 'Pharaoh, let my people go'."

"I'm sorry Mazor," Marduk replied, refusing to acknowledge the name Di Lizardo. "That's out of the question."

"You better let him go, by God."

"I've told you, he remains with us."

"Look, Marduk, I done told you. I don't care what you do with that bastard from the prison. I know you got him too. Don't deny it. But I'm telling you, by God, that you better release Hamster, and I mean pronto. And this is the last time I'm a telling you."

"Or what?" Marduk challenged him angrily.

"Or me and some of my boys are comin' after him."

"Surely you jest," Marduk laughed. "You wouldn't even make it through the front gate before we vaporized the lot of you. So save your idle threats for somebody else. I've offered to send you a check in any amount you wish. I suggest you take the check and mind your own business lest some unfortunate accident befall you."

That was it for Di Lizardo. Marduk, the robed one, his former friend, had just threatened him. As far as he was concerned, Hamster was as good as liberated. Surely that space-dressing freak couldn't have forgotten that Di Lizardo himself had designed and installed the security system for the entire compound. Be that as it may, he didn't want to show his hand, so he pretended to cool down. "Okay Marduk, you win. I'm in business to make money. I'll settle for $10 thousand, and you can keep the bastard."

"You've made the right decision," Marduk replied, cooling down noticeably. "Anyway, the FBI was pursuing him at the time of his accident. He wouldn't have lasted another two weeks before he was detained and imprisoned. He's better off with us."

"Perhaps, you're right, by God, after all," Di Lizardo said quietly.

"I'll pray for you," Marduk said sarcastically.

"Good. I can use the prayer, and you can use the practice. I'm telling you, I'll forget Hamster, but I want my money, by God."

"Does Marduk really think I can't spring somebody out of the Wildman Sanitarium?" Di Lizardo asked himself. "Those bastards couldn't 'vaporize' a cup of cappuccino, by God. They wanna talk 'vaporize,' by God, and I'll 'vaporize' some shit all right." Di

Lizardo no longer had any sympathy for the Secret Chiefs or their ridiculous causes. He'd take their check all right, just to throw them off the trail. Then he'd liberate Hamster.

23.

LOVE COMES A KNOCKIN'

Chip had been offered the opportunity to remain with these freaks, as had Marvin Hocker. The offer no doubt came at the right time as far as the freaks were concerned, because Chip knew for a fact that Hocker was within a matter of days of blowing out the back wall of the laundry, making his escape, and continuing to Florida, where he would resume his life without delay. It wasn't really much of a call for Hocker. What else did he have going for him? He was flat-headed, violent, and crazy, and the cops were looking for him everywhere. This place suited him fine. He'd be able to do what he wanted, come and go as he pleased, and basically live the life of luxury. His opinions and intelligence, what there were of them, would be actively sought and valued. Hocker accepted their proposal on the spot.

They'd both been offered the same deal, at a big meeting of the ten Secret Chiefs. It had sounded fun, but the fact of the matter was that Chip was a young man with a busy agenda. There were things to do, money to be made, cars to be acquired, and women to be loved. He wasn't prepared to settle down just yet, especially not to live in some cement laboratory with strange people. It didn't matter how much money they had, or how luxurious the surroundings. In the first place, he was used to luxury, so that aspect of the deal was not any great inducement. In the second place, he wasn't interested in any scientific research or anything else that might require a great deal of thought or force him to remain at any one place. He liked freedom of movement.

So how had he answered the Chiefs? First of all, he thanked them for their gracious hospitality, and for saving him from what, without their kind intervention, would surely have been certain death in a watery grave. He did everything in his power to charm the Council without, of course, seeming artificially solicitous. The reason for this was that, as far as he could tell, these people were stone ass crazy. They were intelligent, educated, and rich, but considering their mental state of high excitation, combined with the aforementioned virtues, a potentially explosive and dangerous situation existed. Of course he didn't wish to live the remainder of his young life with a bunch of crazy freaks. Duh, no shit. He didn't refuse their offer outright for fear they might have killed him. Instead, he requested some time to think on the matter. He wasn't threatened, and no threat was even implied, but he wasn't offered his freedom either. He was basically a bird in a gilded cage, but a bird anxious to fly the coop.

"Take as much time as you need," Marduk had suggested, "and feel free to ask any questions, but of course not to anyone outside this area, and to wander around the facility and familiarize yourself with our work. As you know, we aren't all work and no play. We have a gymnasium, a music room, whatever you want. You are not a prisoner here. We want you to remain with us."

There was one other very serious consideration in requesting time to deliberate the situation. There was that lovely understudy, Dr. Davis, Dr. Debbie Davis. As far as Chip was concerned, it was truly a case of love at first sight. She had been there at the meeting with the Council and had taken notes as questions were asked and answers given. It was different from anything he'd ever felt before. Yes she was slim and physically desirable, with all of the womanly attributes that he held in such high esteem. But for the first time in his life, he was not even consciously aware of her body. It was there, no doubt, but that was the least of his concerns. He was much more aware of her face, particularly her eyes, as they looked into his, across the large conference table. He wondered how her hair smelled. She was truly the most beautiful woman he'd ever seen. Her beauty made him feel insecure, despite the fact that he had logged, so to speak, a great deal of experience with beautiful women all over the world. This was something entirely different. He wanted to talk to her, but at the same time, didn't want to spend any time fantasizing about being with her. She was probably crazy too. If not, why would she be here in this freak house at all?

Chip's number one short term objective was to get out of the place and return to Nashville. On the other hand, what was the hurry? If what the Secret Chiefs had told him was true, the FBI was probably looking for him right now. Before he could take any corrective or defensive action, however, he had to find out what was really going on. To do that, he needed access to the outside world. He needed to make some phone calls, and yet he was reluctant to do that either, for several reasons. In the first place, any outgoing phones were most likely either blocked or bugged by the freaks. Chip's house was probably bugged also, by the FBI. He needed to take some action, but there wasn't much he could do here. He had to get out, that much was certain. There wasn't any immediate hurry though. He needed to at least formulate several different strategies, and then there was that beautiful Dr. Davis. He should at least find out if she was crazy before he split.

The Gods now prepared to smile upon Chip, a welcome relief from having his father murdered, his Rolls-Royce destroyed in a car crash, and being held as a prisoner by a group of maniacs. This favor was to take the form of Dr. Davis, whose aid had been solicited by Marduk, in persuading Chip to join their ranks as one of the Secret Chiefs. As a result of this request, Dr. Davis would be afforded the opportunity to speak with someone from 'the outside' without arousing any suspicion.

From what they had told her privately, Chip was an only child from a wealthy Nashville family who had squandered his inheritance in a very short period of time. He had gotten himself in some legal trouble as a result of some shady dealings in the automobile business, and was the subject of an ongoing FBI interstate bank fraud investigation. As a result of the car wreck, he and Hocker had been more or less delivered to their doorsteps as replacements for the two departed Council members.

"But what if he decides he doesn't wish to remain here?" Dr. Davis had asked the Council, in reference to Chip.

"We'd prefer not to consider the alternative Deb-O-Ra," Bustokus had said, addressing her by her new name.

"But why can't I become a member of your group?" she asked. "I have an excellent scientific background. Furthermore, I'm already here, and I want to stay here."

The fact was that Deb-O-Ra didn't want to be there either, not one bit more than Chip did, but she had no choice. She now knew that if Earth was to be spared this approaching catastrophe, she must remain and find a way to disable SS396. There was no one else who could even hope to accomplish this task. Consequently, she sought to even further remove any suspicions the Council might have regarding her motives and purposes. Not that they suspected anything, but she didn't want them to even think about beginning to suspect anything.

Personally, she didn't care one way or the other whether Chip Hamster joined their group. What was it to her? It was a moot point. There was one thing she still couldn't figure out. Why would these people want to destroy Earth if they were going to be here when it happened? It just didn't make any sense. Maybe Bustokus had told her the truth, maybe SS396 was just an illusion.

Nope, she knew better than that. SS396 would destroy the planet if it wasn't somehow stopped first. There could be no doubt about it. Maybe the Council had some sort of really deep underground bunker that would enable them to survive such a major disaster. It was unlikely, but even if possible, what would be the point? Some piece of the puzzle was still missing, something which would explain everything, but what was it?

In the meantime, there was Chip Hamster. He was attractive enough, she thought, but not her type. She wanted someone who looked like Cary Grant, someone who went to work everyday in an expensive business suit, someone who took life seriously. From what she could tell, this Chip Hamster was more or less a beach bum, and didn't take anything seriously. She wanted a stock broker type, a showpiece. For these reasons her interest in him was not romantic in nature. She hoped, however, that she could trust him enough to tell him the dire and dreadful nature of her discoveries.

This place has its advantages, Chip thought, as he put the 9 foot Bosendorfer concert grand through its paces. The piano wasn't designed for honky-tonk, blues, or New Orleans music, but it lent itself admirably, nonetheless, due to the extra octave of notes on the lower end of the scale. It hadn't been twenty minutes ago that Chip had played piano and joined in a few numbers with some of the regular inmates of the Wildman, in an ass kicking blues session. It was amazing, he reflected, how music seemed to calm the insane.

They had all played together for about thirty minutes before the guitar player slid back into the mental netherworld and had to be hauled away. He'd dropped his guitar pick in the middle of a particularly heavy riff, and it had fallen into the air vent. This was all it took to set him off. All he had to do was grab another pick from the plastic container on top of the amp. But no, he suddenly changed from as professional a guitar player as Chip had ever seen on any stage, to some screaming psychotic. By the time the big meats in the white suits carried him away, he was again quiet, but this time withdrawn, and mumbling to himself, his eyes all glazed over. Since it was close to lunch time, the orderlies rounded up the other musicians too, and hauled them away. They'd been instructed to leave Chip alone, so they went about their business as if he wasn't even in the room.

But the band had been great. The organ player was some black guy about twenty-five years old. He'd obviously received some classical training somewhere. The singer was very strange too. He didn't look at anybody, like he was real shy, but, when the bass player and the drummer started up, he joined right in and let it rip. He had the power and range of Robert Plant, but with a deep lower end, something the former Led Zeppelin singer lacked. The bass player also had a vacant look, as though he had been hypnotized, while the drummer laughed hysterically the entire time they played. He was still laughing in fact, when the two orderlies led him away. When the guitarist flipped out over his dropped pick, the drummer laughed so hard he literally fell off his stool, knocking over several drums and a cymbal as he fell. They were all crazy as hell, in the medical sense, but they played together as a unit extremely well, and had a sound that was greater than the sum of their considerable individual musical abilities.

"Those bastards should be recorded," Chip thought. "If I wasn't involved in the car business, and wasn't wanted by the FBI, and wasn't being held prisoner in the bug house, I might think about being their manager. They really are that good. With my incredible executive abilities and business knowledge," Chip reasoned, "I could make them superstars overnight."

As these thoughts passed through his mind, he continued playing the piano. What a magnificent instrument. He would miss having something this fine to mess around with. While he absentmindedly ran his fingers over the keys, the heavy sliding door to the music room opened silently. Dr. Davis slipped in unnoticed and quietly took a seat in an exquisite Belter side chair. After about ten minutes Chip rose from the piano and turned to leave the room. As he did so he noticed Dr. Davis, and was very surprised to see her.

"You're pretty good," Dr. Davis said, breaking the ice.

"I didn't see you," he replied with some embarrassment. "How long have you been here?"

"Just a few minutes," she replied with a smile, causing him to relax.

"What are you doing here?" he asked. "I mean at this sanitarium."

"I came here to study under the Secret Chiefs," she replied. "They are brilliant scientists."

"So what are you doing here, I mean in this room?" he asked, sizing her up. As far as Chip was concerned, this woman was working for them. Unless he found out otherwise, he intended to treat her cautiously despite her incredible beauty.

"Are you being held here against your will?" she asked bluntly, catching him completely off guard.

What the hell kind of question was that? It was highly personal, and presumed an intimacy that did not exist, at least not yet. He deliberated a moment before answering.

"Look," he said, "I really don't know anything at all about you, other than that you were sitting at the table with the Secret Chiefs at the meeting the other day. I conclude, therefore, that you are one of them. Since you are likely to report my answers to any questions, I can only say that I haven't made up my mind whether to join your organization. Under the circumstances, it certainly sounds attractive, but it's a big move for me, and not a decision I intend to make in a hurry. I hope you understand."

"I certainly appreciate your reluctance to answer me, but I must know," she said.

"This is some kind of Mexican standoff," he replied, looking into her beautiful brown eyes, and suddenly wanting to tell her anything she might ever want to know about anything in the world. "But like I said, I don't know who you are, or what your agenda may be. You, I gather, already know a great deal about me. If you want me to tell you anything beyond my name, rank, and serial number, you'd first better tell me: A, about yourself, B, why I should trust you; and C, why I should tell you anything at all about my plans."

Chip looked at her, still very much aware of her beauty, but numb for the moment to its influence. This was a life and death matter, as far as he was concerned. He didn't imagine for a moment that they intended to release him again into the general public if he decided not to join their band of merry men. They would most likely kill him and toss his body into the river, where it would float downstream and be found a few weeks later, 'finally having turned up after the accident.'

For Dr. Davis, it was a time of decision. She certainly understood his predicament, since he had much more to lose than she did. It was also a calculated risk for her, if she decided to tell him everything she knew. At least, though, she was certain that Chip wasn't one of them. He, on the other hand, did not know whose side she was on. In light of these considerations, it was obvious that if anything was going to be accomplished, she would have to take the initial risk. She would have to make that leap of faith. Furthermore, she would have to take that risk right now.

"I'm waiting," he said coldly.

"I have no choice but to trust you," she said. "I don't have time for a Mexican, or any other kind of standoff. What I'm about to tell you will sound so far-fetched that you probably won't believe it, but I have to take the chance. There's really nobody else I can even talk to about it. I'm sure, at least that you understand that much."

"I'm not a complete moron," Chip said defensively. "I can probably grasp the essence of anything you might have to say, if you keep it simple enough."

"Jesus," she thought. "Another prima donna."

"Look," she said, "I didn't mean that you wouldn't understand what I'm going to tell you, I only meant that it sounds unbelievable, and that you, of all people, would understand why I couldn't talk to anyone about it."

"All right then, lay it on me."

"OK. Until a short while ago I worked at an observatory in Iceland as an astronomer. By accident one of my associates knocked over an empty Double-Cola bottle. It fell to the floor, rolled around, and came to a stop directly under the eyepiece of our telescope. As soon as the concentrated light hit the bottle, strange things started happening. There were loud piercing high pitched sounds accompanied by powerful light beams that destroyed much of our lab in a matter of seconds. The bottle was accidentally knocked out from under the telescope and the disturbance ended as quickly as it had started. When the bottle cooled down, we examined it thoroughly and determined that someone possessed of superior intelligence had intentionally constructed this refracting lens in the bottom of the Double-Cola bottle."

"Interesting theory," Chip mused, "but so what?"

"Well, the lens is so far superior to anything that exists currently, that...let me put it like this. This lens is to astronomy what a jet would be in terms of transportation, to a pedestrian."

209

"OK," Chip conceded. "You found a high tech lens in a Coke bottle. I got that, but so what? What does that have to do with anything?"

"With the increased technology available to us with that lens, we determined that there is a large celestial body that has been intentionally manufactured by some person or group, which has been specifically constructed for the purpose of destroying Planet Earth."

"What do you mean?"

"I mean," she replied, "that a gigantic celestial formation of undetermined composition, is moving toward our galaxy at this very minute, and that Earth is its ultimate target."

"You're right," he laughed. "That is very far-fetched. In fact it's crazy. Uh, excuse me, I didn't mean to use the 'C' word."

"Hey, this isn't some joke," she snapped angrily.

"Well," Chip observed sarcastically, "they still let me watch the news, and I believe something of that nature would have been noticed by somebody, somewhere. Besides, even though I flunked general science, I still know that it would probably take millions of light years for anything on the outside of this galaxy to reach the solar system we inhabit. By the time that happened, everybody on this planet will have been dust for zillions of years. I don't think you have anything to worry about."

"You don't understand," she replied hotly. "Don't be such a smart ass and listen to me."

Chip didn't care for her tone, and despite her obvious physical beauty, she somehow suddenly seemed less desirable to him just now. Another ball-busting, pseudo-intellectual feminist who wanted all men to pay for something weird in her childhood. Maybe her father played too much golf.

"Look," he said," you asked me a question. Now I'm going to answer you. I'm stuck in a maximum security nut house and I'd much rather be just about anywhere else. Plus, the FBI is after me. Now if that asteroid, or meteor, or whatever it might be can be made to land on the gate and destroy it, then I can get the hell out of here. Otherwise, it has nothing to do with me."

"You idiot!" she blurted unintentionally.

That was it for Chip. "You know, you might be happier back in Iceland. The broom closet is down the hall. There are probably several to choose from, and I'm sure one of them has got your flight number. Bon voyage." He rose and started in the direction of a large Hammond Organ, leaving her sitting on the chair.

This is just great, she thought, now I have to humor some spoiled brat in order to save the world. "Wait," she said, "I'm sorry. It's just that what I'm telling you is real. These people fully intend to destroy Earth. This isn't something they're planning, it's already in motion. As soon as this thing, whatever it is they've created, hits our galaxy, it will accelerate at a rate faster than the speed of light. It will also most likely become invisible at that instant. In other words, nobody will be able to track it, or even see it."

"Alright," Chip said turning to face her. "Assuming that what you are saying is true, why are you telling me this?"

"Who else can I tell? I can't talk to anyone around here about it. I doubt that I can make any outside phone calls. And even if I could, who would I call? What would I say? The only people who know about this at all are my colleagues, and they can't help, not without the Double-Cola lens. Besides, they don't know where I am. The rest of the scientific community doesn't have the equipment or technology to even grasp what I would have to tell them. There is no way they could believe or even understand me. Furthermore, I am here because the people who run this place abducted me."

"Well it looks like you took to them fast enough," Chip said.

"I'm telling you, I didn't have any choice. They created this thing. It's targeted at Earth right now. If it's going to be stopped, that is, if it even can be stopped, it has to happen here, and if my calculations are right, it has to happen now. I think this planet will be destroyed in less than a month."

She definitely had his attention now. "But why...?" Chip asked, stopping to collect his thoughts.

"Assuming that what you have said is true," he continued, "and that it's possible, why would they want to blow up their own planet? The place where they live? It just doesn't make sense."

"I haven't figured that part out yet," Dr. Davis replied dejectedly. "I don't know."

"Maybe you need to spend some time working on an answer to that question before you get too upset," he suggested.

She said nothing, but just sat there, realizing that she really was alone. She'd hoped she might receive some help from Hamster, but it seemed that he was just some spoiled yuppie, after all.

"OK, then," Chip asked, sensing that he perhaps had been a bit too hard on her. "What do you want me to do about it? I don't know anything about space. I'm trying to find a way out of here myself without getting killed. What can I do?"

"I really don't know. It's just that...that..." Dr. Davis started sobbing, suddenly overcome by emotion, crushed by the hopelessness of the situation. She didn't know how to stop this thing, there was nobody she could trust. It was almost too much. Instinctively, Chip placed his arm around her shoulder in an inept attempt to comfort her, but this gesture only served to increase the outpouring of her emotions. "The weight of the world is on my shoulders," she cried. "Nobody can help me, there's nobody to talk to. I'm not smart enough to stop this thing myself. It's just terrible. I thought you would help me, but you don't believe me. It's just...."

Chip was no different than any other man. He was greatly moved by the woman's tears, and his protective instincts kicked in immediately. "Look," he said firmly. "Look at me." He knelt down on one knee and looked directly into her teary eyes. "There isn't anything that can't be worked out. Anything that has been created can also be destroyed. Forgive me for being skeptical, but in light of my personal circumstances, I'm sure you understand. I honestly don't know whether to believe you or not. What you are talking about is so far above my head that it's hard to imagine. I can't even program a DVD recorder, so bear with me. Be patient."

She felt a little better now. His presence, in this protective and reassuring mode, was comforting even in this apparently hopeless situation.

She was definitely more intelligent than he was, and Chip realized it immediately. But there are several different kinds of intelligence. She was book smart, he was street smart, two different but complimentary orders of intelligence. He would help her figure this out. As he looked at her, his heart almost melted. If there was a woman on the planet more beautiful than she was at just this moment, such a sight would be difficult to imagine. Her chin still quivered and her eyes had a pleading 'help me' look that he couldn't have resisted even if he'd wanted to. He would right now willingly sacrifice his cars, his life, and everything he now possessed or ever would possess, to see her truly happy, to be a hero in her eyes. This sudden rush of powerful and conflicting emotions was something for the most part unknown to Chip Hamster, playboy, wildman, and lover of women. He looked at her sitting before him in her tight fitting checkered suit with a patch that read 'Deb-O-Ra,' and he was helpless. .

It was the dawn of a new era for Mason Charles Hamster. He would put his own wishes and desires aside, at least for the moment. He would gird up his substantial and mighty loins, and with this woman, would save Earth from the evil machinations of these monster, space-dressing freaks. His purpose was clear now. The same blood that flowed through the veins of his ancestors, the same intuition which discovered the treasure upon which his family's fortune had been founded; the same intelligence that had created the giant Amalgamated Cheese and vanquished all competitors; these powers were all available to him now.

"How can I help?" he asked.

This was the answer she'd hoped for. "I don't know yet," she replied, wiping her eyes on the sleeve of her jumpsuit." I guess for right now, I just need a sympathetic ear. I need you to listen to me and help me formulate a plan. We don't have much time."

24.

BREAKOUT

Di Lizardo was quite angry, and it was more than just the money. It was also more than the fact that they were holding private citizens against their will. The source of the junk car dealer's rage was probably the smug, self-righteous attitude of those pedantic academic dropouts, the Secret Chiefs, and Marduk, the Supreme Leader, was the worst.

It all seemed so far away to Di Lizardo now, as he sat in a lawn chair inside the Tiki Hut, caressed by the fragrant smoke of a White Owl Ranger, a most exquisite cigar, with "a substantial degree of non-tobacco ingredients," whatever the hell that meant, probably rodent droppings. That's it, he thought, it 'seemed' so far away, the Wildman, the pretense, the stupid space names. The fact of the matter, however, was that the Council was again interfering with his personal life. The check had come from those bastards, $10 thousand, as promised. He would cash it at the bank this afternoon after lunch at Shapiro's Deli, just to throw them off. But did those fools, in their arrogance honestly believe that would be the end of the matter? $10 thousand dollars was a drop in the bucket to them. They spent more than that a year on coffee. He was going to spring Hamster out of that place. Why? Because he could, of course. It was a matter of principle. Di Lizardo had his money, now it was time to take action.

"Golden Loaf," a rustic voice practically shouted into the receiver. It was Gloria, the ex-wife of the Loaf's owner. She was big and fat and yellow, a bit jaundiced perhaps, but just the size that a country boy liked 'em. She was, however, constitutionally incapable of speaking at a normal conversational level. She yelled to, and at everybody. The loud background noises indicated that it was lunchtime, an inappropriate time to be calling the Loaf, unless one were either placing a to go order, or looking for the Loaf's owner, Tomtom.

"Get me Tomtom," Di Lizardo shouted over the loud sounds of plates being slammed down. The Golden Loaf was essentially a large log cabin which had once served as the restaurant, office, and tavern of Honest Abe's Motor Court, a theme motel of the type commonly seen in the 1930s. Rural native Georgian, Abe Lefkowitz had built the place as a tourist stop for visitors to famous Lookout Mountain, back before the Second World War In the beginning, it had consisted of individual log cabins which served as vacation cottages for the many visitors to this highly scenic area. As time passed, however, the out of towners were replaced by a local crowd possessed of a more sporting nature. Honest Abe's became known as the "Big Three Court," the big three, of course, being gambling, whiskey, and women, not necessarily in that order. The large Abe Lincoln neon sign still stood, as it had for the last seventy years, but the paint was now faded almost white and the broken glass of the neon tubes dangled precariously in several places. A couple of the original log cottages still remained, but they were moss covered and collapsing, with rusted 1950's vintage cars rotting away in their individual garages.

"He ain' cheer," Gloria shouted, giving the standard reply to any request to speak with the restaurant's owner, Tomtom Thompson. It could be an ex-wife, a girlfriend, the po-lice, the Feds, a bill collector, or any one of several dozen undesirables seeking to waste the time, money, or energy of Tomtom.

"Get him, Gloria, by God. I know he's in there. It's Ron Di Lizardo on the phone. I need to talk to him right now."

"Jest a minit," Gloria screeched, recognizing Ron Di Lizardo as one of the elect who could speak to Tomtom at any time, provided, of course, he was actually on the premises.

Tomtom Thompson was a descendant of the first Honest Abe, not Lincoln, but Lefkowitz, the man who built the joint originally. When the interstate had cut off the main road into Chattanooga back in the early 1960s, many of the old time tourist courts bit the dust. There were a few still remaining at the base of Lookout Mountain, but they were run down, and now owned by Arab-Americans, the kind who had several veiled wives, carried scimitars, and drove large, late model Mercedes sedans. The Mighty Gospel Mountainaires, Thompson's gospel group, referred to these Arab Americans generically as 'towel heads,' a most odious and disrespectful reference to a group of Americans who possessed so many fine cars, such beautiful women, and so damn much money. Anyway, after the interstate had cut off the main road into Chattanooga, people just drove straight into downtown, bypassing Lookout Mountain altogether. Seeing the writing on the bathroom wall so to speak, Tomtom had decided to close the motel and had turned the place into a very successful 'meat and three' diner, specializing in 'home cookin' and patronized mainly by locals.

The 'Golden Loaf,' as it was now called, was not only the most popular restaurant in north Georgia, it was also the hangout for the Mighty Gospel Mountainaires, perhaps the most famous of all the vocal groups to emerge from the area. The Mountainaires were well known nationally and regionally, and had a busy touring schedule, which took them by tour bus everywhere from Florida to Minnesota. All four of the Thompson brothers sang in the Mountainaires, but Tomtom, was unquestionably the group's leader. While the group was financially successful to the degree that all the brothers had relatively new Lincolns, this was nothing compared to the money they made running their own distillery.

It was in their capacity as distillers of fine sour mash whiskey, that the brothers initially made the acquaintance of Ron Di Lizardo, proprietor of Mid-South Intergalactic Auto Brokers. There was nothing quite like a Mercedes Benz radiator for the final stages of the distilling process.

Since they'd started buying their tubing, compressors, and radiators from Mid-South, there had been no accidental poisoning deaths, and only one alcohol related blindness in the last year, compared with three the previous year, and five, the year before that. Di Lizardo was a bit strange, and nobody really knew where he was actually from, no matter what he claimed, but he was 'people.' He had told Carp Thompson that he was originally from Florida, but it seemed unlikely.

The main thing was that Di Lizardo had stumbled onto the business end of their illegal operation accidentally one day, and had the opportunity to turn them in to the Feds, but hadn't done so.

"I'm a businessman," he'd told them, as soon as their shotguns had been lowered. "As such, by God, I'm in business to make money. If I was to rat out one of my best customers, I'd stand to lose a substantial amount of my local business. Besides," he hesitated, "I love a nice clear mountain whiskey."

Di Lizardo had been permitted to live as the result of his open minded attitude, and now served as lookout, since anyone approaching that area by land had to first pass by his place of business. Over the past year a genuine friendship had developed between the Thompson brothers, the crowd that frequented the Golden Loaf, and Ron Di Lizardo. For this reason, it was this group that the junk car dealer decided to call when he needed a favor that might require a bit of muscle.

"Yeah boy," Tomtom answered with his standard greeting, "I thought you was coming over for lunch today. Now listen here. I got fresh mashed taters, kidney beans with Cajun spices, black eyed peas, macaroni and cheese, pork cooked greens, and cream style corn. None of this shit's canned. You know that, Ron. You better get your Yankee ass over here 'fore I run out of catfish. Come on now."

"I got a little job I need some help with, Tomtom. I was hoping, by God, that you, Carp, Sol, and Jeeter could round up some of the boys and help me with a little business matter."

"I tell you what, you come on over to the Golden Loaf and we'll talk about it. We got cousin Tadpole in from Statesboro. Now he's one tough somitch. He was in the navy back at 'Nam, you know one of those eels, or something. They's a arrest warrant on him, so he's up here for a few days laying low till things cool down. Tadpole used to drive for us. He's got a '70 442 Oldsmobile that'll do a hundred fifty, and can hold a hundred gallons of Lookout Mountain Lemonade. He ain't never been caught neither. Sol and Jeeter's both here right now. You come on over. You know I don't like to talk no shit on the phone."

"I'll be right over, by God," Di Lizardo said. "You save me some catfish now." Di Lizardo jumped into 'Redbird,' a dented and beat up 1969 red Cadillac convertible, cranked it up and stomped the accelerator, creating great clouds of brown dust, and throwing gravel sixty feet behind the car. "Does it get any better than this?" he shouted at the universe, thrilled to be alive on this incredible day. Already his blood was running hot at the very thought of the approaching battle. Boy would Marduk be surprised when these rowdy hillbillies descended upon their command post, by God, like a swarm of beer drinking, shotgunning locusts. Three quarters of a mile down the road, Di Lizardo slammed on the brakes, sliding his car in the loose dirt and gravel for about thirty feet before stopping precisely next to a black king cab pickup truck with a couple of hogs snorting and rooting around in the pickup bed.

He waited until the big cloud of dust passed, hiked up his shorts with both hands, and strutted into the Golden Loaf like he owned the place. There were several unfamiliar truckers seated at the counter, and some of the locals were busy playing cards and drinking iced tea down by the jukebox. The waitresses all looked up as he entered, startled by his striking good looks, and tanned, muscular arms. He looked a great deal like a younger version of 1950s actor Victor Mature, only much taller, a resemblance he was quite proud of. As he surveyed the inside of the Golden Loaf, he saw Sol, Carp, and Jeeter, down by the pool table. They looked up as he approached.

"Ron," Jeeter said, "this here's cousin Tadpole, from down South. He's here for a few days visitin' the Mountainaires."

"Pleased to meet you," Di Lizardo said, extending his hand and sizing up the newcomer. He was a big one, by God, with a neck like a Clydesdale and real big arms. He was probably every bit as tough as he looked.

"Hey, Gloria," Sol shouted, "Git Tomtom. Tell him that the junk man Lizardo is here."

While they waited for Tomtom, Di Lizardo ordered up a good country style lunch with all the fixins,' and listened as the Mountainaires planned their next series of performances.

"Naw, naw," Sol stated firmly. "We're gonna have to find a different venue in Birmingham. That church we played last time had some funky sounding organ. I don't know what it was, but it wasn't a Hammond."

"Yeah, man. That was the First Church of Christ the Holy Reedemer, Incorporated. It was some old Conn organ. Sounded like somebody was cranking a cat's tail, sure did, and the damn piano was out of tune. We don't have to play no shit houses anymore," Jeeter continued. "We're the hottest gospel quartet in the South. If we're gonna have to split the take with the host church, then we need to play as big a facility as possible. We're there to make money."

"Didn't you play some snake handler place, by God?" Di Lizardo asked.

"Boy that snake church sure was a mess. It was some place outside of Knoxville. Jesus almighty." Sol was excited by the memory. "There were three teethed-women, people who were missing arms, fingers, and hands from snake bites. Men were yelling and raising rattlesnakes in the air, women too, shaking them around, and all. The snakes had a right to be pissed off."

"No shit," Di Lizardo agreed.

"Yeah, think about it." Jeeter laughed, "Most of the women around here have at least seven teeth, three for bitin,' four for holdin.'"

"Well God damn," Sol exclaimed, "I didn't know you could count that high Jeeter."

Their laughter was interrupted by the arrival of Tomtom, a beer-bellied lout of a man, sporting a head full of what can only be described as 'gospel hair.' Like the ones on TV, portly polyester-clad men with gold chains hanging from their necks, pouffed up dyed blonde hair about a foot tall, not one hair of which would move an inch in a tornado. Tomtom fell into that category.

"Naw," Jeeter continued, "I mean it. Now listen. I ain't shittin' yuh. Some snake is lying out on a rock in the woods, minding his own damn business, just sunning hisself. Next thing he knows, some sumbitch snatches him up without any warning, mind you, and shoves him into a dark tow sack with a handful of other snakes he doesn't even know. Next thing, he's hearing some real bad music. The sack opens, the light floods in, and some jerk grabs him and starts shaking him around in the air, yelling, and raising all types of hell, treadin' on him, and beating his head against the floor. I'm surprised more of them ain't bit. If I was a snake I'd bite the first son of a bitch that touched me, and take the lockjaw on his ass. They'd have to prize me off the bastard with a damn crowbar. I mean it."

"Me too, by God," Di Lizardo agreed.

"The only reason more of them ain't bit," Carp speculated, "is that the snakes 're too damn stunned to believe what's happening to 'em. Even a rattlesnake knows he's pizon. I think the poor bastards are just too damn shocked and surprised to bite somebody right at first. I think they's the ones scared, at least in the beginning."

"You might be right about that, but you're wrong about a snake knowing he's pizonous," Tadpole observed. "A snake just bites. That's what he does."

Tomtom listened to the discourse and then interrupted. "Look boys, that was a accident. The Mountainaires ain't playing anymore snake joints. I told you that was a accident, now why do I have to keep hearing about it? Let's talk about this shit later. Lizardo here has got a problem and he came by to see if we could help him."

"Ok, boy," he said addressing their guest, "tell us what's on your mind."

"A few months ago," the junk man said, "I entered into a car deal with a friend of mine from Nashville, by God, a man named Chip Hamster. You might have heard of him. Now, here's my problem. His car ran into the river a month or so ago and he hasn't been seen since."

"Is that the Hamster that's a cheese magnet?" Tadpole asked.

"Yeah, same guy" Di Lizardo continued, "Well anyway, he's being held prisoner, by God, at the damn Wildman Sanitarium, and I want to break him out. I wonder if you guys could help me out. I'll pay you whatever you feel is fair."

"Now wait jest a minit," Jeeter interrupted. "I heard on the T V that he was swallowed up by some big fish. That is, if we're talking about the same guy."

"Bullshit!" shouted Tomtom. "The only thing down in that river big enough to eat a man is a catfish or a big turtle, and everybody knows a catfish won't go after a live man."

"It could be a gar," ventured Sol.

"Naw, 'tain't no damn gar," Jeeter answered authoritatively.

"Is too, God damn it."

"It ain't no damn gar. Now I done told ja," Jeeter stated firmly, hoping that was the end of the matter.

"Is too, I done seen one seven God damn feet long swimming out where they pour all that mercury and shit into the river. I shot the son of a bitch with my 22. He just smiled and kept on swimming. I'd uh had to get my 45 to sink the big son of a bitch."

"I'm telling you Sol, it wadn't no God damn gar. The big ones don't come this far north, now let's drop it. It wasn't a gar, and that's that."

There was a moment of silence, and everybody relaxed waiting for Di Lizardo to continue, glad that the matter had been settled.

"Well, what was it then?" Sol asked quickly, trying to get the last word. "The damn Loch Ness monster?"

"Listen by God," Di Lizardo shouted. "Nothing got Hamster except the people at the Wildman. I'm telling you boys that they're holding the son of a bitch prisoner in the bug house," the junk man shouted. "They told me they had him, and that they weren't, by God, gonna let him go. That's a direct violation of his Constitutional

221

rights."

"You just say when, God damn it, and we'll take a little trip down there and get him back," Tomtom stated. "And you don't owe us nothing at all. Ain't that right boys?"

"Damn right," Sol agreed. "You done been a friend to all of us, providing us with much needed parts for our business, helpin' keep our tour bus on the road, guarding us against intruders and all. Whatever you need Lizardo, all you got to do is ask. 'Eternal vigilance is the price of freedom.' It'll be our high pleasure and honor."

"You got that shit right Sol," Jeeter agreed.

"Is them beans tender enough for you?" Tomtom asked their guest.

"These are most delicious indeed, by God," their guest replied.

"They didn't come outa no damn can neither, hee hee hee," Jeeter laughed, removing the toothpick from his mouth, flicking it across the room, and spitting on the floor.

"Well, then, it's done," Tomtom stated authoritatively, looking from face to face to be certain all were in accord.

"I can't tell you how much this means to me," Di Lizardo said, deeply touched that these fairly new friends were willing to help free an imprisoned fellow human being, someone they didn't even know. Of course, he neglected to mention, there was more than a slight possibility that several of them might be vaporized by the high-tech defensive laser weapons employed by the Secret Chiefs.

"When do you want us to spring him?" Tomtom asked.

"Let's see. Today is the 15th. I think we ought to get him out on the 20th. I've got to draw up a map of the Wildman, so that we can plan this out, by God, so that everything turns out right."

With that, Di Lizardo finished his lunch, guzzled down a Double-Cola, gobbled a triple decker Moon Pie, and returned to the Tiki Hut to plan the rescue in detail. The good news was that the Chiefs, having sent Di Lizardo the ten grand, wouldn't be expecting an invasion. The bad news was that they have the most precise, advanced, and deadly weaponry on the planet.

25.

LET'S ROCK!

D-Day: Dec. 20, 11:00 P.M.   Golden Loaf: Lookout Mountain,
Georgia.

To complete a successful rescue operation in enemy territory, under
hostile circumstances, there are several minimum requirements.
There must be a clearly defined objective, a specific plan of action,
and the means of accomplishing it. Ideally, this plan would include
a backup in the event there are unforeseen circumstances. In light of
these weighty considerations, Ron Di Lizardo met with the
Thompson Boys, a.k.a. the 'Mighty Gospel Mountainaires,'
complete with country cousin, Tadpole, at their hive, the Golden
Loaf, which had been established as an interim command post for
the execution of their mission. Tomtom and the boys had made
certain that their expedition was well armed. First and foremost,
there were eight one-gallon gas jugs filled nearly to the top with a
highly flammable home brew. Under the top of each jug was a piece
of cloth that would serve as a fuse.

"This oughta be like Desert Storm, by God, the ol' in and out, a
surgical strike," Di Lizardo observed, seeking to establish the tone
of the mission.

"Yeah," Sol countered," but we ain't got no planes to loosen `em
up before the ground troops strike."

"We are the ground troops," Jeeter said, smacking Sol in the back
of the head for emphasis.

"That may be," Carp Thompson replied confidently, "but that was
a much bigger operation. We're just doing a rescue. We ain't there
to blow nothing up." He looked over at Ron, as if seeking
confirmation.

"Well what the hell am I doing here if we ain't gonna blow up
something?" Tadpole asked. "I'm trained in pyra-technics. I thought
I was gonna at least get to blow something up," he said, obviously
disappointed.

"Don't worry," Di Lizardo reassured him. "I've got specific plans, by God, for your skills."

"That's good, cause I came prepared," Tadpole smiled, reaching into his hunting jacket and producing four sticks of dynamite. Di Lizardo also noticed the handle of a 21-shot Glock sticking out of his belt.

"Hey, wait a minute, Ron, you said you was gonna get us some donuts, God damn it, Krispy Kremes, too," Jeeter interrupted.

In Jeeter's estimation, Krispy Kreme donuts were the best on Earth, and certainly an essential part of any commando type operation. Few, if any in their distinguished aggregation would take exception.

"Pipe down," Di Lizardo snapped. "They're in my car, by God. I said I'd bring `em, and I did. Now let's get back to the business at hand."

"Jeeter ain't worth a shit, until he gets his donuts," Tomtom stated matter of factly.

"But while we're on the subject of eats, I got some fine P-can pie in the ice box. I got the best damn little green onions you ever tasted, too. They's fresh picked. Jeeter, run out to the car and get them donuts so you can pay attention. Now," Tomtom resumed. "I can fix up some greens. I still got some left from dinner."

"I'll take me a slice of chess pie," Sol said. "That is, if there's any left."

"Coming right up. Anybody else? Come on now Ron, don't be shy. This is the Golden Loaf Restaurant! Now I know there's something on the menu just a callin' your name. 'Ron, it's me callin, it's your favorite dessert, come on Ron, eat me'." Tomtom called, imitating a female voice. The rest of the boys laughed as Ron deliberated.

"All right Tomtom, you got me by the nuts. I'll have me a slice of that chocolate pie, by God."

"Me too," Tadpole shouted.

"Gimme one of them donuts Jeeter, you stingy bastard," Sol demanded. "Don't hog the box."

"Coffee, Double-Colas, Krispy Kreme donuts, pie, and a bunch of good friends gathering around the welcome table at the Golden Loaf, north Georgia's most famous restaurant," Tomtom stated, tears of joy glistening in his eyes. "This is a moment we shall all remember. Now I think it's time to offer a prayer for the success of

224

our mission tonight. The Lord's been mighty good to the Mighty Gospel Mountainaires, and to the world famous Golden Loaf."

"Here here," Sol agreed.

"Pre-e-e-e-e-ch !" Tadpole shouted.

"Yes, yes, yes." Jeeter agreed.

"Hey, God damn it," Carp interrupted. "Put down the....Tadpo... excuse me, Tomtom, but Tadpole's drinking our Molotov cocktails. Put that shit down, Tadpole. We need it for the God damn mission."

"Hell, I was just having me a little, there's seven and a half gallon jugs left. I'm sorry."

"Cut that shit out, Tadpole," Tomtom said gently, "Now let us pray. They all bowed their heads.

"Lord Jay-sus," Tomtom called, "We who are gathered at the world famous Golden Loaf tonight, humbly thank you for our many blessings. We especially thank you for so generously equipping us with dynamite, guns, and other weapons necessary for tonight's sacred mission, that of rescuing a poor, private citizen held prisoner, against his will, by evil terrorist infidels at the insane asylum."

Gentle words of affirmation, such as 'Amen', and 'yes, yes, yes', were quietly expressed by the small group of battle ready commandos.

"We humbly pray, oh Lord," Tomtom continued, "that we might complete this mission with a minimal loss of life on our side, the side of good, justice, honor, and the American way. We also pray, holy Jay-sus, that you might offer us, that is, we your humble soldiers and servants, your divine help and guidance in seeking out and destroying every last one of these filthy heathen terrorists, that they might be delivered straightaway to that burning hell, which you have so graciously prepared for them, as an eternal place of torture and regret, that they might forever, throughout all eternity know and realize the grave error of having bet their lives and souls on the wrong horse in this great cosmic race. Amen."

"Amen, amen, yes, yes, yes."

"Furthermore, we ask that you let them fry, roast, burn, and otherwise suffer greatly for violating the Constitutional rights of this Godly and holy servant of yours, who we venture forth to rescue tonight. Let us serve as your hammer to smite these filthy heathen bast..., I mean idolaters. Thank you merciful Lord. In Jay-sus holy name, Amen."

"Yeah."

"Alright," Tomtom said, "let's go kick some towel head ass."

"I don't believe they'll be any foreigners there, by God," Di Lizardo observed. "Besides," he continued, "the place is a hospital for the insane. We aren't there to kill anybody, per se. I think that what we should do, is to probably liberate the whole place. We should get our man first, and then free everybody, all of those inmates who have been abandoned by society, whose greedy sons and daughters have left them there to die."

Actually, (and nobody knew it better than Di Lizardo), the Wildman Sanitarium was, without doubt the most luxurious facility of its type in the nation, if not the world. There were indoor and outdoor tennis courts, swimming pools, tracks, and basketball courts. There were computer games, a $7 million flight simulator, gourmet cuisine, personal servants and trainers for each of the inmates. The place was almost a paradise. It was doubtful that even ten percent of the inmates would want to leave if given the opportunity. Nonetheless, in consideration of the very real danger from the advanced weaponry of the Secret Chiefs, it was necessary to stir up the Mighty Gospel Mountainaires so that they would be prepared. The fact of the matter was that the Council, despite its high tech weapons had never had reason or opportunity to use them. There had never been any military training or even defense exercises. Still, the lasers were certainly capable of destroying any intruders instantly. There was no reason to suspect that despite their lack of training, the Secret Chiefs couldn't utilize the lasers in the auto defense mode. This was most likely what they would do, simply push a button activating the laser auto defense system. They could watch the whole thing from the monitor screens in their sector, go to sleep whenever they got tired, and turn it off the next morning. One thing for sure. They wouldn't call the police.

The guidance director had to be destroyed. Di Lizardo would take care of that himself. There was no need in frightening these volunteers unnecessarily by telling them there was some slight possibility that they might be incinerated. "Here's the plan," Di Lizardo stated. "The first thing is for Tadpole to create a disturbance at the power plant back behind the tennis courts. No, on second thought, we need the problem to be closer to the dormitory, so that there will be an evacuation. A kitchen fire would be ideal. Since it's still fairly warm outside, chances are that the general population will be evacuated through the rear side door, marked 'A' on your maps.

226

Does everybody see that?"

"We got it," Tomtom replied.

"Good," Di Lizardo continued, "There can't be anything suspicious about this. It must be an electrical fire, in a refrigerator motor, circuit box, or some other major appliance."

"I'll hit the fuse box," Tadpole said. "I've got a transformer off a Pabst neon I use to shock fish with."

"God damn he shore does," Jeeter interrupted. "The son of a bitch tried it out on me before he lexicuted any fish. Hooked it to my bed one night. When I got up in the middle of the night to drain my lizard, sure enough, the minute my feet hit the floor, my head hit the ceiling, by God. Shocked the ever living shit out of me."

Everybody laughed.

"Oh yeah, you bastards, go ahead and laugh. I'm gonna get him back one day, you just wait. Then you all will all be laughing out the other side of your face. If he intended on lexicuting fish, by God, he should have tried it out on Carp. He's the one named after a fish. Taught me a lesson though, God damn it. I don't get into no bed anywhere without first touching the springs with the end of a screwdriver. If sparks jump out, I ain't jumpin'in. And that's all there is to it."

The men continued laughing, now becoming hysterical. But Jeeter was obviously getting really pissed off. He just stood there with an angry look on his face, staring at all of them. The madder he got, the more they laughed. Whenever Jeeter got angry or excited, his speech impediment kicked in "Alright God ndamn it," he cursed.

Di Lizardo hoped he could get these stooges to concentrate on the business at hand long enough to learn the plan, but this really was funny. He finally succumbed, broke out laughing, and rolled out on the floor.

"All right God ndamn it, I'm ngonna nget nall of you for this. Let nthe ngood nLord bless yuh, nand nlet nthe nundertaker, ndress yuh God ndamn it!"

Finally things calmed down, and everybody got back to business.

"Ok," Tadpole resumed, still grinning, "I think that the best thing to do is hook the transformer to the main circuit, bypassing the fuse box, and then hit the juice. That should start a fire in that part of the building. But is it enough to get the place cleared out, or do we need something else?"

"No, that should do it," Di Lizardo replied. I know you guys are taking some iron, by God, but don't be shooting up the joint, until after it has, by God been secured from the inside. If you start blasting before everybody is out of the building, they won't come out at all. If people are shooting at you, it's only natural to seek cover. I don't want those inmates, by God, hunkering down under their beds like a bunch of sniveling, by God, cowards."

"Yeah," Carp shouted, "we're trying to free these bastards. They can't get free if they're still in the building."

"I got a better idea," Tadpole said. "Why don't I just sneak into the kitchen and thow in a Molotov cocktail at the base of the refrigerator, or in the electrical room? That Lookout Mountain Lemonade is highly flammable, and it don't leave no fumes like gasoline."

"That might be the best thing," Di Lizardo agreed. "Okay then," he continued. "Here it is. Tadpole, you and Jeeter take the access road to the left, as soon as you get in the gate. Follow it on around until you pass the tennis courts and then hang a right. After you make that turn, the road dead ends into the rear delivery door. I got a key for that door. Use it, go inside, and start the fire."

"Got it boss," Tadpole stated confidently.

"But I wanted to go with cousin Tadpole," Sol complained. "I wanna' blow up something."

"You get to go with me in the 'Command Vehicle,' Di Lizardo stated, "and I promise you that'll be a lot more fun." What a bunch of morons, he thought.

"No shit? Really? The 'Command Vehicle?' All right."

"Okay," Di Lizardo continued, "Me and Sol are going around the other way. As soon as the fire starts, the fire alarm will sound. I figure it will take at least ten minutes for the fastest fire engine, by God, to get here from Chattanooga. Before they arrive, Sol and I will have rescued Hamster, we'll have freed the prisoners, and we'll all be on our way back up the mountain."

"How are you gonna' do that?" Tomtom asked. "And where do you want me and Carp to be?"

"As soon, by God, as Tadpole and Jeeter start the kitchen fire, the alarm will sound all over the compound. In exactly thirty seconds from the time that we first hear the alarm, by God, Sol and I will hook the chain to the bars on Hamster's bedroom window and jerk the whole damn wall out. There's only one place in that compound where they could be keeping him. We have to be ready and in position when that alarm sounds. If not, Hamster, and everybody else in that part of the building, by God, will leave their rooms to go see what's happening. If Hamster ain't in his room when I pull the wall out, the mission, by God, will have failed. This has to be right the first time."

"As soon as we snatch Hamster, we're coming out the same way we came in, only we ain't stopping for nothing. Me, Sol, and Hamster will meet you boys back at the Loaf. By this time, the yard on both sides of the driveway should be filled up with the inmates. Now Carp and Tomtom are gonna be in the school bus up by the side parking lot, hidden over in the trees by the river. Look at the map. I got it marked with a red X. Tomtom's gonna' drive, and Carp, well, you get to have all the fun. You get to shoot the machine gun, by God." Di Lizardo was referring to a rather large belt-fed, water-cooled .50 caliber deck gun, stolen from an army depot in Memphis during the 1968 riots.

"Now," Di Lizardo continued, "don't start shooting until we have passed you. In other words, by God, when I, Sol, and Hamster drive by you on our way back to the gate, then start firing. Remember, don't shoot anybody. Just shoot over their heads. We're there to free these people, not, by God, to kill them."

"You know, boys," Tomtom interjected. "I feel like we are doing a good thing here. It gives me a kind of warm feeling, praise Jesus, to free these people. It's kinda like Moses freeing his brothers from the evil towel headed Egyptians."

"Are there any questions or comments?" Di Lizardo asked.

"Before we start this mission," Tomtom said, standing and placing his hand over his heart, "I'd like to say a word for our fallen comrade Walter 'Tweet' Wilson."

At the mention of that sacred name, the Mighty Gospel Mountainaires, and cousin Tadpole, stood solemnly en mass, waiting for a comforting word from their leader. Tweet had died jumping out of a bedroom window not too long ago, when the woman's husband had come home early from work. It had been a terrible blow to all of them.

The delay bothered Di Lizardo, but it wasn't nearly as irritating or as offensive as the name 'Tweet.' What the hell kind of person would permit himself to be addressed, by God, as 'Tweet?' If his parents were still alive, they should be shot.

After about ten minutes of extolling the virtues of their dearly departed cousin, the Mighty Gospel Mountainaires were ready to descend upon the Wildman Sanitarium.

"It's 11:30 p.m.," Di Lizardo stated calmly. "Everybody knows their duties. It should take us ten minutes to get there ten minutes to accomplish our objectives, and ten minutes to get back. I'll see you all here in half an hour. Then, by God," he continued, casting a glance at Tomtom, "I believe I will have me some of that fine lemon ice box pie."

Tomtom's face turned red as a beet as he smiled his approval. "Let's hit it men. We're in 'Redbird,' Jeeter. You and Tadpole next, and then Carp and Tomtom bring up the rear in the bus. Let's kick some ass."

Chip Hamster had gone to bed as usual, about 11:00, just a bit after the news. There was definitely a great deal on his mind. First and foremost was what Dr. Davis had told him. It seemed absurd enough, but she had no reason to lie. On the other hand, if the Secret Chiefs were preparing to destroy Earth, why would they give a damn whether he joined them? It just didn't make any sense from either perspective. Everybody in this whole place was probably crazy anyway. If not, why would they be here to begin with? Dr. Davis couldn't substantiate any of her outlandish claims. She couldn't prove anything. She was probably telling the truth, but in this place, who could say? That whole bit about the FBI could be bullshit too. There was no way to find out without getting out of this place and back to Nashville, where he belonged. He wondered about Ioveena , Cissy, Rene, and now, the lovely Debbie Davis. If she was a liar too, and crazy as the rest of them, it didn't matter. If he had to believe her to be with her, it was probably worth it, or so he thought.

Chip closed the book he'd halfheartedly been trying to read, placed it on the bedside table, then reached over and turned off the light. He placed his head firmly upon a big feather pillow and fell asleep easily in a matter of minutes, but was suddenly awakened by the flash of the emergency lights in the hallway, as they flooded his room through the little rectangular chicken wire glass panel in his door. This was immediately followed by the dimming of the lights and the loud whining of the diesel motors cranking up the power plant's auxiliary generators. The loud scream of the hospital's fire alarm brought him fully awake. No sooner had the alarm started than the emergency lights shut off and the generators stopped. Everything was silent except for voices in the front of the compound. What in the hell's going on in this bizarre house of freaks?

"Hamster, Hamster, you in there?" a voice whispered loudly, through the screen. "It's me, Di Lizardo. I've come to break you outa this joint, by God."

Chip could see the dark silhouette of someone's head and shoulders at the window, but he couldn't tell who it was. There was a loud grating sound followed by the sound of metal locking onto metal. He didn't know what to think.

"Hamster, it's me, Di Lizardo, I'm busting you outa' here, by God. Stand back away from the window!"

"Who? Ron?" Hamster asked, trying to whisper.

"Get away from the damn window now! That's an order, by God." Di Lizardo shouted. Immediately there was the sound of the Cadillac's 472 engine winding up outside the window.

"Stomp thu somitch!" Di Lizardo shouted. His words were followed by the screech of tires and the smell of burning rubber as the car accelerated. When the chain had stretched out all of the way, it caught the bars over the window with a strong jerk, and wrenched them out of the frame in one motion, accompanied by a loud grating sound. There was then a loud metallic crash as the four by eight foot steel grate fell to the concrete driveway.

"Jump Hamster! Let's get the hell out of here. Come on!"

Hamster jumped and Ron Di Lizardo caught him by the torso, threw him into the back seat of the Cadillac convertible, disconnected the chain from the car, jumped into the passenger seat and yelled, "Move it, by God!"

The Cadillac sped down the side of the road that skirted the river, moving quickly around the side of the building and toward the front gate. Chip looked back and saw that the lights had come on again. A great cloud of dust and debris was still hovering around the hole in the wall that used to be his window. The light flowing through it gave an eerie, almost solid look, like some kind of ghostly monster whose shape changed even as he watched. Looking ahead again, Chip saw the parking lot for the hospital's visitor center to his right. People in their bedclothes stood out by the side door. Suddenly there was the loud and unmistakable blast of machine gun fire originating slightly behind the car to his left. He instinctively hit the floor of the car and, looking up, saw the bottom of the arch that spanned the two stone gateposts as they passed beneath it. The car jerked and lurched as it sped down the road away from the Wildman Sanitarium. In the distance, Chip heard an approaching siren which was getting louder with every passing moment. Suddenly the volume was piercing, and Chip rose placing his hands over his ears, to see a large fire engine pass close to the car at a high rate of speed, with lights flashing. The excitement made Chip suddenly feel nauseated and cold. He was shaking like a leaf, and his teeth were chattering.

By the time the three vehicles involved in the rescue mission had made it back to the Loaf, Chip realized that this had all been done on his behalf, and was truly grateful. After a large glass of iced tea and a big plate of greens, Chip regained his composure and felt it necessary to thank his rescuers. He rose from his table to address them.

"Ron," he said, looking at the junk dealer, "first of all let me say 'thank you.' If you hadn't organized this rescue party and come when you did, I really don't know what would have happened. Those lunatics wanted me to join their 'council of the twelve,' or some bullshit like that. All I wanted to do was get out of there. They kept telling me that I must choose to remain with them of my own volition, and that I was free to leave whenever I wanted. But every time I mentioned getting outa there, they stalled me with statements like, 'It would probably be best for you to think it over for a few more days.' I was beginning to wonder if I was ever going to get out of that place. Who are those people anyway? How did you know I was there?"

"I knew you were there because your car was towed to my place. When they didn't find your body, I suspected they had you."

Since the mission had been successfully concluded, there was no point in telling the boys anything they didn't need to know. There was no reason to risk reprisals from the Secret Chiefs. As matters stood, no real harm had been done aside from the one wall at their part of the facility that had been damaged. There was no doubt that the Chiefs knew Di Lizardo had engineered the breakout. And yet, they also possessed a certain sense of fair play, and would most likely not take any counter measures unless further provoked. The Council members knew they had been holding Hamster against his will, in direct violation of their own charter, and most likely wouldn't be too upset about the rescue, as long as Di Lizardo returned their $10 thousand, and paid to have the wall repaired.

On the other hand, if there was talk around town and it was traced back to the Mountainaires, they would conclude that Di Lizardo had been running his mouth and might, at their option, decide to fry this entire part of Lookout Mountain. The less said, the better.

"Those people," Di Lizardo replied, "....and you guys didn't see any of them," he said, looking in the direction of the Mighty Gospel Mountainaires, "are some very strange and rich inmates of the hospital. They are both crazy and dangerous. The reason you didn't see any of them is because they live at the rear of the compound. They are very rich, much more so than anyone who lives in Chattanooga. As the result of their excessive wealth, they are able to bribe, buy, and pay off the doctors who run the hospital, as well as the staff and anybody else. They have basically turned the place into their own country club. They dress up in robes and costumes, and play with some old discarded radio equipment left over from World War II, and pretend to be scientists, trying to save the world."

"You mean they really aren't scientists? That they're just a bunch of dressed up idiots?" Chip asked.

"You look surprised?"

"Well," Chip answered, "I am. I thought they were crazy at first. I still think they are crazy now, but I met this girl, some astronomer from Iceland. She was talking some real horseshit about how she had found some lens in the bottom of a Double-Cola bottle, and that she had used it to discover some giant meteor that these people had created to destroy the Earth. She said it was going to hit us at any moment. I guess that is crazy. She said they'd captured her snooping around the Double-Cola plant. She's probably crazy too. What a pity," he said with a wistful sigh.

"Wait a minute," Di Lizardo exclaimed, suddenly very interested. "Tell me that again, only this time more slowly, and in greater detail."

"Ok, I met this scientist at the bug house. At first I thought she was working for them, but she said she wasn't. She said they had abducted her from the Double-Cola plant, had taken her somewhere underground, and had then brought her to the command center to find out how much she knew about some Double-Cola bottle. She said that she had discovered back in Iceland that some star, or whatever it is they created, is heading toward us. She said that, according to her calculations, as soon as the thing crossed into our galaxy, it would be invisible, and that it could literally destroy this planet in less than two weeks.

"The problem is that nobody on Earth, according to her, has

sophisticated enough instruments to even see this thing. She was very upset about it and said that I was the only person she could talk to, considering the rest of them were in on it. I felt sorry for her, and offered to help, but what the hell could I do about it? I'm just thankful to all of you for getting me out of that place. I really appreciate it. And, of course I've heard of the famous Mighty Gospel Mountainaires all the way over in Nashville," he lied. "I mean hell, who hasn't? Anyway, thanks again."

This was truly a joyous occasion, and Tomtom rose to give a speech. Suddenly Di Lizardo interrupted, "Look, I'm sorry boys, but we got to get outa here quick. I think I left the stove on back at my place. Come on Chip, let's roll. Thanks again guys, I'll be here for lunch tomorrow, by God, and there better be some damn catfish left."

"What was that all about?" Chip asked, as soon as they were out the door.

"We're going back," Di Lizardo said

"Going back where?"

"To the Wildman Sanitarium."

26.

LET'S ROCK AGAIN!

"I don't understand," Chip said. "Why do you want to go back there?"

"We've got to snatch your scientist girlfriend, by God, and bring her back to the Tiki Hut."

"Why?" Chip asked. "Why right now?" not that he particularly minded.

"Well," he replied as he pulled into the gravel driveway of Mid-South Auto Brokers, "I suspect that everything that woman told you is true. I didn't want to say anything in front of the Mountainaires, but these people have the technology and the ability to create anything they want out there. If she said that they are planning to destroy the planet, by God, she's probably right. If she mentioned the Double-Cola lens, there's little possibility of doubt."

"How is it you know so much about this Double-Cola lens?" Chip asked.

There was a moment of silence and then Di Lizardo replied, "Hell, I invented it."

"You?" Hamster asked in amazement. "You're a junk car dealer," he stated, as if reorienting himself. "What would you know about astronomy?"

"Maybe someday I'll tell you," Di Lizardo replied. "Right now, we've got work to do, and not much time."

"Ok, but why would anybody want to destroy their own planet?" Chip asked. "It just doesn't make any sense. If they blow up this planet, or radiate it or whatever they're planning on doing, they'll be destroying themselves, too."

"They're way too smart for that. Knowing how these people think, my guess is that they're planning to leave the planet before it hits."

"Leave the planet?" Chip asked, scarcely able to believe what he was hearing. "Leave the planet? Where are they going, Mars?" he laughed. "Jupiter?"

"No," Di Lizardo answered seriously. "They won't be that close. They'll leave this solar system altogether," he said, noticeably omitting the affectation 'by God,' which he had appropriated as a conversational aid to grease the flow of communication in this part of the country.

"Do you realize what you're saying?" Chip asked.

"Yeah," Di Lizardo said, sliding to a stop. "Wait here."

In the blink of an eye, he emerged from the shed behind the Tiki Hut with two large automatic pistols and a shorter machine gun with a thick wire looking stock.

"What's this?" Chip asked.

"Back-up," the auto broker said, shifting his car into reverse and stomping the accelerator.

"It's good that it's a dark night," he said, halfway speaking to himself as the long Cadillac convertible sped down the gravel road, kicking up dust and rocks in its wake.

"So what Davis said about these people is true? And all of that stuff about the Double-Cola bottle isn't a bunch of horseshit?"

"You got it," Di Lizardo answered.

"Well, who in the hell are these people?" Chip asked.

"In the old days," Di Lizardo replied, "they were called 'Gods.'"

"Gods?" Chip asked.

"That's right. Higher beings, adepts, masters, the Great Brotherhood, the true Rosicrucians, the Magi, those possessed of 'Christ Consciousness,' the elect, or the Secret Chiefs, as they call themselves. They are known by many names. They are truly the masters of the universe. They control the fate of nations, wars, diseases, medical discoveries, the weather. You name it."

"This is insane," Chip said, half laughing at the absurdity of it all.

"No," Di Lizardo replied, "It's not insane, but it is peculiar. As far as what they're doing right now though, it's serious, dead serious."

The Cadillac skidded to a stop, before sliding from the gravel road onto the asphalt of the regular highway. Then Di Lizardo hit the gas pedal again and the car surged forward.

"I wouldn't want your Exxon bill, by God," Chip laughed. The auto broker smiled. But Chip Hamster didn't know what to think. Here he was, riding down some two bit highway in a dirty old Cadillac convertible, holding his nuts with one hand and a machine gun in the other, getting ready to challenge some super race of alien madmen to a fight. It was way beyond crazy.

"Shit, it's warm for December," he yelled into the wind, "even for here."

"That ought to tell you something. Get ready, we're going in." The big Cadillac hit a rise in the road, jumped like a fish and then slammed hard, back down on the ground, beside the main drive. The car slowed now as Di Lizardo whispered instructions. "I don't know what we're gonna find here, but the directive is shoot first and don't wait for a second chance, these bastards have weapons you've never even thought of. The good news is that we have the element of surprise. They've never been attacked before, at least at this installation. They most likely know that I'm the one who got you out, so they won't be expecting anything else. They won't bother me, but that doesn't mean they can't or won't kill you, so shoot first. Now when we stop, follow me. We've got to get that scientist out as quickly as possible." Di Lizardo reached across Chip's lap and pulled back the stiff bolt of the machine gun, and then killed the headlights.

They took the road to the right side of the installation and as they passed under the gate, they could see that the fire engines were still there. It appeared that the inmates had been returned to their quarters. A few men stood around talking in front of the fire engines, but everything else seemed back to normal. The auxiliary generators had been shut down, and the regular power had been restored throughout the compound.

This was still too risky. They'd have to ditch the car by the river and go the rest of the way on foot. Di Lizardo drove through the freshly mowed grass, down toward the river bank and the row of trees, which he hoped would hide the car. They heard voices near the hospital entrance, but there were no police cars, which was a good sign. It meant that Di Lizardo was right, so far. They wouldn't want any publicity of any kind. The hospital director, Dr. Langley, had probably been called to the scene from his house, or some party at the country club. He no doubt explained that there had been an electrical overload, a grease fire, or some other accident. The fire department would not be permitted to linger or investigate. Langley would get them out of the building as soon as possible, and then kiss their asses in the parking lot. That's what appeared to be happening.

They abandoned the car and stuck close to the tree line, moving parallel along the side of the building toward the rear of the compound. Di Lizardo seemed to know exactly where he was going. It was really uncanny.

"Hey Ron," Chip whispered, "How come you know so much about these people? And how is it that you know your way around this place so well?" Chip could never have imagined the answer he was about to receive.

"I was one of them myself, once," Di Lizardo answered calmly.

"Here's the door, let's go," he said, stopping Chip from asking anymore questions.

Di Lizardo lifted a large metal flap to the left of the door and placed the palm of his hand on the illuminated green screen. It looked like the old sonar screens they used in the Navy, Chip reflected. Di Lizardo didn't think they would have had his hand print removed from the entry scanner....too much trouble to reprogram. Fortunately, he was right. The door slid silently and quickly into the wall, and then closed again as soon as they were inside. They were in some type of equipment room, part of a long hallway which was dimly lit by black light fixtures placed near the low ceiling, every ten feet or so. It reminded him of being in a submarine. There wasn't much room, and there were transformers, tubes, wires, pipes, and other lighted pieces of unfamiliar electronic equipment all along both sides of the hallway, as well as on the 'overhead' as they called the ceiling on a submarine.

"Follow me," Di Lizardo whispered. Di Lizardo led them down the hall, took a right, ascended two flights of stairs, and proceeded down a long corridor with glass walls on either side from floor to ceiling.

"Okay" he said, stopping. "We're going to the guest quarters. Here, put these on," he said, reaching into the bag hanging from his shoulder and withdrawing two sets of Russian night vision glasses.

"Cool," Chip whispered, as he put them on, fastened the strap on the back, and took a look around. Everything was sort of a fuzzy green, but quite visible. He noticed that when he turned his head rapidly from side to side, the light streaked, reminding him of an LSD trip.

"From this point forward," Di Lizardo warned, "be on guard. There's no telling what we might run into, so be ready. The main electrical power substation for the lab is just ahead. I'm going to spike the box and short circuit the auxiliary generators. That will also cut the power to the living quarters. Hang close and cover me while I'm in the electrical room. If anybody or anything moves, shoot to kill. What we're doing here is that critical. Here, use this as back up if you need it," Di Lizardo said, handing Chip a Nazi era Walther P-38 with a silencer on the end of the barrel.

"Let's move it."

The protruding pin, just above the hammer, indicated to Chip that there was already a bullet in the chamber. He flipped the safety lever up and was ready for action.

There's too much light in this place, Chip thought, adjusting the knob on the side of the night vision glasses. He wasn't afraid, but might as well have been. He was cold, and shaking all over. He'd never shot anyone before, at least not intentionally.

Di Lizardo slipped quietly through the door into the power station with Chip right behind him. After about thirty seconds the lights in the rear of the sanitarium went out. The generators began to crank, but shut down immediately. If it weren't for the night vision glasses, Chip wouldn't be able to see anything at all. He felt safer now, in the dark, knowing that he could see without being seen. They continued walking.

As they approached another hallway, the lenses on their night vision glasses indicated a web of criss-crossing infrared beams. Chip looked at Di Lizardo, awaiting his instructions.

"Get down on the floor and crawl under them," Di Lizardo said. "If one of those beams touches you, it will set off the alarm, and cause all of these doors to lock. In other words, we'll be stuck here."

Chip slid very carefully under the beams, following Di Lizardo. They then stood, turned a corner, and continued down yet another narrow passageway. The place was a maze. Suddenly Di Lizardo stopped in his tracks.

"Don't move a muscle," he said. Chip looked up and saw a very large Doberman at the other end of the hall, less than thirty feet from where they stood. The dog was very edgy, probably because it couldn't see anything. But it was growling, shaking its large head from side to side and slinging saliva, its sharp and plentiful teeth clearly visible, even in the dim green light of the night vision glasses. The dog was moving toward them slowly. It knew they were there, but more importantly for the intruders, the dog knew that they didn't belong there. It was growling loudly now, and inching toward them slowly, in a crouched position, alert and totally unintimidated.

"Damn," Chip thought, "This is the biggest, angriest dog on

Earth." Ron was still between Chip and the dog, thank God for that. It would rip out his throat first. The fool was still advancing, moving down the hall, in spite of the dog. With every step, the dog moved that much closer, still crouching close to the floor. Suddenly Di Lizardo stopped, turned back and tapped Chip on the arm, and pointed to some more infrared beams. Chip sized up the situation up immediately. If the dog lunged for them, it would set off the alarm, the doors would lock, and they would be trapped in this hallway with an angry dog and no possibility of escape. It was a no win situation. If either of them shot the dog, the bullet would pass through the beams and set off the alarm. Either way, they were stuck.

The dog moved closer toward the intruders, and toward the red pencils of infrared light, its growl becoming louder and more menacing with each step.

This was just too much for Chip. He knew the dog could literally smell his fear. His life flashed before him. He remembered sitting on the back porch with Therpis drinking Blatz Negaritas, riding in his Rolls-Royce with the top down, and making love to Ioveena on the beach in Key West.

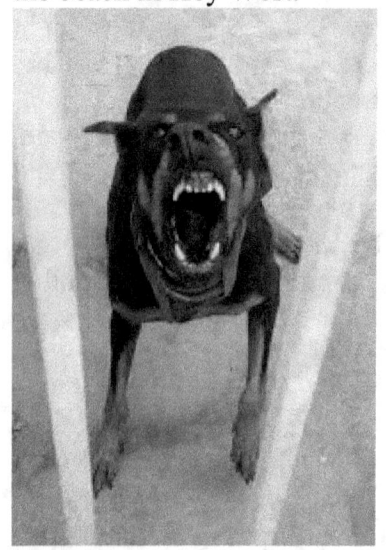

Suddenly the dog stood up on all fours and bared its teeth. This sight brought Chip back to the present immediately. He looked at the dog again. It was pissing as it continued its approach, the final phase before it ripped them to shreds. This was it, he thought, they were dead. He closed his eyes, and waited for the inevitable.

Suddenly Chip smelled Brut, the formerly rare and desirable fragrance that was now sold at chain drug stores in rubber bottles. He opened his eyes to see Ron crouched down on the floor, a spray bottle of the after shave aimed at the dog. What is this madman doing? The dog crouched down again, ceased its growling and crawled slowly toward Di Lizardo. "Come on Steve, it's me, Mazor, come here little Stevie Wonder. Come here, baby." The crisis was over. "I thought we might run into Steve," Di Lizardo said casually, as if they hadn't been on the verge of being devoured, "so I brought some Brut. It's his favorite."

"Well thanks a pantload for telling me," Chip said. "This little incident took ten years off my life."

They ducked beneath the light beams and continued making their way slowly down the hall. Chip had no idea where in the hell they were, and couldn't have found his way out if his life depended on it. Di Lizardo had expected to see somebody up and about, even at this late hour, but nobody was stirring. They kept walking, but there was no one there. The place was deserted.

"Nobody's here," Di Lizardo said, sticking his pistol back in its holster. "This is really strange, but hell, nobody's here. Let's go get your friend," he continued, "then let's get the hell out of here. They'll be back any minute. If they find us here, under these circumstances, we'd both be better off dead."

The two located Dr. Davis in her room asleep on top of the sheets, dressed only in a bra and some bikini panties. What an exquisite sight. Their unannounced arrival initially caught her off guard, but as soon as she realized that they'd come to rescue her, she threw on a robe and left with them quickly, not asking any questions. They left the way they'd entered, crawling beneath the light beams, with the big dog, Steve following them.

Well, they were almost free. The door through which they had entered was less than ten feet away. Di Lizardo lifted the steel plate, exposing the screen that stood ready for his hand print, but suddenly he hesitated, as if sensing danger. Instinctively he drew his pistol, quietly instructed Chip to forget the P-38 and get the machine gun ready, and told Dr. Davis to stand behind them. He looked at the monitor screen above the metal door frame. The camera on the other side showed the area surrounding the door. All was quiet. There appeared to be nothing out of the ordinary. He pushed the scan button on the control panel, and the images coming through on the monitor screen began to shift as the camera on the other side of the door panned in the search mode. Nothing. He hesitated a moment longer, then placed the palm of his hand firmly on the surface of the screen. The door slid quietly into the wall and Di Lizardo stepped through, ahead of the others.

"Well, well, well. It's Louie the Pencil, a.k.a. Mazor, Secret Chief, emeritus," a familiar voice spoke, shattering the silence. Marduk was facing them, and in his hand was an aural accelerator pistol, a very deadly weapon, but one that was only able to effectively deal with one target at a time. Marduk saw Chip's machine gun aimed at him as well a pistol in the grip of Di Lizardo.

"It appears we have a Mexican standoff," Marduk said.

"We mean you no harm," Di Lizardo replied. "Let us go."

Marduk was tempted to blast Mazor, but let the feeling pass. It would be easy enough, but Chip Hamster would return fire and probably kill him with the primitive but effective weapon he was holding. Besides, the Secret Chiefs were leaving. By this time tomorrow, they would all be gone, well on the way to another dimension, leaving Earth to its certain and rapidly approaching destruction. What difference did it really make whether these three died right now or in two days? There was no point in forcing a confrontation. As the two titans stood facing each other, Marduk suddenly remembered Mazor's sense of humor and his silly pranks, and was inclined to let them pass. Of all the Council members, he had liked Mazor most. This was the last time they would meet. He lowered his weapon, raised his hand, and said, "Go in peace."

Di Lizardo immediately replaced his pistol in its holster, dropped to one knee, and bowed his head as a sign of respect for the order and its supreme leader. "Aboogala," he said, after the practice of the ancients. He then rose silently and quietly instructed Davis and Hamster to follow him. Mazor turned for one last look at Marduk, but he had vanished.

"Come on Little Stevie," he called, and the dog joined them. In less than fifteen minutes the three, and their new found pet, were back at Di Lizardo's residence atop Lookout Mountain, none the worse for the experience.

27.

THE SHOW MUST GO ON

Back at Di Lizardo's place Dr. Davis answered his questions about the recent activities at the Wildman compound. She explained her initial findings, how she'd reached her conclusions, why she'd come to Chattanooga, how she'd been abducted, and why she'd asked to study with them.

"So this really isn't a bunch of horseshit?" Chip asked.

"Not at all," Di Lizardo replied, seeming preoccupied. He turned to Dr. Davis and asked her if she had witnessed any unusual behavior, or anything out of the ordinary, that might provide any clue to their intentions, beyond destroying the planet.

"When everything is unusual," she answered, "it's difficult to cite any one particular incident or thing. They've been spending a great deal of time away from the Wildman lately, basically for the last couple of weeks. There's really nothing unusual about that though," she continued. "I imagine that they've been working on their float for the Christmas Parade."

"Christmas parade?" he laughed. "I doubt that. The Secret Chiefs fall under the category of what locals would call 'pagans,' or 'heathens.' They certainly are not Christians by any stretch of the imagination."

"All I know, is that they have a Christmas float, and that it's going to be in the Christmas Parade. They're going to be dressed as Magi. That's all I know about it. Supposedly the float is at some warehouse and is being prepared for their...."

"For their departure," Di Lizardo interjected, ending the sentence for her.

"You mean they're building a space ship?" Dr. Davis asked, amazed.

"Of course they are," Di Lizardo said confidently. "It all makes sense now. They've created something that will knock Earth into another orbit. Nobody will even know it's coming. But first, they'll board their craft, leave here, and then watch the destruction from another location, beyond this solar system, but probably still within this galaxy. That's why they let us go tonight. If they were staying around, we'd never have succeeded in breaking you two out of there. My hillbillies would have been decimated."

So far, Chip had listened in silence to the conversation between the astronomer and the junk dealer. What they were talking about sounded crazy to him. As if some people from an insane asylum could actually create something in outer space that would be big enough to knock Earth out of its orbit, but would, at the same time be invisible. Yeah sure. He lit a cigar and looked into the night sky. It was still dark, but through the clouds it was possible to see the stars. This was all too absurd. These two, the junk car dealer and the scientist, might be crazy themselves. Hell, didn't Di Lizardo say he used to be an inmate at the bug house? And Dr. Davis was in the bug house when Chip met her. Hell, she could have been there for years. She might even be one of them herself. There was no real way to be sure. He decided to just listen to what they had to say. After all, it was fairly amusing.

"What I don't understand," Dr. Davis said, "is why they would want to target Earth. Why don't they just leave, if that's their intention?"

"Oh yeah," Chip said silently to himself. "Sure. Why don't they just saddle up their rockets and ride off into the sunset. Please, give me a break."

"It's about basic philosophy," Di Lizardo answered. "The Secret Chiefs have done all they felt they can to save the planet from its inhabitants, but nothing's changed. The ozone layer is depleted, the air and water have become polluted, animal species become extinct daily, and the population increase still continues to erode the natural resources. Make no mistake, Earth has a consciousness of its own, and creates its own diseases when things get out of hand. Look at all the plagues in the middle ages. It's like a dog shaking water off its back. The Earth is shaking itself now, by God, to get some of the dead weight off its back. This shaking takes the form of strange, new, and basically incurable diseases. The diseases don't care who gets 'em, as long as some of the dead weight is removed. Do you understand what I'm saying?"

"Yes," Dr. Davis replied, "I understand what you're saying but I..."

244

"The Council is just attempting to speed things up a bit. It's like Earth's resistance is lowered due to the presence of too many human parasites. It can no longer kill people fast enough to survive. The Council, by striking Earth with this celestial body, will by God, literally kill millions of people, both during the impact, and later, by God, when deadly gasses and radiation emerge from Earth's center. Earth will, as a result of the impact, be moved out of its natural orbit. This will result in a number of associated changes in gravity, and other so called 'natural laws,' which are only constant under specific conditions. It may sound strange, but in their own minds, they are doing the planet a favor. In a sense, they're right. There won't be any factories or manmade pollution for possibly several thousand years. This, in conjunction with a greatly reduced population, will give Earth an opportunity to bounce back, to, by God, build up its resistance. Those who do survive and adapt will lead the way into an eventually brighter future, not that I really think it matters to them particularly. The thought might in some small way make them feel good about themselves."

"They must be stopped," Dr. Davis stated firmly.

"Yes and no," the junk man answered. "Yes, we need to see if we can destroy whatever it is they're sending this way. While their intentions may be laudable, it doesn't fit with my twenty year business plan. No, we don't need to stop them from leaving the planet. Good riddance. My guess is that they'll leave on the 21st, the equinox. That's today, by the way. They've most likely programmed the thing to hit us within a week after their departure, just in case they needed some extra time to prepare."

"After SS396 becomes invisible, it's probably too late to stop it," Davis observed.

"Well, you're right about that, but we can't go back and look at it tonight by God, You mentioned your friends in Iceland. You better call them right now, and see if the thing is still visible."

Dr. Davis called her associates, Entutu and Henry, at the Thompson Observatory in Iceland.

"Observatory." It was Dr. Henry.

"Clarence."

"Debbie, where are you?" he asked, recognizing her voice immediately.

"It's a long story. I'm still in Chattanooga, but I don't have time to tell you about it right now. You won't believe what's happened

245

down here. I stayed with them under the guise of wanting to be an understudy until I found out exactly what their intentions really were. Everything you said was true, they do intend to destroy the planet, and they certainly have the ability, but we'll have to talk about it later. Right now, we've got work to do. Just tell me if SS396 is still visible through our telescope."

"Of course it's still visible, I looked at it last night." he replied. "Why wouldn't it be? Hey listen, are you all right? What's going on down there?"

"I'm fine," she said, "but it's been real strange. I can't wait to tell you all about it, but there isn't time now. I'll call you back later but stand by. Please do me a favor and don't leave the observatory for the next 48 hours. And don't ask any questions. The fate of this planet literally depends on what happens in the next two days. Just stay there. Right now, though, I've got to get going. See you."

"As long as it's still visible, we're okay, but I'm not sure for exactly how long," Di Lizardo said. "If they're leaving here on the 21st, that's today. When is the Christmas Parade? Is that today?"

"Yes it is," Dr. Davis replied. "It starts this afternoon, but I'm not exactly sure at what time."

"They'll most likely leave after dark," Di Lizardo speculated. "This means, by God, that there are two possibilities as far as SS396 is concerned. They're are so arrogant they might think nobody will even figure out what it is, let alone how to stop it. In that case, they'll leave it on its present course and schedule, and it will strike at the pre-programmed time. Another possibility is that they'll attempt to speed it up right before they leave Earth. They're so smug that they'll most likely just leave it wherever it's set right now. In that case, it'll get here in its own sweet time. That could be anywhere from ten hours to two weeks. I wouldn't think that it would be any later than that though. On the other hand, and much more likely, it will be within less than 24 hours after their departure. We'll hit the compound tonight, as soon as they blast off, after the parade"

"So what are we going to do?" Dr. Davis asked.

"We should go to bed, get some sleep, and deal with it after they vacate the compound for good, after dark. There's nothing we can do about it right now."

"Yeah, I agree with that," Chip said, rousing from his reverie. "This all still sounds strange to me. It's really hard for me to believe any of it, even now. I remember standing out on the balcony of the

Sky Harbor Motel and looking down at the Wildman, and wondering about what you'd said. It seemed like an interesting fantasy, but nothing real. I had no idea that I would ever actually be inside the Wildman, or that a governing body of the elect actually had a base there. And to think, they actually wanted me to join them. If I had, I might be riding out of here on a spaceship. I wonder."

"If you had joined them, you would be riding out of here, by God," Di Lizardo observed, "but don't get the big head about it, because they were down two members when you washed up into their compound. If it had been your buddy Therpis, they'd have taken him. Now listen, I hope you all won't think me rude, but I'm gonna' go to sleep. I wasn't planning on company when I got up this morning, but there are two couches here, blankets, sheets, and pillows in the closet over there. Bathroom's down the hall. I'll see you in the morning. Good night."

"Wait a minute," Chip said. "There's something I forgot to say."

"Yeah, by God, and what's that?"

"Thanks for getting me out of that place. I didn't think they were going to let me go, and I damn sure didn't want to join them."

"Me too," Davis interjected.

"You're both welcome," Di Lizardo said. "And you're right. Neither one of you would have left there alive if you'd tried to escape on your own. Creatures who have no hesitation in killing millions of people, don't worry about killing one or two individuals. The fact that Marduk let us leave there tonight clearly indicates to me that they're leaving, by God, and that they fully intend to wreck the planet. I'm going to sleep now, so good night. We don't have much time, and it's going to be a long day tomorrow."

So there they were, alone together. There was an awkward moment of silence before Dr. Davis broke the ice.

"When Bustokus told me that some hillbilly thugs had broken you out of the sanitarium," she said, "I didn't know what to think. I was confined to my quarters electronically when the gunfire erupted. When I found out that you were gone, I didn't know if I'd ever see you again."

"I didn't know you cared," Chip smiled, thrilled at the implication of her words.

Dr. Davis blushed. "Well, I ..."

"It happened kind of fast," Chip said, interrupting her. "I was asleep in my bed with the window open, and woke up when the alarm went off and the lights started flashing. Then I heard somebody calling my name. I didn't have any idea who it could be. The next thing I knew, the wall was literally ripped out right before my eyes, bars and all. Suddenly there was a gaping hole. I jumped, Di Lizardo grabbed me, and threw me in the back seat of his car, before I even knew what happened. On the way out I heard machine gun fire. Then, about fifteen minutes later, we ended up at some restaurant on the other side of Lookout Mountain, with a bunch of his rowdy friends. I told him that we had to come back and get you, that I couldn't just leave you with those people," Chip continued, stretching the truth just a bit to fit the circumstances.

The awkwardness they initially felt upon realizing that they were alone together, and no longer under close scrutiny diminished quickly, and was replaced by feelings of a different nature. Dr. Davis was still dressed in the loose fitting robe she'd grabbed in her haste to escape the sanitarium. As she sat down on the couch beside Chip and turned toward him, the top of her robe opened slightly, exposing her right breast, veiled lightly within a black lace bra. He also noticed the curve of her neck, where it joined her smooth shoulder, and observed the way her honey colored hair framed her face, and flowed down over her breasts in the dim light of the room, like liquid silver. Her skin was soft, smooth, fragrant, and inviting. This was really too much for him. Despite his lengthy experience with women of all types, this woman before him was truly the most beautiful sight he'd ever seen in his life. The sexual attraction between them was obvious, but it was much more than that for him. He wanted to experience her totally, to make love to her with his body, mind, and soul, to know her simultaneously on each of those levels. He really wanted and needed to love her, right now. She was talking about some aspect of the Secret Chiefs' discoveries, but Chip wasn't hearing a word she said. He meant to, and wanted to, but he was simply overwhelmed by her presence. He watched her mouth as she spoke, and wanted to bite her ripe full lips, ever so gently, to open them. He looked at her eyes and wanted to kiss her closed eyelids, then to see them open wide, somewhere between pain and pleasure, when he first came into her. He wanted to kiss her stomach, to kiss the inside of her thighs, to inhale her fragrance. And her perfume, what was it? Slight but sweet, just a trace, just enough to pull him closer until her own natural essence completely enveloped him. He was truly in another dimension already, just from her nearness, in a state somewhere beyond time, beyond space, beyond even life or death. He was totally immersed in the here and now of the moment. There was nowhere else, there was nothing else, just him and the one he loved.

"Excuse me," he said, as he pulled her to him midsentence, unable to wait another second. He kissed her open mouth gently and passionately. And she returned his kisses, each one requiring an answer, given back in the same way it was offered. He reached to turn out the lamp on the table beside the couch. Her sharpened breathing, sighs, and soft moans only served to increase his ardor. Nothing in his whole life matched this moment, and yet the moment was passing before his eyes, even as time stood still.

"Shit. It's too dark, by God," Ron Di Lizardo cursed silently, as he vainly attempted to watch the motions of the two lovers through the narrow keyhole.

ELSEWHERE

"All right," Marduk said, addressing the other nine Council members. "It's been an interesting day, but it's late. I think we should 'knock off ship's work' until tomorrow morning. I urge all of my fellow Council members to take a good long last look around and reflect upon our work here. We've accomplished a great deal in our time, and the Earthly civilization has advanced on many fronts as the direct result of our efforts. Regrettably, our best efforts have been inadequate. You can't free people who fail to recognize that they're imprisoned. More importantly, it's impossible to liberate cattle, which, sadly, is the class most mortals fall under. May the strong survive."

"I had hoped that their civilization might be spared," Ahmedis lamented. "'If but for one man,' we all agreed, but alas, under the circumstances, there wasn't time to search."

"There have been millennia," Marduk replied. "Let's drop the sentimentality and get down to the business at hand. Besides, if one truly great man shows up and disarms our system, they'll all be spared. But that's very unlikely. Let's move onto something else, and then get the hell out of here. I'm tired. Is there anything else?"

"Before we adjourn, would you tell us what happened with Deb-O-Ra, and Hamster, Your Excellence?" The Titan requested.

"Very well. While you were still at the foundry, tonight," Marduk explained, "and some of you know about this already, Louie the Pencil.....I mean Mazor, and some of his outlaw hillbillies, descended on our compound and liberated candidate Chip Hamster. As you know, Mazor had claimed last week that Hamster owed him some money arising from some nefarious and vile business arrangement. We sent Mazor a check for the amount he claimed Hamster owed him, and I thought that would be the end of the matter. Apparently, I was mistaken. Mazor and his band of whiskey-swilling thugs raided our installation while we were on site at the foundry, preparing our craft for departure. Later, Hamster and Mazor returned for Deb-O-Ra. I apprehended them leaving the building through the access door. I could have detained them, but what was the point? We're leaving in less than twenty-four hours. Hamster didn't want to be a part of our group anyway, and we were planning to leave Deb-O-Ra behind. I was the only Council member here, and I did what I thought was appropriate under the circumstances."

"Well," the Corsican replied, "it is unfortunate that we will be leaving with only eleven of the required twelve members, but I suppose that under the circumstances, there's nothing to be done about it. I'd hoped Hamster would work out, but I think he's just too young. There are too many things he wants to do."

"Well, at least Hocker, that is, Meeztor, seems to be working out," Alexander observed.

"Quite so. Now, let's move onto some last minute matters and details," Marduk suggested. "First, does everybody know where they're supposed to be and when? I'll quickly review the plan of the day right now, but you should already be familiar with it. You're on your own time until dinner at 3:30 p.m., about twelve hours hence. Take advantage of that time to attend to last minute details and to gather any smaller personal items you might want to take with you. Remember, everything in your inventory, at least the larger items, have already been sampled, so I urge you not to waste needed space on our craft with items that will already be there when we arrive. At 4:30 p.m.," he resumed, "we board the underground transport for the Double-Cola plant. From there we'll be taken by bus to the Aquarium parking lot between Broad and Market Streets, which is the starting point for the parade. You will see our float in the parking lot. It's the last one in the rather lengthy lineup.

We'll disembark together from the bus in full parade gear, and then load onto our craft, which has been designed to resemble the 'Yellow Submarine,' from that stupid Beatles cartoon, except for the orange and white colors of the UT football team. As I've already mentioned, our spacecraft will be the last float in the parade lineup. The parade begins in the Aquarium parking lot at 6:00 p.m., proceeds down Market Street past Warehouse Row, and the Choo, then turns right, dead ending into Broad. We then take a left on Broad, proceed past Abe Shavin's Hardware, past the Double-Cola Plant, the Bar B Que joint, and then take a second left, passing the former Confederama, the Winn Dixie, and then on toward the St. Elmo entrance to Lookout Mountain. The parade will make its loop in St. Elmo, turning right at the bottom of Lookout Mountain, passing the Incline on the left, heading back over to Broad, and then all the way back to the Aquarium parking lot.

"Behind us will be several police vehicles as a rear escort. We'll then experience 'unexpected mechanical problems.' This will be at the furthermost part of the parade route from the point of origin.....that is, directly in front of the Lookout Mountain Incline. At this point," Marduk continued, "the children will be removed from our float, loaded into the police cars, and taken back to the Tennessee Aquarium parking lot. The trailer transporting our spacecraft will back up to the Incline and unload our craft directly onto the tracks, facing the top of the mountain. We will then be secured to the tracks and readied for launch. Are there any questions so far?"

"So we will all be on board the craft from the time the parade starts straight on through to launch time, is that right?" Cybrion asked.

"That is affirmative. We'll all be on board at this time, and will not exit the craft. When we reach the Incline, Ken and Irby, from the foundry, will secure us to the launching rails with chains. The chains will be tightened from controls within our capsule, and we'll be slowly pulled into a secured launching configuration.

"After we're in launching position," Marduk continued, "the chains will be released, we'll fire up the engines and move into position. As you know, these engines were built here at this foundry and fitted onto the nacelles affixed to our craft at the Skipjack Yards, down in Louisiana. They've been thoroughly tested. We'll employ the tracks already existing and in use daily by the Incline's cars. With almost a mile of track, we should comfortably be able to clear the top of Lookout Mountain, and easily depart. As you know, every detail has been covered. Any possible exigency, no matter how remote or unlikely, has been anticipated and prepared for. Gentlemen, we are ready."

"Now what about the police?" Bustokus asked.

"The police who will be following us, have been informed that our vehicle is to be placed on permanent display at Rock City after the parade, and that the only way to get it to the top of Lookout Mountain, considering its size, is to transport it straight up the incline tracks to the top. They will certainly receive a surprise when our rockets activate and melt everything across the street, including that funky ice cream joint. Are there any questions?"

The Council members looked back and forth at each other, and seemed satisfied that everything was in order.

"Splendid," the Supreme Commander of the Secret Chiefs replied. "Sleep well. This time tomorrow, this place will be just a dot in the rearview mirror."

"One other thing, Your Excellence," Atlas interrupted, "and maybe I missed this because I came in late, but what was decided about the facility? Are we going to destroy it or what?"

"For our creation to strike Earth, it must continue to be energized artificially with our aural particle accelerator, at least until it actually crosses into this galaxy. After that happens, it requires no further attention. It will follow its program. Until it reaches that point, I repeat, it must be energized by our projectors. Should there be a power failure of any sort, the emergency generators will maintain the proper lever of aural particle acceleration. It won't even miss a beat," Marduk replied confidently.

"Yes, Your Excellence, I understand that," mighty Atlas replied. "I just wondered if perhaps we should take any additional security measures to safeguard the projectors, prior to our departure."

"I don't think really think any further precautions are in order," Marduk replied. "I have taken the liberty of visiting Dr. Langley. I advised him that we would be entering a week long period of silence as soon as the parade is over, in celebration of the equinox. He was informed that we would remain within our compound during that time, and most strongly cautioned to see that we are not disturbed by anybody at all. Bustokus has attended to other details in this matter. Perhaps he will favor us with a report at this time."

"That's right," Bustokus stood to address the gathering. "At 2:30 p.m. this afternoon, Cybrion and I will begin shutting down and disabling our defense systems. We will spike every piece of equipment. There will be nothing left that will be usable, all the way down to the toaster. The only things which will remain operational are the aural particle accelerator projectors. These, of course must remain functioning until 'our little disturbance' crosses the threshold into this galaxy. The oxygen level within the projection chamber will be reduced to a level incapable of supporting human life. Furthermore, the atmosphere in that area has been positively charged with the radindocrinator. Should that door be opened, intentionally, or inadvertently, the first person crossing the threshold will introduce a negative charge into that area and instantly become a lightning rod. That would serve as an example to anyone else who might wish to enter the room. The area is definitely secure. Cybrion and I have both reviewed our departure plans and feel that everything is in order. We do, however, welcome any additional ideas or suggestions, and our plans are available for the perusal of anyone in this room."

The Council members nodded their heads in approval, and Bustokus took his seat once again. "Remember," Marduk reminded them, "if you have any laundry, or if you want to order lunch, make phone calls, or anything else, you must do this prior to 2:30 pm this afternoon. After that, everything but the projector will be shut down."

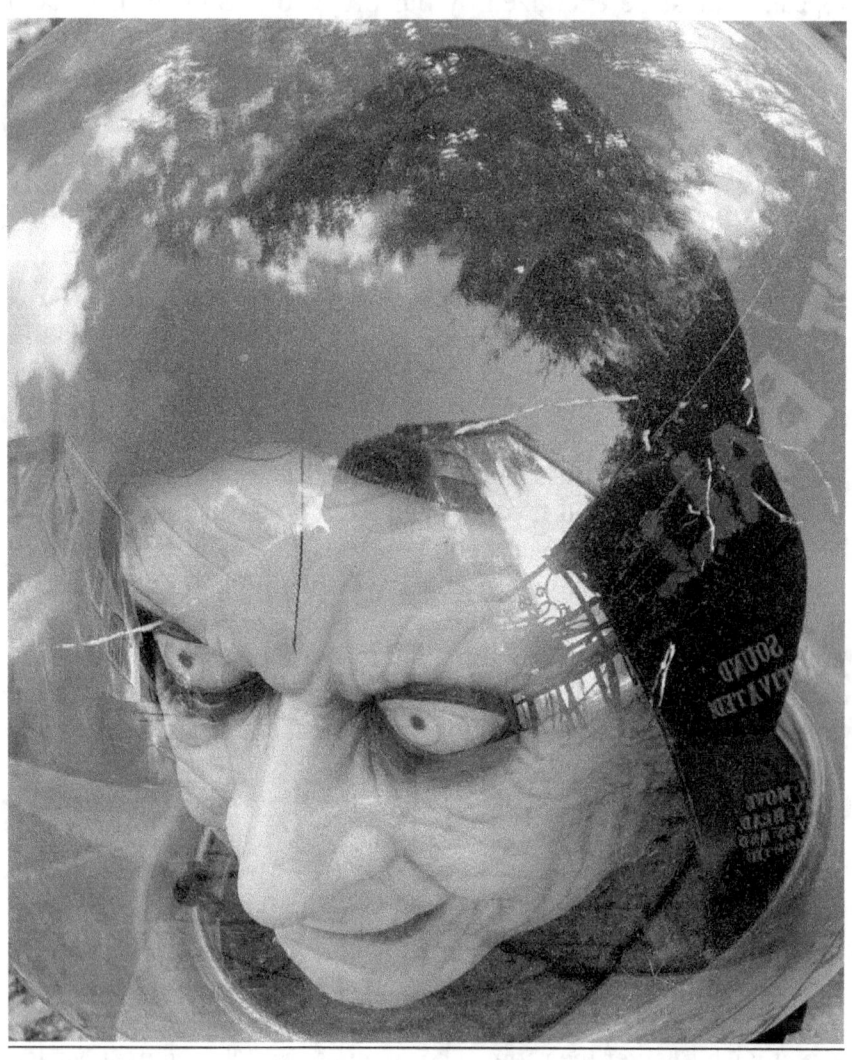

28.

10-9-8-7-AND COUNTING

Dr. Davis and Chip Hamster didn't get much sleep, but what they did get was most excellent. Around noon things got stirring at Di Lizardo's as the three began to weigh the seriousness of the task that lay before them......nothing less than saving the entire human race and possibly the planet itself. One of Di Lizardo's several live in women offered to fix them a big country ham breakfast, and Di Lizardo, of course, suggested the Golden Loaf. Since it was the first day out of captivity for both Hamster and Dr. Davis, they felt like going somewhere in public. There was some initial fear on their part that they might be seen out and about by one of the Chiefs, and possibly captured. Di Lizardo, however felt that this was rather unlikely.

"They're too predictable," he said. "You can bet, by God, that they're hanging around the hive getting ready and taking care of last minute details. We need to go on into town anyway, by God, to have a look at their so-called parade float."

They settled on a Hindu joint on East Brainerd called the India Mahal. It was there that they made their plans to save the world, three brave souls who staked their lives, fortunes, sacred honor, and asses, on the success of the mission.

"I don't want to underestimate the Chiefs. Marduk and his boys are very intelligent, resourceful, and thorough. Although I've more or less lost contact with them since I left, I do know, based upon what you've said," Di Lizardo paused and looked at Dr. Davis "exactly what they intend to do. They won't be likely to make any mistakes. This whole thing has been planned in great detail. We'll have to be very careful."

"Do you think that your rescue of us last night would tip them off that you might be planning anything else?" Davis asked.

"No, I really don't. I've thought about it a lot, by God, and I don't think so. They all think I'm crazy anyway, running a junk car lot and all, after being one of the so-called elect. Hell, what can I say? I like cars. That's all there is to it. They think I rescued Hamster here cause of a business deal he and I had going. That action on my part, fits well within the psychological profile, by God, they have of me."

"That explains your rescuing me," Chip observed, "but how do you account for coming back after Dr. Davis? I mean, wouldn't the Council view that as suspicious, she being a scientific understudy?"

"Aw hell no. They'd just think, by God, that I brought Hamster back for his girlfriend. If anything, that action would avert suspicion."

Hamster and Dr. Davis looked at each other sheepishly, a look that did not escape the keen observation of Di Lizardo.

"So you don't think they've booby trapped the place?" Dr. Davis asked quickly, feeling strangely ill at ease over Di Lizardo's most recent observation.

"I imagine they've secured the rooms that house the equipment necessary to keep SS396 headed this way," Di Lizardo speculated, "but I doubt they've gone much beyond that. Of course that depends on whether or not you gave them any reason or indication, by God, to suspect that you had any idea what they could be up to," he continued, addressing Dr. Davis.

"I can't recall anything I might have said or done that could have made them suspicious of either my motives or intentions," Dr. Davis replied, scanning her memory for any conversations pertaining to SS396.

"If they asked me about anything requiring specialized knowledge, and I knew the answer, I told them. I was there to learn as much as possible. I had no idea when I joined them that I would be fortunate enough to run into someone on the outside, who'd actually been one of them. I thought it would be up to me entirely. I really don't know whether I could have handled it all on my own. In fact, I doubt it."

"All three of us may not be able to handle it. We might as well face that possibility and factor it into the equation," Di Lizardo said. "This is some serious shit, by God. There's no telling what they've planned. The whole place, hospital and all, may blow off the face of the Earth as soon as we open the door. Despite their incredible intelligence and power, they really are crazy. I don't think you fully realize that fact. They're crazy. Anybody with enough intelligence and technical ability to have come this far isn't about to risk the

256

desired outcome in the interest of saving a few hundred or even thousand lives. I'm sure they liked you, enjoyed showing off for you, and were glad to have you around. But make no mistake, by God, they'd just as soon kill you as look at you, if they perceived any kind of threat to their plans."

"That's chilling," Davis observed. "They seemed so nice."

"Another thing," Di Lizardo remembered. "They weren't particularly fond of the hospital's director, Dr. Langley, and probably wouldn't hesitate to blow up the hospital just to ruin his day. On the other hand, they'll need to keep their equipment running until SS396 hits our galaxy, so who knows?"

The three concluded that the only possible course of action as far as disabling SS396 was concerned, was to expect anything, and attack the problem one step at a time, once they reached the Wildman. All the speculation in the world wouldn't enable them to guess what specific measures, if any, the Secret Chiefs had taken to protect their interests.

With that, Di Lizardo, Hamster, and Dr. Davis left the Indian joint and proceeded back toward town, stopping en route at the Krispy Kreme to secure the necessary provisions for their upcoming mission.

The parade site at the base of the Aquarium was already filling up with people by the time the three arrived at 2:30, and all of the floats were in line, even though the parade wasn't supposed to start for another couple of hours. The plan was for the parade to make the first half of the loop in the daylight hours, and the return trip as it turned dark, so that the lights on the various floats, as well as those strung between the street lights, could be fully appreciated by the spectators.

This was indeed Chattanooga at its finest, Di Lizardo reflected, as he led his group in the direction of a street corner preacher who was spouting some vile pseudo-Christian doctrine against the parade and the 'barbaric idolaters' who had engineered this 'abomination in the eyes of the Lord.'

"This is the Bible," he shouted angrily. "It's been on the bestseller list for two thousand years. Read it! Y'all can read can't you? Read your Bible! It ain't nothing in it about pagan trees and phallic worship. It ain't nothing in it bout 'lectric lights, parades, and all that kind of stuff. It ain't nothing in it about a Christmas turkey. Jesus didn't eat no Christmas turkey. It ain't nothing in it 'bout

257

buying up a bunch of 'lectric trains and bikes, and all that kind of stuff for your children. It ain't nothing in it about women dressing up to look 'foxy,' with diamond-o-rings, mink fuhs, and all that kind of stuff. Women ain't supposed to be 'foxy,' they supposed to be holy! The Devil's the one that wants lights. The Devil wants the big turkey. The Devil wants you to dress your women like harlots.

"Y'all ain't liking me," he said, looking at Di Lizardo. "I can't help it. I'm not here to be liked, I'm here to save you. I ain't here for no parade, I'm here to save you. Jesus didn't eat no Moon Pies!" he said pointing at the line of floats "Jesus didn't drink no Double-Cola! And Jesus didn't ride no rocket ship, neither!"

Hamster, Di Lizardo, and Dr. Davis looked over at the line of floats, and sure enough, there was a sinister space like machine at the end of the procession, looking very different from the rest of the parade entries, despite its yellow color, orange UT lettering, and a sign on the side of the trailer which read 'Santa's Helpers.'

"Yeah," he continued, "y'all go ahead and look. That's a spaceship if I ever saw one. Those floats are evil. Santa's helpers? Do you really believe that? It's Satan's helpers! And aw yeah, there's big fat Santa Claus, himself. Ain't he cute and jolly, in his red suit? Wake up somebody! The Devil wears a red suit! That white beard of Santa's represents smoke from the fires of hell! Wake up! Santa Claus is known as 'Ole St. Nick.' Nick is another name for the Devil! And you telling children the Devil's coming down their chimney? Get back Santa! Get back Satan! Get back Devil! I'm preaching now. I don't want no Devil coming down my chimney. Amen, Holy Ghost. I don't want no Devil in my house! Ayyyyaah! Get back Devil! Get out of my house Devil! Amen Holy Ghost."

"Let's go have a closer look," Di Lizardo said, turning toward the floats on the other side of the block.

"That's the wildest thing I've ever heard," Davis said, truly shocked. "How could anybody think that way about Santa Claus? That preacher is the barbarian."

"If you live in Chattanooga, you get used to street corner preachers. They come down from the hills on Saturdays and preach. It's part of their training. After a while, you get used to it. I like them. They're colorful."

As they walked in the direction of the floats, the preacher called after them. "Don't turn your back on the Lord! Don't walk away from Jesus!"

It was a spaceship all right, no doubt about that. They walked around it once, secured a map of the parade route and left. The Chiefs could arrive at any moment. "Yep, that's it" Di Lizardo said, "They're gonna launch from the bottom of the Incline, by God, using its tracks. Let's get back to the Tiki Hut, and get ready."

29.

HURRY UP AND WAIT
COMMAND CENTER: TIKI HUT
DATE: DEC. 21 TIME: HOURS

Jap Harley, The Lookout City's highly respected television news journalist.

There was nothing to do but wait. The parade coverage was about to begin on TV, hosted by a major network's local affiliate anchorman. In this case, it was Jap Harley, the Lookout City's 'Most Respected News Journalist.' Chip had been watching him lately on the evening news at the compound. He was baldheaded like the Wizard of Oz, only Jap was also a big tub ass. The opening camera shot each night began with the viewer looking at a full screen picture of what appeared to be the cratered surface of the moon. This always was accompanied by dramatic music, usually the stuff that fat Elvis always started his show with in Las Vegas, the same music from the film '2001.' Just as the viewer began to think he really was looking at the surface of the moon, the camera would back off slowly, revealing, not the moon, as imagined, but the side of the newsman's head. At just that instant of recognition, the newsman's head dramatically turned from the side angle, to face the television audience head on.   Immediately Jap broadsided the television audience with something stimulating, like a bus wreck in India, or a top local story; an axe murder, for example.

"In a late breaking story, a local Chattanooga resident received a dreadful surprise today. What started with a flat tire, ended with the horrible discovery of a beheaded corpse found stuffed in his trunk.

While police have not ruled out foul play, the actual cause of death is not being released just yet, pending identification of the body. We'll keep you informed as the case develops." Duh, no shit! The victim was 'decrapitated.' Jap was a serious news journalist and didn't smile often. When he did, it was awkward and ill-timed, as was the case with former president Richard Nixon. Chip was glad that Jap was going to be covering the parade. It was nice of him to come down for the night, when he could have been out laying pipe or watching live studio wrestling, two of his favorite sports.

"Welcome to our live coverage of the Lookout City's annual Christmas Parade. I'm Jap Harley, of course, and this evening I'm being joined by well-known Chattanooga socialite and great philan....philanthropist, Page Wainwright. Welcome Page, to our live coverage. What do you think so far?"

"Well Jap, it certainly is a pleasure to be here tonight, although with the temperature in the mid-seventies, it doesn't feel much like Christmas."

"You're right about that, Page, but you know, regardless of the temperature, we can be sure of a wonderful parade. The view you are seeing now," he addressed his television audience, "is from our famous 'Eye Hi Cam,' positioned high atop Chattanooga's tallest building, the twenty-seven story Yoni Mining Tower. We're looking at the Tennessee Aquarium, the starting point of this year's parade. Page, would you describe some of what we're looking at for our many friends in television land?"

"Of course," Page replied, "but first I think we should thank some of our local sponsors."

With that the camera moved in on Jap's head as it turned sideways, and then closer yet, still magnifying the pores on his head until they again resembled lunar craters. Then the scene shifted to some commercial about cat piss and 'your cat's urinary tract health.'

"That goofy son of a bitch must get dizzy turning his head back and forth like that every few minutes," Chip observed.

"Silly," Dr. Davis laughed. "He doesn't do that every time, it's on film."

"Naw, I think he likes to do it, but either way, it's amazing to me that the people of Chattanooga watch this ridiculous charade every evening and don't think there's anything unusual about it," Chip said. "Or is it just me?"

"It's the vortex," Di Lizardo replied. "What's strange elsewhere, by God, is normal here." And so they sat around Di Lizardo's crib drinking Double-Colas, snacking on Moon Pies, and monitoring the parade. It wouldn't be long now.

It came as no surprise when the float called 'Santa's Helpers' experienced mechanical troubles, about an hour and a half into the parade, at the farthest end of the route, just below the Incline. A brief announcement was made about the float's 'unfortunate withdrawal,' and the coverage continued, following the rest of the floats, all the way back to the Aquarium. When the parade moved on, leaving the float called 'Santa's Helpers,' at the base of the Incline, it was time to return to the Wildman and try to stop SS396 from destroying the planet.

30.

LAUNCH
COMMAND CENTER: WILDMAN ANNEX
DEC. 21   HOURS

"You've done a great job with the weather, boys," Hocker laughed as the Council members solemnly walked through the tunnel to the underground transport tube. "It feels like Miamuh Beach out here," he continued unaware that they were leaving the planet Earth, never to return. 'Meeztor,' as Hocker had been renamed, liked being a probationer to the order of the Secret Chiefs. There were many great perks associated with the job, not the least of which was being able to walk through the main part of the asylum and having those burly smart aleck orderlies all but kiss his ass. It was also cool to dress in robes. They didn't do that at prison, and it was a shame that they didn't, he reflected as they walked, but it didn't matter now. He would soon be a full-fledged Council member himself, and assigned some real important duties, that's what mattered now. He'd been told of their impending departure, but some of the more insignificant details of the forthcoming trip had been unmentioned, such as their destination, for one thing. Hocker was under the impression that they were going to fly over to Knoxville for a big 'Volunteer Christmas' at UT. Consequently he was dressed appropriately in a hideous orange and white robe, with a bright orange and white 'UT' embroidered on the back. He was cool and he knew it.

As they filed through the cave toward the underground transport, its doors opened horizontally with a loud hiss, and they boarded the capsule. The doors sealed, and the craft lifted off the ground, hovering for a moment, before speeding through the tunnel and arriving at the docking station underneath the Double-Cola plant, five minutes later. The Council disembarked from the tube, ascended to the ground level, by way of the escalator, exited through the front door, and immediately boarded a large tour bus. It was a very exciting time for the Secret Chiefs, the end of an era, but also the beginning of something else, the dawn of a new day. The streets were lined with well-wishers and spectators, each of whom sought a glimpse of whatever famous person or persons might be on that big hillbilly tour bus. The police escort accompanied the bus, with lights flashing, all the way from Double-Cola to the parking lot of the Tennessee Aquarium, where the other floats and participants were assembled and waiting for the parade to begin.

The scene was reminiscent of a Democrat pep rally, with marching bands from area high schools tuning their instruments and practicing their musical selections. Politicians passed out barbecue sandwiches as scantily clad baton twirlers, and regal looking drum majors practiced their moves. All of the crowd excitedly awaited the mayor's dynamic annual Christmas speech. Nor did he fail in his duties as the city's chief executive and spokesman, proudly explaining how the 'Lookout City,' had survived the horrors of reconstruction, and bilked hundreds of thousands of northern tourists out of money owed to the citizens of this great Southern city, resulting from damages inflicted by those heathen invaders, not so very long ago. As a result of many unspecific advances of all types, Chattanooga has "again regained its position as the main 'jural' in that Tennessee Triple Crown, comprised of Chattanooga, Knoxville, and Johnson City."

With that, the mayor cut the ceremonial ribbon with a giant pair of scissors, and the first marching band began the procession down Market Street, beating a large number of drums in a loud and decidedly sensual manner. The drum corps were proceeded by a dozen lovely brown-skinned majorettes, excitedly shaking every part of their young and shapely bodies that could be shaken, as the parade began its trek toward the old train station.

The Oscar Mayer Weinermobile was a likely candidate for `Best of Show.'

The first float was the famous Oscar Mayer 'Weinermobile,' perhaps, at least from the masculine perspective, the most desirable vehicle ever made. It was understandably saluted, praised, and adored, not only by the male members of the audience, but by giggling adolescent girls who looked at it between blushes through the fingers of their covered faces. It was truly an exciting float, a likely candidate for the 'Best of Show' award presented each year by the Chattanooga chapter of the Daughters of the Confederacy.

The second float consisted of a large trailer with two upright, rotating 'Moon Pies,' truly a sight to behold. There was another area high school band, which was followed by the parade's third float, a giant Double-Cola bottle reclining on a flatbed truck, surrounded by prancing mini-skirted cheerleaders.

The American Legion, the Chattanooga Branch of the French Foreign Legion, the Sons of Confederate Veterans, and many other notable organizations, each had unique and decorative floats, all surrounded by nubile adolescent cheerleaders and baton twirlers. All in all there were twenty-three separate entries, as well as eleven different marching bands, and three divisions of drum corps, certainly the largest Christmas Parade in the Lookout City's proud history.

Bringing up the rear, was the most unusual of all the floats, a mock up model of something that looked like a cross between the Beatles' 'Yellow Submarine' and the submarine used in the Disney film 'Twenty Thousand Leagues Under the Sea.' This strange float, the parade's largest entry, was mounted on a very long and wide flatbed truck, and secured by extremely heavy steel chains. The presence of bright flower strands woven among the massive chain links only served to accent the visual peculiarity of this particular entry. While it resembled a submarine, there were also definite similarities to a spaceship, specifically the three large clusters of machined, stainless rotanium rocket engines affixed to the rear of the float. The other entries seemed much lighter by comparison, being constructed mainly of plywood, and chicken wire, and pulled by small lawnmowers or tractors. This last float, however, was obviously extremely heavy, since the trailer supporting it had five rear axles, with eight very large wheels per axle, and still groaned under the weight. When the other floats passed, the spectators all waived and cheered. When the last float passed them, however, they mainly stared in bewilderment as it cast dark shadows on both sides of the street.

People who had offices along the parade route viewed the procession from the roofs or windows of their buildings. In one particular office, near the point at which the parade was to begin its return loop, Freddie Ganzler, a geologist with the Environmental Protection Agency, was working late, checking the radioactive levels of some recent soil and rock samples from the area. He had stopped his research long enough to have a cup of coffee and to call his girlfriend. As they planned their tryst for later that evening, the geologist was disturbed by the sudden loud noises made by his Geiger counter. He attempted to ignore its loud insect like buzzing but it quickly reached maximum volume.

"Look, something's come up. I'll call you back in a few minutes," he said, quickly hanging up the phone, and grabbing the instrument. He pointed the chrome plated cylinder in several different directions, from floor to ceiling, but there was nothing radioactive in his immediate environment. Whatever it was that was making this instrument of his go crazy, was outside, and close to his building. He rushed to the window just in time to see the passing starboard side of some strange and gigantic submarine or spaceship being hauled on a long steel trailer. The shadow it cast darkened his walls, giving it an even more sinister appearance. It was massive, whatever it was, and most likely the source of the high radioactive readings. The geologist ran down the stairs and out of the building, chasing the slowly moving 'float,' and catching it easily. He held the meter and pointed it in the direction of the trailer. The vu-meter pegged immediately to the highest reading and the instrument emitted noises at maximum volume. Whatever this thing on the trailer was, it was highly radioactive, dangerously so. Radiation at this level posed an immediate health hazard to anyone within a mile of it. Something must be done, and right now, to protect the public from this deadly menace, but what? And what was this thing?

For a moment the young man just stood there in awe as the gigantic, whatever it was, continued moving slowly down the street, followed by two police cars with flashing lights. He ran back into the building, bounded up the stairs to his office and called the Highway Patrol. He attempted to explain who he was, and what he wanted, but got nowhere fast.

"Look buddy," the trooper said, breathing heavily into the phone, "What do you want me to do about it? I could send a unit over there, but what's he gonna' do when he gets there? I think for this type of thing, maybe you'd better call the National Guard. Besides, if what you said is true, there ain't no real hurry, is there? I mean where the hell's something that big gonna go, anyway?"

Something had to be done now. The geologist couldn't simply drop the matter and walk away. He called the Center for Disease Control in Atlanta, but there was nobody there he could talk to at this hour, on a weekend night. The next call was to the National Guard. Finally, he connected with someone who understood what he was trying to say. Fortunately, if not miraculously, it was Lt. Walter Harwood, a former fraternity brother from UT Chattanooga.

"National Guard, Lt. Harwood speaking."

"Walter?"

"Yeah," the officer replied cautiously, recognizing the voice, but not being quite able to connect it with a name or face, "Who's this?"

"It's me, Freddie Ganzler."

"Ganzler?" he asked, "What are you up to? I thought you'd gone to Zimbabwe, or someplace like that to study rocks."

Lt. Harwood hadn't seen Ganzler in at least two years, and was understandably surprised by the call.

"Listen, Walter. I've got to tell you about a potentially dangerous situation, one which concerns the public's health, and its exposure to very high levels of radioactivity."

"What are you talking about? Slow down, and tell me all about it."

Harwood knew that his old school buddy was one of those wild academic types, about half 'Earth person'...that is, overzealous environmentalist.....and about half normal. He wasn't crazy though, and if he had something to say, especially anything scientific, he was probably right. He'd been one of those pencil toting nerds who made straight A's and drove a Volkswagen van, one of those underpowered things that looks like a loaf of bread and always holds up traffic.

The geologist explained what had happened, and what conclusions he'd reached given the information available at that moment.

"Get back out there Freddie, and see if you can catch that thing. I'll check the parade route and be there in a few minutes. Stay with it, keep it in sight, and I'll see you as soon as I can get there."

As soon as he could get there turned out to be over half an hour later, and by this time it was already dark. Lt. Harwood had first called the police department and received a detailed description of the parade route, as well as a list of the participants. The last float in the lineup was entitled, 'Santa's Helpers,' and was registered to a company called Atmospheric Transports, a company for which no records or listings existed. There was no telling what this thing was, whether it was occupied, and if so, what the intentions of its occupants were. The best thing was to take a half dozen fully armed men in a Humm V, to the parade sight, and pose as part of the parade. There was no reason to frighten the public at this stage. Ganzler could meet them there, show him the readings from his Geiger counter, and if what he'd said was true, they would arrest the float's occupants, and impound the vehicle, on the spot.

Ganzler had caught up with the float in less than half a mile, but by the time Lt. Harwood and his troops arrived, the float had been left behind by the rest of the parade, backed up to the base of the Incline, and secured to its tracks by several burly dock workers. He'd asked the police what was happening and they had replied casually that the float was 'some sort of display for Rock City,' something which, due to its size, was too large to be moved by road.

Instead, it would be raised up the Incline's tracks to the top of the mountain. There was clearly no point in talking to the police about the matter, so the geologist anxiously awaited the arrival of the national guard, checking his Geiger counter periodically, and staring, awestruck at the sight of this giant, futuristic piece of equipment, marked apart from the UT logo, only by a bumper sticker on one side that read 'See Rock City.'

When Lt. Harwood arrived at the base of the incline in the Hummer, Ganzler approached him quickly and showed him the meter's reading. As soon as it was activated it pegged to the right side. This thing was literally exuding radioactivity.

"I brought my own, just to be sure it wasn't an instrument or calibration error," Harwood said, handing his Geiger counter to Ganzler.

"Same thing," Ganzler said, the meter pegging all the way to the right as soon as it was turned on.

"What do you think we should do?" the National Guard officer asked, puzzled.

"I don't know," the geologist replied. "The first thing to do is to secure, evacuate, and quarantine the area. There should be nobody within a mile of this thing."

"What the hell is it, Ganzler?" the Lieutenant asked, looking perplexed.

"Hell, man, I don't have the slightest clue."

"It sort of looks like a submarine, but I don't know. Those pods on the stern are definitely jet engines, but what for? Is there anyone in it?"

"I don't know," Ganzler answered. "It appears to be seamless, like a big fuel tank. I don't see any doors, and nobody has gone into it, or come out of it, at least while I've been here. The people who unloaded it from the truck seemed to be speaking with walkie talkies, but I don't know whether they were communicating with someone on the inside, or just talking to each other. I don't see them now, what do you think?"

The police still stood casually beside their cars, chatting with each other, smoking cigarettes, and drinking coffee from the Crapdonald's drive thru, generally oblivious to the strange looking thing poised menacingly at the bottom of the Incline.

"The first thing we need to do is stop it from moving up the side of the mountain," Lt. Harwood suggested. "It doesn't seem to be moving though. Maybe they planned to take it up tomorrow during daylight hours. How did it get hooked up on the tracks?"

"Well," Ganzler replied, "the people who brought it here hooked it onto the tracks and then left. I tried to talk to them but they wouldn't answer any questions, and went about their business like I wasn't even there. I don't think anyone should be within five hundred feet of it for any reason. In fact, we should probably back away from it ourselves. You don't want radiation poisoning, I can guarantee you that."

While the two men stood there looking at the spaceship, and wondering what they should do, there was a sudden 'puff' sound, like when a gas heater comes on. The back of what appeared to be rocket engines slowly began to glow, and very rapidly turned to bright red, then just as quickly shifted to a deep blue color.

"What the hell is that?" the guardsman asked.

"I'd say the damn thing's firing up its engines, getting ready to launch," Ganzler exclaimed, "or at least move up the tracks. We should stop it."

"Stop it? With what?" the guardsman asked, moving further away from the increasingly loud whine of the engines.

A thin green pencil sized beam of green light suddenly darted from the side of the spaceship, and focused on one of the police cars, to the amazement of everyone in the small group of bystanders. The beam lingered for a few seconds and then the police car exploded, lifting off the ground several feet and slamming back down to the asphalt, engulfed in flames. This happened so suddenly and unexpectedly that the men didn't have time to react. The two policemen nearest the destroyed car were knocked to the ground by the tremendous force of the explosion.

"Head for cover!" Lt. Harwood shouted to his men, "let's take this thing!" The Guardsmen spread out, taking positions behind whatever cover was available. "Fire!" Harwood shouted, and three of the Guardsmen fired machine guns at the craft with no effect whatsoever. Another thin beam of green light focused on the other police car, lingered, and then moved to the Guardsmen's Hummer. Both vehicles exploded, showering the area with burning, twisted debris. One of the guardsmen held a shoulder mounted rocket launcher in place and fired a heat seeking missile toward one of the spacecraft's glowing engines. The rocket went right into the engine and exploded but did no damage at all. Instead the engines revved up faster and louder, sending a scorching fifty foot flame from the end of each power plant, incinerating everything the flames touched, and setting fire to a row of 1920's era buildings across the street from the Incline's entrance. The noise level was incredible, and the ground shook as the huge craft began moving slowly, climbing the tracks up the side of Lookout Mountain, pulling away from the street.

In a matter of seconds the spacecraft was halfway up the track, accelerating faster the higher it climbed. Within three more seconds, it had plowed through the Incline visitor's center at the top end of the tracks, and lifted off into the air, leaving a trail of burning foliage and debris in its wake. The Guardsmen and police watched in amazement as it continued to distance itself from them, now just a large bright blue spot in the night sky. Suddenly, there was an explosion, and the spaceship appeared to disintegrate, with burning pieces of its first stage falling to Earth in a flaming shower from the dark night sky above the top of Lookout Mountain.

Back on the street in St. Elmo, several large brick buildings were burning out of control, three vehicles had been destroyed, and the policemen and guardsmen stood by helplessly, shocked at the destruction, unable to even call for back up or assistance.

"Look out!" someone shouted as a huge ice cream cone tumbled from above the entrance to one of the burning buildings, crashing to the ground, and raining flaming plastic drops all across the street.

"Good God," Lt. Harwood said to Ganzler as they looked at the burning remains of their vehicle, the two police cars and the buildings on the other side of the street. "I've never seen anything like this. Summer Guard Camp in Hattiesburg never addressed this type of emergency."

"Me neither," Ganzler replied, standing there with a blank look on his face, still in shock from what he'd witnessed. Sirens were now blaring loudly in the background. At least help was on the way.

The Sunday edition of the *Chattanooga Times*, under strict orders from the Defense Department, and in the interests of national security, would report the incident as a 'fire of undetermined origin, possibly the result of a ruptured gas line.' The charred and empty remains of the large spaceship would soon be found in sections on the other side of Lookout Mountain, and a fight would erupt between the states of Tennessee and Georgia over ownership of the pieces, in much the same way as they had fought for nearly a century over the ownership of the civil war locomotive, 'The General.' Ultimately, and in relatively short order, the Government would resolve the feud by stealing the evidence, just as it had in the famed Roswell case, and maintaining that the event had never happened at all. Before the investigation was over, however, everyone from The FAA, to KFC would have something to say about the matter, but no definite conclusions would be reached.

The Geiger Counter showed high levels of radiation emanating from the float from Atmospheric Transports

31.

IT MAY ALREADY BE TOO LATE

"Let's head on down there," Di Lizardo advised. "I've got my tools. I don't think we'll need any firepower, but I've got 'Sparky,' just in case. Let's move it."

As they loaded their equipment into Redbird, there was a bright flash up in the night sky, like an explosion.

"That's them," Di Lizardo said. "They've launched. They're gone."

"There are pieces of the spaceship falling from the sky," Chip said excitedly, "It looks like the Challenger, like they blew up!"

"It looks like it, sure enough, by God," Di Lizardo observed casually. "But it's most likely the first stage of their launch power plant falling back. Whether they're alive or dead has nothing to do with us. Let's move it. We've got work to do. Wherever they are, or might be, they're not down here anymore, and that's all that matters to us right now."

They drove the red Cadillac convertible down the mountain, around the corner, and up the driveway, coming unexpectedly upon a hastily erected guardhouse, obviously a hospital security precaution against any further invasions. As they arrived, the guard exited the shed quickly and approached the car, motioning for it to stop.

"May I help you?" the guard said coldly, but courteously.

"Yeah, I'm here to pick up some stuff around back," Di Lizardo answered, not recognizing the guard, and not being able to think of anything convincing on short notice.

"Let's see your pass," he said, reaching out his hand.

"I don't have a pass and I don't need one," he said, quickly losing his patience.

The guard immediately assumed a stiff and defensive posture, and casually unhooked the leather strap covering his pistol.

"I'm afraid that I can't let you in if you don't have a pass."

"I tell you what," Di Lizardo said, hoping to avoid a

confrontation. "You call Dr. Langley and tell him that Mazor is here to pick up some of his belongings."

"Dr. Langley's in town at the Christmas Parade sir," the guard replied sternly. "You need to turn your car around and exit the property the same way you came in."

Di Lizardo was starting to get pissed, and didn't feel like fooling with some halfwit power crazy guard. The guard was one of those big beefy looking oafs with an attitude, someone who'd never properly had his ass whipped, due to his intimidating size. Di Lizardo decided then and there to whip some ass, and started to open the car door.

The guard pressed against the door with his considerable bulk, holding it shut. "If you don't leave right this moment sir, I'm going to have to teach you a lesson," he advised, just hoping for the opportunity to test his steroid pumped strength against someone he imagined he could easily whup. Di Lizardo pushed the car door halfway open, in spite of the guard's presence. The next thing Di Lizardo knew his arm, indeed his whole body was reeling with pain as the guard touched him with one of those hand held electrical tazers. Di Lizardo started cursing loudly. He was obviously incapacitated.

"That ought to teach you, you son of a bitch," the guard said laughing. "I told you not to fuck with me."

"I can't drive," Di Lizardo said to his companions between gasps of breath, as the guard walked back and stood outside the door of the guard shack, lighting a cigarette and waiting for Di Lizardo to recover enough to drive out of there the same way he came in, like the guard had told him to do in the first place.

"Get 'Sparky,' my accelerator pistol," he whispered to Chip, "It's under the seat. Get it and shoot this bastard."

"I...I don't... I mean I don't want to kill the guy," Chip said.

"I told you," Di Lizardo repeated. "Get the pistol and shoot him. It won't kill him. Now do what I told you God damn it!" Di Lizardo shouted, obviously in extreme agony.

Chip reached under the seat slowly, withdrew a strange looking pistol and called the guard over. "Hey fat boy!" he shouted, "Get your big fat lard ass over here, I want ask you a question. Is it true that your nuts shrink up from all those steroids you morons take, and that you can't get it up?"

"No, Chip, cut that shit out!" Di Lizardo laughed. "I can't take it. I can't laugh. It hurts too much."

"You dumb asses must want some more shit," the guard said angrily, reaching for the car door. "Your buddy got off easy," he said to Chip, "but you? Hey, I'm gonna personally whip your ass. Honey can you drive?" he asked Dr. Davis. "Cause you're Gonna' have to drive these two pussies to the hospital in a few minutes," he laughed.

As the guard pulled the heavy Cadillac door open, Di Lizardo leaned back, Chip aimed the gun and pulled the trigger. A silent red beam struck the rent-a-cop in the chest, immediately knocking him unconscious and silently backward at least eight or ten feet. He landed on the ground and didn't move.

"You drive," Di Lizardo said to Chip, moving over to the middle of the car.

"What a gun, I must have this," Chip said. "No smoke, no noise, just power."

"We'll talk about it later. Let's roll."

With Chip at the wheel, they drove down the road to the right of the Wildman, past the main driveway, and around to the side door, the same one they had used to rescue Dr. Davis. Di Lizardo lifted the metal security screen door and placed his hand against the glass.

The door opened silently and they stepped through into the passageway, which this time was very well lit. Di Lizardo led the way through the mazelike configuration of the Secret Chief's inner sanctum, as they passed through a large tropical garden, down a short hallway, and stepped onto a large freight elevator. Again Dr. Davis had no idea whether they were going up or down, there was only the sense of rapid movement.

The elevator door opened, revealing a large equipment room of some sort, with walls lined floor to ceiling with large transformers, amplifiers, and other instruments. Each time Dr. Davis had been here before, all of the equipment in this room had been operational. This time, there were pieces of glass strewn across the floor, and the only things electrical in the room still working were the overhead lights, which fully exposed the destruction the equipment had suffered.

"Good God," Chip exclaimed, "what happened here?"

"They spiked all of the equipment," Di Lizardo observed, just in case. They didn't want anyone else using it, or figuring out what they were up to. It's a standard precautionary measure, but they sure did a good job, by God. Don't step through that door. My guess is that the equipment room is charged. Stand back."

Di Lizardo tossed a screwdriver through the door of the equipment room. There was an immediate flash and the screwdriver disappeared.

"Just as I expected. But that's it. Let's go," Di Lizardo shouted. "They forget I'm the one who designed all this shit," Di Lizardo said, looking sadly at the carnage. "But somewhere in this room there is another transformer," he continued. "One that hasn't been destroyed. They had to keep it working to drive the aural particle accelerator. It may not be lit up, so look carefully. Unless we find it, there's nothing we can do. So start looking. And don't touch anything still connected to the wall by any kind of power cord."

It was a fairly large room, so it took all three of them to look through the transformers and other equipment. Whoever had worked this stuff over had done a very thorough job, having either torn it from the walls and thrown it on the floor, or left it in place and smashed it with axes or sledge hammers. After about thirty minutes, Chip found the working transformer, still connected to the wall. It was hidden carefully under a pile of other smashed and broken ones, with sliced wires hanging out the back.

"Hey Ron, this one looks like it's still working," he called.

"Don't touch it!" Di Lizardo shouted. "It's probably wired to kill anybody who moves it, by God."

Di Lizardo jumped over several piles of destroyed and twisted instruments and transformers, and very carefully approached the one Chip had located. The instrument lights were out, but Di Lizardo could see that it was lit up on the inside. This one was still working, but had been thrown in the pile and covered up, to make it look like all the others. Di Lizardo examined it carefully. There were no wires connected to it other than those running from the back of it into the wall.

"This one's grounded," he said. "If they'd wired it to kill whoever picked it up, it would most likely have shorted itself out in the process. They obviously aren't expecting anyone in here until after the accelerator has completed its mission. My guess," he continued, "is that Marduk instructed Dr. Langley not to disturb them for a week, since it's the equinox, a traditional time of silence for the Council. That means we have no more than a week's time at best before SS396 crosses into this galaxy, by God, and becomes invisible. We could, on the other hand, have as little time as, today, or even right now. Good work Hamster. Now let's move."

The group proceeded further down a narrow, dimly lit passageway for several hundred feet, going deeper beneath Earth's surface, before exiting at the underground transport boarding station.

"We've got to take the tube from here," Di Lizardo said.

"What tube?" Chip asked. "Where are we?"

"We're in a cave, at the bottom of Lookout Mountain. Ruby Falls is the first level. There's another cave beneath that, and we're in the one below that, at the third level."

So far there was nothing to suggest any kind of booby traps. It was entirely possible that the Secret Chiefs, in their smug scientific arrogance, didn't feel it necessary to take any unusual precautions. They took the tube for a several minute ride toward the observatory. Chip was most impressed, especially when the underground transport moved from the horizontal to the vertical and began its ascent.

"I had no idea any of this even existed," Chip said. "This is incredible. What a place. I feel like James Bond."

"This would have all been yours if you had joined them," Di

Lizardo laughed, "…for about ten minutes."

The tube leveled off and they exited from its side, and walked down another hallway through several locked doors, each of which opened as soon as Di Lizardo placed his hand on the security screen. They kept moving, and soon ended up in a large recording studio. Di Lizardo reached under the console, felt a button, and punched it. Immediately, one of the studio's walls disappeared, revealing a wall of blank TV monitor screens.

"These are usually activated," Di Lizardo explained. "Focused on different parts of the cosmos, but then you know that already 'Deb-O-Ra'," he said, jokingly. The Celestia-Sphere's direct TV monitors were also off when the three entered the telescope's control room. Turning them on was easy enough. Di Lizardo quickly examined the screens for anything out of the ordinary, and finding nothing unusual, placed his hand on the third monitor from the left, second row down. Immediately the screen lit. "Access Denied."

"This ain't right, by God," Di Lizardo exclaimed angrily, taking a seat at the large console. "I designed this son of a bitch, and there ain't nobody else smart enough to reprogram this bastard but me. No brag, just fact. Now what's wrong with this pop-eyed son of a bitch?"

He stared at the screen for a moment, got up, punched the reset button and again placed his hand on its glass surface. "Access Denied. Do Not Attempt To Reset."

"All right you son of a bitch," Di Lizardo cursed, and then inserted his fingers on each side of the TV and slowly pulled it from its housing in the wall. It was still connected by a power cord, and a cable. Di Lizardo disconnected the TV from its power source, set it on the floor, and had it completely disassembled within a few minutes. Davis and Hamster stood by and watched, feeling more or less helpless until the Celestia-Sphere could be accessed.

"Do you know how to operate this thing?" Di Lizardo asked Dr. Davis.

"I'm familiar enough with the Celestia-Sphere Mark I, but with their high tech modifications, I don't know. I'm not sure. What do you need?" She asked.

"What channel is SS396 on, and what are its coordinates? There are over five thousand settings for this thing. We definitely don't have time to look for it on our own, by God. That could take days. We don't have that kind of time."

280

"I don't remember," she said honestly, "but I'll try. Is there anything I can do now, while you're working on the monitor?"

"Yeah," he answered. "Go over to that red door, open it, and get me an extension cord. By the time you get back, this will be ready."

"What are you doing?" Chip asked him.

"Despite what I thought, somebody must have reprogrammed the access code and removed my hand print from the acceptable code signature module. It ain't no big deal though, by God. Like I said, I designed this bastard. All anybody's hand print does anyway, is to complete a circuit. I can do that myself by touching two wires together and bypassing the scanner altogether. Get me that extension cord. Yeah, that's it," he said to Davis. "Now plug the son of a bitch in, and hand it to Chip. Ok, Chip, now you take the wire from her and plug in the TV. That ought to turn the somitch on."

As soon as the connection was made, another wall disappeared, exposing a section of the Celestia-Sphere. He sat down at the console and began turning dials and pushing buttons. "None of these screens are working," he said absent mindedly, still pushing new and more complex combinations of buttons and numbers, but to no avail.

Across the room, Dr. Davis removed a panel from the side of the Celestia-Sphere eyepiece, exposing the Double-Cola bottle held firmly in place by two brightly polished rotanium clamps, one on each end. The light was passing through the soft drink bottle from the small opening at its top, churning around inside the bottle, and exiting in a much wider series of beams from the bottom of the bottle, that part of the bottle which served as the refracting lens. This series of beams, instead of reflecting into a mirror, and then into the eyepiece, as in any other telescope, narrowed in focus to a point, with all the beams converging onto a metallic plate at the entrance to the aural particle accelerator.

"This thing's on," Davis shouted across the room to Di Lizardo. "What do you want me to do?"

"I told you," Di Lizardo replied. "I need the coordinates to SS396. Don't touch the telescope. Come back over here."

Chip felt like a fifth wheel. He had no idea what either of them were talking about. "I'd like to help," he said, "but I don't know what to do."

"Just don't touch anything, honey," Davis cautioned him. It was nice, he reflected, to hear her call him 'honey.'

Dr. Davis returned to a chair at the large console next to Di

Lizardo.

"These screens are dead," he observed, "most likely disabled the same way everything else has been destroyed around here. The Celestia-Sphere is still working because it's hooked to the aural accelerator, and transmitting instead of receiving. It's operating in reverse. I should have suspected that's why they wanted my lens. They intended to use it as a projector, not as a receptor."

"Wait a minute," Chip said, "I'm no scientist, but tell me if I understand you correctly. Instead of light coming through the outside end of the telescope, the part aimed at the sky....Instead of light coming through it and into the eyepiece of the observer, the light is going from the observer in the opposite direction, and out into space. Is that it?"

"You got it, Hamster. Through the power of the aural particle accelerator in conjunction with my lens, they have created something out in space, and targeted Earth. This is an incredible accomplishment, even for the Secret Chiefs. I'm impressed, by God. But like I said, these bastards are crazy, they've gone over the edge this time. I don't know what's wrong with them, but this thing has got to be stopped, right now. I don't think we have much time left."

"What are we going to do? I mean how can we stop it if we can't see it?" Dr. Davis asked.

"These monitors are operated by the transformers and amplifiers in the destroyed solar equipment room," Di Lizardo said. "The one transformer still working, by God is running the accelerator. There isn't anywhere near enough power left over to run this bank of screens, and they're all on the same circuit, an obvious engineering design flaw on my part, by God, or so it seems now."

"What if...?" Dr. Davis hesitated to even suggest something so absurd in the presence of such an incredible scientific mind.

"What?' Di Lizardo asked.

"This will probably sound stupid, because it's so simple, and they've gone to so much trouble to keep this thing running, but what if.....?"

"What God damn it?" Di Lizardo shouted angrily," I don't have time for playing 'What if.'"

"What if we just shut down the power altogether, remove the lens from the Celestia-Sphere, and stop the accelerator from projecting at all? Wouldn't that cause the disappearance of SS396 altogether? That is, if it's really artificially objectified anyway."

Di Lizardo sat at the console looking stunned. He could scarcely believe the suggestion he'd just heard. Dr. Davis waited anxiously for some reply. It probably was a stupid thing to have said, but it seemed logical at the time.

"You mean simply unplug the son of a bitch?" he asked. "Is that what you mean, just unplug it, just like that?"

"Well, I.....Yes, that's exactly what I mean," she said.

"Dr. Davis," Di Lizardo replied, "You're brilliant. It won't be quite that simple, but in principle, that is what we're talking about." He grabbed the phone off of the side of the console. "We got a dial tone, by God, they forgot to disconnect the phone. A criminal always forgets something, some minor detail, which usually proves to be the cause of his undoing. Call your friends in Iceland, and let's get them to look at SS396 through their telescope. They're gonna have to walk us through this thing, by confirming the results of what we're doing down here. Call 'em up," he said, handing her the phone.

"Where are you Debbie?" Dr. Henry asked.

"Listen Clarence," she said urgently. "I don't have time to explain right now. I'm alright and I'll tell you everything that's happened later. First, I need you to get SS396 in focus. All of our screens are dead. This is an absolute priority one emergency. We may be too late already."

Within less than five minutes they were on the speakerphone with both Drs. Entutu and Henry, who had SS396 in focus. It appeared to be unchanged overall, except that a small portion of its left side had disappeared.

The implications of this sad situation were apparent to Di Lizardo and Davis. It meant the part of SS396 that was invisible had already crossed over into our galaxy. It was now objective and invisible, with mass as well as acceleration. In a very short time, possibly even minutes, it would be all the way into Earth's galaxy, uncontrollable, unstoppable, and invisible.

"Quick! There's no time to lose. I'm going to shut off the power to that lone transformer, by way of the console here. Hopefully we aren't too late." Di Lizardo moved a couple of knobs, punched in some numbers and a light appeared on the console meter board.

'LOSS OF POWER: TRANSFORMER 36452.'

The accelerator immediately shut down with a loud metallic clanking sound and the light passing through the Double-Cola bottle disappeared.

"What's happening up there?" Di Lizardo asked, talking into the speakerphone. "It ought to be invisible. Can you still see it?"

"It's still there," Dr. Entutu said, "and it's still moving to the left, apparently crossing into our galaxy right now."

"Son of a bitch!" Di lizardo shouted. "Davis, I want you to go to the Celestia-Sphere, remove the Double-Cola bottle and reverse its direction, and then lock it back in place. Now move it. We may not even have a minute left!"

Di Lizardo started punching keys on the recording console attempting to bring as many transformers as possible on line and switch them over to power the accelerator.

"Have you got it yet?" he shouted, still pushing buttons. "Come on Davis! Move it!"

'36452: STANDBY; 36453: LINE MALFUNCTION; 36454 LINE MALFUNCTION; 36455: LINE MALFUNCTION; 36456: LINE MALFUNCTION.'

"The problem is that it takes a hell of a lot less power to sustain SS396 than it did to create it. It probably required every transformer in the equipment room to feed the projectors, whereas it only took one transformer to keep SS396 in position and on course. On the other side of our galaxy, energy increases of its own nature, by God, sort of like 'An object in motion will remain in motion.' On the other side of the galaxy, and object set in motion will increase its velocity. Energy can be created over there. Come on, Davis move!"

"It's in," she yelled from across the room.

Immediately Di Lizardo hit the power switch and the Double-Cola bottle lit up as the power surged into the aural particle accelerator.

"What's going on up there?" he shouted at the speakerphone.

"We're re-calibrating now," Dr. Henry said. "It looks like you slowed it down appreciably, but it's still almost halfway off the screen. It may be too late."

"I don't accept that, by God," he said as he kept seeking other power sources to channel into the particle accelerator. The only thing I can do is to try to suck it back into its previous position. I'm

284

going to take all of the power from the hospital's power station and reroute it through this board. When the auxiliary generators kick in, I'll take that too. Hopefully, that will be enough to reverse the projectors. It's just a guess, but it might work. It's our only hope. Davis," he continued, "go back into the closet and get us some flashlights. Now! When I kick in the power, we're gonna' lose everything, including the lights."

'SUBSTATION REROUTING: STANDBY....POWER TRANSFERRING; TRANSFER COMPLETE; WARNING OVERLOAD HAZARD! WARNING OVERLOAD HAZARD!'

The lights went out and immediately the auxiliary generators kicked in, activating the emergency lights, but Di Lizardo shut the emergency lights down throughout the entire installation, including the hospital, sucking every bit of electricity available. The red warning lights on the console kept flashing. Except for the light passing through the Double-Cola bottle, and the flashing warning lights on the console, the observatory, the entire compound was without electricity.

"That's all I can get," Di Lizardo stated flatly. "There ain't no more. If this doesn't get it, we're through. Son of a bitch.''

"What are you people doing down there?" It was Dr. Henry on the speakerphone.

"I'm trying to reverse the accelerator and force SS396 back out of our galaxy. Has there been any change?"

"Yes," Henry replied cautiously, "it appears to be regressing, that is withdrawing to its original coordinates, but it isn't there yet, it's just moving back. Good work."

Suddenly an alarm sounded loudly and the console lights flashed red.

'FIRE: SECTOR SEVEN! FIRE: SECTOR SEVEN!'

"Don't you think you better shut it down?" Dr. Davis asked.

"I can't. It has to keep going until it's all the way back in place. If any part of it remains within our galaxy when the accelerator shuts down, even the minutest fragment, it will move back into our galaxy automatically as soon as the power shuts off."

Chip and Dr. Davis were both sweating nails.

"I smell smoke," Chip said.

"Me too," Davis agreed, shining the flashlight toward the door. "There's smoke coming under the door, we've got to get out of here now."

"Go over to the door, put your hand on it, and see if it's hot," Di Lizardo instructed.

"Yeah, it's hot," Chip said.

'FIRE: SECTORS SEVEN AND EIGHT! FIRE: SECTORS SEVEN, EIGHT, AND NINE! HAZARD: SECTOR NINE! EVACUATE SECTOR NINE!'

"Keep cool," Di Lizardo said, "it's too late to get out of here the way we came in, by God. We're gonna have to climb the side of the telescope. It's that or fry. Let's go. You first Davis, you know your way around the Celestia-Sphere. Hamster, you follow her up the side of the telescope, by God, now move it!"

"What's going on down there?" Dr. Henry asked.

"We've got an equipment fire." Di Lizardo replied calmly, "It's no big deal. Is SS396 still moving?"

"It's almost back to its original coordinates," Henry said.

"We can't leave you here," Dr. Davis said, crying. "You have to come with us now. Please, this place is on fire!" she pleaded. "Now!"

"I ain't gonna fry, but there's one other thing I've got to do before I leave. Now you two get the hell out of here! I don't have time to rescue you. Now get moving. Beat it!"

Dr. Davis led the way up the side of the telescope and Chip followed her. He didn't like climbing the side of the gigantic telescope. It was solid as the Rock of Gibraltar, thank God for that, but there was no guard rail of any kind, and the sheer drop was not one that Chip cared to consider. They were climbing a multi-story structure holding onto nothing but slippery twisted steel loops, each only a foot wide. There was hardly enough room to even get one's toes on the ladder. Worse still, it was dark. All he could see of Dr. Davis was the dim outline of her dark silhouette against the early morning sky.

"Come on man!" Chip called to Ron, as he continued to climb, but there was no reply. Chip could see orange flames licking the bottom of the control room door, and the smoke passing by him on its way up and out of the observatory was becoming thicker and blacker every moment.

"Don't let the light beams touch you," Dr. Davis shouted back at Chip.

"No shit," Chip thought.

"Ok, we're near the top of the telescope," she shouted back at him. "There's a rail surrounding the opening where the telescope protrudes. It's about four feet from the side of the telescope. When we get to the very top, we'll have to jump for it. Don't miss."

Dr. Davis jumped like a squirrel from the side of the telescope and grabbed one of the rails. There was nothing holding her to the rails except her hands. Her feet dangled below the opening in the side of the mountain. She easily pulled herself up to the next rail, then flipped over the side and landed on the ground.

Chip was right behind her. This really sucked. Four feet had never looked like such an incredibly long distance. There wasn't much of an area to spring from, just another steel loop step. He reached the top rung, balancing precariously on his heels and crouched down. The idea of dropping to his death seventy feet below was not an acceptable outcome. He had to make it the first time. He jumped, but as he did, the telescope shifted with a loud crash, causing him to lose his balance in mid jump, as his left foot slipped.

"Oh God!" Davis screamed as Chip fell.

He dropped several feet before grabbing one of the steel rungs, just about jerking his arms out of their sockets in the process, but stopping his descent. The telescope's shift had caused it to move from the center of the opening all the way to one side. Chip climbed back up the ladder, swung around, grabbed the rail with both hands and flipped over, landing on the ground. Dr. Davis leaned down and put her arms around him and kissed his face, glad that he was still alive.

"What about me, by God?" Di Lizardo asked, climbing over the rail."

Dr. Davis jumped up and threw her arms around his neck.

"My hero!" she laughed. And indeed he was.

"Let's get the hell out of here," Di Lizardo shouted. "The cops, fire department, or somebody else will be here soon, and I damn sure don't feel like answering any questions."

32.

HOME

Chip was understandably tired, but too excited to sleep. The knowledge that he was less than a hundred and twenty-five miles from home, and that he could be there in a couple of hours, was a wonderful thought. He wanted to call Therpis right now, but thought his phone might be tapped. It was probably better to wait. Chip would see him soon enough. The first thing he should most likely do is call his attorney, Mr. Filcher, and start to clear up the financial mess he was in as a result of his car title scam. Filcher's phone probably wasn't tapped, although if the FBI was really serious about catching crooks, tapping the phones of all lawyers was the obvious first step in reducing crime nationwide.

"Ron," he said, "I need to make a call to Nashville, is that cool?" Di Lizardo's phone probably wasn't tapped.

"Yeah man, call whoever you need to call."

Chip dialed the number. "Law offices," the receptionist answered.

"Mr. Filcher please," Chip said.

"May I tell him who is calling?"

"Yeah, Chip Hamster."

"Will he know what this is regarding?"

"Yeah, it's regarding me. Just tell him I'm on the phone." Here, I've been gone for months, abducted by madmen, helped save the universe, almost been roasted alive, nearly tumbled to my death, and I've got to explain what I want to some twenty year old receptionist. Give me a break! Chip didn't imagine he would have to wait long, and he didn't.

Filcher answered the phone immediately. "This is a surprise," the attorney stated coldly. A most unpleasant one actually. He'd hoped, and believed the foolish bastard was dead, in which case, as executor of Chip's father's estate, and as administrator of trusts, and in the absence of any heirs, he would have ended up with the big house in Belle Meade, as well as certain other substantial assets. That this foolish bastard was still alive, and had resurfaced after several

289

months, was a most unpleasant surprise indeed. "Where have you been?" he asked.

"It's a long story. After the accident I was captured by some madmen from that sanitarium outside Chattanooga, and held prisoner. It was horrible. The good news is that I'm free at last. The bad news is that I understand some legal difficulties of a financial nature have developed in my absence. I guess we need to talk about that. When can I see you?"

"Where are you now?" the lawyer asked.

Chip hesitated before answering, not wanting to give his location, just in case the phone was bugged, not that it couldn't be traced anyway. He evaded the question. "I've got some personal matters to attend to, but I'd be free anytime after around three o'clock today."

"Why don't we meet and have dinner somewhere?" The lawyer said. "There are several important matters we need to discuss, and I have some additional papers that require your signature. I'm involved in a lengthy corporate closing meeting at two, and doubt that I'll be free before, say, six-thirty. Come by my office after dark, say, around seven, and we'll decide where to go when you get here. And one other thing, it would probably be better if you came alone, since some of what we need to discuss is rather personal in nature. Also, in light of your present status resulting from those car loans, it would be best if you avoid anyone and everyone who might recognize you, at least until we get these problems straightened out. You shouldn't be seen in public right now, if you know what I mean, so don't let anyone, anywhere know that you're back, or even alive, until we can meet and straighten all of this out."

"Okay," Chip said, "I'll lay low in the meantime, and will look forward to seeing you then."

He slowly put down the phone and turned to Dr. Davis. "That was a strange conversation. He wants me to meet him at his office after dark, and to come alone. I got a weird vibe about that."

"Well, you said he's been your family lawyer for over forty years. This is the same guy, right?"

"Yeah, it's probably my imagination, but he always was a real slime. He'll…never mind, it's probably nothing. He handles a lot of big corporate crap. He probably is tied up all afternoon. It's not like we've never had a dinner meeting before. The cheap bastard actually billed me for dinner one night. I mean it. He insisted that we eat at some real expensive joint, then he ordered a couple of bottles of high dollar vintage wine, and hung me with the bill. I wasn't upset by that, so much. I'd expected to pick up the check for dinner. What irritated me is that he billed me three hundred dollars for the two hours we spent at dinner. Can you believe the audacity of that bastard?"

"What did you do?" she asked.

"About what?" Chip answered, assuming a very stupid facial expression. "Just kidding," he laughed. "I was too angry to even talk to him. What I did, after a few days, was call his secretary and tell her to deduct that time from my bill, which she subsequently did."

"Filcher never did like me, not from the day I was born. He told me, after my father died, that I was a spoiled deadbeat, and all that kind of crap. He has no idea how hard it is to be a writer in a place like Key West. On the other hand, he might have billed me for dinner like that, in retaliation for something I did to him a few years ago."

"Oh, and what was that?" Debbie asked, a small smile tugging one corner of her mouth.

"Well, one time, Filcher, my old man, and I went to dinner at the country club. I was about twenty-eight at the time. At the club we all ordered the traditional house favorite, the 'Surf and Turf,' which included steak and lobster. Filcher was particularly snide that night, so I snuck the lobster head out of the restaurant and stuck it under the seat of his car."

"You what?" she laughed, almost on the verge of tears. "Why would you do that? How could anybody even think of such a thing?"

"Hell, it was there. I couldn't let it go to waste, a big lobster head like that. I had means, motive, and opportunity. I laughed about it all the way home. The more I tried not to laugh, the harder I laughed. I could see the old bastard scowling at me in the rearview mirror. I bet his car stank for two weeks before he reached under the seat, felt those antennae poking out, and recoiled in horror."

Dr. Davis laughed uncontrollably.

"Hell, I may do it again tonight. The old bastard knew it was me."

"Are you ready, by God?" Di Lizardo interrupted.

"Yeah," Chip answered, "we're ready. Let's go, I'm starved."

"Well," Di Lizardo said, "you better gird up your loins, by God, and get ready. I've done called Tomtom, and he's expecting us. We're gonna put on the feed bag, by God, with a real breakfast. I mean country style. Grits, country ham. You want fat, calories, and cholesterol, by God, they got it at the Golden Loaf."

They hopped into a bright red Ferrari 360 with the whole passenger side smashed in. "Jump in, we're gonna take 'Smiley.'" Di Lizardo had a name for everything, which was really kind of cool in a way. Dr. Davis slid in and perched on top of the center console.

"Chip, you'll have to hold the door shut so's not to fall out. I also suggest you put on your seatbelt, just in case. I wouldn't want you to flip out and land in the gravels. You ready?" he asked. Di Lizardo didn't wait for an answer but launched the dirty red sports car like a rocket, sending a cloud of flying dust and gravel in its wake. "E-e-e-e-eo-w-w-w-w-! Son of a bitch! Ain't it great to be alive today and free of those bastards!" Di Lizardo screamed.

"Yes it is," Dr. Davis replied, nudging Chip with her elbow.

And indeed it was great to be alive on this incredible day, Chip reflected. The warmth of her shoulder pressing against his chest, and her captivating fragrance were intoxicating to Chip. The thrill of being close to the one he loved, and speeding down a dirt road in a beat up, but fairly new Ferrari. Could there be anything better? No, this was it.

It was just a hop, skip, and jump, down the winding dirt road to the Golden Loaf, but Di Lizardo was always able to reach at least eighty mph. Before he had to start slowing down, no matter what kind of car he was driving. He just reached the desired speed a little faster in the Ferrari.

"Wups," he said, stomping the brakes. "This somitch sneaks up on me sometimes." The car slid sideways through the parking lot, but there was a new rut Di Lizardo hadn't seen, so the car hit it, jumped up, and then slammed down hard before sliding to a stop. The cloud of dust following the car engulfed it like a brown fog, coming in through the gaping hole where the window had been, and causing his two passengers to cough and wipe their eyes.

"Does he always drive like this?" Dr. Davis asked.

"Only when I'm in the car," Di Lizardo answered. "See, I got good ears, by God. I can hear a snake in the grass thirty feet away. Come on, they're probably waiting."

And so they exited the car, and pushed open the rusted screen door and entered the Golden Loaf, Di Lizardo leading the way, strutting in like he owned the joint.

"Hey buddy," he waved at a rustic looking fellow at the end of the counter. The man returned the greeting with a toothless grin and a wave of his arm.

Dr. Davis looked around the dubious surroundings, her nose keenly aware of the pervasive odor of stale grease.

"Wasn't this place used in that movie `Deliverance?'" she whispered to Chip.

"I heard that too," Di Lizardo called, turning around and giving her a wink.

"No, don't be alarmed by appearances, this place is great," Chip answered. "These guys are Di Lizardo's minions. They rescued me the other night. They're the ones who came down, guns blasting, engines roaring, and sprang me out of the Wildman. As if that weren't enough, they're really great cooks, and I'm told they can sing too.

"Chipper!" one of them called.

"Tomtom. Tadpole, what's for breakfast, baby?" he shouted in reply. "This is gonna' be great."

They walked over and sat down at the big table reserved for the rural elite. Di Lizardo introduced Dr. Davis to everybody, and the visitors seated themselves.

"Gloria, let's eat!" Jeeter shouted.

"Chip's gonna be back to Nashville for awhile," Di Lizardo said, "and he's taking Dr. Davis here with him."

"Hell, we already know he's leaving, and that's why we're having this big country style breakfast in his honor," Jeeter shouted.

"Amen," interjected Tomtom. "We're even gonna' sing for y'all."

"All right," Di Lizardo shouted, stomping his foot loudly on the floor. "Can you believe it? The Mighty Gospel Mountainaires, the world famous Mighty Gospel Mountainaires, are gonna' sing for us right here, at their own home base, the Golden Loaf. This is like seeing Elvis perform at Graceland. Hell" Di Lizardo exclaimed, slapping his thigh excitedly, "the Mountainaires opened for Elvis one time, they sure did. It was at some fair in Memphis, by God, before he got fat. Hey Carp!" Carp was busy up by the kitchen getting some ice tea. "Hey Carp!" he shouted again, but Carp still didn't hear him. "Jeeter would know, by God. Hey Jeeter! Didn't you boys open for The King one time?"

"No man, we ain't never toured outside the good ole USA, but we might someday, if we get over there. We might just do that."

"No, by God, I mean the real king….Elvis."

"No, I don't think so. Well, now, wait a minute. Seems like that was before I joined the group. It might have been Tomtom who opened for Elvis, but he was in another quartet then. I think it was when he was with the Telestial Tremolos, but you know that group broke up when the tar truck rolled off the edge of Monteagle Mountain and flattened their trailer. It had all their instruments. Bill and Eddie thought that was a sign from God that they shouldn't be playing music, especially for money. It was sort of like the Church of Christ, you know they don't allow no music. Eddie, hell, he moved down to Florida, I heard, and is singing with somebody else, some no name group, not famous like the Telestial Tremolos had been. Now Bill, he went on over to east of Knoxville where they tell me, he's taking up serpents, you know, a snake handler. You'd have to ask Tomtom about the King though."

That was a little more detailed answer than Di Lizardo really needed. "Yeah, thanks," he said, shaking his head.

"Coming through," Gloria yelled, pushing her considerable girth through the swinging kitchen doors with a big tray of breakfast selections. "Ron, Jeeter, now you boys get out of my way if you wanna' eat."

And so it went, a great big breakfast for all. Country ham and biscuits, dripping red-eye gravy, butter soaked grits, glistening golden brown fried potatoes, and pancakes, with bacon on the side. This delightful repast was punctuated with fond recollections of going down to the Wildman and springing Chip from those `towel-headed heathens.' Last but not least, the guests were treated to a truly stirring rendition of `Mine Is an Angry God,' skillfully rendered by the Mighty Gospel Mountainaires.

At length Chip stood, feeling a need to address this rough, but good natured crowd of hillbilly Americans, this last remnant of a rapidly disappearing segment of the once great national heartland.

"Guys," he said, wiping gravy from his chin, "Cousin Tadpole, Jeeter, Tomtom, and Carp, all of you. I just have to say thanks again. You guys came down into that strange, God-forsaken enclave, positioned in the very center of this provincial outpost, and rescued me from some of the most savage heathens who ever captured and detained an American citizen. If it weren't for your heroism and bravery, I might have been killed right along with the rest of them in that aborted space launch last night. If you're ever in the Music City, do not hesitate to call upon me. I would be thrilled at the opportunity to personally escort each of you to the Grand Ole Opry."

"Well, well. Mighty fine," Tomtom replied, as the official

spokesman for the Mighty Gospel Mountainaires, "It was our great pleasure, since any friend of Ron Di Lizardo's is a friend of ours. And you know, Chip, you're now an unofficial member of the Mighty Gospel Mountainaires. You should henceforward consider the Golden Loaf to be your home away from home."

With that, they bid a fond adieu to their hosts, and returned to Mid-South Auto Brokers Intergalactic so that Chip could have a look at what was left of his Rolls-Royce convertible.

"It's down the road about a quarter of a mile, sitting off to the right on the paved area with a bunch of other cars," Ron had said. Dr. Davis walked with him, and they held hands as they strolled, stopping here and there for a kiss.

"So much has changed in my life during the past few months," Chip told her. "I guess that I'd been living in some sort of never-never land, like Peter Pan, afraid to grow up. And then with my father getting killed, and the murder still unsolved, it was really a pretty big shock. I guess I never got over it. I know I wasted my money foolishly, buying expensive cars, but now that it's all over, at least that part of it, I don't feel so bad about it though. I've had a good time. Not that many people actually have the opportunity to do what they've always wanted to do. I'd wanted a Rolls-Royce convertible since I was a child. At least I can say that I had one. Not many people are that lucky."

"What are you going to do with your life now?" she asked him.

"I'll meet with my lawyer and see how much trouble I'm really in. As soon as I know that, then maybe I'll start to get out of it. After that, I guess I'll see what happens. Maybe I'll get a job like everyone else, or perhaps I'll have another great adventure. I've always been really interested in the music business. There are some guys at the Wildman, inmates, that is, who are really great musicians. They might be crazy, but that just gives them a leg up on the competition. I might go back, spring them out of the Wildman, and be their manager. Who knows?"

"What are you going to do?" he asked her, "I mean now that the world is again safe for democracy."

"I'll stay with you for a few days, if that's okay, then return to Iceland. I've got some unfinished business there."

"Yeah, I know what you mean." But he didn't know what she meant, not really. What work anywhere is more important than love? But, she was an adult. He didn't want to talk her into doing anything she didn't really want to do. He contented himself with the thought that whatever was supposed to happen, would happen. It usually did. Still, she was everything he'd ever wanted. He hoped that she wanted to wrap things up at the observatory and come back to be with him.

Chip's ruined car, a terrible sight indeed!

There it was in the distance, his wrecked Rolls-Royce convertible. It was ruined, a terrible sight indeed. The passenger side front was really smashed, with the front wheel almost torn off. The top and windshield were in surprisingly good condition. The entire passenger side was crushed and dented from front to back, and the door was jammed and wouldn't open. It was lucky nobody had been killed in the wreck. The leather interior was, for the most part, still in pretty good condition, but the top of the back seat was beginning to crack from exposure to the sun. Chip walked around to the driver's side, opened the door, and slid inside, as a stream of ants scurried around a pool of water gathered in the back seat floor well. The driver's seat was broken, and tilted backward at an unusual angle. The dash was bent and pulled apart, with the beautiful burled walnut cracked and splintered. This was truly a sad ending for such a beautiful car, but after what had happened with the Porsche, Chip had made sure the Rolls was insured, so hopefully the money was still available. This would all have to be attended to, and soon.

"I think I'm gonna' have Ron tow this thing back to my house and put it on a slab of concrete right in the middle of my back yard, sort of like a monument," Chip said, "I think that's what I'll do."

They walked slowly and silently back to the Tiki Hut for a last bottle of Double-Cola before leaving for the Music City. Strangely, it was a melancholy time for all of them. Each had benefited in his own way from the unique experience. Debbie had learned a great deal, not only about science and astronomy, but about herself as well. She'd learned that no work is worth sacrificing her life, that Iceland was indeed a horrible place, and that she wasn't happy there. It had taken this trip down South for her to realize that her life had been wasting away. Whatever she did, she wouldn't be staying in the frozen wasteland any longer than it took her to pack her bags and say good bye to her friends. Last but not least, she again felt like a woman. Her self-confidence and her desirability as a sexual person had been reaffirmed by a night of passionate love making. She had neglected this part of her life for too long.

Chip learned that nothing that isn't gained honestly is ultimately worth having, and that something which has been obtained fraudulently, or at someone else's expense, is likely to slip away. He'd also learned that maybe it was possible for him to love someone other than Ioveena . Last but not least, he'd begun to suspect that growing up wasn't really such a bad thing after all.

Di Lizardo now had the security of being free from the Secret Chiefs forever. Finally he could live beyond the possibility that one night they might sneak up with some powerful weapons, take him prisoner, and drag him back to the sanitarium. He also possessed the satisfaction of having helped save the world, something he could reasonably be proud of for several years to come. It was true that he would miss his new friends, but Ron somehow felt that he'd be seeing them again soon. Hell, it had been a wonderful experience all the way around.

"Seriously, we'd better hit the road," Chip said reluctantly. "It takes about two and a half hours to drive to Nashville from here, that's assuming we stop at Manchester for a big ice tea from Crapdonald's. It's twelve now. We'll gain an hour on the way back, but I want to stop by the house, see Therpis, and take a nap before I meet with Filcher.

"Who's Therpis?" she asked, "That's about the strangest name I've ever heard."

"He's a distant cousin or uncle, or something. I'm not sure who he is really, but he's been at the house as long as I can remember. He's one of my best friends, but I'll tell you now, in advance, he's a little strange. He's what is referred to in the Deep South as a 'Peckerwood,' but he's a great guy. You'll like him. He lives in a house out back with his wife, Matti Pearl. He gets drunk and rowdy, and then she beats the hell out of him."

"Sounds like an interesting family."

"Yeah," Chip smiled fondly. "I'll be glad to get back home. I can't wait to see Therpis, that simple son of a bitch. He's the only family I've got."

Ron was kind enough to let his friends borrow a new black Mercedes S 65 sedan. The car had been submerged under water in an unusual accident for a week or so, and Ron had acquired it from some insurance company. After the fuel system had been unclogged and the mud pumped out of the interior, it had cleaned up pretty nicely, not that it looked like a new car. Everything at Mid-South Auto Brokers was covered in several layers of dust and dirt. That's the way Di Lizardo liked it.

And so they made the short drive back to Nashville, taking the old two-lane road, and passing through some of the most beautiful rolling hills and smaller mountains in America. Dr. Davis had never felt better or happier. It was like really being free for the first time, free from the societal expectations of the people whom she'd permitted to set her agenda for the past fifteen years.

"Don't be surprised if we're stopped and I'm arrested. There could be some warrants out on me over this financial bullshit," Chip warned his companion casually, as they took the Harding Place exit off I-24 and headed across town to Chip's place. "It's not likely, and I don't want to alarm you, but it is possible." The closer they came to his area of town, the better the scenery, and the more expensive the houses.

"Do you live in this area?" Dr. Davis asked, impressed by her surroundings, as they passed several large and magnificent homes.

"Yeah," Chip answered, turning right on Belle Meade Blvd., driving half a mile, and turning right into a driveway leading to an imposing neo-classical structure. As they pulled around the house toward the back door, Chip saw a window shade open in the guest house. By the time they exited the car, Therpis was standing there with his hand poised over his pocket, the place where he always kept his pistol, and a happy look of disbelief on his face.

"Where've you been Mistuh? They said on the TV that you was resumed dead. Had a big article in the paper too. I saved it fo yuh. I knew you'd be back."

"Well, Chip laughed, "I was captured by spacemen and held in an underground prison, rescued by feral hillbillies, and finally set free. Here I am, it's great to be back."

"Well, it's sho' good to see you Mistuh. I told `em all. I said `that man ain't dead, he's just hiding out.' That Mr. Filcher came over, said he was your lawyer and demanded to be let in the house. Fo I could stop him, he and that big fat yellow secretary of his shoved me out of the way and went on in. They were snooping around, but I followed them all right, and they didn't leave with none of the silver."

"Good job Therpis. What did he want?"

"He said you was dead, that he had to take care of your estate. I said that I did the lawn, washed the cars, and took care of the estate myself, and would continue to do so, just like I always done, leastwise until you came back. He said you wasn't coming back. I told him that if he said that again, his teeth was gonna' be smiling at him from out in the yard. Look, that man may be your lawyer. I ain't saying he is, and I ain't saying he ain't. I am sayin' he's a slippery little son of a bitch," Therpis concluded sagely.

"I'm beginning to think you're right, noble Therpis. By the way, permit me to introduce my friend, Debbie Davis. Debbie, this is my distant relative, twice removed, thrice reinstated, and frequently incarcerated."

Dr. Davis laughed.

"Who got you out of the slammer while I was gone?" Chip asked. "I know you been in there."

"Aw now Mistuh Chip, I ain't done much but smoke a little weed. I been staying away from the hard stuff."

"You mean to tell me that you haven't been arrested the entire time I've been gone?" Chip asked, scarcely able to believe this leopard had changed its spots.

"Well, I didn't say that now. I did get thrown out of the Kwik Sak, and they put me outa Springwater. Yeah, and last Tuesday I went crazy, howlin' at the moon, cursing everybody on the street, you know, doin' like I do. The po-lice took me downtown, held me for about six hours and turned me loose again. When I got home, Matti Pearl whupped me senseless with that big chrome vacuum cleaner pipe. You see the black and blue marks on my arm don't you?" he asked, rolling up the sleeve of his left arm to substantiate his account of the incident.

Dr. Davis laughed, then turned away, pretending to cough.

"That Sidney Von Snocker, he got me out another time," Therpis continued. "All in all, I stayed pretty clear of the po-lice. I saved all your messages too. You got a whole box full. That Filcher and his evil ass ho wanted to see your messages, but I said no to that, and they left in a big huff. I told him that next time he wanted to come over he'd better have a search warrant. He said he was the executioner of your estate and that he didn't need permission from anybody to do a gat damn thing, especially from my ass. He furthermore said that if he was me, he'd be looking for someplace else to live."

"I don't like the son of a bitch myself," Chip replied, "but I have to use him for the time being. You did the right thing, though. Good work. Hey, do we have any Blatz?"

"Yes suh. I've been drinking them fo yuh so they wouldn't get stale, but every time I drink some, I replace them with some fresher ones."

"Good work pal," Chip said, slapping him on the back fondly. "I'll see to it that you are properly rewarded for your diligence tomorrow. Right now, Dr. Davis and I need to go in and freshen up a bit. Why don't you join us for dinner later? I want to hear what happened to you after we crashed, what you did, how you got home, and what you've been up to. I'm supposed to meet Filcher at his office at 7:00 for dinner, why don't you join us. Since neither one of you like each other, it should make the evening much more interesting. I'll fetch you at 6:30."

Leonard Filcher; "A slippery eel," Therpis observed sagely.

"I appreciate the invitation, but I don't like that slippery eel. He reminds me of an embalmer with that pale white skin of his and those big, pointy teeth. The son of a bitch spooks me Chip, he really does, but I guess he ain't gonna try nothin' on me with all of us there. Besides, I could really dig a real big dinner somewhere. I'll see yuh then."

"That Therpis is one wild and crazy son of a bitch," he said to Dr. Davis as they walked through the back door of Chip's house. "Nothing surprises him. I could have just as easily walked in after an unexplained absence of five or ten years, and it would have been all the same to him. Here," he said. "Let's go inside."

"This place looks like a museum," she said as they passed through the kitchen and into a long hallway. "Look at the furniture, and this art is incredible. Some of these paintings look like old masters."

"You mean old bastards," he laughed. "But if you really appreciate art, just wait until you see my collection of fine Mexican velvet paintings. I probably own the most complete Velvet Elvis collection in metropolitan Nashville. In fact, I have concentrated the entire collection in one room, surrounding a very large and trashy round bed topped with a hideous golden crown as a canopy. I know you'll love it."

She didn't know whether he was kidding or not. Sometimes it was hard to tell, so she answered evasively. "I'm certain it's as nice as everything else."

"I hope that you're favorably impressed," he replied, "since this is where we will most likely live when we are married."

Again she didn't know how to respond, or whether he was serious, so she kept on walking and pretended not to hear.

"Did you hear me?" he asked.

"Yes, I heard you, but with you, I never know whether you're joking or not." It was a wonderful thought, but she really didn't see Chip as the marrying kind.

He gently grabbed her arm, spun her around, and looked into her eyes. "I'm serious. You are the most wonderful person I've ever met. I've been in love with you since the first time I saw your face through that small window outside the music room at the Wildman. I love you completely, body and soul. I want to be with you. I want you always."

Dr. Davis didn't know what to say. Chip was a wonderful man and an incredible lover, but there were some things about him that bothered her. If he was that good in bed, which he was, it was undoubtedly the result of having spent a lot of intimate time with many women. He was probably the type of guy who slipped around. Secondly, he didn't have a job. It wasn't a question of whether he had enough money or not, it was that perhaps he lacked purpose. She'd always had this picture in her mind of a man who looked like Cary Grant, someone who wore a suit, and played tennis at the country club. By his own admission, Chip didn't even know how to knot a tie, and for that matter didn't want to.

On the other hand, he was wild and free, and with a very commanding personality and presence. He wasn't gay, wasn't a mama's boy, and didn't have a bitchy ex-wife…three very rare attributes these days. She really didn't know what to think. In the meantime, here she was in this magnificent house with this wildly independent and interesting man, at the end of a most remarkable adventure. She could see in his eyes that he meant the words of love he was speaking to her. At least he thought he did, and at just this moment, that was good enough for her.

"You are the most fascinating person I've ever met, Chip, and I want you in my life. But right now," she said, "why don't we go to your room, take a look at your velvet Elvis paintings, and see what comes up?"

32.

FILCHER

"Look, I know Filcher wanted me to come alone, but he works for me, not the other way round. I don't work for him, so I don't care what he wants. I changed my mind. You and Therpis can go with me to dinner somewhere nice, kind of a 'Save the Universe' celebration. I'll go by his place, you and Therpis can wait in the lobby, and then the three of us can go to dinner by ourselves. All he wants me to do is sign some additional papers. As my legal representative, I'm certain he's already aware of the business about getting loans on junk cars. I can just tell him the details, see what he wants me to do, and then leave."

"Well, I've got to admit that yours was a brilliant idea," Debbie stated, looking at Chip thoughtfully. "That is, from a purely conceptual standpoint. I can't believe that anyone would actually attempt to put it in practice in the real world," she laughed. "I mean who would be stupid enough to loan money on cars they hadn't even seen?"

"Banks do it all the time. Besides, I can be very persuasive when I need to be," he smiled.

"I can personally attest to that."

"I was truly ahead of my time," Chip reflected proudly. "If I hadn't had that accident, there's no telling what might have happened. Well, for one thing, we'd have never met."

"Just think," she reflected, kissing him softly on his chest. "If we hadn't met, we wouldn't be lying here now. In fact, we probably wouldn't even be here at all. If you hadn't brought Di Lizardo into the picture, we would've all been destroyed. There's no way I could have known what to do by myself."

"It was cool the way your friends in Iceland described it," Chip replied, "but tell me about it again. You know I don't really have a scientific mind. Did the thing blow up or just disappear? And what happened to the Secret Chiefs? Also, did Lizardo tell you anything more about being one of them? He wouldn't tell me a damn thing."

"Slow down, you impetuous boy," she laughed. "One thing at a time, and first things first. Now, Ron was able to basically force SS396 back out of our galaxy by reversing the projections of the aural particle accelerator. After it was completely back in the other dimension, he simply turned off the power that had created it in the first place. When the power source was removed, it simply ceased to exist. That wouldn't have been possible once SS396 had fully crossed over into our galaxy. At that point, it would have become real, in the same sense that all the planets are real. That is, SS396 would have become tangible and objective, but at the same time invisible."

"I see what you mean, sort of," Chip replied, "but I still don't understand how something can be real on one side of some imaginary line, and unreal on the other side of that line. I don't guess it really matters one way or the other."

"Let me see if I can explain it better," Debbie suggested.

"No, that's okay. Instead, why don't you tell me what you think happened to the Secret Chiefs? I mean, did those people really build a spaceship so sophisticated that they could just pack a picnic lunch and head off to some other dimension? Or did that thing explode in the sky after takeoff, and fall in pieces to the earth, incinerating all of them?"

"Chip," she said looking truly puzzled, "I don't know what to think, and I've thought about it a lot over the past two days. It looked to me like the thing exploded in midair, and if that's what happened, nobody got out of there alive. On the other hand, the explosion we saw, and the remains that were found on the ground may have merely been what was left of their first stage rocket booster. I think they're gone, that they're not here any longer, not on Earth. I seriously doubt that they're dead at all. In answer to your question, yes, they could pack a picnic lunch and travel to another planet, or to another galaxy, for that matter, as easily as we could drive down to the store. They really are that technologically advanced."

"Well, who were they, or are they?" Chip asked, still finding it difficult to believe that people like the Secret Chiefs actually inhabited the planet, and had lived as close by as Chattanooga. "Are they from outer space and disguising themselves as humans, or are they human, and just highly evolved? And I can't help but wonder, are there other people like them still here, living in Knoxville, or Memphis, or somewhere else nearby? It's too strange. And what about Di Lizardo? He was one of them, himself. He seems normal enough, or is that also just a disguise? Does he possibly have seven beady red eyes and eight hundred pointy little teeth? Shit, who knows?"

"I have no answer to any of these questions," Debbie reflected. "I spent time with all of them, but I can't say anything certain about them one way or the other. The only thing that I know absolutely, is that they were so advanced scientifically, that if this planet survives human meddling, it will take us possibly thousands of years to even conceptualize the principles that they used in day to day operations. They used light and sound in ways that we can't even begin to imagine. They also had colors and sounds that are unknown to us. I have no idea who or what they were, or are," she said, "and I guess I'll never know. This is sad to say," she continued, "but in light of what I've experienced studying with them, I don't think I can ever be a scientist again."

"What do you mean?" Chip asked, raising up sharply, somewhat surprised by this unexpected revelation.

"I mean now that I'm aware such knowledge exists, I don't think I can plod along any further one inch at a time with people still working with what, in light of my observations, can now only be deemed vestigial concepts. I just don't know. This has been a big shock to me psychologically. It's like someone somewhere is working on inventing the wheel, and feels pretty happy with his progress, until he finds out that another scientist somewhere else has already built an operational 747. In a way, it's like my life has been a waste up to this point, at least my career."

"No," Chip interrupted, "I don't see that at all. Look at it this way. If you hadn't been doing what you were doing when you were doing it, the entire planet, and possibly everyone on it would have been destroyed. I don't mean might have, or could have, I mean would have. I don't believe any other scientist in the history of knowledge has accomplished as much in the scientific field as you have. As Peter Fonda so eloquently expressed it, in that classic film 'Easy Rider', `you're doing your own thing in your own time, you should be proud.'"

"You're silly," she laughed, and then leapt from the bed in terror. "What time is it?" she asked looking desperately around the room for a clock.

"It's 4:30," Chip answered casually. "We've got plenty of time."

"No we don't. I've got to take a shower right now, and then you must take me shopping. I have nothing to wear. Here, we've been lying around in bed talking and fooling around, and I don't have anything to wear tonight."

"Women," Chip sighed fondly.

By the time they'd shopped and she'd dressed, it was a little past 6:30, and already almost dark. Therpis strolled in through the kitchen door, walked through the pantry, into the hall, and shouted up the stairs, "I'ze here Mistuh Chip. It's after 6:30. I washed the car off," he shouted, "and it looks better, but there's still mud all over the floorboard. Where you been driving that thing?"

And off they went, heading east toward downtown Nashville, about eight miles away. The lights of the city twinkled as they got closer to the main business district. "There sure are a lot of restaurants here," Debbie observed casually as they continued toward town on West End Avenue.

"Sure is," Therpis agreed. "Look, it's a Captain D's on the right up ahead. Some somitch stobbed a young woman in there something like 43 times one morning, killed her sho' enough. Thu' po-lice said they ain't never seen such a brutal stobbing, blood and gore all over the place. Turned out to be the woman's husband done it. That was about ten years ago. Somitch probably out, got his own restaurant by now. They shoulda lexicuted his ass. Now it's a Starbucks. Look over here on the left," he continued, "right before the McDonald's, there used to be a pizza joint. Now listen to what happened. Some somitch came right on in there and there's a cop standing at the cash register, see, jes picking up his order. This somitch snuck up on him, pulled his pistol out of the holster and shot the damn po-lice right there. A friend of mine was there having dinner when it happened. He saw the man shoot the po-lice. He witnessed it. I'm telling yuh, a friend of mine saw it happen."

"Now up ahead on the right, there's a Wendy's. Some big fat waitress shot another waitress and killed her deader'n a fish, sure did, and right at lunch time too, in front of everybody in the place. Can't even eat in peace no more."

"Therpis," Chip interrupted, "I don't believe Dr. Davis wants a guided tour of Nashville's most popular murder sites."

"Well excuse me, I was just…oh yeah, alright. I gotcha. Now over there on the left is the Parthenon. It's uh exact replica, that's what they say it is, an exact replica of the Parthenon in Greece. Theirs is

306

all beat up and falling down though. I don't know why they don't fix it up. Too cheap, I guess. But ours is in good shape. They call Nashville the 'Athens of the South'," Therpis observed. "That's right, cause of the Parthenon, but since they's already an Athens in Georgia, and another one in Alabama, one in Texas, and one in Tennessee, they called us Nashville instead of Athens. We're the only city with a Parthenon, except for the one in Greece. The Athens in Alabama, the one in Georgia, and even the one in Texas ain't got a Parthenon. They shouldn't be allowed, on accounta that, to even call themselves Athens. It's an affront to Nashvillians. It is."

"Well you certainly seem to know your geography Therpis," Dr. Davis said, complimenting their tour guide. "I'm impressed."

"I sure do," he observed excitedly, his face beaming at her approval.

"Filcher has a cool office," Chip said. "It's right downtown, in an old building from the 1920s. It has its own fenced in parking lot around back, both for security and privacy. There shouldn't be anybody there but us. Here we go," he said, turning down an alley in the center of the downtown business district, and then pulling into a small courtyard surrounded by spiked wrought iron posts. There were no other vehicles in the parking lot except for a big orange Winnebago, and Filcher's new Lincoln. "Why don't you both come in with me and wait in the lobby? This shouldn't take more than fifteen minutes."

"I think I'll wait out here in the car, Mistuh," Therpis said, backing away. "You know me, I can't sit still."

"Well," Chip replied, not too pleased with the prospect of leaving Therpis anywhere unattended in public. "Please don't get into any trouble, and be here when I get back."

"You the boss and I'm the hoss," he replied. "I ain't going nowhere. I want some of that big supper you promised me. Ole Therpis'll be here, don't you worry bout that."

"I can't tell him what to do," Chip said fondly to Debbie as they walked through an expensive looking iron gate. "The problem is that he's liable to get drunk or wander off somewhere. If he does either one, I'll leave his ass right here, I mean it."

"Oh stop it. He's precious, one of a kind. He'll be all right," Debbie reassured him.

They came immediately to a locked security door and Chip pushed the button on the intercom. "Yeah," a cold and raspy masculine voice answered, which Chip recognized as Filcher's.

"It's me," Chip said. A buzzer sounded, he pushed the door open, and they found themselves in a short hallway which opened into a beautifully appointed lobby. Chip expected to see somebody, but there was no one there, not even the usual security guard. He was probably wandering around upstairs somewhere, making his rounds and checking the building.

"Filcher's office is on the third floor," Chip said, pushing the polished brass elevator button on the wall. "Why don't you come on up with me?"

"No," she said, pushing him away gently. "He wanted you to come alone. I'll just wait down here and keep an eye on Therpis."

"Okay," Chip said, kissing her gently on the cheek. "I'll be back soon."

Chip always observed how important it was for attorneys to appear solid and stable. Their offices usually have rich walnut or mahogany panels with dark worn leather chairs and sofas. The idea is to make it appear to the client that the law firm has been there forever, that it is rich, solid, and successful. The fact of the matter is that, with a few exceptions, most lawyers don't have two nickels to rub together. It's all a big front, a big pretense. The giant law firms with hundreds of names listed down the side of the page are more pretentious, and even worse. The names on the left side of the page, if noticed by the client, would be seen to be in a constant state of flux, like ants at a picnic. Filcher had money though. He'd made it in the days before Perry Mason. The old bastard must be at least seventy by now, but he'd still just as soon sell his mother into bondage as actually go into a courtroom and do what lawyers were supposed to do.

The elevator was stately, like everything else, Chip reflected. Polished brass, rich dark rosewood panels, all most elegantly understated. A bell rang, the elevator stopped, and the door opened silently, exposing a receptionist's desk in the center of a large room, and a glassed conference room with open curtains behind the desk.

"This way," a voice spoke, shattering the silence and seemingly coming out of nowhere, definitely catching Chip uncomfortably off guard. It was Filcher, dressed to the nines in an expensive dark striped suit, and cool as ice.

"Please follow me," he said, extending his hand, which Chip reluctantly shook, only out of social necessity. The hand was cold, white, and smooth, not like a man's hand at all. Chip glanced at the lifeless thing he'd just touched and beheld a large but pale hand, almost translucent actually, punctuated only by a lightning like pattern of blue veins and sharp, polished nails. "So nice to see you," the lawyer hissed through bloodless lips, his eyes conveying a message other than the expected joy of finding an old friend still alive after having been presumed dead for several months. "You came alone, I trust?"

"Yeah," Chip answered, after all, he did come alone into this office. That should be good enough for Filcher.

They stepped into the large, but comfortable office Filcher had used for as long as Chip could remember. In a way, it reminded him of home. He'd spent many hours here as a child, crawling around on the dark, rich carpet, accompanying his father to business meetings with Filcher, the family lawyer. The familiarity of the worn leather chairs and the shelves of books promoted a soothing and calming effect, which enabled Chip to relax. In no time at all, he was back to himself, joking irreverently with the stiff and unduly formal Filcher.

Chip's casual demeanor was welcome to Filcher as well. He was used to dealing with an adolescent idiot who signed and did whatever he was told. He didn't want to have to suddenly waste time with someone who thought too much, had an opinion about anything, or felt like asking any questions about matters well above his intellectual level. Chip thought he was here to talk about his unfortunate financial problems, but all of that petty stupidity had already been resolved by Filcher. Chip was here to sign some papers, and that was it, period.

"First, of all," Filcher said, walking to his desk and removing a stack of papers, "I'm genuinely thrilled to see you. There was never any doubt in my mind whatsoever that you would be back. Only next time," he said jokingly, and completely out of character, "don't wait so long to call me. We should be in touch weekly. You know, Chip, I've always regarded you like a son, like the son I never had, in fact. I know I've been hard on you from time to time, too hard perhaps, but that's only because I recognize the full measure of your potential. You are every bit as sharp as your father was, and I see the same characteristics in you which he also possessed, the very same traits that allowed him to accomplish so much during his lifetime."

Chip was a bit stunned. He didn't know what to think about any of this. He'd wished for a father figure so badly, he'd almost be willing to fall for it, maybe even have to fall for it. The words of Therpis, however suddenly returned to his mind, haunting him. "He said you were never coming back, that you were dead." No, Therpis must have misunderstood the lawyer.

"I really don't know what to say, Mr. Filcher," Chip said, unwittingly warming up. "Actually I never thought you liked me. Despised me, in fact."

"My God, son," Filcher said. "How could you ever think that?"

"Well I know that you know that I'm the one who put the lobster under your seat, and I know you think that I'm the one who got your daughter pregnant."

"No, no. Don't worry about that, Chip, water under the bridge. That thing with the lobster head did irritate me at first, but I slid it back in there and my mother in law found it when she and Barbara were out shopping. You see that I'm a bit of a jokester too. It turned out alright. Now my daughter, that was another matter, but let's not talk about that. She married a big executive with Genesco, so that turned out alright too. Like I said, water under the bridge.

"It's hard growing up in the shadow of a man like your father, but I have every confidence that you will eclipse his accomplishments with even greater ones yourself, at the appropriate time. Mason was a bum until he hit forty. Before that he lived off the inheritance he received, wasting it on expensive cars and loose women. He finally settled down and started Amalgamated Cheese, among other things and turned out very well after all, so don't worry."

"Well," Chip replied, honestly touched, "I don't really know what to say. I never...."

"Look, you don't have to say anything," the lawyer replied.

"I'm a little embarrassed by the trouble I got into with those car titles. I know it was a stupid thing to do, and then that bank loan from Mark O' Lepty, I really don't know what got into me, I mean it. I really don't."

"Well, look," the lawyer said, "I had to get your father out of a lot of shit, let me tell you. He was always punching some loudmouth at a restaurant, setting somebody's foot on fire, or borrowing another man's wife for a weekend. I got him off, and he paid me well for my services. I expect the same from you. As far as the business with the bank, and those awful title pawn places, the matter has been favorably resolved. It's all over."

"But how?" Chip asked. "How did you take care of all of that?"

310

"One of those many papers you signed at the will, was a limited power of attorney which permitted me to act on your behalf in your absence, or in case of an accident. Furthermore, there was an additional $150,000 that I didn't tell you about which was placed in another account in an out of state bank as ordered by your father. Given your nature, we thought you would most likely need it someday, probably sooner than later. It was just a sort of extra little insurance policy. It's a good thing I held that money back for you, or it would most likely be gone as well."

"You mean I'm off the hook? Really?"

"Yes, Chip you are. I charged you $60,000 for my services, and I don't apologize for that either. I paid off all of your known debts, both legal, and illegal, made a few calls downtown and got the heat off you, took my fee from the account, and transferred the balance to a new account in your name. I think you still have around $20,000 remaining."

This was all too good to be true. He was a free man, once again. Maybe this was why his old man had kept Filcher around for so long. Maybe he really is that good after all.

"Well what do I need to do?" Chip asked. "Is that it?"

"You need to sign another stack of papers before you leave. I have them all right here."

"What are they?" Chip asked, rising and approaching the desk.

"They're basically mutual indemnification releases against any possible lawsuits arising out of the transactions involving your car title scams. A couple of those companies wanted to file charges of fraud against you even after the loans were repaid. I told them that I would sue them on your behalf for any number of reasons, some of which might have even been actionable. Two of the other title loan places were quite willing to forget all about it as long as the money was repaid. The local branches didn't want someone from the main office finding out that they'd foolishly been duped into making loans on cars that didn't exist. In other words, you're both agreeing not to sue each other now or at any time in the future."

"Ok," Chip said, briefly glancing at one of the papers before signing an entire stack.

"What are these others?" he asked.

"You have a couple of signature cards for the new bank account, another letter closing your account at the first bank, and another letter making you responsible for paying your phone and electric bills from this point forward. I'm getting out of the accounting business once and for all," Filcher said.

Chip signed all the papers and Filcher visibly relaxed. Often clients wanted to read something before they actually signed it. While this is a good idea in theory, it is in reality, a decided waste of a lawyer's valuable time.

"Is that it?" Chip asked, ready to leave.

"Well," Filcher said, "I think we should have a celebratory dinner in honor of your safe return. Where would you like to go?"

Getting out of going to dinner with Filcher was going to be much more difficult than Chip had first imagined, especially in light of all the attorney had just done for him.

"Mr. Filcher," Chip said dejectedly, "I'm sorry, but I can't go to dinner with you tonight. I'm really sorry, but I'm dead tired. You know I just got home today. I sincerely apologize, but let's make it another time, say the first of next week?"

Filcher glanced at the floor, looking sadly disappointed, as if this was something he'd been counting on for quite a while.

"All right then," Filcher relented, "Mason and I always concluded our business with brandy and cigars. It's a family tradition. Before you go, let's have a drink. And I know you smoke cigars. How about a very large Cuban Partagas?"

This was indeed an offer that Chip couldn't refuse. He sat down on the leather couch again and Filcher handed him the cedar lined humidor. Chip buried his face in the exotic aroma, a unique mixture of cedar and fine tobacco, a fragrance not unlike the tack room of a stable. Chip set the open box beside him and selected several large cigars, rolling each one carefully between his fingers, seeking the most loosely rolled. Sometimes a burr or a knot will cause even the finest cigar to burn down one side unevenly. A cigar that is too moist, or has been rolled too tightly will burn hotter than one rolled correctly. A cigar which has been rolled too loosely, on the other hand, will burn too quickly. It's a delicate balance. After several attempts, he found just the right cigar. While Chip punched a hole in the end and slowly lit the cigar, Filcher stood at the bar behind the couch, preparing him a very special brandy, precisely warmed to the correct temperature.

"Most exquisite," Chip said, genuinely thrilled that someone as famous as Filcher was in legal circles, would take such a personal interest in him, after all this time. "I owe you a great debt of gratitude," Chip said, hoisting his glass toward the lawyer. "I've always respected your work....that is, what little I knew about it."

"Well, I certainly appreciate your kind words," the lawyer hissed. "But it is I who owe you."

"Oh no, no, no. I owe you."

"Very well," the lawyer replied, "then tell me what really happened in Chattanooga, where you've been since the accident, and how you finally managed to get home."

Outside in the parking lot, Therpis had exchanged greetings with some wino and the two had adjourned to the garbage cans in an alcove beside the Winnebago for a light libation of Golden Harvest. Therpis recognized the man as being from the famed Bordeaux region of Nashville, out by the Clarksville Highway. Therpis contributed to the reunion with two toothpick-sized joints of reefer he'd got from Purvis, the next door neighbor's yard man.

"Ah bo boo booo," he exclaimed in approval, shaking his fleshy jaws rapidly from side to side. Ooooo Weee! Now that's some good shit mistuh!"

Downstairs, Debbie had begun to grow impatient. She hadn't eaten anything since this morning, and was really getting hungry. She began pacing back and forth, then decided to step into the restroom for a moment.

Back upstairs, Chip was beginning to rapidly feel the effects of the brandy. "So you fell in the water after the wreck?" Filcher asked.

"Yes, when the car went into the water, I went out of the car," Chip laughed, feeling more light headed with every passing moment.

"You ignorant bastard," Filcher said with a smile.

"What?" Chip asked. "I don't think I heard what you said."

"Oh, I'm sorry," Filcher replied. "I said, 'what an unfortunate accident'."

"Oh," Chip laughed, "Imagine that. I thought you said 'ignorant bastard.' Oh God, what's happening here?"

The office door swung open silently revealing Filcher's mistress, lover, and business partner, the dark-skinned German postwar baby, Frau Ioveena , scantily clad in a tank top, using maximum polyester restraint to hold her very large breasts in place.

"Is he ready?" she asked coldly.

"He's ready for a swim in the river, where he should have stayed in the first place," Filcher seethed.

"I vill check back in a minute," she said. "Zee narcotic usually takes five minutes."

Now Chip knew he was imagining things. For an instant he thought he'd actually seen Ioveena , the love of his life. But whoever it was, she was gone now. She said she was coming back though, and he just knew she would.

"Ioveena , Ioveena , my love," Chip called, but he didn't know if he actually said anything. His lips were numb now, and his whole face felt like a big slab of rubber, like a mask. He tried to get up, but found he couldn't move at all. It was a strange thing. At first his mind had been foggy, like he was drunk, but now he could hear and understand everything. He now knew he'd been drugged, and was keenly aware of his surroundings, only he was unable to do anything about it. He couldn't move at all, and could hardly talk.

"Ioveena ," he mumbled.

"You stupid bastard," Filcher said, kicking Hamster's legs. "How could you possibly imagine that I could tolerate you, even for a minute? You are about the dumbest son of a bitch I've ever seen. Do you think I cleaned up your financial mess because I like you? If you really believe that, then you are even more stupid than I've imagined, and I seriously doubt that's possible. I cleaned up your stupid deals with those trashy title pawn shops so there would be no claims against your estate, or should I say, my estate. It's a good thing you can't read, because you signed over everything you own to me. When your rotten, putrescent, fish-eaten corpse turns up way, way down the river from Chattanooga in a few months, I'll end up with everything.

"You seven up pitch..." Chip said, but he couldn't talk, or even move. He could only listen helplessly as Filcher unburdened himself of years of rage.

"Your father was stupid, just like you. All because your grandfather found some painted turtle, he inherited a fortune. Your family fortune rode in on the back of a turtle, a God damned turtle! Your father managed to piss most of that money away, until I sent Frau Ioveena to Mexico to finish him off. He wasn't as stupid as you though. He wouldn't sign anything without reading it. In fact, he wouldn't sign anything at all. We got tired of waiting, and Frau Ioveena terminated the simple bastard. All of that money of course went to you, but not before I skimmed off a large part of it. I wanted the house though, the money wasn't enough. And then you drove into the river, like the idiot you are. But your carelessness was our good fortune. Everything would have been fine if you'd just stayed dead. But no, you had to fuck that up too, just like everything else you've ever done in your entire wretched, miserable, useless life. But it's too late now. You're gonna go for a big swim."

Glancing at Chip's mute amazement, he continued. "At first it was just business between Frau Ioveena and myself. I met her through an international banker in New York, one of my shadier friends, who'd used her on occasion for some highly specialized contract work, if you know what I mean. At first, we agreed to split the money, but I was to get the house. That was the deal, but then we fell in love. It wasn't something we'd consciously planned. A rich and suave man like me, a big, beautiful, hot-blooded international criminal like her. Well, there were bound to be sparks, and then the burning white hot flame of passion. She never loved you, you fool, you were just part of the game. If you'd just stayed dead, we would have both just retired, lived at your house, traveled some, and enjoyed the good life, but no. This time you won't be back, and that swimming merit badge you got in the Boy Scouts won't save your ass now. Idiot!" Filcher shouted, looking down at Chip with undisguised contempt and loathing, then bitch slapping him across the face.

So that was it, Chip thought, it was all a lie. Ioveena hadn't been rescued by a porpoise, it was all a set up by her and Filcher. She'd never really loved him. It had all been about money, all of her sex, love, and affection, just a game to get some money. And the worst possible thing of all, she loved Filcher. Oh God, how horrible. The thought of her plump legs bent at the knee, and that mortician-like Filcher's little pale white ass grinding away on the woman he loved, was just too much. She would have killed Chip too, most likely. It was really too horrible. It was one thing to think of her pining away somewhere, really loving him and missing him. But she'd actually killed his father with a frying pan, no less, and sought Chip out also, hoping and planning to kill him, to run away with that filthy bastard Filcher.

The door opened and there, standing in the light, was the dark and shapely outline of Ioveena , her hands on her hips, and her legs spread apart, an impressive sight, even under these circumstances. All woman, no doubt of that, all woman, and everything that a woman could be to a man.

315

"He's ready now," Filcher said coldly. "And he signed everything. I'd backdated it all and he was too stupid to even look at the dates on the papers he signed, let alone actually read them. Load him into the Winnebago and I'll join you there in a moment, after I lock up. The world is ours now my darling," Filcher said, sliding a cold, clammy hand between her dark, hot thighs.

"I vill take him zhere," she said bending over the limp body of Chip Hamster.

The last thing he saw was the very large line between her gigantic breasts. "Heaven," he sighed, now slipping completely out of consciousness.

"Vhat a fool," she laughed, as she leaned over Chip's limp body.

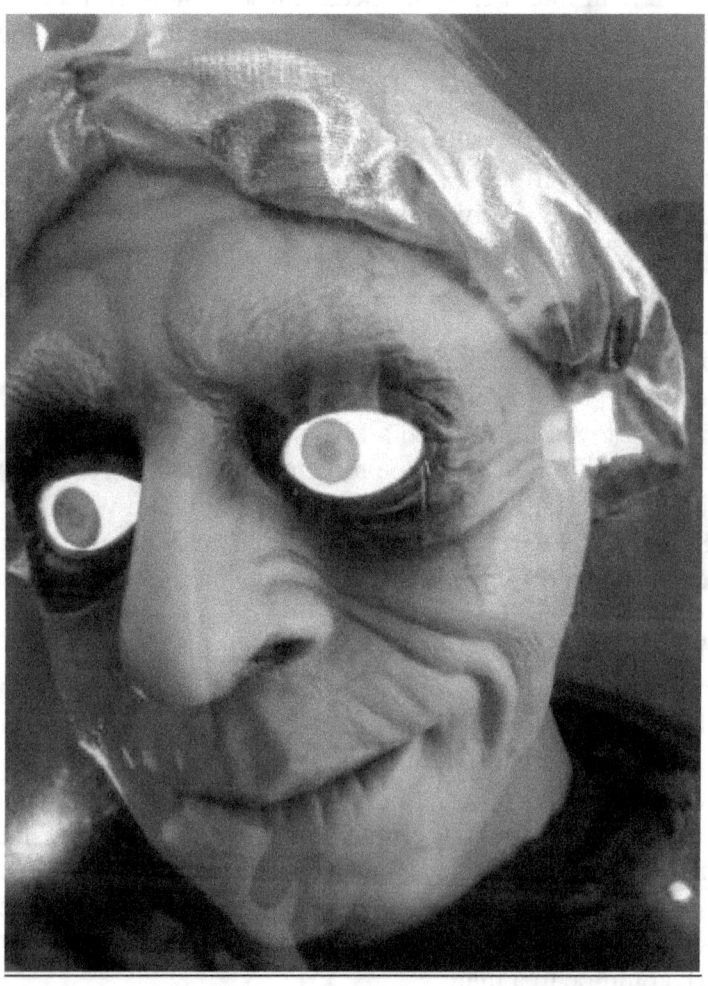

33.

CEMENT SHOES

Frau Ioveena easily hoisted Chip over her shoulder like a big sack of feed, and started down the third floor hallway to the elevator. It was a good thing Filcher had made certain the security guard had the night off. It would be smooth sailing from here on out. She would personally drown Hamster in the camper's deluxe toilet with her own bare hands, just as soon as they got out of town. Then they would dump him down river from Chattanooga, and that would be the end of it. Nothing personal, just business, all in a day's work. Filcher was fairly thorough on his own, but still, Frau Ioveena always, by reputation, double checked everything herself. That way she could be sure there were no mistakes. One simple mistake, one stupid miscalculation or omission and the greatest plan was ruined.

Chip seemed heavier than she remembered, but then his weight had been more evenly distributed over a larger area of her body on other occasions. The elevator door silently opened and Frau Ioveena stepped into the lobby, looked around, and proceeded to the rear of the building. She scanned the parking lot, looking for any sign of activity. Nothing. It was time to move. She slid out the back door into the dim light of the parking lot, with Chip draped over her broad fleshy shoulder like a long colorful shawl. When she reached the motor home, she struggled to open the door, but somehow managed, stepped inside and casually dropped Chip on the floor, not even bothering to lay him out properly.

"My God, what was that?" Dr. Davis asked herself. It looked like some big, fat, cross-dressing bastard with someone thrown over his shoulder. As soon as the back door slammed shut, Dr. Davis raced to the window for a better look. It looked like Chip as far as she could tell, given the poor lighting. Whoever it was had taken him into the big camper. But was it Chip? She had to be certain. And whoever it was, was he dead or alive? She couldn't let this vehicle leave. There was very definitely something strange going on here, something strange, and sinister.

"Uh oh." She ducked behind the stairwell as the big woman or drag queen, or whatever it was shut the rear door of the camper and returned to the building. As the figure moved closer to the building, Davis could clearly see her features, though just for an instant. If it was a woman, she was a big ugly mama, one built more for comfort than speed, if her size served as any indication. Her bared arms were as big as country hams, and there was a horrible angry look on her face that was truly frightening to behold. She entered the building quickly, and headed straight for the elevator, taking it to the third floor and stopping there, no doubt at Filcher's office.

Dr. Davis sprinted to the orange Winnebago and tried the back door. It was unlocked, so she opened it and quickly stepped in. There was Chip lying in a heap on the floor. It was dark in the camper, but it was definitely Chip, and he was out like a light. She bent down in the darkness, felt for his wrist and checked his pulse, normal. He'd either been poisoned or drugged. There was no way to be certain. She had to get him out of this camper, but how? And where was Therpis? Suddenly she heard the voices of a man and a woman talking right outside the back door of the camper. It was too late, she was trapped, and there was no way out. God help her if they opened the back door. She walked down the hall in the darkness as fast as she could, quietly feeling along the wall with her hand as she moved. She touched what seemed to be a shower curtain, and slipped into the space. The hard and sharp faucet knobs jabbing her in the back confirmed her suspicions.

"I got zee keys," Frau Ioveena said, reverting to her natural dialect. "I vill drive his car and follow you to Chattanooga. First I vill kill him, but not until vee are out of town. You vill drive this camper. Did he sign everything?" she asked again.

"He signed everything without question," Filcher said joyously. "The world is ours now, my darling. I can retire and we can be together forever."

"Yes, my dear," she said, grabbing his crotch, and giving it a squeeze, "but first vee must finish this nasty business. Give me zee briefcase," she said, taking it from the lawyer and placing it in the trunk.

Davis heard the back door of the camper open.

"Just checking," Frau Ioveena said to Filcher. "He vill be out for about two hours vith the dose I gave him. In this case, he vill never wake up. I vill kill him first. No loss, he vas stupid anyway. Vhat a

318

fool."

"I just want to be sure that there's no chance of him waking up at all," Filcher said.

"Don't vorry about that," Frau Ioveena said, closing the camper door, and returning to give Filcher a good bye kiss. She pressed close to him, grabbed his ass with both hands and ground him against her voluptuous body. Filcher's pale, death-like face actually flushed crimson for a moment at the thought of the Earthly pleasures that awaited him. She could truly rock him until he felt like his back had no bone. What a woman. His type of woman, none of that lukewarm Belle Meade stuff, just good, hot, wet, backbreaking sex.

"Lord have mercy!" he whispered silently.

She hopped in the Mercedes, checked the console and found a loaded Glock 17. In the glove box was yet another pistol, a Walther P-38.

"Hmm...he likes zee 9mm," she reflected, as she started the car. She, on the other hand preferred the lowly .22 caliber round, the most underestimated bullet in the world. While it was true that the .22 lacked the stopping power of a .45, or even of a 9mm, it was an irrelevant consideration for Frau Ioveena, a moot point. What kind of idiot needed a .45 to kill someone? Only an amateur needs a round of that size. She'd made that discovery on that job in Bolivia in 2008, the first time she'd used a .22. It had been an accident really, she'd been given a custom built .22 sniper's rifle by her employer. At first she refused to use such a lowly round, but the hit had been so clean that she'd insisted on the .22 from that time forward. It was now internationally known as her signature. If someone was killed by one precisely placed .22 bullet between the eyes, it was assumed that Frau Ioveena had been there. She would never be apprehended anywhere in the world, she was certain of that.

Frau Ioveena waved her arm out the window at Filcher, signaling her desire for him to go first. He pulled out slowly into the alley, and then turned onto Third Avenue North, moving slowly downhill toward Broadway, and taking a left. "The moron," she thought. "He's going to get us stuck in all that traffic. Vhat an imbecile. Vell, hopefully he vill go all the way to the river, take a right and cut over. Son of a vitch!" she shouted loudly. "He's turning left on Second Ave. Jesus, vhat a dumb ass!" They sat through the same two traffic lights twice before things started moving again.

Suddenly there was a flashing blue light in the rear view mirror.

Frau Ioveena reached into the console and withdrew the 17 shot Glock, placing her foot gently on the brake as she pulled the slide back, making sure that there was a bullet in the chamber. She was set. If the cop came for her she would fill him so full of holes that when the wind blew he'd whistle.

"Okay vitch!" she shouted quietly under her breath, expecting the worst. Suddenly the police car pulled around her to the left, turned on its siren, and moved down the center of the street into the turning lane, stopping a car full of rowdy, good looking girls. They saved his life, she mused, replacing the pistol in the console, and continuing to drive slowly down Broadway toward the river.

It was all that hillbilly tourist traffic that was slowing things down in the lower Broadway area. People were crossing the street indiscriminately, walking in between cars and ignoring the traffic signals. They were yelling and shouting as if there was no tomorrow. It was those stupid hicks coming out of the Hard Rock Cafe, and in and out of the Wildhorse Saloon, milling around like idiots in their cowboy hats and boots. At last she was finally able to turn left. There was Filcher up in the distance in the bright orange Camper with the white UT symbol on the sides and back. Tennessee football fans were shouting their approval and beating on the sides of the camper as it passed them slowly, barely moving an inch at a time.

"Great," she cursed under her breath, "there's some son of a vitch filming something, interviewing people on the street. I vant to get out of all this traffic, now." She was getting antsy and edgy, and felt her patience slipping. She was capable of anything at any moment. Anything could set her off; a look, a car moving too slowly, or someone crossing the street in front of her. She fought to keep her cool, but she was rapidly reaching her own personal bottom line.

There were motorcycle police all over the place, but they were mainly watching the girls instead of taking care of business and smoothing out the traffic problem like they should've been. She looked contemptuously at three fat cops standing by their inferior, mass-produced Japanese motorcycles, and thought how useless and disgusting they were. There was an instant look of recognition as her eyes unintentionally engaged the glance of one of the police officers. The other two kept on chatting, but this one looked directly at her. She looked away, and then looked back. He was still looking at her, not a good sign at all.

"Son of a vitch!" she shouted silently under her breath. She looked in the side mirror as she passed and noticed that he'd picked up his radio transmitter and was checking out her license registration with the home base. If that's what he's doing, and she thought it was, he'd better hope it checked out all right. "If he comes after me, he's dead, and so is anybody else who tries anything."

She kept watching as the officer hung up his phone, tapped his partner on the shoulder, then straddled and started his motorcycle, pointing to her car. This was the moment of decision. Should she make a run for it now, or let him come to the window and see what he wanted? If he came to the window, she could shoot him there, or let him go, depending on what he wanted.

She decided to wait and see, first of all, if he came after her, and secondly, what, if anything, he wanted. Then, if she decided to shoot him, she could get him point blank, without wasting ammunition needlessly. 'Precision and economy are the marks of the good operative,' at least that's what she'd learned in the CIA training camp she'd attended, the one that supposedly didn't really exist. 'Never use two bullets if you can get the job done with one.' It wasn't that there weren't enough bullets available, it was about training for that once in a lifetime situation, where you only have one shot. You have to learn to make a kill with one shot every time, so that when that one time comes up and you only have one bullet, you don't choke on the situation and go down yourself. It was the most practical advice she'd ever learned, and she generally made every shot count.

She looked in the rearview mirror and saw the motorcycle slowly snaking its way through the crowd and gaining on her. Its blue lights weren't flashing yet, lucky for him, but when he moved closer, he turned them on. When he made this most likely fatal error in judgment, Frau Ioveena calmly reached into the glovebox, removed the P-38, and checked to see that there was a live one in the chamber. 9mm. It wasn't her style, but then neither was shooting redneck policemen in provincial, backwoods places like Nashville. How she longed for Hamburg or Berlin.

She pulled to a complete stop, activated her emergency flashers, and lowered the window awaiting his arrival.

"Do you know that you have a tail light out?" he asked, leaning in the window, and casually looking around.

"No sir," she replied attempting to seem feminine and helpless. But her blank expression was not convincing at all, and the cop became suspicious.

"Miss, may I see your driver's license and registration?" he asked calmly, now shining his flashlight around the inside of the car. It picked up a reflection off of a metallic object on the floor. They both looked down at the same time and saw, to her surprise, the business end of an UZI submachine gun sticking out from under the front seat. There was that instant of inaction, that calm before the storm, as both the officer and the driver froze and decided what to do. At this point, things seemed to suddenly shift into slow motion. It was a duel for time, one that either of them could lose. He tried to reach for his gun, but held the flashlight in his shooting hand. The cop had the instincts of a player, or he wouldn't have tuned in to her vibe in the first place, but he didn't have the experience to back it up. He'd rashly assumed that since he was doing light duty crowd watching, he wouldn't encounter any serious problems. He should have kept his shooting hand free at all times. Now this slight error in judgment could cost him his life. Before he could even unhook his holster, Frau Ioveena fired four times, striking the officer dead center in the chest and knocking him back several feet. So much for economy. Immediately there was a loud gasp from the crowd and people took off running as fast as they could go, scattering in all directions, and completely closing the street behind her.

Cursing, she hit the gas pedal and the big fuel injected Mercedes V-8 sprang to life, pushing several smaller cars up onto the sidewalk as she sought to escape. Immediately, the other two officers started their motorcycles and began pursuit, but were slowed by the crowd. Another officer on foot patrol rushed to the downed policeman and attempted to stabilize him until help could arrive. Fortunately, the cop was wearing a vest and only been stunned by the force of the bullets' impact. Up at the top of Second Avenue, Frau Ioveena could see the big, lumbering, orange Winnebago moving along slowly, oblivious to the action going down behind it. She flashed her lights, wanting Filcher to know what was happening, but he'd probably figure it out himself as soon as she went racing past him with the cops in pursuit. The two policemen trailing her hadn't had time to radio for back up, they were too busy dodging pedestrians. These next few seconds were critical. She reached down to the floor, retrieved the submachine gun and stuck it out the window, sending a wild spray of bullets across the street. She had to get to the top of Second Avenue, across the bridge and over to Main Street.

Meanwhile, Dr. Davis had been hiding in the shower behind the curtain, but peeking out every so often to see what was going on. She could see the outline of Filcher at the wheel, and guessed by the beating on the side of the camper and its slow progress, that they must be somewhere crowded, perhaps on Nashville's version of Bourbon Street. The camper was barely moving at all, due to the incredible amount of both automobile and pedestrian traffic at the top of the hill. People were milling about everywhere.

Suddenly she heard police sirens and machine gun fire. She stuck her head slightly out of the shower and looked through the back window, surprised to see the Mercedes charging up the hill, knocking smaller cars out of the way as it came. The large woman was steering the car with her left hand, and had her right arm crossed over, and was shooting wildly behind her as she drove. God, what a weird scene. Davis ducked.

Suddenly the camper stopped altogether. This was the best possible place to make her move, but fear held her in check. She didn't have a plan, and had no weapons other than a small can of hairspray and the thin metal fingernail file, which she carried in her purse. She must think and act quickly. If she could just drag Chip out of the camper and onto the street or the sidewalk, they would both be safe. Filcher wouldn't be able to get them. She could call upon the crowd for help. On the other hand, if they got moving again, they'd be lost. It would be much more dangerous, if not impossible, to stop something this big going down the interstate at 70 miles an hour. She had to act now. This was it.

She withdrew the hairspray and the file and lowered her purse quietly to the floor. The sirens, gunfire, and screams of terrified tourists now created all the diversion she needed. She left the shower, calmly and precisely, and walked to the rear door of the camper, stepping over Chip's now semi-conscious form. As she did the Mercedes sped past her, and its driver glanced briefly into the camper's rear door. Their eyes met for an instant, as the car sped up the hill and away. It was truly one of the most frightening glances she'd ever received. There was such an intense hatred in those eyes. It was bone chilling.

Dr. Davis opened the door all the way. The sudden burst of light must have hit the rearview mirror and caught Filcher's attention. He immediately put the camper in park, jumped up and started coming toward the rear of the vehicle, assuming that the door had either come undone, or that some rowdy tourist had opened it and was planning to jump in. For an instant their eyes met, and both stood there wondering what to do. Filcher didn't know who she was, or what she was doing in the camper.

"Out! Get out of here," he said angrily.

"Not until I got what I came for," she replied coldly, stepping fully into the camper, and leaving the rear door swinging. She grabbed Chip's arm and started to drag him toward the open door.

"Oh no you don't, you little bitch!" Filcher said, lunging toward her. As he reached out his arm to grab her, Dr. Davis sprayed him directly in the eyes with the hair spray, causing him to step back for a moment.

But this was a matter of life and death for Filcher. He had no intention of letting this woman, or anyone else upset his plans. Chip Hamster was a dead man, period. Filcher wiped his burning eyes and came toward her again, reaching out and grabbing her arm, but shielding his face this time. Dr. Davis took the metal file and stabbed him with all her might on the inside of his wrist, causing him to immediately release her and recoil in pain. She hoped she'd hit an artery, but wasn't so lucky. The file was buried in his muscle, but had unfortunately missed an artery.

Filcher was tired of fooling with this inconvenient woman, and decided to go get his pistol and just take care of her. Desperate circumstances call for desperate measures. This thing was not going according to Hoyle at all. He'd seen Ioveena speed past him, firing out the window as she drove. Something was terribly wrong.

"Damn!" He should have kept the money with him, but had foolishly entrusted it to her. The $150,000 in the trunk of the Mercedes in the brown alligator briefcase, was as good as gone. And now some crazy bitch was trying to rescue that stupid bastard Chip Hamster. What the hell else could go wrong?

"Wait right here," he said to her, as he raced to the front of the camper to find a gun, the pain still shooting through his arm like flames.

"Yeah," she shouted after him, continuing to pull Hamster ever closer to the door. "I'll wait right here so you can go get your gun and shoot me. Yeah, I'll just wait right here, take your time." Hamster had been regaining consciousness for the last several minutes, and was now starting to come to physically as well.

"Where am I?" Hamster mumbled, trying to assess the situation.

Filcher was really pissed. He'd been sprayed in the face and stabbed. Now Hamster was starting to wake up. Ioveena had said Hamster would be out of it for at least two hours, more than enough time to drown him in the toilet. And now, on top of everything else, some bitch was trying to rescue the stupid bastard. It would do her no good, though, for Filcher was back in a flash with some type of very large pistol held firmly in his right hand.

"Don't move!" he growled.

Dr. Davis was now fully outside the camper with her feet on the street.

"Now," he said, aiming the pistol directly at her, "why don't you step back in slowly and shut the door behind you. Now, there's a good little girl."

She knew that if she stepped back into the camper, she was dead, and so was Chip. But Filcher was desperate and dangerous, and capable of anything. She hesitated, thinking maybe she should slam the camper door from the outside and run for the police. She quickly decided to do what the attorney said. After all, he had the gun.

"Now, move very slowly," Filcher said again, beginning to feel in control of the situation. He might as well kill both of them now. With all of the pandemonium outside on the street, a couple of pistol shots would scarcely be noticed. "So long bitch, whoever you are." As Filcher pulled the trigger, Hamster, in an uncharacteristically selfless gesture, lurched upward, throwing himself fully in front of Dr. Davis, shielding her from the bullet with his own life.

The shot tore through Hamster's left shoulder, its force knocking them both against the rear door of the camper, which opened as Dr. Davis fell against it. There was no time for anything but immediate action. Dr. Davis rose from the street where she had fallen, and slammed the door of the camper shut, leaving Chip on the floor inside and Filcher standing there with the pistol still in his hand. It was a calculated risk. Hamster might already be dead, and if not, Filcher might finish him off. There was no way to tell, and there was no time to weigh the options. Her actions were instinctive. The only possibility was to get to the police immediately and hope that Chip would stay alive until they returned.

"Wretched whore!" Filcher shouted angrily. He was in some deep shit now. He wouldn't be able to drive out of here, at least not quickly. There wouldn't be any fast getaway. As he stood there trying to figure out his next move, he became suddenly aware of the sound of someone laughing. It was a stupid and annoying laugh, slightly familiar, but he couldn't place it. It reminded him of....there it was again, it was coming from somewhere in the camper. Just then there was a knock on the front door of the camper, and Filcher knew it wasn't Ioveena . The knock was followed by the sound of a loud address over the police bullhorn. "Drop all weapons, open the door and come out slowly with your hands in the air." The girl must have gotten the police immediately. This was one hell of a mess.

The command was repeated. There was nothing else to do. He'd have to surrender. Filcher had seen too many police shows. He knew that even now a SWAT team could be moving into position, lining the roof across the street with sharpshooters, ready to blow his head clean off. Filcher seethed with rage. His whole life had been ruined by the Hamsters. Mason Hamster, Chip's father, had poked Filcher's girlfriend back in high school. Oh yeah, Filcher knew about it, alright, but had to pretend he didn't, in order to get old man Hamster's legal business. And now, when revenge was within reach a Hamster ruined it again. The stupid little bastard.

"Come out with your hands up, and you won't be hurt." It was the third warning. He made the decision to exit the camper, and threw the gun into the darkness of one of the curtained bunks lining the side walls of the camper.

"Oh baby," someone laughed, "Don't be hittin' your man with no rolling pin. Oh come on now baby, you know she didn't mean nothin' to me. Why don't you give `ole Therpis a little sugar?"

Filcher slid the curtain back and found that drunken imbecile Therpis, moaning and mumbling to himself. How did that son of a bitch get in here? What else could possibly happen today? Thinking quickly, Filcher retrieved the gun, emptied the bullets on the floor and replaced it in the aged valet's drunken grip. Therpis was now waving it around and cursing. Great, this might work. Filcher quickly moved to the front door, opened it slowly with his foot, holding his hands high in the air, and shouted "Help! There's a man in there with a gun! He was holding us hostage. He shot someone already!"

At that moment, an officer instinctively grabbed Filcher and pulled him quickly away from the door, and out of the line of fire.

"Are you all right sir?" he asked, as several fully armed policemen stormed the camper simultaneously through both doors.

"Yes," Filcher answered, attempting to look frazzled, "There's another man in there. He's been shot. They kidnapped me from my office parking lot. It's a lucky thing you guys showed up when you did or there's no telling what could have happened. I disabled one of them, but there's another one in there with a gun."

This is working, Filcher thought, as the officer released him. "Stick around because we're gonna' need a statement from you just as soon as you calm down."

Filcher turned to slip quietly away in the confusion. This would by no means solve his problems, but he could go back to his office, destroy the incriminating papers he'd had Chip sign, and deny that any of it had ever happened. He could stand safely on his well-respected and scandal-free reputation, and come out smelling like a rose.

Dr. Davis had rushed back to check on Chip, but sensing that he was alright, turned her attentions to Filcher. Hopefully by now he'd confessed everything. She went around to the front door of the camper and saw that the police had handcuffed Therpis. Where had he come from? She scanned the sea of faces for Filcher, and sure enough, there he was across the street in front of the Italian restaurant, slipping away undetected. She rushed back to the officer holding Therpis and quickly explained the situation. The officer picked up his radio and directed a car to secure the perimeter from Third Avenue, to the top of the block, while several others on foot tracked down the fleeing lawyer, and finally found him cowering like a slinking dog beside a Toyota Lexus, on the third level of the parking garage across the street.

Chip was transported to Baptist Hospital where he was treated for a minor flesh wound, and a drug overdose, then released to Dr. Davis several hours later. Filcher was arrested and jailed without bail, pending trial on three counts of aggravated kidnapping, multiple counts of fraud, harboring a fugitive, unlawful possession of Class III weapons, conspiracy, attempted murder, and a number of other lesser charges, a fitting end for any attorney.

34.

EPILOG-A NEW DAY

Chip Hamster awakened to the sounds of birds chirping outside the second story window of his stately Belle Meade mansion. The sun pierced the curtains brightly, casting moving shadows across the pale yellow walls. As the Chambers Brothers said, 'It's a new time, a new day.' That slimy lawyer Filcher was finally in jail where he rightfully belonged. Hell, Chip reflected, even Perry Mason couldn't get the son of a bitch out of the slammer, that is, if there really was a Perry Mason. Well, no matter, Chip had been exonerated of all bank fraud charges, despite his obvious guilt, not for his own sake, but as part of Filcher's evil plan. There was no question whatsoever that Chip had been let off the hook, and he felt extremely fortunate. The old Chip would have felt he deserved to be released, if for no other reason than the simple fact, that he was a genius, and should therefore be above the law. All that had changed now, and Chip was truly humbled, at least to some degree. The laws of this great American nation should be applied equally to all citizens, regardless of their wealth or status in the community. Chip had gotten off lucky, and he knew it.

The mystery of his father's murder had been completely and satisfactorily solved. But who would have ever thought that a lawyer with the wealth and reputation of Mr. Filcher, would have risked everything he had worked for all of his life, just to get a bit more money? As if he didn't have enough already. Well, it hadn't been completely about money after all, had it? 'It's still the same old story, a fight for love and glory, a case of do or die...' It had been about passion, about raw emotion, about uninhibited sex. Filcher had been overwhelmed by Ioveena in much the same way Chip had, but to a much greater degree. Chip was a pipester, a ladies' man, and as such could have his choice of any number of beautiful and passionate women. This being the case, his body and psyche were not shocked to quite the same degree that they would have been if he was an old bastard like Filcher, and hadn't had any lately.

But even considering that, Ioveena was still the most incredible woman Chip had ever met. Who could blame Filcher? There was no man alive who could resist her sexual powers, her 'charms,' as they are referred to in polite society. She was like the snake that stares into its victim's eyes, paralyzing it so that it can't escape. The victim sees the snake coming, knows that it will die, but still can't break free. It's a psychic fascination. Even in light of all that happened, it still came as a surprise that she turned out to be an international terrorist. There were no telling how many men she had destroyed, or governments she'd toppled. Maybe she'd have killed Filcher too, sooner or later, the same way she killed Chip's old man, the same way she'd planned to kill Chip.

And yet, except for her violent nature, she was really the perfect woman. No woman could even come close sexually. She could out cook any famous chef anywhere, could drive a car as good as any man, and could assume any identity she wanted, spoke seven different languages, was also an explosives and munitions expert, a skilled marksman, and flight trained as a fighter pilot, with multiple jet engine rating. Good God, what more could any man want, or even imagine?

Filcher had no idea who he was dealing with, anymore than Chip had. Still, it's possible nobody would have ever really known who she was if the ATF hadn't started snooping around because of the machine gun the Chattanooga police found in the abandoned Mercedes. When they lifted prints off of the car and ran them through the system, boy, did they get a surprise. Frau Ioveenavitch, was wanted in seven different countries for crimes including, but not limited to first degree murder, terrorism, extortion, manslaughter, armed robbery, theft of a military airplane, arson, possession and use of Class III automatic weapons, kidnapping, burglary, assassination, impersonating an officer, international flight to avoid prosecution, destruction of property, forgery, conspiracy, fraud, unlawful removal of mattress and cushion tags, and parking in the yellow lines. As soon as the police found the car where she'd left it, in front of the Read House Hotel, a massive manhunt was conducted, but they never found her. They never would.

But who knows? Maybe she'd really been in love with Filcher after all. She'd gone to the prearranged place to wait for him, but he'd never made it out of Nashville.

Oh well, Chip reflected, it was unlikely that she'd return to the Music City to kill Chip. He'd rather think of her out and about, wild and free, loving a host of other lucky men, than rotting away in some dark prison cell. Still, what a woman.

He stretched deliciously, enjoying the feel of the crisp cotton sheets against his skin. Life would be simple again, like it had been before he had loved...her. He could barely bring himself to speak her name, even now, even after she had proved so untrue, after all that had happened. "Ioveena ." He spoke the name anyway, softly like a prayer, feeling a wave of powerful emotions overwhelm him. Her love for him had been an act after all. She'd never loved him. This was the hardest thing of all to accept, and yet he'd never be completely sure. She had been so passionate, so loving, and so full of hope for tomorrow...forever. This uncertainty cut like a double edged sword. The only woman he'd ever truly loved, an evil Jezebel, a Delilah. A ho. Well, the evidence was incontrovertible. Facts don't lie. On the other hand, the suffering she had caused him had given his personality a depth that it never possessed before. Now, his life could be imagined as a tapestry, with each of the events, his father's murder, his own brush with death, the accident, being imprisoned by alien madmen, being shot, Dr. Davis, and the loss of Ioveena , his one true love, all interwoven in a deep, rich, and colorful pattern.

She'd broken his heart, and though he felt utterly and totally abandoned, there was also a strange sense of power beginning to emerge. He knew now that he would be alright, that he would survive, and lift himself up, and that eventually, all would be well. His strength came from the knowledge that nothing any woman could ever do to hurt him in the future would matter quite as much as it had this time. It was like the mumps, or the chicken pox. Having been through these things, he was now immune forever. He knew intellectually that he would love again someday, but, never like he had loved Ioveena . It all seemed far away now, but someday, he would love again. As his father's Gene Pitney record had so eloquently expressed it, some decades ago, "Only Love Can Break A Heart...Only Love Can Mend it Again." That day would come.

He wanted to run to her even now, to forgive her for his father's murder, for plotting his own death, for everything. Women are made for love, he reflected, to love and be loved, and Ioveena , most of all. Well, no matter, it was never to be. Women really are different from men, a different species entirely. They're probably smarter too, look at Dr. Davis, for example. Therpis was right when he said that women know more than men because men come out of a woman's body. "They can just read yuh." There was something to that.

That was the good thing about Cissy, he reflected, she was all woman. She wasted hours in the bathroom, had shoes all over the house, was utterly incapable of being anywhere on time, misplaced things constantly, talked on the phone incessantly, and was guilty of other things that were equally annoying to any man of steel. And yet these minor irritations were, in the final analysis, part of the eternal mystery of Woman as almost wholly "other." Amazing and truly miraculous if actually observed. The eternal female, an incredible mystery, in one's very house.

Ultimately, it was Ioveena 's lust for wealth and power that brought about her demise. Isn't it ironic, he thought, if she'd stayed with him she would have had everything she wanted? Well, not really. She'd already most cruelly killed his father before they'd even met. She got away with it, too. Chip wanted to marry her, and would have. If that had happened, she would have married Chip, murdered him as well, and run off with that old bastard Filcher. But what did she intend to do with him, Chip wondered? Was she really in love with him? Was it all for him? What did she see in that ancient bastard? Maybe she would have killed him too. Chip would never know. He would have married her too, if he hadn't gone through his inheritance so quickly. Buying that Rolls-Royce and that bug-eyed Porsche had probably saved his life. When he'd received the news of his father's death, he'd at first intended to come to Nashville, settle some business matters, and then return to Key West immediately. He would have married Ioveena sooner or later....sooner no doubt, if he hadn't wasted his money. Waiting to get married had most likely saved his life.

And what about Dr. Davis? That was another story. She'd decided that she would return to science after all, and had already taken a job at an observatory in California. It had been fun while it lasted, but the truth of the matter was that she'd dropped Chip like a hot brick because he "didn't know what he wanted to do with his life." Hell, he was only thirty-five. How the hell did he know what he wanted to do for the rest of his life? What an absurd idea. She had saved his life though, and she was really a wonderful and brilliant woman, perhaps the most intelligent person he'd ever known. She'd also helped Chip by placing another notch on the bedpost between him and Ioveena . And he had saved her life too. The score between them was even.

He lay there on his back, with his head resting on his folded hands, and stared at the ceiling. A magnificent old Century fan turned slowly, lazily, hardly moving the warm spring air. As he looked upward, he suddenly became aware of a large hornet angrily flying around the room. He watched for a moment as it dashed against the 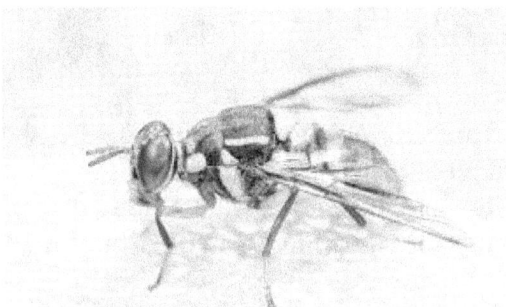 glass, and then got caught in the curtain. It buzzed loudly and furiously, outraged to have its freedom so restricted. Chip lay there a moment longer before jumping out of the bed and preparing for his day. He'd learned his lesson, and this time didn't wait around to be stung. He opened the window the rest of the way, gave the curtain a shake, and the hornet flew off into the morning sky.

Chip Hamster was really a new man, with a second chance at life. He would go out now, and make something of himself, make a contribution of some sort to civilization. The world was once more truly his...er, uh,...oyster. There were many great things to be accomplished; books to be written, women to be loved, important business deals, and millions of dollars just waiting around the next corner. While he wasn't exactly sure where that particular corner might be, he knew that he could never return to Key West. Well perhaps someday, but not now.

The memories of Ioveena were still too fresh. Mallory Square, the intimate kiss she afforded him on the Conch Train....it was still just too much to bear. He was overcome instantly by a nostalgic rush of emotional distress and longing for something which will never be again.

Alas that was then, but this is now. And while the world was truly his stage, Nashville would always be his home base, and what was Nashville most famous for? No, not the famed Goo Goo Cluster, not Varallo's Chile, not the Gerst House, not the former Houston Oilers, excessive taxes, or even its high murder rate, but....country music. Here Chip was, positioned right in the very Mecca of the music business, Music City, USA. Fate had placed him here, and finally led him back to the birthplace of his ancestors, the home of his youth, Nashville, Tennessee. He determined then and there to become a music business mogul. How difficult could it be for a man of his abilities?

"Therpis, bring me a Blatz!"

"You's the boss and I'm the hoss," the aged relative replied. "How's that shoulder today?'

"It hurts like hell. It isn't everyday a man gets shot, although it could be these days."

"Well Mistuh Chip, you are one tough son of a bitch, taking that bullet the way you did, and saving that girl's life. You know what, I think you just might be a hero. I ain't sure, but you just might be."

"I could be. I don't know, myself. I might have just stood up at the wrong time. I really don't remember that much about what happened. I woke up and saw Filcher coming after her with a gun. I didn't have time to think about it. Anybody would have done the same thing under the circumstances. Filcher was desperate, like a roach drowning in a urinal full of hot piss. He would have killed her. It was funny in a way though. She kept taunting him. I think that's what woke me up. But hell, like I said, everybody thinks I'm a hero, and that's what matters. I do know one thing though, I am one tough son of a bitch. You're right about that."

"You sure is. I can't argue with that."

"No...I'm serious. Think about it. My father was murdered, I was cheated out of my inheritance, betrayed by the only person I trusted completely....other than yourself, of course. As part of a vast conspiracy of truly international proportions, I was set up to be assassinated by my true love, the same woman who'd killed my father. Then I miraculously survived a grinding, near fatal car wreck, drowning in the Tennessee River, and being devoured by giant radioactive mutant catfish, only to be captured by alien madmen and held for several months at an asylum, under such horrible conditions that I cannot bear to speak of them even now. After my own liberation, I selflessly returned immediately to the very place where I'd been held prisoner, and personally rescued Dr. Davis. One can only imagine the unholy plans those perverted madmen had in store for her. On the way out of that bug house of freaks, I valiantly faced down their leader, the criminally insane genius, Marduk. No sooner had I freed Dr. Davis, than I had to single-handedly stop the approach of the giant death star asteroid targeted for Earth. Searing flames roared around me everywhere in the burning laboratory, nearly roasting me alive, as I bravely stood my ground alone at the console of the aural particle accelerator, struggling to save the planet, and all of its inhabitants.

"Finally, a free man at last, after enduring months of incredible atrocities, I returned to the city of my birth only to be drugged, kidnapped, and betrayed once again by my closest family friend, attorney Leonard Filcher. Next, I courageously took a bullet meant for Dr. Davis. I am one tough son of a bitch. In fact, Therpis, I could be one of the toughest men who ever lived."

"Now hold on a minute Chip," Therpis interrupted, "I ain't no slouch my own self. You done seen me all roughed up and bruised before from that big chrome vacuum cleaner pipe Mattie Pearl beat me with. I'm pretty damn tough myself. If I had a dollar for every time she whupped me over the head, or the police smacked me, I'd be as rich as any man in Belle Meade. If you want to talk about tough, now, you go right ahead on, but just don't forget who you talkin' to. I done told you, I ain't no slouch."

"Being beat up by one's wife hardly ranks with saving the world, in terms of sheer courage. I don't think....actually, being beat up repeatedly by the same woman sounds masochistic to me, if not actually downright cowardly. That isn't tough at all. It's stupid. I don't think there is any comparison," Chip reflected casually.

"Well, I don't know about that," Therpis replied indignantly, raising his voice. "What about the time...maybe you're right. Forget about that. I know you done been shot, but look here," he said bending over and proudly showing Chip a small scar on the back of his neck. "You ain't never been stobbed. This bitch snuck up on me one night at the Elks Club in Richmond, Indiana and stobbed me in the back of the neck with a penknife. So help me Jesus, the woman would've killed me sure enough, if fat George hadn't stopped her. And what about the time a brick came loose from off the old National Life building, and fell on my big toe from fifty stories up? My toe got big as a tomato. You didn't hear me whining about that did you? No, I took it like a man. So just remember who you're talking to if you want to be talking about being tough. I am 'Mr. Tough.' Now I'm through with that."

The discussion was interrupted by the sound of the ringing doorbell. "Therpis, see who the hell that is. It's probably some bastard trying to get me to change long distance phone service."

Therpis returned momentarily carrying a large package wrapped in brown paper. "It was the UPS man...or woman. I couldn't tell for sure....whether it was a man or a woman. Either way I wouldn't want to mess with 'em. Now, we was just talking about tough. That UPS driver, man, woman....or beast, looked ten times tougher than both of us put together," Therpis laughed.

"Why don't you take that package out in the back yard and open it up out there," Chip said, "I don't want all of that dust, paper, and crap in the house." The package probably wasn't a bomb, but why take any unnecessary chances.

Chip waited for a few moments, but since no explosion was forthcoming, he stepped outside and found Therpis standing on the back porch sipping a cool Double-Cola, taken from the open package; a case of the delightful beverages packed in dry ice.

"Oooo-wee this is some good shit," Therpis exclaimed excitedly.

On the table next to the open box lay a large, white, sealed envelope addressed to Chip. On its upper left hand corner Chip noticed the brightly colored symbol of the madman formerly known as Marduk. A sudden chill fell upon him like a shadow, at the recognition of the space freak's distinctive trademark. Chip carefully retrieved the envelope from the glass top of the wrought iron table and held it cautiously between his thumb and forefinger, examining it closely from all sides. Would he never be free of the bullshit which had plagued him throughout this past year?

"I wouldn't drink that if I were you," Chip suddenly remarked. "There's no telling what's in it."

"I know Double-Cola when I taste it," the aged valet replied. "It's the 'Nectar of the Gods.'"

"Well," Chip mused. It was already too late. If the bottle had contained some acid or poison, Therpis would be clutching his throat and rolling around on the driveway at this very moment. Chip replaced the still unopened envelope on the table and reached for the empty Double-Cola bottle. Aiming the bottle skyward, he looked through the open end as if it were a telescope. The bottle immediately manifested peculiar but specific light refractions, indicating that it was one of the 'special' bottles, like the one discovered by Dr. Davis and her colleagues in Iceland.

This discovery presented several possibilities. The entire case of Double-Cola might be comprised of these special bottles, but to what end? How, or why, would Marduk have anything delivered to Chip? Especially if the Secret Chiefs were in another dimension, or on another planet. As a souvenir of Chip's great adventure? It was doubtful. The implications were darker and far more sinister. And yet, nothing had happened to Therpis when he drank the first bottle. Chip, in his usual casual manner, concluded that the case of Double-Cola posed no immediate deadly threat. There was no 'why' anyway, as far as the Secret Chiefs were concerned. They did as they pleased. He might as well see what the envelope contained. Besides, if the crazy bastards wanted Chip dead, they would have already had him killed by now.

"Therpis, open that envelope for me will you, and tell me what it says. I don't have my glasses with me."

"You don't wear no glasses, Chip."

"I know, but just open it for me anyway, will you? This glare is horrible."

"No dice!" Therpis answered, getting suspicious. "There might be a bomb, or something else in that somitch. Uh, uh. Naw, I ain't that type of ape. You open the somitch....and I'll just stand over there out of the way and watch."

"What the hell," Chip said, more to himself than Therpis, as he picked up the large envelope, "Marduk and his bunch of space freak thugs don't have any beef with me. If the envelope explodes, it explodes. Hell with it." Chip reached into his pocket, pulled out a switch blade, and slipped the point into the corner of the envelope, making a clean incision along its top. "Nothing." This was a good sign. Reaching inside, he withdrew what appeared to be a large greeting card. "Nothing out of the ordinary here either," he mused, replacing the envelope on the table. It was just a greeting card, though obviously not one from Hallmark. On the front of the card was, of all things, a pretty, water colored depiction of the Washington Monument.

"These bastards really are crazy, Therpis, I swear to God they are. Therpis..."

Therpis was standing behind a tree about thirty feet away, out near his wife's clothesline, his face peeping around a large branch.

"Get your ass over here. It's just a greeting card from some people I used to know."

"Okay, Mr. Bastard, I'm coming back, but if it blows up and kills me, I'm gonna' kick your ass."

Chip opened the card and found himself face to face with a very lifelike eight by ten inch color photograph of the exceedingly dim-witted stooge, bird-brain, and former prison escapee, Marvin Hocker, the flat-headed moron, and new Council member, now known as Meeztor.

"Great God almighty," Therpis exclaimed. "That somitch looks like the Imperial Wizard of the Ku Klux Klan. Is that who it is Chip?"

Before Chip could reply, the photograph abruptly came to life, as if on a television screen, its closed eyes suddenly opening eerily. "Charles Mason Hamster," the image spoke, "We will return for you at the appointed time and place, 'Track 29, boy, you can give me a shine'."

There immediately followed a large puff of foul-smelling, sulphuric, yellow smoke, causing Chip to involuntarily drop the card to the ground. A loud, hollow, laughter suddenly seemed to permeate the back yard, emanating from nowhere in particular. Within an instant, no trace of the greeting card remained, save for a small pile of smoldering ashes, which were quickly dispersed by a sudden breeze, along with the fading sound of the hysterical laughter.

"You got some strange friends, Chip. I think you better stay away from those folks. I don't believe they're from our part of town, if you know what I mean."

"Yeah," Chip replied.

ELSEWHERE

And elsewhere, at an undisclosed location in another dimension, an ancient and withered hand closed a giant ledger book, its rich, grey, dinosaur skin cover emblazoned in large gold letters with the name 'Charles Mason Hamster, III.' The dusty book was returned to the same spot on the shelf from which it had been removed, well over a year ago.

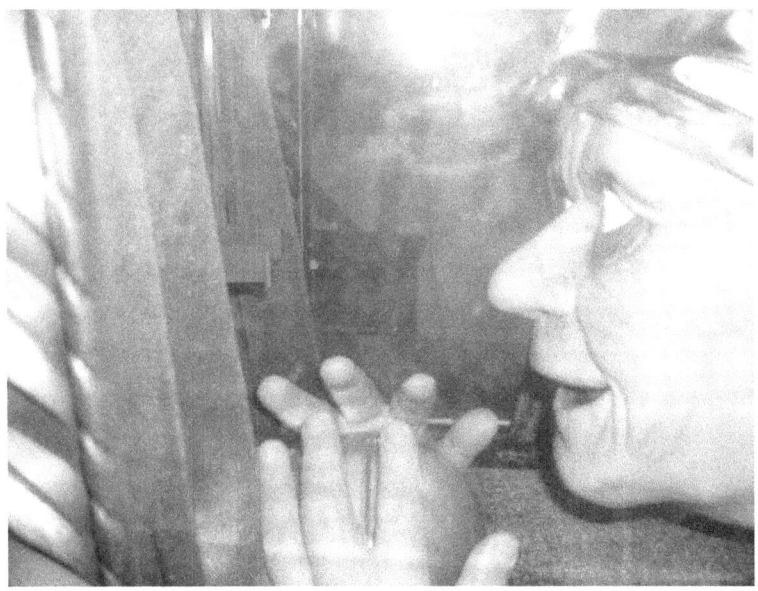

"Who's next?"

I don't know. I've got to think about it. In the meantime, let's get some lunch. How about Mexican?"

"I could go for Mexican. Yeah, Mexican would work."

About the Author

I started in the music business right out of college as an agent for the newly formed Nova Agency in Nashville. Within six months this company, which consisted of two other agents, was the exclusive agency for Jerry Lee Lewis, Waylon Jennings, Jessi Colter, Tompall Glaser, Dr. Hook, and David Allan Coe just as the `Outlaw' phase of country music was beginning. After that, I worked at the Lavender-Blake Agency, the exclusive agency for George Jones, Tammy Wynette, Ray Price, Johnny Rodriguez, Johnny Paycheck, the Statler Brothers, Barbara Mandrell, Johnny Duncan, Joe Stampley, Johnny Bush, and others. I then moved to Dick Blake International as one of four agents, the exclusive representatives of Barbara Mandrell, Louise Mandrell, Merle Haggard, the Statler Brothers, Don Williams, Ronnie Milsap, Brenda Lee, Ricky Skaggs, Carl Perkins, and many others.

By 1983, I was president (and part owner) of In Concert International, the exclusive agents of Mickey Gilley, Ronnie Milsap, Johnny Lee, John Anderson, Lou Rawls, Johnny Rodriguez, James Brown, Johnny Paycheck, Jerry Lee Lewis, Fats Domino, as well as numerous Jamaican reggae acts, and manager of country legend Ray Price.

After twenty years I was burned out and wanted to do something else. My first book, `Music City Babylon, Inside the World of Country Music.' (1992) chronicled my life behind the scenes. Since then I've primarily written about subjects which interest me. I enjoy mountain biking, music, art, architecture, antiques and vintage cars. I currently split my time between my home outside of Nashville, and 1840s Grey Gables in Mississippi.

My books so far:
Music City Babylon, Inside the World of Country Music. Birch Lane Press, New York, 1992
The Branson, Missouri Scrapbook. Citadel, New York, 1994
The Complete Guide to Riverboat Gambling. Citadel, New York, 1995
Making it in Country Music. Citadel, New York, 1996
Nashville, Gateway to the South. Cumberland House, Nashville, 1998
New Orleans in Vintage Postcards. (Images of America). Arcadia Publishing, Charleston, SC 1999
Nashville in Vintage Postcards. (Images of America). Arcadia Publishing, 1999
Memphis in Vintage Postcards. (Images of America). Arcadia Publishing, Charleston, SC, 2000
Chattanooga, Best of the Lookout City. Milton Publishing, Chattanooga, 2001

Beer Signs for the Collector. Schiffer Publishing, Atglen, PA 2003

Cameras for Collectors. Schiffer Publishing, Atglen, PA. 2001

The Peabody Hotel. Arcadia Publishing, Charleston, SC. 2002

The New South. (Contributing author) Insight Guides, London 2004

Porsche, the Ultimate Guide. KP Books, Iola, Wisc. 2005

The Hammond Organ. Privately published 2008

The Hammond Organ. Backbeat Books, Hal Leonard Books, 2011

Vignettes from the Modern Era. DeathcatMedia, Nashville 2017

 The Arlington Resort Hotel & Spa. DeathcatMedia, Nashville 2017

Siren. DeathcatMedia, Nashville 2018

The Peabody, the South's Grand Hotel. DeathcatMedia, Nashville 2019

Pilgrimage of Darkness. DeathcatMedia, Nashville 2020

Car Crazy! DeathcatMedia, Nashville 2021

Porsche 928, an Introduction. DeathcatMedia, Nashville 2021

For further information on these books as well as reviews, pictures, and upcoming books, check out my website: deathcatmedia.com All are available on amazon,